THREE A.M.

TOR BOOKS BY STEVEN JOHN

Three A.M.

THREE A.M.

STEVEN JOHN

A TOM DOHERTY ASSOCIATES BOOK
NEW YORK

THREE A.M.

Copyright © 2012 by Steven John

A Tor Book
Published by Tom Doherty Associates, LLC
175 Fifth Avenue
New York, NY 10010

www.tor-forge.com

Tor® is a registered trademark of Tom Doherty Associates, LLC.

ISBN 978-0-7653-3116-8

First Edition: March 2012

Printed in the United States of America

0 9 8 7 6 5 4 3 2 1

For my wife,
as all things are

ACKNOWLEDGMENTS

First, I must again thank my wife, Kristin, without whom this book might have been cast aside unfinished. Her loving support and encouragement kept the fire beneath me; kept the words coming.

Without Russell Galen, my superlative agent, even the finished manuscript might well never have found its way to print. I'll let the word "superlative" stand on its own and not bother with many other adjectives, appropriate though they are.

To my brother and parents, the first editors of this book, and the first supporters of a lifetime of endeavors, I shall likewise avoid tossing about adjectives (and waxing maudlin—I can do that on my own time and not drag all these nice people through the process), so suffice to say I thank and love you.

Without the vision, skill, patience, and creative mind of Eric Raab, my editor, this would not be the book it is. (Maybe I'd still be happy with the story and the characters and the whatnot but . . . would you? I feel safer having left it to the experts.) Eric's pondering and editing, and his dialogue with me, discussing and suggesting and debating, have helped smooth and tighten and mold and on and on—many thanks are due, and given. Katharine Critchlow, thanks to you, too, for steering us home.

The other half of my family, my parents- and brother- and sisters-in-law, deserves thanks, too. They brought (and bring) love and support such that one could scarcely hope to find in blood, let alone in marriage.

Ryan Ariano . . . you're a fine writer and a sharp reader, sir. You helped me with this one a helluva lot. Good hiking and jogging and talking and sipping with you, too.

I must also thank Brendan Deneen, my first agent, in many ways my first editor, and the first "book world" professional to take real interest.

And no, I didn't forget you, Osborne. Jim gave me the nudge that started the snowball rolling. I'll buy the next round.

For all of you.

Glendale, CA
2011

THREE A.M.

MY LEGS GAVE OUT AFTER LESS THAN A BLOCK. I CRAWLED FOR maybe a hundred yards and then pulled myself along with just my elbows for a few feet more. The pavement behind me was streaked with blood. I figured I was in the last few moments of my life, so what the hell—stop crawling.

Rolling onto my back, I looked up at the sky . . . the blue sky. There were a few clouds and the sun was bright, warming. I lay there staring upward for a long time. The buildings around me were all dilapidated above their first few floors—cracked paint, boarded-up windows, old signs, and bare flagpoles that no one had seen in years.

It was warm and bright in the sun and there wasn't a soul around. Everyone was terrified and hiding. So I had the street and the sky to myself, and I lay there, bleeding and broken and probably moribund, and I was happy as hell. I had never felt such joy, in fact. Ever. I was . . . satisfied.

1

SHE WAS BLOND, OF COURSE. EYES AS GRAY AS MIDNIGHT FOG and lips stained red. Her dress matched her lips and hugged her hips and chest, and my eyes kept drifting to where the crimson silk stopped and her thighs began. Christ, what a beauty. And oh how she knew it. And she knew I knew she knew, and it didn't matter a bit.

She waited so long to start talking, I was lost in her beauty by the time she started playing her game . . . trying to hook me. She almost did. No one ever actually did, though—at least no one had in years. Sure, she was gorgeous, but I would just as soon have put a knife in her back as I would have put her back on a mattress. She wasn't innocent . . . wasn't clean. I could see it as clear as the skin between her breasts where her dress took a plunge. I don't care who you are—a young beauty or some old tough—if you smell corrupt, I'll take you down if someone hands me enough dollars.

And she was deeply corrupted. Lost in her own darkness. I sat there, feeling coy and looking passive and letting my eyes drift from her chest to her legs and every once in a while to her face. I wasn't going to say a damn thing. It was her move, her game, and I knew how to play it. She did too, as I learned— and better than I would have expected from a girl barely pushing twenty-six, but just the same, she was good.

I hunched over my scotch and she lounged behind her vodka. I smoked and looked at her and she looked at me and she knew I was waiting and she let me. The place was mostly empty. It was late on a Tuesday—just folks like me who don't have a schedule to keep. All burgundy paint and wood and always dark, but the vents were good and it was never all that smoky.

So I lit another cigarette and almost laughed when she actually broke the silence with a husky "Can I have a light?"

I held out my lighter, meaning for her to take it, but she leaned in and waited, a long black cigarette between her dark lips. I lit it for her and she touched my hand and it was all such a fucking cliché.

"So," I said.

"So . . ." she said back. No way. I wasn't giving her an inch. I turned back to my drink. When I looked up a second later at the mirror behind the bar, she was staring right at my reflected eyes. She smiled slightly. Beautiful. Dammit. All right, then . . .

"Okay," I said to her reflection. "What is it you want to talk about?"

She laughed and it seemed genuine, pure. It sounded all wrong in this dark-walled bar. People here never laughed like that. She took a long drag of her cigarette and put it out well before it was done. "I thought you'd never ask." A long pause. "I'm Rebecca."

"Hi, Rebecca."

"Hi, Tom Vale."

I fucking knew it. I nodded a few times, looking down at my

drink, a wry smile turning up the corners of my mouth. Must have been the whiskey; I was not amused.

"You know, Rebecca, I have an office."

She smiled, leaning closer to me. I turned to face her. "I've stopped by many times in the past few days. . . . You're never there."

"Yeah, well, that's still where I like to do my work. I come here to do my drinking."

"Well, then, let's just drink. We can do business some other time."

I sighed silently, stubbing out my smoke. "Seeing as that's not what you're here for, let's just have it."

"This place seems a better office for you anyway."

I couldn't fault her there. I've been coming to Albergue for years. In fact, I did most of my work from the very barstool where I was sitting. Usually, though, I was alone here. Albergue was where I sat to think about things or to drink until I didn't have to. It was small, off an alley that wasn't even off a main street. No one new tended to find the place. Which didn't make the lovely Rebecca's presence any more comforting. It was one of the few bars around that still had cases of the scotch I like. The guys behind the bar knew not to talk to me too much unless I started talking to them. There were pictures of fields rolling beneath blue skies on one of the walls. It was perfect for me. Until this.

"I want to hire you, Tom."

"No," I said flatly.

She pulled away, looking slighted, but it was bullshit. "Won't you at least hear me out?"

"I'd rather not."

"Well, let me buy us another round and just listen. Please. Then I won't bother you anymore if you still don't want to help me."

She finished her drink and waved the bartender, Adam, over to us. He caught my eye with a subtle smile the girl would not recognize as out of the ordinary. I looked down, shaking my head slightly. His slender, pocked face was placid again as Rebecca ordered another vodka martini for herself and a glass of Cutty Sark on the rocks for me. She knew my drink. She wanted me to know she knew my drink. Adam served us and she slid her glass toward mine and clinked the base of hers against it. A few drops of her vodka spilled into my scotch.

"Okay. You've got me for a drink. Let's get to it. You know my name, you know my whiskey, and now you know my office is here, not the room with a number written next to it. Who are you . . . how and why do you know about me . . . and what are you going to propose that I'm going to say no to?"

She took a long sip from her glass and then closed her eyes for a moment. She opened them slowly, her irises following her lids upward until they locked on to mine. "If I offered you fifty thousand dollars for a month's work, what would you say?"

"Probably yes."

She smiled to herself and turned away from me. The last few patrons got up from their barstools and left. Now it was just me and her together with our reflections. She was studying mine, I could tell. I kept my eyes down, looking at the wood of the bar. It had been scratched and revarnished countless times. I'd stuck a knife into it myself once or twice on angry, drunken nights.

"A man named Samuel Ayers was killed last month."

"Go to the police, sweetheart. We're done here." I turned away.

"I did . . . or I mean—someone did. . . . His wife, I think. And they found the guy who shot him and tried him and he's probably on death row already."

She pulled a cigarette out of her handbag and picked up my lighter. Her hand trembled a bit as she lit it, and though I couldn't be certain, it seemed like the unsteadiness was intentional, practiced.

"The man they have didn't kill him. I know it."

Typical. So goddamn typical, I could have screamed. Instead I talked.

"Rebecca, do you have much experience with this kind of thing? This wronged-man kind of thing? No? Well, I do. A lot. Forget it. Forget him—your boyfriend in jail or whatever. He probably did kill your Mr. Ayers, and if he didn't, sorry, he's gone anyway. No way out. The system wins; you don't. Apologies, but it's your life, your problem, not mine."

"I'll pay you the fifty thousand even if you can't change a thing. If you'll just try."

That was a lot of money: twice as much as I had to my name. Too much for me to write off out of hand even if she was dirty. So I finished my scotch and decided to get involved. But I wasn't going to let her know yet—I was too far into my cups to play it cool right now.

"Okay. Here's the deal. Give me your number in case I think of any questions for you, and come to my office in two days. I'll hang around there in the early afternoon."

"How about I keep the number to myself and come tomorrow?"

"No. I'm getting drunk tonight. Tomorrow's all for me. Two days, afternoon. And keep the phone your little secret for all I care—pretty eyes or no, I want you to finish up your drink and leave now. I like to be at my bar alone."

She seemed hurt. I didn't give a fuck. Fifty grand or no, I was hating this situation already. I'd been paid to find things out and take care of problems for more than a decade, and the good ones never talked money before they talked facts. The good ones were never beautiful. But money spoke louder than morals.

I watched her go and she knew it.

* * *

I WANTED TO STAY AND GET DRUNK, BUT REBECCA HAD SCREWED up my thinking. As I tried to reason through the few open cases I was working, all I could think about was her lips and her legs and her money and wonder what was behind it all. So I decided to go home to my little apartment and drink the same scotch there anyway and be done with Tuesday. Or Wednesday. Whatever.

Tossing some bills onto the bar, I nodded to Adam and headed for the exit. I pulled open the first heavy door and stepped into the alcove beneath the loud, massive vents. Shutting the iron door, I paused and waited until it was sealed, and then pressed open the second door and stepped out into the fog.

Mist swirled around me and I was still for a moment to adjust to the fog-blindness, leaning against the bricks of Albergue just like I did most every night of my life. I could see three orbs tonight, and set off heading south after lighting a cigarette.

The orbs in this part of town were placed about ten feet apart from one another. I laid my hand on the first as I walked past it. The luminous, yellow orange sphere was warm beneath my palm. There had been a slight breeze up right when I'd left, but it subsided now and I could see only one orb ahead of me and one behind as I turned onto Sixth Avenue.

My brow grew damp with the mist and I wiped at it with a dirty old handkerchief, picking up the pace a bit. I hated the cold, clammy feeling I got all over my exposed skin at night. Eighth Ave had blowers and they would likely still be on at this hour, so I headed that way, cutting down an alley. There were no orbs in the alley, but I knew it well and ran my hand along the wet bricks of the wall as I walked.

I crossed Seventh and passed two people. A woman and a man—that much I could tell by their silhouettes. Another short alley and I came out onto Eighth Avenue, where, sure enough, the blowers were still running.

The fog swirled and danced ten or fifteen feet above street level; higher than that was thick gray. But on streets like this, when the blowers were all on, you could almost see clearly. I passed one of the massive fans as I walked up the street and gripped my coat closed against the wind. Behind it was a small dead zone, where gray wisps drifted downward, out of reach of the blower fans a few blocks north.

I paused there for a minute to light another smoke. The ten-foot-tall fan hummed, impressively quiet when you weren't on the business end. As I took my second drag, the hairs on the back of my neck stood up—just a bit and only for a fleeting moment, but I'd learned to take them more seriously than anything else on earth. Subtly, pretending to stretch and roll my shoulders, I looked all around me.

I couldn't see a soul. Not on the street and not in any of the first- or second-floor windows of the nearby buildings. The only sound was the blower's hum. I decided to write it off, but made careful note of where I was and the time anyway. Just before midnight—the witching hour, I thought to myself with an internal smile. If someone was watching me, no need to convey any sardonic thoughts. Or anything at all.

Abruptly, I set out walking north again. Though all seemed normal, I had already made up my mind to take a snaking, illogical path home. I passed through dark alleys, up streets lined with softly glowing orbs, and down a couple of the larger, clear-blown boulevards. Rebecca and her red lips kept drifting into my thoughts, and before long, I was more wandering than evading.

She was still on my mind as I sat in the chair beside my threadbare mattress drinking a glass of scotch with no ice. And she stayed in my head as I slept on top of the covers.

2

I AWOKE AROUND THREE IN THE MORNING, JUST LIKE ALWAYS.
Through the gray sheet tacked over my window came pale yellow
light from the sign of the shop below. It sold clocks and lamps
and all sorts of bullshit. Shelves piled high with coffee mugs,
hammers, picture frames—whatever they found they put up for
sale. Asian guy and his wife. Not too old, but beaten down . . .
He always used to cast his eyes on the floor and mumble when
I'd greet him. So I stopped saying hi. The wife would lean against
the front window all day, her face pressed between the retractable iron cage that had never been slid aside.

She would peer out into the few feet she could see before the
mist got too thick, and then, whenever someone materialized
out front she leaned back, staring at them with her little black
eyes. I'd never heard her say a word. I hadn't been in there for
over a year. I got my sun sphere there: a fancy model with a luminous clock built into it. That's how I always knew it was three.

For a long time, I had gotten it into my head that something
was waking me. It was too precise for a body clock phenome-

non. Certainly not my body, at any rate, which was usually full of booze and nicotine and whatever and never went to sleep at the same time two nights in a row. So I picked random nights and stayed up. The first night of my little experiment, I tried to read, tried to listen to music. . . . It was all too tedious: trying to pass time made time go slower, so I had just sat there in my chair, glancing from the white wall glowing yellow in the shop's light to the sun sphere and the blue numbers glowing inside it.

Nothing. Three A.M. had come and gone without so much as a breeze outside.

The following night I awoke at 2:58.

I had stayed awake and sober at least ten other times, watching three in the morning slide silently by. But still, five nights out of seven, I woke up.

Sighing, I eschewed the half-empty bottle of scotch on the table and walked stiffly, naked, into the kitchen/living room. The only other room in my place was where I shit, showered, and shaved. I spent most of my time home half-awake in the bathtub or half-asleep in bed. The rest I spent in the twelve-by-ten room where I occasionally had food and had a small cloth couch and a pressboard table. There were also some cabinets and drawers, and in one of those drawers were the pills I took some of the nights I couldn't sleep. Actually it was most nights. And I'd been taking two or three of them at a time recently.

They were technically for manic-depressives, but they let my brain shut the fuck up and my body go limp, so what the hell, I used them. I got them from a guy named Salk, who was some sort of pharmacist and sold whatever he could sneak out to a few loyal buyers. He gave me a good price because he knew what I did for a living and that I could have him busted hard anytime. I had helped him out of a few jams because he knew I was buying pills illegally.

I hardly remember how our unique business relationship began—a bar and some drunken conspiring, I'd wager. It certainly was strange: All he had on me was that I bought government-controlled substances, and all I had on him was that he sold them. It was a vicious, beautiful cycle that kept us both fucked and both safe.

Those were the best kind of partnerships to have.

I popped two pills and sat down on my ratty couch to have a smoke. It usually took about two cigarettes' time until the drugs got to work. Those few minutes always got very strange. Right before I passed out, almost invariably, I thought of life before the fog.

I had been twenty-eight the last time I saw the sun. Fifteen years ago. And that had been just a chance parting in the mist. It took months for it to go from clear to hazy to socked in. I was so used to it that it rarely occurred to me just how different things were. But those first days—those had been horrible times. Everyone gripped by a sense of despair. Suicides ran rampant. Fear was everywhere. As the sickness spread and they started shutting down cities, quarantining us by the thousands, the fog started in and changed everything. Fucked everything up.

I hadn't driven a car, thrown a baseball, lounged on a bench . . . nothing like any of that in a decade and a half. It's amazing how little you can do when you can't see a goddamn thing.

The pills started taking hold before I was finished with my cigarette, but I still wanted a second so I lit another off the embers of the first and inhaled deeply. I loved that little burn at the back of my throat when I took in a lot of smoke. Let me know I was doing something. Killing myself, sure. But fuck it—I was in charge. I was aware.

I pulled open the window and lay on my back in the middle of the floor. After a minute, damp gray air crept across my body. It was cold tonight. I smoked my cigarette and looked at its little orange tip, my own personal orb, glowing in my own personal haze. My thighs and stomach grew chill and wet as the heavy air passed over the hairs of my body. I shivered, smiling like a half-wit, and ran my left palm across my chest and down along my torso, blowing smoke into the mist.

The sun always used to bother me. When it shone in my eyes, I hated it. As a carefree kid, I hated when it heated my shoulders, or later baked my fatigues while I was out on exercise runs . . . when it cooked our backs while we did push-ups out in the grass.

And the grass made my flesh itch. I missed diving into cool water, though, stepping into the river, being wet and cold all over. I ran my hands over my face and thoughts and shoulders and clinched the cigarette butt between my teeth. Fucking sun. I had hated it and the grass, but I missed it all. I would gladly have gotten a thousand little cuts and itching, sticking grass all over my body and rolled in the sun now, but it was never anything but the mist and no more cool blue lakes and no more deep blue. Just fog and a world at arm's reach. Around the corner was a million miles away. So fucking pathetic. Goddamn disgusting just blubbering and jacking off there lying on the floor in the fucking mist in my own little chambers and running hands all over my body until I was lost in the pills and dreams I never recalled after a few minutes when I'm awake and grasping for them and they drift away. . . .

OATMEAL AND COFFEE AND SOME BAR THAT WAS SUPPOSED TO have fruit and vitamins and shit in it. All I tasted was the shit. That was my morning routine. That followed by pushing the heels of my hands against my head to hold the pounding headaches at bay. I knew I did it to myself, but somehow the painful pragmatism of avoiding morning hangovers never beat out the gratification of a good drinking session at night. Ever.

For some twisted reason, I did my best thinking hungover. So in a backwards way, enjoying myself at night usually led to a productive day. If drinking alone and stumbling around in alleys and popping pills can be called enjoying myself, that is.

I had a beer with the last bites of my bland-ass oatmeal. "I need a woman to keep me from doing shit like this," I mumbled aloud. A woman would have been nice for sex too. And, well, companionship. I got over the sentimentality of the latter thought fast enough whenever it popped up. *Keep it down, Tommy. It's just you and the bad people out there in the foggy city.*

I had been finding myself more work as a strongman than as an investigator. Clients paid to have me scare people into paying up, or into not straying too far from their marital bed, or to stop asking questions.

The one actual case I had been working before Rebecca came along was a robbery. A big one that had taken a whole hell of a lot of planning. Over four years, in fact. The police had given up and so the guy had come to me. Eddie Vessel. Thin shoulders and pale skin. He ran a business that housed information for other businesses and for individuals, and someone had been stealing info and money. And staplers and pens and such, but that wasn't why he hired me.

See, the police either tried really hard and didn't quit until they nabbed a perpetrator—it didn't matter much if they were guilty or not—or, if the case didn't affect the government, they dusted a door handle for prints and then said, "Good luck, asshole. Investigation closed." And there weren't many cops. Or at least not walking the beat or taking down reports. Military squads patrolled the streets now and again, just enough to make their presence known—and believe me, when forty men in dark gray uniforms holding rifles across their chests materialize from the fog, you think twice about your next move.

Granted, there were transients and bums out there, but it's not exactly squatting when you're hiding out in a misty abandoned building with broken windows and no electricity. Sure, there were plenty of would-be thieves lurking, but what did it matter when there was nothing worth stealing? Or buying. Even if you could get your hands on a pile of cash, the only commodities worth much were food and drink. That's all I ever saved up for, at any rate, with a heavy focus on the latter.

The police, on the other hand, weren't so much there to protect people from danger as they were to coerce us into not causing trouble in the first place. They were the ones who came to you by night, not some thief or killer. I guess they got the job done in their own twisted way, though. People kept pretty much in line. And when something did go bump in the dark, when someone got beaten or stabbed or, every once in a while, ended up dead, a man like me was a pretty hot commodity. I'm goddamn good at what I do. In a city afraid to ask questions, I made my living asking them.

Following people around in the foggy streets, putting together profiles of their movements. Their habits. Who they talked to and when and all that detective stuff. Research, I guess—that word makes it feel more legitimate. But at the end of the day, I usually solved things by asking people questions they didn't expect and watching them squirm. It's amazing how much you can get out of people if they think you already have it. And it gets almost too easy when one slap or a good shaking is enough to terrify.

Eddie Vessel had maybe fifteen, twenty employees, and one of them had been stealing a few things a month for years and lots of things a day for weeks. The police accused the Eddie of robbing himself and advised him to leave them alone. He had narrowed it down to a few guys, and I narrowed it down beyond that. It was either this stupid-looking tall drink of water named Watley or a dark-haired, dark-skinned guy named Thurmond. They both had access to the company ledger, both had access to all the files, and both had a motive to steal: The world sucks. I had no idea why so many people still fell in line.

Watley was a family man; Thurmond, a drunken loser. So I figured Watley was the crook. Thurmond could get drunk enough off his salary. But if you had more than one mouth to feed, that could lead a man to rob the place he worked. With everything grown in greenhouses and every drop of water run through purification plants, it got more expensive to eat all the time.

I had no interest in the case, but I felt sorry for Eddie. Most of his business came from ordinary citizens, folks trying to preserve memories. His warehouse was full of audio recordings and paper documents and pictures that families wanted kept safe. I had dug through the place a few times on weekends, Eddie wringing his hands and following me around, dusting here and organizing there and trying to keep busy. Everything he stored was pre-fog. Pictures of husbands holding wives in bright, sunlit fields. Old videos of beaches and oceans or mountain ranges. That sort of stuff. Depressing.

I guess really it wasn't that I had no interest, but that the more time I spent there, the more knotted up my stomach would get. Seeing all that . . . beauty . . . from the past. I don't know how he and the people who worked there took it. I guess one asshole couldn't. At first I thought maybe it was sentimentality. Of the few government or business files Eddie housed, only one file had been tampered with, and it seemed nothing had been stolen. Some cash, but not much, had gone missing too.

If there had still been functioning banks or insurance agencies or whatever, it would have been much easier to lock the situation down. But there was only cash, and it had been that way for years . . . maybe ten, eleven years, in fact. I never really understood the factors of inflation and free market economies, the bullshit that mattered in the global world I grew up in, but in the mist, a dollar was a dollar: a piece of paper I held until I spent it on scotch or stuck it in a hole next to my bathtub.

I liked it that way. The last bills were printed well over a decade ago, so whenever you'd exchange money, you were guaranteed it would be worn, soft, and faded. It was oddly comforting. A touch of before. Seems like it should have been worthless, but we were all so damn nostalgic for some semblance of order that we bought it, so to speak. Funny what a few rectangular pieces of paper can do. Or make one do.

I sighed, resolved to review my notes, and got my little gray plastic tape recorder out of a cabinet, setting it by an outlet next to the couch. There were only two outlets in my apartment. I plugged my sun sphere into one and whatever else I needed rotated in and out of the other. You could see where there used to be five outlets in the place, but with power as precious as it was now, a residence as small as mine got only two. Some buildings had been taken off the grid altogether and left to molder; some—mostly government facilities—were aglow at all hours of the day. Not sure who made the decisions, but the lights always came on when I flipped the switch, so why bother wondering? At least we didn't pay for electricity anymore. My parents used to get on my case for leaving lights on or the television playing. I missed them, but was glad they died before everything changed. When I thought of them, it was in a perfect vacuum of then, never touching now.

They both got sick, like most everyone else, and died mercifully fast. At least Dad did. I hoped she did too. I wasn't with her at the very end. I still wondered sometimes if they had lived longer whether I would have been different. But just as soon as they were gone I joined the service, and deep down I was so fucking bitter about it all that I never thought about them for long. They were from before, after all. Thinking of them meant thinking of it all.

So Eddie. Poor Eddie losing money and data that led to more money lost as tearful, indignant families took their files and pictures and film and videos elsewhere. I flipped on the tape recorder and pressed rewind, planning to relisten to all my notes and observations and then make a decision over whom I'd try to scare a confession out of first.

A few photographs and documents he'd let me borrow lay

littered about on the coffee table. In only one of the dozen-odd pictures was there even a trace of the fog. It was a picture of a gnarled little pine tree. The sun still fell upon the grass around the tree, but it was soft, diffuse. The picture must have been taken in the last few days of light.

I cracked another beer and sat down to listen to my canned voice mumbling out observations and hypotheses. I reused my tapes so much, their quality was always shot and a scratchy, humming white noise played under my every word, but before long, I wasn't paying any attention anyway. I was thinking about her. Rebecca. It's strange how quickly you'll start to assemble fantastic notions about people you don't know from a hole in the ground. Before long, I was picturing things she might say and how I might respond. I pictured her smiling at me, wearing that red dress here in my shitty little apartment. Then she was in blue jeans and a tight T-shirt—nothing fancy— the opposite of how she had dressed and acted, in fact. Laughing, talking to me about things, about life in the past. Christ, I bet she hardly remembered the past. Before.

I imagined her telling me she had no case, no money for me . . . it was all just an act and she was scared and lonely and spent her last cash on those drinks she bought at Albergue. I would hold her and gently rub the small of her back and breathe in her scent and she would be crying when she pulled away from me and would tell me they were tears of happiness . . . relief.

"I need to get fuckin' laid," I said aloud, standing up and shaking my head at the bullshit fantasies. It had been maybe six or seven months, and I couldn't even remember her name. Carol or Carrie or something? I left while she was still in bed, awake, and she knew I was going and was not at all upset by it. I couldn't blame her. It was Carol. I nodded wistfully to myself, remembering her long chestnut hair streaked gray. She was maybe five years my senior, maybe more. We met while buying

the same kind of soup, and in both our eyes was the same simple desire: flesh. After we fucked a few times, it was painfully
clear that behind our eyes were irreconcilably different people.

In spite of everything, she was full of life. Slender and
toned, her skin healthy if a bit thinned by age, she used to
walk around her apartment naked, telling me about the myriad
paintings on her wall. I never once let her into my shithole of a
home. The way she would moan and close her eyes so tightly, a
tear sometimes sliding down one cheek while I grunted and
dripped with stale whiskey sweat above her—I couldn't take it.
I think she pitied me, and that made it all the worse.

It went on for maybe a month. Probably less. The morning I
left, we didn't speak a word. And I'd hardly thought of her in
all the months in between.

I stood before the window wearing just a pair of shorts.
There was a breeze up this morning, and every once in a while
I could make out the street a story below me. The orb posts,
dark for now, pierced up through the mist. Squinting at where
I knew an alley opened onto my street down to the left, I thought
I could discern the shape of a person. The form was unmoving,
and through the slowly drifting mists, I couldn't be sure if it
was anyone or even anything at all . . . maybe just a shadow. I
strained to see but never got a clear look.

I thought of going downstairs and outside to check, just to
satisfy my curiosity as I was sure it was nothing, but decided to
drop it and sat back down beside my tape recorder. At least the
little incident had gotten my mind off women and my under-
used genitalia. I pressed play.

"Saturday, the . . . the sixteenth, and I have now been, uh . . .
it's been three weeks since I began profiling the employees
here. . . ."

I leaned back on the couch, groaning at my own tedium.
Most of the tapes I had so far were filled with minutiae and

fruitless conjecture. Every session ended with me creating more of the same. And when I went down to see Eddie, forget about it . . . hours of fucking notes I'd sit and drink to later.

AN HOUR HAD PASSED, AND STILL I SAT LISTENING TO MY NOTES and scratching down highlights and thoughts on a little yellow pad of paper. Frankly, all my recordings usually came in as nothing more than tokens. I'd play snippets out of context for clients and show them notes scratched here and there on my yellow pads of paper. (I'd bought a massive stack of the notebooks from the shitshop years ago and still never filled them all.) I'd talk about this tendency of such and such person or this bit of anecdotal bullshit and ask a few questions that I couldn't care less about and then I'd stop whoever I thought was stealing or the errant husband or whatever in some lonely alley and shake what I wanted out of them. It worked, so why not? Also, if you surprise someone a few times in the same place, then wait a few weeks and do it once or twice more, they'll be on edge for months, if not forever.

We're so attuned to patterns that it's easy to create them for people. I'd say, "I'll be watching you," do so for a little bit, and then I was. Always. I saw the old Asian woman from the shop below me at the same times every day. She kept a schedule of when to scowl out at the world, to press her round cheeks between the metal slats of the grate and her forehead against the thick glass.

I stuck to my various routines because I wanted to, not because of any exterior pressures. We were all just rats in the maze. Me. Rebecca. All of us. When I was a kid, I spent one afternoon out in a field near my parents' house screwing with this ant colony. I watched them for over an hour as they built a massive anthill. It seemed like it was two feet high, though really it was probably only eight or nine inches. I was barely four feet tall then, so things were bigger to me.

When their work had died down for a while and they seemed satisfied, I jammed a stick in there, plugging up their hole. Suddenly there were more ants than ever, running here and there and digging and scrambling over one another, and in minutes there was a new hole right next to the one I'd blocked. Next, I watched as they filed past one another in a perfect line, one by one maintaining the lanes of their ant highway. I put a rock right in the middle of their path, and at first they all rushed around and over it and then soon they were passing one another again in a perfect line, two inches left of the rock barrier I'd created. To them it must have seemed a mountain, but they just ran around it.

Sometimes I felt bad for the ants I'd crushed and blocked. Sometimes I felt more sorrow for having caused them suffering than I did for having hurt human beings. Any man I'd crossed or injured and any woman I'd slighted or cheated had at least made choices. And I had made choices too, so I could never feel sorry for myself. But for the stupid little ants who just kept running, there was no choice but to do so, and I felt rotten for having played any part in stopping that.

There were very few insects left in the city. There were still ants around, but not like I remembered in my childhood. Every now and then, I'd kill a roach or a fly in my apartment or office. I never felt any moral ambiguity about killing them. They shouldn't have come into my space. I'm not sure if it's boyhood nostalgia that makes me feel like the rocks and sticks in the anthill were wrong but the roach under my shoe is fine. Maybe that's growing up . . . leaving certain memories and sensations in the past. Maybe it's just that then, when those ants built that hill, it didn't seem so futile. I could crush their colonies and they'd keep coming back, as determined as ever.

Before, when you looked down from a building top or high window at the city streets, it was just the same as the frenetic little insects' world. People running around bumping off one another or sitting in traffic and jockeying for car-lengths. Drop a parked cab or an overturned trash can in front of the cars or the pedestrians, and they'd pause for a bit until they figured out which way to scurry around it, and then everyone would fall in line behind them and form a new channel and get on with themselves.

I used to sit in parks or cafés in the days of the light mists and spreading disease and watch people and feel angry as hell. Everyone had a sense that things were changing and government platitudes and optimistic radio announcements and billboards and all the fucking farce had no effect. We knew things were bad and heading south. I'd sit and watch as people had their last few weeks of sidewalk conversations and treetops and glimpses of sky, and everyone knew that it was a gathering darkness but no one said much of it. Like when you sit by the bedside of some moribund cancer patient, it's always rosy snippets from the past or bright cherry blossoms ahead and oh so many smiles and then their multiplying cells win and the sky goes from blue to gray and then there is no sky. Mothers with hollow eyes rubbing ignorant children's heads and forcing smiles for the other mothers who gathered around them: "It's going to be all right . . . right?" "Oh yes!" one says, as if with authority. As if with any fucking clue, with anything to stand on or lean against aside from pathetic, wayward optimism. "Yes . . . it's going to be fine. I can feel it!" Pollyannaism for some; whiskey for me. No fucking clue what the rest wake up for.

That's when everyone started walking with their heads cast down; up was depressing, the ground and the streets familiar. Hardly anyone's eyes met anymore. All everyone was worried about was not getting their toes stepped on. By feet, by life . . . just don't get your toes stepped on or your hands slapped and don't think too much. We'll get through this, folks. The fucked-up thing about humanity is that we always do. We get through things. We're so goddamned adaptable, we can live in ways we were never meant to. The initial depression and the few instances of looting and the tears and rapes and the rending of garments and gnashing of teeth and all just faded away and people accepted it all.

I gave up on Eddie and whatever asshole was stealing his sad bastard clients' memories. I paced around my place, slowly dressing, one article of clothing between sips of cold coffee and cigarette drags as I wandered, muttering. When I was half-drunk, I felt so fucking sentimental and sorry for the people having things stolen away from them. They only wanted to keep their photos from curling up in the dampness, and so they stuck them in Eddie's climate-controlled warehouse. Sometimes I was so sorry for them and sometimes—when cold sober or dead drunk, mostly—I was so disgusted with the lot of us that their innocence and indignation made me sick. A blubbering grandmother or blustery young father bitching about their last trip to a forest being gone and boo fucking hoo. I wanted to tell them to give up . . . curl up . . . die or accept it: The forest is gone. Enjoy the foggy streets and sleep with your vents pumping and drink lots of the few kinds of liquor you can still get.

I STEPPED OUT INTO THE COLD, GRAY MORNING AND STRETCHED A bit. My jeans were rumpled, and I wore just a T-shirt and slate-colored jacket. As I'd gotten out of the mood to work on the memory thief, I'd gotten in the mood to get rough. I decided to visit a deadbeat who owed me money. Heller. Didn't even know his first name. He was maybe thirty—a squirrelly guy who jumped at loud noises and probably did a lot of drugs and had made the mistake of borrowing from me. He had a few different apartments all in his name; one had been a dead aunt's, the other a dead sister's or cousin's, I'm not sure. It was tricky to track him down because he moved around between the places all the time.

I had looked into renting one a few years back. It was about the size of my place now, but it had a little balcony, and I had liked the prospect of sitting outside above the streets, lost in the air. I wanted to sit there naked and drink scotch and soda and listen to people muttering below me and imagine it was London from centuries past and other such nonsense. But Heller had changed his mind while I was there looking at the place. I think he saw me wanting it and then like a petulant child decided he liked it too. Liked it too much to have old Tommy Vale in there.

But he had said he'd take my deposit and think about it. It took me three months to corner him in an alley and convince him that he oughta pay me back. But then for some inexplicable reason, he had come to me later and asked to borrow money. Even more strangely, I agreed. I guess I was so desperate for human contact that I was willing to enter into a deal that would surely have me chasing and beating the poor fuck before long. It was something . . . it was a reason to talk to someone.

I stood outside my building, smoking a cigarette and trying to decide which of Heller's places I would check first. I usually started with the apartment I'd wanted to live in. Sometimes I figured he'd offer it again to have me ease up on the debt, but whenever I caught him, I'd clap him on the back of the head a few times and he'd give me a rumpled twenty or a few tens and it would be enough and I'd be secretly glad to have a reason to come back. Sometimes we actually talked, once the unpleasant business was out of the way.

I started up the street. The pale yellow glow of the shitshop's sign came into view and I slowed as I passed the window. The old Asian woman was there, glaring at me, her circular face pressed between cold iron slats against dirty glass. I stopped in front of her and gave a half smile. She leaned back from the window, leaving her hands gripping the metal grate, and kept staring at me from within the shop, her face impassive.

"What the fuck are you thinking about, woman?" I whispered aloud as I walked on.

I threw down my cigarette and picked up the pace. Each time I passed an unlit orb post, I laid my hand gently on top of it out of habit. I loved the warm glass spheres at night. By day, they were cold and damp; in the evening, they were comforting. A group drew near me, and I could hear their muffled voices:

"If we don't take him with us, he'll never learn," a woman said.

"Look, it's just one week." A man. "I know you don't think it's ideal . . . learn this sort of thing . . . I'm certain." I lost some of what he said, and then suddenly they were before me. It was a family. A mother wearing a dark dress, maybe thirty-five years old, maybe younger and just worn out. The father wore a rumpled suit and glasses, which he wiped at as they came into view. Two young boys were in tow, both dressed in slacks and brown jackets, with pale, slender faces sticking up above matching dark ties. Hadn't seen kids that young in ages. I was strangely unnerved and embarrassed, seeing their little eyes on me.

The mother was startled to see me and almost missed a step. Then she forced a slight smile and dip and took the smaller boy's hand. The father mumbled a hello, which I returned with a nod, never slowing down throughout our three- or four-second encounter. By the time they were six feet past me, we were all ghosts again. I couldn't be sure, but it sounded like they were talking about going to church. I couldn't even tell you when Sunday was most of the time. Day names didn't matter hardly. It all seemed so ridiculous. So antiquated. But for a moment there, I was almost . . . tempted. Not to find one of the few churches that was still open or anything so drastic; rather, I felt a twinge of jealousy at their feeling a part of anything greater at all.

That, and it must have been nice to always have someone to talk to. When you spend all your time alone or with bad people or at best people who want you to go after bad people, your frame of reference gets all screwed up. All the time I found myself snapping at clerks or being short with waiters, rude to strangers. It's not like that was anything unique in this goddamn city, but I wasn't always like that. It bothered the hell out of me to know that I had changed. It bothered me to feel like the person I culti-vated for the first few decades of life was a failed project.

I almost ran into a darkened orb post. I needed to focus. Keep up with all the sentimental shit, and you got so down . . . there was so little in my life to bring me back up that mostly I had to keep my thinking on the level or keep liquored up. Heller. Money. Maybe a conversation.

The fog was especially thick, the air colder than normal, and no breeze stirred the narrow streets up in the northwest part of town, where Heller lived. I traced my fingertips along the brick wall to my right and could barely see my outstretched hand. I slowed to avoid tripping over anything and searched for a street placard. My fingers found it before my eyes, suddenly sliding across smooth, cold brass. I leaned close to the large engraved disc and read 48TH STREET, with a line under it to show that's what I was on, and RIVER STREET, with an arrow by it indicat-ing that it was the next cross street. I took a few slow steps be-yond the placard, running my palm over the damp bricks, until my hand slipped past the edge of the wall and into space.

I turned down River Street. It was a mere three feet beyond the brass sign, and I hadn't been able to see it. The fog was about as bad as it got. I decided to spend some time on one of the blown-out boulevards later—my latter-day equivalent of an afternoon in the park. Heller's building was about a hundred yards ahead on the left side of the street. I crossed slowly, feel-ing ahead with my foot until I found an orb post, and then fell into a rhythm heading up the street. The posts were placed so precisely that I could walk along with my eyes closed, swinging my right arm at a certain speed, taking three long steps at a certain gait, and each time I lowered my palm, it landed on the next post. It was the fastest way to travel on a very gray day.

One post, one two three steps, next post, one two three steps, and so on. Nineteen posts later, I opened my eyes and edged my way up onto the curb and over to the building beside me. I found the door and smiled at my accuracy. Sure enough, it was Heller's building.

The outer door was usually locked, but I'd learned long ago that a solid kick right by the bolt did the trick nicely. I put my ear to the cold iron for a second to see if I could hear anyone within. Just the hum of the vent, so I leaned back, raised my right leg, and gave a hard kick, heel by the knob. The loud thud was dampened by the heavy air, and the door shuddered inward a few inches. Clockwork. I pushed it open and stepped into the alcove.

The old, rattling vents above me wheezed mist out of the tiny room as I shut the door behind me, waited a moment, and then turned the knob on the second, glass door. I always liked how these older buildings—the old walk-ups—had no lobby areas. You came here to sleep and eat and have sex and whatever else life consists of but not to chat in the foyer. I started up the rickety stairs covered with a moldy carpet, trying to plant my feet close to the outer edge of each step to minimize their creaking.

Heller's place was on the third floor. I slowed my upward climb as I passed the second landing to listen between each step. Faint music drifted down from above. I hoped it was him playing it. I wanted to listen. I had thrown away or taped over all my music years ago. It depressed me, but still, every once in a while, I loved to hear a minute or two.

It was sweet, gentle music . . . pianos and strings. I got to the third landing and stood there for a long while, just listening. I wished everything were different and there was nothing to do but hear it. I sighed, put on my game face, and knocked hard on his door.

The music stopped. For a moment there was silence, and then I heard footfalls coming toward the door. Silence . . . then: "Who's there?"

It was Heller. His thin, raspy voice.

"Open up, Heller."

"Who is it?"

"Open the fucking door or I'll kick it in."

"Vale?"

I paused just long enough to let the moment linger. "Vale," I said.

I heard him sigh, and then fidget with the three locks that barred his door. The tumblers on the final dead bolt clicked and he pulled the door open.

Heller wore beige linen pants and no shirt. His pale, sunken chest was rising and falling rapidly beneath his pointed chin. He hadn't shaved in days and was bleary eyed. His dirty blond hair always looked gray contrasted against his sallow, sickly face.

"Hey, Tom," he muttered.

I pushed past him into the apartment. The main room was large and contained nothing but some metal folding chairs; a small, soiled couch; and an ornate mahogany coffee table. Atop the dark wood of the table sat an old tape player, much like mine. Except that next to his was a stack of cassettes.

The door to his kitchen sat ajar, and I could see various cans and boxes strewn about on the countertops. His bedroom door was shut. The balcony I had so craved sat through that room, and before speaking a word inside his home, I had made up my mind to get out onto it for at least a while.

He watched me as I surveyed the place, standing next to the door with his left hand still on the knob, as if I might suddenly decide to leave. I took a few steps farther into the place, toward the large windows off to my left.

Behind me, I heard him let out a long, tired breath and step away from the door. "I don't have any money right now."

"Sure you do," I said matter-of-factly.

I turned to look at him standing shirtless and shoeless in the middle of his messy apartment and gave a big, toothy grin. "Why don't you go grab whatever you've got."

He shook his head in resignation, scratching at his pasty stomach. "I started renting out my sister's old place two weeks ago, but I won't have a penny for a few days yet."

"The place on Forkner Ave?"

"Yeah," he answered, looking up at me for a second, then down at the cement floor.

I nodded as if in thought, which I was not, and then walked into his tiny kitchen. The cans lying around were all for beans or corn or other such single-item foodstuffs. I pulled open the fridge, hoping for a beer or some wine. Anything to drink, really. There was a bowl of pickles floating in water and some old condiment jars.

"High-class living, huh, buddy?" I sneered. I hated acting like such an asshole, but he needed and expected to be treated like this. He'd had plenty of money not more than a few years back. His inheritance now squandered, I figured my tough love and loans were all that kept his emaciated ass in line.

"Only the best." He slinked into the kitchen and walked around me, pressing his back up against the wall, keeping the small table in the center of the room between us. "I don't have cash for you." He paused. I said nothing; expressed nothing. "I'm sorry."

"Don't fret so much, Heller," I said soft and low, drawing out my *F* on the word *fret*. "Got something to drink? I know you have something around. . . . Cash or no, you'd sooner be dead than empty handed there, right?"

He stared daggers at me, nodded.

"Great. Well, grab me something. I'll just poke around." I walked briskly from the kitchen. He moved as if to stop me, but dropped his arm just as quickly. I walked to the bedroom door and pushed it open. His bed was a mattress propped up upon what once was a bed frame, now just a few splintered boards. A pile of clothes sat in one corner; some empty liquor bottles occupied another.

I glanced into the dingy bathroom before turning to the large sliding-glass door of the balcony. It opened smoothly and I stepped outside. The thick fog swirled past me and into the apartment, and I slid the door shut. He had another pair of folding chairs out in the cramped six-by-four-foot space. I sat down in one of them.

A minute later, Heller slid the door open and stepped outside, now wearing a T-shirt and holding a plastic cup in one hand and a coffee mug in the other. The fan bolted to his ceiling hummed behind him. It was angled so as to blow out the door when it was open. I knew what he would say next. He shut the door and muttered, "I wish you'd switch on the fan before opening that door."

I made eye contact with him and held it until he looked away. Looking past him through the dirty yellow glass of the sliding door, I saw wisps of fog as they were caught by his shoddy vents and spread throughout the room.

"Well, kid, I wish *I* didn't have to do this kind of thing." I sprang up from my chair and wrapped my right hand around the back of his neck. Hard. He gasped a bit and almost spilled the coffee mug. I grabbed his wrist, steadied it, and then took the mug from him. I sniffed it. Vodka?

"What are we toasting with?"

"Gin," he coughed out as I pushed his head forward a few inches, squeezing harder and shaking him from side to side.

"Okay, then. Cheers!" I grinned, releasing him and tapping my mug against his cup. I took a pull of the clear liquor. Awful shit. But alcohol nonetheless. I sat back down. After a moment, he sat too.

"You can relax, Heller. I'm not gonna hit you or anything. Just a pat on the back today." He stretched his neck from side to side reflexively, rubbing at where I had grabbed him. I leaned back as I continued talking and realized that he already had a pale violet bruise where my thumb had been. Jesus. "I just wanted to drop by and see how business was. How you were doing." He said nothing. "So, how are you doing?"

"As good as anyone, I guess," Heller mumbled. He took a large sip of his gin and coughed a bit as it went down.

"You're not the picture of health, Heller. Are you getting enough vitamins and iron in your diet?"

"Might be missing a bit of vitamin D, I guess."

I snorted out a small laugh. He was a clever kid, sometimes. "Yeah . . . slight shortage of that these days." We sat in silence for a while. "How old are you, Heller?"

He looked over at me, held my gaze for a moment. "Twenty-five."

Fuck me . . . I'd figured him for at least thirty. Twenty-fucking-five . . . that was right about at the age where the pre-fog world would be clouded by a child's weak memory. "Do you remember the sun much?"

He nodded, took a sip of liquor. "Sure, I remember it pretty well. Enough to miss it, anyway. I look at pictures of sunny days all the time. I guess some of my memories kind of merged with those images. But I remember how it felt. I remember being able to see things. Being outside and . . . I dunno . . ."

"Under the sky," I added for him.

"Yeah. I remember the sky."

"I wonder if I'll ever see it again. I think about it all the time. I know that's not some profound revelation or anything. I know everyone thinks about that all the time but . . . it's like . . . well, fuck, you may be too young for this to even make much sense, but you remember how everyone used to talk about the weather? Like if it was unusually hot or cold or whatever out, whenever you'd be talking to someone you didn't know that well, you'd say, 'Hot out, huh?' or bitch about how cold it was or talk about how nice it was or the rain and all. So now nothing ever changes, right? So what do we talk about? No one talks about this shit"—I waved my hand in an arc out over the balcony wall—"because you only bitch about something that's gonna change, y'know?"

Heller nodded. He seemed lost in thought, and it was pretty clear he didn't want me there. Or at least didn't want to talk much, but I needed something to do other than wander the streets or mope around at home, half-assing my way through yet another depressing case or drinking alone. So I decided to impose on the poor kid.

"Listen, let's go inside for a minute, huh?"

"Sure." He arose looking nervous. I think he felt the other shoe was about to drop. When I asked him for a refill of gin, he took my glass without looking up at me. He walked into the kitchen and I went into his living room. I sat down on one of the folding chairs and looked at the stack of cassettes by his tape player. Bach, Chopin, Sinatra . . . all things I knew innately but had not listened to in years. Maybe a few notes in some restaurant here, a refrain passing a door there—music really does get me down most of the time, but I was in the mood to choke back some more rotgut liquor and listen to the past for a while.

With energy and manufacturing and all at such a premium these days, it was de facto impossible to create new recorded music. Some places had bands or at least individual musicians strumming guitars or plinking away at pianos, but most of them were too classy for my pocketbook and general outlook. Heller entered and saw me staring at his tapes. He set my mug of gin down and I nodded thanks. Without saying a word, he removed a cassette from the player and inserted another. Heller pressed play and from the little speaker came that familiar, comforting sound of a scratched-up piece of tape rolling toward music. Then came a few gentle, almost timid piano notes. Just a few notes every few seconds at first, then a deeper chord came in underneath them and strings crept into the melody and soon an orchestra filled the room with well-loved, scratched-up recorded beauty.

Heller had been standing, leaning against the wall, but now he sat, sliding down the white painted plaster to sit with his legs crossed, staring down at his cup. I realized that I had tears in my eyes. I quickly looked away and wiped my eyes with a thumb and forefinger, as if massaging tension at the bridge of my nose.

"You smoke in here, right?" I asked, fishing out a pack of cigarettes and a lighter.

"Sure."

"Should I get something to ash in?"

He looked up, a weak smile on his pale lips. "You can ash anywhere. My floor's fucking concrete." He shook his head slightly as he lowered it.

I lit my cigarette and smoked it slowly, trying not to but constantly glancing over at him. He was a strange kid, to be sure, but there was something about Heller that made me think he understood a great deal about life. An old soul. He was too melancholy for his age. It wasn't depression, exactly, nor angst or any of a young man's common demons. . . . He seemed to bear the weight of a lifetime on his thin shoulders. He seemed very tired.

I reached out and picked up the case to the tape he had put on.

"Chopin," he said without looking up.

"It's beautiful."

"He was amazing." Heller looked up now as he said this, nodding with conviction as he stared off at nothing. Then he looked over and our eyes met. "You can borrow it if you want."

"No. Thanks. Music . . . it makes me feel rotten most of the time. I can't stand it, not more than once every few weeks."

"Well, if you want, take it. I'm sure there'll be a moment when you want to spend some time with him."

"With who? Shoppin?"

"Chopin."

I took a long drag of my cigarette and looked away, out the big bay windows on the far side of the room and into the gray.

3

I WANDERED DOWN FORTY-SIXTH STREET LATER THAT AFTER-noon. The fog was lighter now, and I could see three orb posts ahead of me even though they weren't yet aglow. I was heading for Saint Anne's Boulevard. I needed to feel some space. I'm not claustrophobic or anything, and I feel sorry for any son of a bitch who is, but I needed some open space. About twenty feet ahead of me, the mist danced and swirled and I knew I was al-most there. I walked into the churning air and for a second could see nothing, and then I stepped through it and onto the wide, clear-blown street.

I stopped to collect my thoughts, sighing as I looked up and down the wide lane. There were at least twenty people in view—more than I'd seen outside at one time in weeks. A strange sense of community washed over me. A young couple smiled to each other as they leaned against a wall. A man with coffee-brown skin in a light gray suit came ambling up the street. Beneath his matching gray hat, he wore dark sunglasses. He was smiling. And whistling. I snorted out a small laugh upon seeing him.

Sunglasses. A tune on his lips . . . Hope springs eternal. Not
for me, of course. Normally I avoided people, but just then I
wanted to say hi to everyone out on this fine, windblown street.
I started to turn around to ask what was on his mind worth
whistling about. Then I thought to ask an older man who was
passing nearby the time of day, and took a step to do so, but I
hesitated and he ambled on. I watched his thin, stoop-shouldered
frame shudder with each step, as if each time his foot fell, it
pained him. His jacket, once fine, was thin and fraying with
holes along its seams.

My sense of connectivity with the world faded as I watched
him walk away, and instead I wondered where he was going
and why. Old people in shabby clothes have always depressed
me. A glimpse of this old-timer shattered my whole mood. It
seemed so unfair that, in a lifetime so rife with injustice anyway, at the end of their tenure, the elderly should have to shuf-
fle about dressed in patchwork rags. Well, fuck it, I guess. I
sighed and figured I'd just get home fast, picking up the pace.
Ahead of me, a few pedestrians suddenly stopped walking and
moved over against one wall. Then I heard it: the low rumble
of marching feet.

I ducked into the closest alley just as the patrol emerged from
a side street, lingering in the dancing mists where I could just
see the squad. There were about twenty soldiers walking four
abreast in lockstep. Pressed grays and polished black rifles. They
turned with parade ground precision and set off down Saint
Anne's the way I had intended to go. Unsure why, I turned the
other way to take a circuitous route home. Sometimes I wish I'd
stayed in the service. It would've been nice to have a routine and
my meals and pay guaranteed. To feel secure rather than made to
feel insecure. I needed to go over my notes from Eddie's case
more, and then I wanted to have a few good, stiff drinks before
I started to think about seeing Rebecca tomorrow.

"Tomorrow?" I muttered out loud, picking up the pace as I

headed south. Murder and suspects and fifty thousand dollars and all of it. It had *no good* written on it in six different languages. But it was a lot of cash, and she was a very, very pretty girl. I was intrigued by her, and a bit uneasy, which only piqued my interest and need to understand all the more. She knew my name, my drink . . . Those weren't too hard to find out, really, but I had the feeling she knew a hell of a lot more.

As I passed one of the giant blowers, I caught a glimpse of a woman with blond hair ducking into an alley. I was squinting against the fan's wind and couldn't be certain . . . but it sure looked like her. I picked up the pace and crossed the wide boulevard, holding out my hands as I plunged through the undulating mist and into the alley. I zigzagged back and forth across the narrow alley, waving one arm outstretched before me and keeping the other lower, feeling for orbs or any trash on the ground. I moved about thirty or forty feet up the alley in this awkward stumble. If it had been her, or anyone who didn't want to be found, they would have gotten away by now.

"Hi, Rebecca!" I called out into the misty evening. Silence. It was worth the try. Probably hadn't been her, anyway . . . just my mind playing tricks on me. I made my way back out to Saint Anne's Blvd as the orbs switched on in the alley. The spheres gradually changed from a pale, flickering yellow to the soft orange glow that would guide me home yet again.

I SAT IN MY APARTMENT WITH A GLASS OF SCOTCH IN ONE HAND and the cassette of Chopin's music in the other. I had decided to take it from Heller after all, reasoning that I might end up wanting to listen to it or, if not, returning it would at least be something to do. An education and idleness just don't go well together.

Having Rebecca on my mind was keeping me from my usual brooding sessions, but the more I thought about her and the more I drank, the more a sense of dread worked its way through my veins. The thing I kept coming back to was not Rebecca, but whoever was behind her. There was no way a pretty young girl walked into Albergue and offered up a huge sum of cash on her own, a wronged-man murder backstory and having done her homework on me, no less. I was staring at the worn, gray cassette as I thought about Rebecca, and twice already I had leaned forward toward my tape player to put it on; twice I'd paused, arm outstretched, and then leaned back into my seat—not yet.

When I talked to her, I knew I'd need to feed her information that would be digested by someone else. But it's hard not to say too much or to ask the right questions when the person you're plugging for info isn't the one holding the hand you need tipped. She was sharp, too. Intelligence lurked behind those smiling gray eyes. But people who think they're smart almost invariably think they're brighter than they actually shine. I could use that to my advantage.

I set the cassette tape down and rose. Pacing around the place, I finished off my glass of whiskey and set it in the little kitchen alcove. I was hungry, but about all I had in the apartment was rice and beans. I tried a few pieces of old, dried-out bread, but it was too moldy. I went for the pills instead.

I popped open the little white bottle and dumped its contents out into my palm. Four pills. Fuck. I had meant to see Salk that afternoon, but a few drinks and a bit more time than I'd expected at Heller's had thrown my plans off. I didn't like having that few meds around. The addictive mind never truly craves something until it's in short supply.

I filled my glass and stood by the window, staring out into the charcoal gray night. I felt bad for having grabbed the kid's neck so roughly earlier. It had turned yellowish by the time I'd left him. Heller had seemed like a strung-out nuisance when I met him; now he seemed more like a lonely, sad-bastard young man. I wondered what he thought about me. He must have hated me to some extent. But I've been changing over the past couple of years—growing less tough, more resigned.

I wheeled from the window and set down my glass. Moving quickly, before I could hesitate again, I shoved the cassette in the player and turned it on. For the next hour or so, I slowly got drunk and more than a few times sat with tears running down my cheeks as music filled the room and my mind. Eventually, around two o'clock, I collapsed onto my bed. I had the rare pleasure of sleeping soundly through three o'clock that night.

AS I MADE MY WAY TO MY OFFICE THE NEXT MORNING, I FELT UN-easiness akin to the apprehension before a first date. But I needed to realize that all the conversations and exchanges that I had imagined might occur between us would not. Any words I had put in her mouth were not going to come out, so all my clever or charming rejoinders were useless. I needed to act the consummate professional I used to be and drop all the preconceptions. I stopped in the dead air behind a blower and lit a cigarette.

"Also," I said aloud, unconsciously gesticulating with my hands as if explaining the situation to an external self, "she won't fuck you, Tom."

Hearing it ring out loud like that straightened my thinking a bit. I took a few drags off my smoke and then walked at a faster pace toward my little closet of an office. The glowing numbers on my sun sphere had read 11:18 when I left home, so it was likely now half-past. I figured I'd have at least a couple of hours to get on my game face.

Anyone would call my office a shithole. And I knew I was not in the right mental frame when the first thing I thought upon entering was that it would make a bad impression on a refined lady. There were stacks of paper and cassette tapes strewn every-where. A few of the photos and items Eddie had let me take as samples were piled in one corner. My chair is a dumpy wood and cloth thing I found in an alley. Tripped over is more accurate. Before finding it, I'd sat on a metal folding chair for almost two years, and that's where I was going to put Rebecca.

The desk, gray metal with rust spots and coffee stains, sat beside an ugly black file chest against the wall opposite the door. No windows. The building had been renovated post-fog. Most of the other chambers in it were either vacant or rented out to government drone types. The more scarce power and water had grown, the more people had been employed to make the getting of it complicated.

I usually kept a negative score when I walked in, starting right after I closed the first air lock door. Each person I passed was a point off. I got a perfect score of zero today; I hadn't passed a soul in the lobby, on the elevator ride up, or on the long, dimly lit walk to my unmarked door. The number next to it—1023—was the only way to know where Thomas Vale pretty much never was.

I cleaned the ten-by-ten space as best I could for about half an hour, shoving everything into drawers without the slightest trace of order. I'd been trying to arrange the photos from Eddie's warehouse chronologically—it seemed like most of his clients were missing material from the same time, when the sky turned from haze to real fog. Hours of busy work was erased in seconds.

I grabbed two mismatched coffee mugs and a little blue plastic pitcher. I figured it would be best to seem prepared for her.

In the kitchen, I lost a point. She was short, fat, and dressed in clean, pressed clothes. Lipstick. Why she still bothered was beyond me. I tried to avoid contact with her dull, watery eyes smiling behind thick glasses, but she wouldn't let me.

"Hi, there! How are you?"

Nappy brown hair and pudgy cheeks and that stupid smile as she filled a large plastic cup at the tap. The fuck was she so happy about?

"Morning," I mumbled.

"Actually, it's just past twelve, so good afternoon," she practically beamed.

"Oh. Good afternoon," I said, pausing after the *oh* and sounding about as pleasant as I felt.

I waited until she left with her tepid water before cleaning out the bacteria cultures growing in my mugs. I filled the pitcher with coffee from the tap in the wall and grabbed a few napkins off the counter. The coffee tap never ran dry. I never had any idea who filled whatever container it came from. It was awful stuff but par for the course no matter where you looked. All the coffee in this town must come from the same greenhouse. Gourmet had long gone.

I went back to my office, sat down, arranged the mugs and pitcher, and waited. For an hour. Then longer.

I smoked cigarettes, tossing the plain white pack from hand to hand then pausing to study it. It had the word CIGARETTES printed across it in black letters. There were no tobacco brands left. God save us if the liquor ran dry. Halfheartedly, I flipped through notes no longer pertinent to Eddie's case. I got up, dumped out the cold coffee, refilled the pitcher, and then waited some more. I nodded off at some point.

I WOKE UP CONFUSED. IT WAS QUIET, BUT I KNEW SOMETHING HAD awoken me. I pressed the heels of my hands against my eyes and shook my head to clear it. Then a knocking sounded on the door, so faint it was almost lost in the gentle hum of the building's vents. I rose, stretched quickly, and opened the door.

Rebecca wore slim khaki pants and a conservative button-down shirt beneath a gray blazer. She was simply beautiful. Try as she might to hide beneath these clothes, she was just as pretty as when she wore that slutty red number. I stepped back into the office and wordlessly gestured for her to come in.

"It's so strange to actually find you here," she said quietly as she entered the room and stepped past me. I leaned close to her blond hair as she crossed in front of me and breathed in before she turned. She smelled sweet, vaguely like honey, but damp. Like everyone always does. We stood there, facing each other for a moment.

Then I turned crisply and walked behind my desk, sitting down and indicating she should do the same. "Coffee?"

"Sure. Thank you," she said. I filled her cup and then my own and then leaned back in my chair, sizing her up. I wanted her to make the first moves . . . set the tone and pacing of our first official meeting. Evidently she was waiting for me to do the same; she looked up at me a few times with those pale, gray eyes, but mostly Rebecca sat, staring down into her lukewarm coffee and seeming very uncomfortable. Fuck it. I started things.

"So let's take it from the top, huh?"

"I . . . yes." She stammered, setting down her coffee mug. "I guess I just . . . start . . ." She looked at me imploringly.

"Talking," I said softly. "You just start talking." I pulled a pack of cigarettes from my desk drawer, took one, and offered her the pack.

"No thanks, I don't—don't want one. Thanks."

Well, that was odd. She had almost covered it up. . . . I made my first note of the day . . . aside from her clothes and persistent beauty.

"Okay. Um . . . Okay, Tom. The dead man. Samuel Ayers. He was murdered about . . . two weeks ago now. Maybe twenty days. I'm not sure, but I can figure it out if you need me to."

"I'll need you to."

"Right. Of course you will. He was killed in an alley off of Eighth Avenue. No witnesses, of course, and I . . . I don't know a motive or anything. . . . I just know that the man they have in prison didn't do it."

"We'll get there. Tell me more about Mr. Ayers. Everything

you know." My eyes drifted to the gentle rise of her breasts, not quite concealed beneath her jacket.

"What? Well . . . not much, I'm afraid. He . . ." She caught me staring and faltered. "He was middle aged; he worked some job for the government. I don't know much about him."

"Where did you get fifty thousand dollars?" I tried to catch her off guard with this. It seemed to have worked, to an extent.

"I . . . don't know if that matters, really. I have the money. I can prove it."

"Rebecca, how? How do you have it? Dirty money stains every hand it touches. I need to know about it. Now."

She took a sip of coffee. I could see her fight not to purse her lips against the bitter, tepid beverage. "My parents were rich. They died and then I was . . . rich. I don't have much left now. But I have enough to pay you and—"

"Why come right out with a number that high? Hmm? Just seems odd to me. You walk in off the street and throw that sum in my lap? Why?"

"Because . . . the police wanted even more to complete their investigation. I didn't have more. So I offered you what I could. Because the police won't want you asking questions about this. You'll want all that money when it's over."

"Well, that's reassuring." I took a long, slow drag off my cigarette and laid it down in the ashtray. It's pewter and shaped like a shallow bowl with a large flat lip and has only one groove carved in it to hold a smoke.

She looked away; her eyes traveled around the room, from the file cabinet to my cigarette to the door.

"Okay, who's the guy in jail?"

She looked up at me. Sighed. Looked like she might cry for a minute. This was certainly a different girl than I had seen two nights ago. But she was smart. Deceptive. I could tell, and knew that likely—very likely—both sides of her were beards for some deeper, hidden person. Some self-serving, self-sustaining core. Hook me with a sexy red dress, soften me with moist eyes, and then snap the trap closed. My guess was that this was a no-money trap. I fucking hated no-money traps. They come, use you, and disappear into the fog. I knew she was using me but couldn't figure out what for. I felt that maybe there was some benefit for me, even without the cash. Maybe an insurance policy. If I knew who was behind her, it might help keep my bones intact.

I repeated myself: "Who is in jail?"

"He's innocent."

"What's his name, and what's your connection?"

"His name is Fallon. We . . . I love him." I leaned back in my chair, taking a drag and then stubbing out the cigarette. Well, there it was. Knew it, called it, got it.

"Right." My face was placid. Eyes cold. It was so strange to see her here, nervous, fidgeting, dressed like a secretary and acting like a scared kid. Even if it was just that, an act, if I had met her today for the first time, I would have been sold. I pulled a pen and one of my yellow pads from a creaky desk drawer and started scratching down notes. No info on Ayers aside from middle-age and government job, police asked for large bribe, Fallon is jailed suspect, lover . . . I noted how she was acting and dressed . . . scribbled all this down for a couple minutes, letting her squirm a bit.

"Okay . . . how are you certain of Fallon's innocence?"

"Well, he was with me the night it happened. Every night. And he'd never hurt a fly even if I didn't have a perfect alibi for him. He—"

"What's his last name?" I interrupted.

She stumbled. "He—his what?"

"His last name. What's his last name? Shouldn't take you so long to answer, kid."

"Samson. It's Samson."

"Okay. It's Samson," I said, jotting that down and noting her awkwardness. "So . . . Fallon Samson is with you every night. . . . Who's blaming him for killing people out in the fog, then?"

"I don't know. He was arrested and they wouldn't tell me anything, because we're not married or anything. And you know what it's like trying to learn about trials and get answers from the government and all these days, I'm sure."

"Yeah. They don't like questions, do they?"

She shook her head, smiling ruefully, and took a sip of coffee. She choked it down, looking at the dirty linoleum floor.

"Rebecca." She looked up. "You don't have to keep drinking that shit to be polite. I know it's awful."

Her smile turned from wistful to bright for a fleeting moment. She set the mug down and dabbed at her lips with a gray woolen sleeve. "It's, um—yeah, it's a bit rough."

"It's horrible. Years I've been renting this little box of an office, and it's consistently the worst fucking coffee you can find in a city full of awful coffee."

She leaned back, seemed to relax a bit.

"How did you know my bar and my drink? How did you find me?" I asked.

"I . . . I watched you. I wore a hat, sat there . . . I watched you from a booth. That's all. I swear. Nothing sneaky, nothing—"

"Spying on me long enough to know my drink and my habits isn't sneaky?"

"I'm sorry. I didn't know what else to do. There's no one that can help people with this kind of thing anymore. You know that. You're a dying breed, Tom."

I nodded, looked away, and pretended to be reflective. Pretended to be satisfied with that answer. But really, I was uneasy: she had not been watching me from a booth in Albergue. I notice strangers. Always. The first time she and I had ever been in a room together, she had been a red-dressed, cigarette-smoking seductress. More lies, sweetheart. Fuck. I needed to see proof of the cash. A hefty advance. Soon.

"Okay. Fine. You watched me. How did you know I was someone worth watching? I find my clients these days; they don't find me."

"Yeah, I thought you'd be concerned about that. Here—" She reached into her jacket pocket and pulled out a carefully folded piece of paper. I took it from her outstretched hand. It was yellow with age, fragile . . . familiar.

"No fuckin' way," I muttered as I gingerly unfolded it. But there it was.

THOMAS VALE
PRIVATE DETECTIVE &
CLAIMS RECOVERY

My old ad. Sure enough, there was my office number—still 1023—and the number of the phone I keep unplugged except when I want to call out. The last phone book circulated, what, five years ago? I think it was five years back . . . the same year I first rented out the cell we sat in now.

"Wow . . . there's memory lane for you. . . ." I held the sheet of paper for a few moments longer and then refolded it and handed it back to her. "Same number and everything."

"I tried to call a few times."

"Yeah . . . the phone hasn't been plugged in for weeks. Maybe months. I keep it in a drawer, in fact." I pulled open the bottom drawer on my desk and raised the ancient beige telephone to show her, setting it down on the desk between us like some artifact to be pondered. "I plug it in only when I want to make a call and then put it away as soon as I'm done."

She nodded. I sat still, looking at her for a few seconds. For a bit too long, actually. She makes that easy to do.

"What else do I say? I mean . . . where do we start? Or do you start?"

"How old are you? Twenty-six?"

Her face flushed slightly, and she swallowed before answering softly. "Yes."

"What do you do?"

"I . . . I don't, really. To be honest. I manage my parents' estate. What's left of it, anyway."

I had to ask the hard question next: "Did they die when the virus struck?"

She looked down, her eyes falling, unfocused, on the phone. The moment hung heavily in the stale air. "My father did. My mother died more recently."

"I'm sorry." I paused. "How?"

"Is it really—? . . . She had a . . . an embolism, the doctor said." She looked up at me while she spoke, and then away again as soon as she fell silent.

"Well, again, I'm sorry." I lit a cigarette and leaned back in my chair. "We start like this: I need to know exactly where and when Ayers was killed. So figure that out as soon as you can. I need to know how he died."

She looked up at me as I exhaled a thin trail of blue gray smoke. "He was shot in the back. Three shots from very close range, they said."

"The police said?"

"Yes."

I leaned forward quickly. "Why did the police tell you a detail like that? They don't tell me shit, and I know some of them. I served in the army with some of them, and they won't give me the time of day when I go snooping around uptown, so how could you know that, Becca?"

"I don't know. I guess I was flirting to get information."

"I can see how that might work. What I don't see is any kind of envelope or parcel or anything in your hands. One with a lot of cash in it, maybe?"

"I promise you'll be paid. If you don't want this, then I'll just leave now."

I nodded a few times and took one last, long drag before violently stubbing out my smoke. I exhaled through my nostrils. "Okay. Good enough for now. I need to know more about Fallon. How long you've known him. Been with him." Her eyes darted down and to the left as I spoke his name. "I need to know everyone you've talked to since this shooting happened. What you were doing and who you saw in the days before. I need to know lots of things. So why don't I go get us more shitty coffee."

4

THE ORBS CAME ALIVE AS I WALKED DOWN SEVENTH AVE. THE FOG wasn't bad, and I could see a full three spheres ahead undulating yellow and ocher before settling into their orange glow for the night. The air was colder than it had been in days. It felt good. I buttoned my heavy gray jacket as a shiver ran through my chest, relishing the bracing temperature. It let me know I was awake, aware.

I crossed a few streets, staying on Seventh. In one of the intersections, an older guy nearly walked into me, focusing on a book he held just under his nose. He let out an awkward gasp as I stopped short to avoid a collision, then composed himself, nodded, and ambled on, eyes back on the pages. I wondered if it was a lifelong habit adapted to the mist or if the old guy had begun his literary strolls in the new world.

When we were first placed under quarantine—the few hundred thousand of us—the city took on the aspect of a prison. A massive, Byzantine prison, but captivity nonetheless. Then, when this gray veil slowly drifted down, thickening until it was a shroud over us all, the feeling of the city as a prison was gradually usurped by a general feeling of directionless wandering. When you can't see ten feet in front of you, the road could just as well go on forever as it could stop after eleven more steps. Landmarks lost their status as points of reference. North, south, east, and west became concepts, unencumbered by attachment to a floating sun or silent moon.

The city became a series of tunnels. You were never held in one place, and you never seemed to be going anywhere specific. All any of us could do was wander around, never quite trapped but with no prospect for escape. It was as liberating as it was crushing.

I needed to sleep. I had been doing too much thinking all afternoon. Without pills and a healthy dose of whiskey, it was going to be a long time before dawn. I was even more confused about Rebecca than before, and had no idea what to make of her story—it was all over the place. She had dodged questions left and right. She changed the subject or answered each question with one of her own. She was thinking on the fly.

We had talked for an hour or so, until I had enough to start putting pieces together on my own. She had been growing more and more nervous the longer she stayed in my office. Fidgeting . . . looking around as if someone might be watching us there in that windowless room. When she finally got up to leave, there was relief in her eyes. I didn't take it personally. And she didn't mean it that way, either. I really did get the feeling that she wished me no ill will. But in a way, that only complicated things. If there was no malice aimed at me, why lie and play games?

I had opened the door for her and moved aside. She smiled and said nothing, stepping past me. I caught her by the left elbow and turned her to face me. She was startled, eyes like an animal about to break and run. I had leaned in close to her lovely face and said, very quietly, "Rebecca . . . I don't think I trust you." Then I let go of her arm and gently placed my hand on her shoulder, ushering her out the door. She stuttered and tried to respond, but I had smiled, almost wistfully, and shut the door in her face.

We were to see each other again in two days. Same time, same place. So that left me time to see what I could find out, to start cross-referencing her facts, check up on her details.

It was not quite nighttime. Just enough light bounced around off the fog, coming down from the sun somewhere high above, to render the streetlights impotent. I always loved the magic hour between light and dark. It reminded me of something from a dream: the way the lamps shine but cast no shadows, the sky blue but sunless and the land still colorful but faded. On the streets with blowers, a bit of that essence remained.

The orbs winked at me from alleys and side streets bisecting Eighth Ave. Little wisps of haze reached out toward me, as if for me, from these darkened roads, and then twirled about themselves, dancing back into the mist or gently dispersing into nothing. I think if I had my choice and I could make the fog go away, the first thing I would want to see would be twilight with just a few stars piercing the blue gray canopy. I wanted to watch night creep over the dome of sky and wrap around us all, and then, in the morning, the sun would rise and I would never again be angry to have it on my shoulders or in my eyes.

I had stopped walking and stood, lost in thought, in the middle of the street. It must have been true night above by now—I cast a shadow in the pale light of the streetlamps, and the soft glow of the few open stores and restaurants spilled out onto the sidewalks before them.

The door to Carol's apartment was close by. I knew she'd let me in. Earlier in the afternoon, I had thought it was what I wanted. What I needed. But as I lingered there in the twilight haze, I couldn't bring myself to take those last few steps. To ring the bell, to make the small talk and drink the wine and see her bright green eyes on me, free of judgment but full of pity.

It must have been Rebecca that drove me the other way down the street. I knew why I had sought Carol—knew I would have pretended she were someone else. It wouldn't help anything. Just make things more complex. I lit a smoke and made my way quickly toward Salk's pharmacy and my bottle of fixes.

SALK WAS, BY ALL ACCOUNTS, AN UGLY MAN. HE WAS FIFTY, MAYBE fifty-five, and had aged with the grace of a bulldozer. His remaining hair was more yellow than gray or white. His skin greasy and sallow—jaundiced. The pores of his nose massive. Just massive. I'd never seen anything like them. If he lived another twenty years, he'd be able to smuggle pills in those things.

He said he was a doctor once. A pediatrician. He was a nice guy in a pathetic, beat-down kind of way. In our exchanges, no matter how brief or protracted, all he tended to do was quietly complain. It wasn't whining. It was more of a lament. He lamented the state of things and took what the world had come to very personally. It was leveled at him, he seemed convinced. He wouldn't say "I wish we could still get tomatoes" or "I miss tomatoes" or anything like that. Instead he would sigh and whisper, shaking his head, "Tomatoes are gone forever."

A depressed, depressing guy. But I wasn't exactly Mr. Shot-in-the-Arm, so usually I was polite but laconic with him. I needed booze, smokes, and pills. And maybe some canned food so I wouldn't have to leave the house for a couple days.

I stubbed out my cigarette on the bricks in front of his store. Every time I passed under the faded sign above the boarded-up window, I'd smile sardonically. In tall block letters on a cracked white display that was once illuminated was the word DRUGS. The vents in the alcove were old and weak, wheezing at the offending air.

I blinked and rubbed at my eyes to adjust to the interior light. A few fluorescent tubes shone above, casting a cold pall across the half-empty shelves of the dilapidated place. An old woman shuffled down one of the aisles, reading the labels on various bottles. The place was empty except for her.

I walked to the far wall and grabbed two fifths of scotch and a handle of vodka. Then I stepped in front of the big, hazy sheet of glass that separated Salk from the rest of us. He sat with his back to me on a strangely ornate wooden chair. It was fine wood—maybe oak—and intricately carved with flowery protrusions along the armrests and back. It was a singularly peculiar sight: this middle-aged man in a fancy chair surrounded by rusted metal shelves stacked with bottles of pills.

I knocked gently on the glass. He straightened up, then set down a book and rose, not yet having turned or looked back at me. Salk stretched his fleshy neck and slowly trudged toward the glass, eyes cast downward. When finally he lifted them and recognized me, both warmth and pity played across his repellent face.

"Thomas. Hello."

"Hey, Salk. How've you been?"

"Nothing has changed. Nothing changes."

"Yeah . . . not even my attempts at friendly banter, right?"

He smiled and inclined his head, eyes closed. "I always appreciate your asking, just the same. And how are things with you?"

"Uh . . ." I legitimately thought for a moment. "Fine, I suppose. I mean I'm still here . . . still alive and in one piece. That's about as good as it gets."

He stood behind the thick glass etched with spiderweb cracks and said nothing for a moment. "Still having trouble sleeping?"

"Oh, only every night."

"That's too bad. Well, I'm sure we can help. Let's just . . ." He subtly pointed to the elderly lady, who seemed to be through with her searching. I nodded and stepped aside as she shuffled up to the glass and held aloft one item for Salk to price. A large, brightly colored candle. *Well, that's pleasant,* I thought to myself. As soon as the thought was fully formed in my head, I was struck by my own cynicism. It's the little things in life, right? All the minute pleasant details that add up to a nice day or all the individual frustrations or contentions that lead to a life poorly lived—the sum of those equals the whole. So fuck me, not her.

I ambled around the store, feigning purpose. All I really wanted at this point was to get home and get not-sober fast. Salk's canned goods section got as much action from me as any grocery store. I preferred dumping cans into pots and eating out of the latter with a spoon to multi-step, multi-ingredient preparation anyway. *Fresh* had become a relative term.

I picked up a rickety metal basket from a small table by the door, dropped in the bottles of booze and grabbed a few cans of this, a few of that. Whatever looked, from the label, like it had the most ingredients in it. To balance things out in the old digestive system. I stuffed as many foodstuffs as I could in the basket. Then I grabbed a few small candles. They smelled like apples. I grabbed a carton of cigarettes too.

The old woman was gone, so Salk and I got down to business. I heard several bolts click and rattle, and then he emerged from a narrow door beside the window. Salk surveyed the contents of my basket briefly, and then said, "Let's call it thirty dollars."

"Hey, I appreciate it, but the liquor alone must—"

"Thomas," he interrupted gently, "everything here is subsidized by the government. I'm a licensed pharmacist—a civic employee, after all. No one has checked my inventory in years." He rubbed the bridge of his nose, eyes shut tight as if fighting a tension headache. "And frankly, hardly anyone comes in anymore anyway. I've grown to not much mind it, though. I take what I want and sell what I can for however much I feel is fair." He looked up at me. "And then, of course, there's . . ."

"Yeah." I handed him thirty dollars in rumpled bills and accepted a paper bag he handed me. I continued speaking while packing my cans, bottles, smokes, and the candles. "I need more. More than last time."

THE ALLEY BEHIND SALK'S PHARMACY HAD NO ORBS AND NO streetlights pierced the swirling fog here. The air was gray black, and anything more than three feet from your face impossible to see. A very good place to do this kind of thing. Salk was convinced that the ancient camera in one corner of his store still worked and that the government knew who had prescriptions and who did not.

I was sure this was batshit, but there was no reason to ever press the issue. I stood leaning against the wet bricks next to the pharmacy's back door and waited for him to emerge. After a minute or so, the door clicked open and pale yellow light spilled into the void. He leaned out, saw me, and then stepped into the alley and sealed the door behind him. I heard the rattle of a pill bottle in the darkness. His hand found my arm, and then he pressed the bottle into my open palm.

"It's quite full."

"Thanks."

"You know, Thomas, I used to feel like I really helped people. Really . . . really connected . . ." He sighed and looked away.

"You help me."

Salk laughed under his breath, a bitter little sound. "I do what I can. I like the sense of routine. What else is there?"

Not knowing how to respond, I dug in my pocket for a couple of bills. "This is a fifty and a twenty."

"That will be fine, Thomas. I thank you," he said with an almost noble, resigned air as he backed away. I heard the door click open, and then yellow light again softened the darkness. Salk said nothing more and did not pause or look back as he shut the door behind him and left me standing in the blackness of the alley, clutching a paper sack full of liquor and canned food in one hand and a bottle of pills in the other.

* * *

I SAT STARING AT THE TAPE PLAYER. CHOPIN WAS POISED AND ready to fill the room and reduce me to a blubbering pile. I was drunk, but not very. I looked up and thought to rise and eat something, to bathe—anything to keep me from pressing play and unleashing the music on myself. Unconsciously, my eyes locked on to a black smudge on the wall across from my thread-bare couch. I sat staring at this little patch of filth and hummed to myself off-key.

The ash from my cigarette snapped me from a trance as it fell onto my fingers. The smoke had burned itself out. I shook my hand, startled, and then threw the wasted butt into the over-flowing ashtray. I rose and yanked the tape player's plug from the wall, resolved not to listen to music tonight. I paced around the small room, needing something to do.

Nothing added up about what Rebecca had told me. I con-sidered backing out of the whole thing. Eddie was a poor, honest sap—if I could figure out who was ripping him off, it'd pay the bills and keep me drunk for a couple of months and I was sure to find some desperate, spurned wife or a debtor to shake down or something. I'd lived by my instincts all my life. More so after the fog settled in. Most everyone looks out for themselves—it's depressing, it's bitter, it's true. There were still a few churches out there and some support groups and places where people could gather and actually talk to one another, but none of it was right for me. I'd never been able to trust people; and it was even harder now. I walked over to the window and stood mumbling to myself, half out loud, at times silently. Noth-ing felt right, and really, the only reason I'd agreed to meet with Becca a third time was curiosity. And a little sense of excitement, I guess. And hey, I could always run off down some gray street and never look back when the walls started closing in.

She had told me more about him. Fallon. Told me lots of non-intimate details. He sounded like an asshole to me. He sounded like a pushover—worked in a big office of the power company. A drone. I had already come to hate this man because she loved him. Because he had something beautiful. But regardless of that and regardless of her description, office drones don't end up framed for murder. They shopped at the grocery stores on big, blown-out avenues and spent money at bars in one of the few restaurants uptown. There was more to him. And I was going to find out about it.

Then there was Samuel Ayers. . . . There was at least one advantage to the ever-centralizing, growing bureaucracy of this city: the bureaucrats who answered the phones were experts at inadvertently giving away information. If you wanted to find someone you called the city. Every call for everything started at the same place: City Central. One of the thousand glassy-eyed, soulless pen pushers at Central took your call. You asked for an individual, a department, a business—anything. More often than not, that's where your search ended. They hardly ever gave you the info you needed; they gave a curt take on *fuck you very much,* and you're left holding a dead phone to your ear. But if you were looking for a government employee, things were a bit easier.

I had called Central shortly after Rebecca left my office and asked for Samuel Ayers. The woman on the other end mumbled and clicked at her console and eventually said that rarely heard word: "Transferring." I had interrupted, asking to which department, and she replied, "Science and Development Research. Transferring."

Once I got the phone-answering drone in the Science and Development Department, my trail had, not surprisingly, gone cold. When I had asked for Ayers, the man on the other end of the line clicked at his console, then asked me to repeat the name. He typed more, the line was silent for a minute, and then he came back on, saying, "We have no information to distribute on a Samuel Ayers. Good day."

I'd learned long ago not to start making assumptions when the facts aren't in, as often one will start to treat the two as equals, but still it brought up intriguing questions. Was he a scientist? They didn't tend to have many enemies.

I stood looking out at the gray curtain sliding past my window, doing what I did best—drinking and letting my mind wander. I decided on going to the Science and Development Research Department the next day and trying to talk my way into more information on Ayers. I'd go to the police station and hit up the few guys who didn't shut doors on me for details on Fallon. But for now, I was done working. Done focusing. With a real case like this—not some shakedown bullshit work—I put the pieces together mostly when I wasn't trying to. I'd often wake up with a new idea or click two pieces together while finishing a scotch at Albergue.

I drew a deep, tepid bath and lowered myself into my rust-stained tub. The cool water felt excellent—refreshing and relaxing. It was funny how often on nights when the fog was bad I'd get home damp and sweating, and immediately get into the shower or bath. Water washing away water. I think part of the reason I like bathing so much is that it forces you to do nothing. Or at most very little. Cigarettes and tubs go very well together, especially with a glass of whiskey on the side. But you can't really work; if you think of something you want to do, it's a process— get up, dry off, dress—so anything that can be put off is.

Head back, I closed my eyes and dipped the smoke I was holding into the water, and then tossed the butt away. My mind was blissfully blank. I sat perfectly still in the cool water for a long time.

WITH A RAGGED GASP, I AWOKE AND SAT BOLT UPRIGHT IN BED. MY eyes went immediately to the Sun Sphere—3:00 A.M. on the dot. I caught my breath and dropped back down onto the sweat-soaked mattress, throwing the rumpled sheets and blanket off my body. Had I just been dreaming? I felt thoughts slipping away from me . . . images in the offing and memory on the horizon. A bright green field. People walking toward me from very far away . . . Heller's face.

I let out a long, slow breath, giving up. Whatever had been in my head, I'd lost it. Which was just as well—usually my dreams were less than pleasant. I was pretty sure I knew what dream it had been anyway, and I tried not to think about it. But sleep would not take me back, so in the familiar haze of Salk's drugs, still working their way throughout my bloodstream, I let the thoughts in.

The worst thing I've ever had to do was shoot the sick. I'd cursed myself a million times for not joining the army at nineteen like I had originally planned; had I not put it off those few short years, I would have been done and out by the time the virus came. They stationed us out on the roads and made it very simple: People heading out of the city were to be turned back—people approaching the city were to be shot.

No one knew what it was, but it spread fast, and the afflicted seemed to melt from within over a few short days. Hair falling out, skin turning moist and gray and then shedding off. Bones and teeth brittle and cracking. I've almost suppressed the last glimpse I caught of my mother, frail and rotting, as she was loaded onto a bus and driven off to die. Dad was gone when I woke up the morning before.

I had enlisted within forty-eight hours. Push-ups and square meals and cots. Within the month, as the virus spread ever farther, ever faster, my cursory training was over and I was rated with a .223 rifle and small arms and detonators.

They gave us gas masks and lots of ammunition and the captains spoke with the sergeants and then the sergeants shouted at us. So along with a bunch of other teenaged or twenty-something young men, I laced up my boots, pulled down my mask, and climbed on top of a truck parked across the highway. It had been a pleasant late winter, early spring day. The air was cool but the sun was warm.

When the first few of the dying approached, we fired into the air above them, waved our arms at them to go back. It was a group made up of three women and an older man. Stumbling, they inched ever closer, weak and delirious with sickness. When they were less than a hundred yards away, one of the younger guys, just a hothead kid too young to buy a beer, opened up on them. Then like rabid dogs unleashed, we all did. Shot and killed them where they stood.

At first I tried to blame that kid who opened fire—who opened the way for me to do the same. . . . But really, I should have thanked him. He freed us all to do what I suppose we had to. And it was mercy, really, shooting those sorry bastards. If he had shot my own mother and father, I would have thanked him. It was awful, what happened to those people, what happened to most everyone. I guess that helped me square up what I thought was righteous against all the rotting, living bodies I'd filled with bullets.

By the third day, things were organized enough to blow the bridges. While some soldier-children kept scanning the roads and occasionally picking off the walking dead, a few other guys and I were lucky enough to be ordered to lay down our arms and scurry around placing charges on each concrete pylon that ran down into the river. No sooner had we finished connecting all the detonation cables than a stone-faced captain connected two wires, flipped a switch, and—not even looking—brought the last bridge crumbling down into the water below. The blast was deafening. As it thundered across the land and a great cloud of dust curled up into the sky, none of us knew how final that act of destruction would prove to be. From that moment on, we were cut off.

I was sitting on the edge of my bed, feet on the cold floor. Pressing the heels of my hands into my eyes, I rose and walked stiffly into the living room. I clicked open the locks on the window and slid it open a couple of feet. Then I pushed the coffee table to one side and lay down flat on my back. The fog crept slowly into the room.

Sometimes in some truly horrific chapters of history you hear about survivors envying the dead. I guess a lot of that depends on how they died. It may be selfish, but beyond my family and the few I was close enough with to call friends, I wouldn't have traded any life for the agonizing days of that death. Envying the dead, though . . . who knows? Maybe there is a heaven or a hell. Maybe both. Probably neither, but I knew goddamn well that this life was purgatory, peopled by the lucky few—the saved, the spared . . . the survivor captives. Out of the fire and into perpetual gray. The funny thing is the suicide rate reached its plateau after only a year or two. At least a doctor told me that during my discharge physical. I doubt anyone had conducted a study in years. Still, we managed to adapt fairly well to the sensory depriving maze. Yet even in the gray new world, every once in a while, people got shot in the back in alleys, just like they always have.

I took in long, slow breaths of the damp, heavy air. My palms found my chest and thighs and cheeks and I let myself believe they were not my hands. They say the first real job was prostitution? Wrong. The first real job was killing in the dark and taking what you wanted.

IT WAS 7 A.M. I WAS DRUNK, SITTING ON THE JOHN, TAKING A SHIT. Sleep had not come back, so I had turned again to the bottle. Whiskey had kept me company all through the early-morning hours with one shot of vodka on the side. The vodka was a sort of houseguest. It was just passing through my routine, and I felt sick and pathetic for having bought it. In my mind, a red-dress-wearing Rebecca would be sitting in my candlelit box of a home, sipping liquor and smoking black cigarettes.

But she didn't smoke. Probably didn't drink vodka, either. It was just an illusion she had spun that first night, and I didn't know her from Adam but I had bought the vodka and more food than I had in months even after she'd shown up wearing the trousers and blazer of a prep school prude.

I swayed back and forth on my lonely porcelain throne humming without melody. Then came the worst part, wiping, as bad as it can be. I got the littlest bit of shit on my hand. I almost had a goddamn breakdown right there on the can. I was so fucking pathetic. "Hi, Rebecca," I said aloud, waving at no one with my fouled right hand. I took a long, noisy pull off the fifth of scotch sitting beside me and then washed my hands repeatedly.

I stumbled into my living room and toppled down onto the couch. Diffuse gray light filled the room, and I thought to rise and take the seven or so steps to bed, knowing I'd soon pass out, but it was just too much.

THERE WAS A POUNDING ON THE DOOR. I DIDN'T REALIZE I WASN'T dreaming until I was already fumbling with the locks and it was too late to stop. I looked down, established that I was dressed, and then slapped myself once good and hard across the face before opening the door slowly. Eddie stood there on the landing, looking like hell. I never gave anyone my home address. . . . Had I given it to poor old Eddie? Too foggy, I had no idea what to make of it. Still drunk and confused. I played it cool.

He came right in. I shuffled aside awkwardly and stood there unsteadily as Eddie surveyed my living arrangements. There was a bottle of scotch lying on its side on the table, uncorked and with a few belts left in it. The rest had poured into me or onto the floor. A pill bottle lay open beside it. Eddie looked at me with deep, sorrowful eyes. His dark brows pressed together as he repeated, "It's so awful, Tom. It's just so awful."

I shut my door and lurched past him, dropping roughly onto the couch. Head pounding . . . my mouth tasted like pennies and vinegar. Dry as a bone. My right hand kept trembling, and I was sure he was staring at it.

"What, uh . . . What seems to be the problem, Ed?" I mumbled hoarsely.

"It's all gone now. So awful. All of it gone or thrown across the floor. My life has been taken from me and thrown across the floor. I can't believe it."

"Care for a drink?" I smiled beneath bleary eyes, righting the whiskey bottle and sliding it toward him.

"It's nine thirty in the morning!" he exclaimed with dignity free of disdain.

"Well, don't tell my dead mother." I winced immediately after saying this. Nonetheless, I took a long pull off the bottle and then was racked by ragged coughs. I doubled over, spitting and choking as Eddie stood there, looking like a priest in a whorehouse. *Trust this sorry son of a bitch?* he must have been thinking.

"Sorry, Ed. Not at my best in the mornings." I lit a cigarette, despite every bit of logic piercing through my drunk-cum-hangover haze telling me not to, and sat upright. "I'm okay, though. I'm okay. What's going on?"

He looked away for a while, as if weighing his options, and then looked me square in the eyes. "Every single bit of material I have left has been stolen, destroyed, or just . . . just thrown on the warehouse floor."

"Fuck," I muttered.

"It's thousands of things. Thousands of papers, pictures, discs, film reels, books. Lord, you name it." He sat down on the edge of the table, carefully avoiding the spilled whiskey. "There's no way, Tom, no way that any one person could have done this in one night. I was there until eight yesterday. I got in at seven this morning. It's awful. I'm all finished now. Ruined."

He sat still for a long while, staring at the gray void outside my window. Then he slowly, deliberately raised both hands to his face, lowered his elbows onto his knees, and cradled his head in his palms, swaying gently from side to side.

This was madness. Impossible. The place was huge. It would take all night just to open every file much less rifle through them. I was worthless right now—operating at 20 percent or less. I needed sleep, water, a shower. Time. I was confused, and frankly, I was frightened. *It's just the booze and the pills,* I said to myself, taking a few feverish drags off my smoke and then dropping it, still smoking, into the crowded ashtray. I had to get Eddie out of here. Had to clean up and then get the facts straight. And Rebecca—I had to deal with her shit. Nothing much in my life for years and then fuck. I was slipping—but it felt more like being pulled.

"Ed . . . how did you find me here?"

"Hm?" he muttered, his face still covered by his hands.

"How did you know where I live?"

"You told me. And your note," he said as if I had asked him what my own name was. He straightened up, reached into his jacket pocket, and handed me a small, tightly folded piece of paper. On it was my address. My building, my floor. It was my shitty handwriting. When the fuck did I give him my address?

I shook my head. "Okay. We'll see, all right? We'll see about it all." I rose and told him I'd come by later. At the door, he looked past me once more at my rotten little place, and then at me.

"You found the place okay, right?" He looked confused. "My apartment, I mean."

"Oh . . . yes. Of course."

"Great. Good. Okay . . . I'll come by—I promise."

He left and I shut the door. Locked it back up. Stumbled into my bedroom and collapsed. *Too hazy to think right now.* Sleep was coming. *What's going on here, Ed?* There were no numbers on my apartment's door.

5

I PAUSED AFTER STEPPING OUT OF THE WINDY VESTIBULE TO WIPE the dampness off my skin. The lobby of the Science and Development Research Department was a barren affair. You could see where a long reception counter once sat on the linoleum floor of the enormous, empty room. Now it was just a gray outline replaced by a handwritten sign reading, *Research Dept.—Flr 6.*

I looked around for cameras, windows—any signs of life in this cavernous tomb. But it was just me and the boarded-up windows and a bank of elevators. The two-story glass street wall of the lobby must have looked nice in years past—now it was plywood and nails.

The yellowed floor clicked beneath my shoes as I crossed toward the elevators. A nice pair of brown loafers at the bottom of my crisp gray suit; I hadn't been this well dressed in longer than I could remember. There was no need to attract attention, so I had donned the outfit of a government worker. I'd shaved, clipped at nose hairs, and dragged a comb across my salt-and-pepper scalp.

More gray than I thought. It's funny how whenever you wear clothes in which you don't feel yourself, it seems the world can tell. I sucked in a sharp breath and missed a step as one of the elevators nearest me opened unexpectedly.

Two suit-wearing men and a smartly dressed woman stepped off and walked past me, talking among themselves in hushed tones. Not one of them so much as looked up at me. Still, I stuck out. As I stepped onto the elevator and pressed the cracked plastic button for floor six, I kept repeating to myself two words: *They know.* . . . The elevator button did not illuminate, but I started upward nonetheless. Science and Development once occupied this whole building . . . but now there apparently was so little left to research that they were down to one floor. *They know, they know* . . . it became my little mantra as I rose in the trembling elevator.

HE WAS DRESSED JUST LIKE ME. ACROSS FROM THE ELEVATORS behind a cheap-looking wooden desk sat a pencil-necked man with a weak chin and eyes set too close together wearing a gray suit. He plinked away at a computer, the pale green glow of the text on his screen reflecting off his glasses. I walked toward him slowly, trying to make it look natural and get a sense of the place, take it in for a moment. There wasn't much to see. A few halls lined with closed doors. Behind the consummate bureaucrat was a large room full of other pale-skinned people clicking away at their workstations. The ceiling was low, and the whole place, lit by harsh fluorescents and smelling faintly of ammonia, was fabulously oppressive.

"Hi, there!" I beamed as I stepped in front of the reception desk.

"How can I help you?" His thin voice matched his birdlike frame and dour little face. He didn't look up.

"Well, I'm hoping you can. I'm looking for a gentleman who works here."

"You need to check with City Central, I can't—"

"Oh, no—see, that's where I'm from. The fellah works here and I need to get something from him and bring it back on over to Central, in fact."

He let his annoyance show as he sighed slowly, typed a few more words, and then looked up at me. Retentive little fucker, this one.

"All right. Let's see what we can do. Who are you looking for?"

"Great! Thanks. It's Sam Ayers. Or Samuel, I should say. Gotta be professional, right?" I flashed my biggest shit-eating grin, hating every second of this exchange.

"Samuel Ayers?"

"Yes," I said flatly.

He typed away at his computer. Then a quizzical look spread across his sallow face. "That's . . . unusual . . . There is a record, but it seems he . . . hmm . . ."

Just then, the telephone on his desk rang. He picked it up and listened, saying nothing. I heard a voice on the other end but could not make out words.

"It seems he . . ." I led him, leaning close.

"Well, it seems . . ." He cupped a hand over the mouthpiece, but then just hummed for a while, studying the screen. I pictured all the different things a broken liquor bottle could do to this peon's face as he hemmed and hawed and pecked at his keyboard. He swallowed.

"Well, it looks like there's no record, actually. There's not a Samuel Ayers employed here."

"But you just said there is a record."

"What? No, I must have misread—"

I stepped swiftly around the high desk and leaned in over the man. He was momentarily shocked by my invasion of his space but made no protest, just sputtered slightly and almost dropped the phone. On the screen was what looked to be a full record of the late Mr. Ayers: a picture, text—lots of things I wanted very much to see. But there was no time.

As the bureaucrat regained his composure and rose to place his thin body between me and his computer, I caught the last few words spoken to him over the phone line: "Don't say anything. Find out who's asking."

"Excuse me. Step back. Please. Sir, please step back."

"No, it's all right, thanks," I said, smiling as I put a hand on his shoulder and easily pushed him aside. I pressed a thumb down on the phone's receiver, ending the call, and studied the screen as intently as I could, soaking in details and the grainy image of Ayers's face. I stepped back around the desk and grinned.

"Geez, y'know, I'm sorry! Wrong guy! I thought you were just pulling my leg, but no, this must be the wrong department. I'll head over to Power and Light."

I walked quickly for the elevators and mashed the down button repeatedly. The little man stood, leaning over his desk with both hands clutching its sides and glaring at me. His shoulders rose and fell as he sucked in breath to call after me.

"Just one moment! Just wait a second, please! I'm sure we can help, sir! Please just come on back over here, and we'll look again."

I smiled and waved. "No, thanks. I need to get back to Central anyway. My soup will get cold. Where are the stairs?"

I looked for any promising doors but saw none and turned back to the elevator. Every eye in the room was trained on me. The incessant clicking of keyboards had gone silent and the room flickered in fluorescent tension. Then, in an instant, everyone was typing furiously. They kept looking from side to side down the hallways. My heart was thumping.

Then the elevator popped open. I practically leapt inside, rejoicing that it was empty. Once more the little gray man shouted, "Wait!" But the doors were already closing. As they did, I caught a glimpse of another man. This one was tall. His skin was olive, healthy. The man's shoulders were held high, and his suit was a rich, deep blue. His dark, piercing eyes locked on to mine as he walked toward the elevator just before the last inch of space between us was sealed and I started down. He had not run to stop me—just taken a good, careful look.

I SLID BETWEEN THE OPENING DOORS OF THE ELEVATOR AND WAS surprised and relieved to find the lobby empty. I walked as quickly as I could without breaking into a run for the exit. The first door reluctantly strained open against the vacuum of the vents, and I stepped in and pulled it closed behind me. It clicked shut. A second passed in an hour before the outer door unlocked. I let out a breath I'd not known I was holding in and barged onto the street.

It was one of those rare times when I was eternally grateful for the fog. It swirled and enveloped me as I set off down the street at a jog. I mussed my hair, pulled off and pocketed my tie, and unbuttoned my dress shirt while cutting down alleys and across streets. No particular direction. Just away from those dark eyes set in that tan, handsome, chilling face. He looked like no one I had seen in years. He looked composed, healthy . . . out of place.

Thinking better of stopping so soon but unable to ignore the compulsion to do so, I pulled out a pen and sheet of paper and started scrawling down everything I could remember from the profile. I leaned against a damp cement building to catch my breath and held the paper against it, scrawling down notes. *Samuel Ayers . . . birthdate . . .* So he'd died at fifty-four. Well, that was too young. Sorry, Sam. He had looked strangely familiar, which was extremely discomforting. I never knew any scientists.

I shoved the paper back into my pocket and started sliding along the wall as fast as I could go silently. Someone was coming down the alley. Most people avoided alleys, which was why I favored them. Two sets of footfalls. They drew closer. I needed to find a recess in the wall, a pile of trash—something. The fog was as thick as ever, but the alley was narrow. Maybe six feet from wall to wall. Closer. My left heel fell too sharply and clicked on the uneven pavement.

Silence set in. I was sure they would hear my heartbeat, so thunderous was it in my own skull. I inched along. Still no sound. Then almost inaudibly through the swirling mist came a man's whisper: "Arms out. Go." And much more softly than before, two sets of feet began walking again.

I set off at a dead run, praying nothing would block my path. No stopping. No thinking. I ran as hard and fast as I could straight down the alley, my hand trailing against the wall to my left.

The skin on my palm grew raw as I dragged it across the cracked cement of the building. Then suddenly it was hanging in space, and I turned ninety degrees to my left, knowing I was on a cross street. I ran headlong down it, dodging orb posts as they burst into view mere feet before me. Keep going. Keep running.

A right turn here, a left there. Maybe it was for five minutes, maybe fifteen, but I ran until my lungs howled at me to stop. I slowed and staggered along at a quick walk, wheezing and doubled over at the waist. Then I slumped against a wall and tried to hear over my own ragged breaths. Silence. Just the cold, heavy air and my stifled smoker's cough to keep me company.

As I sat there, leaning against an old brick building with an impending sense of dread, something occurred to me: I didn't know how to get ahold of Rebecca. No phone number, no address. Nothing. I hadn't even thought to ask since that first night at the bar. Fuck me. At that moment, I really, really wanted to run some questions by her.

* * *

"THIS IS FROM THE DRAWERS OVER THERE, THESE PAGES CAME from a safe against the far wall . . . this disc was one of maybe fifty or sixty . . . all gone now. See this photograph? I swear it was ripped in half by hand. Deliberately. Carefully. These shelves were stacked entirely full of old ledgers. . . ." Eddie went on and on in his low, mournful voice. He strolled aimlessly around his ransacked warehouse, pointing to various overturned desks, scattered pages, broken shelves and cabinets. . . .

The place was a mess. He had been right when he told me that one person couldn't have done all this in one night. It seemed like most everything had been taken and what little was left had definitely not been overlooked, rather intentionally disregarded. Some random papers were strewn about. They ranged from children's school reports to old bookkeeper's accounts to newspaper clippings. No pattern at all. Likewise the pictures and film reels and data discs came from across the spectrum of his erstwhile clients.

I glanced down at the torn picture he'd handed me. A blond woman in her thirties smiled, a man's arm around her shoulder. The man had been ripped away, as it were, leaving her alone on a sunny street. Alone in the past.

Eddie rambled on as he meandered through the wreckage of his life and I let him; I was paying no attention anyway. It seemed therapeutic for him to lament. For me, I needed to find out why I had been chased out of the Research Department after asking one question. One. It normally took days of nosing around before someone tried to rearrange my face in an alley. I tried to subtly drop the torn photograph and look at the notes I'd jotted down after leaving Science, but Eddie turned to face me as I studied the scrap of paper. He cast a quizzical eye.

"I'm going to make a few notes, if that's okay."

"Of course. I'll get out of the way." Eddie walked past the

door to the front room, where he kept his desk, leaving the door open. I scribbled a bit on my pad, hardly even attempting to write anything of substance, just a few nouns about what was on the floor. Then I walked toward his office. I was going to shake down Watley for answers to Ed's troubles. That had been the plan since I first met the slim, shifty-eyed fucker. I'd scare him with a few dirty words and a slap or two, read his response, and if it seemed off, well, then the other employee, Thurmond, was to blame. Or at least in on it.

It was an inside job, no doubt. No forced entry, efficiency that pointed to lots of planning and foreknowledge. As much as I had my own business to deal with, at least I was finally going to take things up a notch for sad-eyed old Eddie. For weeks, I'd been half-assing my way through what seemed like a string of petty thefts—now it was major. Now it was a heist.

I stood before his desk. He looked so tired there in his metal chair with shirtsleeves rolled up and brow knit down.

"I'm fucked, Thomas. Totally and fully." I'd never heard him swear before. "It's a confidence business. Now I'm out cash and confidence. I swear . . . I swear it was the goddamn government. . . . They hate operations like this. Want everyone to forget and shut up and hunker down. Just to . . . to stumble through the mist. Go to work and then go home and shut up and sit down. Well, anyway, it's the end of me, Tom. It's the end of me."

"Don't talk so fatalistically. If I find a living room full of your stuff, it may yet work out for you—could be the end for some-one else."

He looked up at me. I read the question in his eyes and shook my head. "No summary justice here, Eddie. No violence here. Even the police will reopen a case if you put the proof under their noses. I'll find out what's going on if I can. If not . . . Christ, at least we're all getting used to despair, right?"

* * *

IT WAS ONLY NINE O'CLOCK, BUT ALBERGUE WAS ALMOST EMPTY. Every few minutes, Adam would walk over and wordlessly check on my drink. He seemed confused and maybe even concerned to see me nursing a single glass of scotch for so long. True, it wasn't my style, but I had business tonight, and I wanted to be clear headed. Killing time here beat doing it at home alone.

Another sip of watered-down liquor and I checked my watch. Nine after nine. Time was moving at a crawl. I'd planned to drop in on Watley at half-past but had already been waiting here for nearly an hour. It wasn't like Watley and I had a sched-uled date. I threw a few rumpled bills down on the bar and nodded to Adam as I turned to go.

He nodded back, half-waving, and I pulled open the inner door. A fine mist played around me as I shut it behind me, got a cigarette ready, and then struck my lighter and inhaled as I pushed open the outer door and stepped into the evening haze. Cold tonight. The air was thick. I blinked for a while, leaning on Albergue's wall for the millionth time, and then set off down the narrow street, the orbs leading my way.

Watley lived only a short walk from the bar, which was par-tially why I had chosen to wait there. Frankly, though, I was nervous to spend too much time at home or at the office until I had a handle on my situation. Figured I must be on some kind of shit list.

Eddie had given me John Watley's address, and I had walked past the building earlier, pausing for less than three seconds to confirm the numbers in the afternoon haze. I took long, slow drags off my cigarette as I walked down one street and then paused, checked a brass nameplate, and turned onto his road. It was a wide avenue—just short of being blower-worthy, I fig-ured. It was all residential, and many of the buildings had large, fancy facades on them. The kind no one had bothered making in years. I stumbled more than once over steps leading up to the lobbies of fine apartment buildings. Nice area. Would have been very impressive with its marbled foyers and glass doors, pre-fog. It seemed nice enough still, despite the fact that its fancy floors and chandeliers were now blocked behind large double-door ventways. It was all a bit confusing, this neighborhood.

I got to Watley's building, double-checked my info, and went up to the outer door. To my surprise and relief, it was unlocked; I hadn't really made a contingency plan. Well, that part was easy. I stepped into and through the vent chamber and into just what I'd expected: a large, well-appointed lobby. A few oil paintings, an ornate—albeit unoccupied—reception desk, carpets with dark floral patterns: the works. No one around. It was silent save the hum of the ventilation system.

His apartment was on the second floor. I bypassed the elevator and jogged up a wide spiral staircase. My footfalls echoed off the granite steps as I took them two at a time. When I got to his floor, I was momentarily dazed. There were only two apartments on the whole floor. I'd assumed the place had been gutted and packed full of little rat's nests. But no—this place was pristine, elegant; it was lost in time. There was no way he could afford this working for Vessel.

I lit a cigarette and took a deep drag, then crammed it into the corner of my mouth. Three deep breaths. I punched each fist into the opposing palm a few times. Get angry. Get ugly. Then get answers.

I hammered down on the door marked *2* with the heel of my hand five times. Waited about ten seconds. Three more loud knocks. Then it opened.

Watley stood framed by the large doorway wearing a rich, embroidered robe over slacks and leather slippers. His middle-aged face looked more intrigued than confused beneath carefully combed graying blond hair. His lips parted slightly as if to speak, but he did not.

I took a long drag of my smoke. "John Watley?"

"Yes," he said, answering my rhetorical question flatly.

"Vale. Remember me?" I jammed my palm against his chest and gathered folds of his robe and shirt into a fist, pushing him back into the apartment as I entered. I kicked the door shut behind me. Watley wrapped his hands around my wrist but did not so much struggle as he did lead me a few more feet into the room. He backed up against a crimson leather chair and sat down roughly, shoving my hand away from him as he did so.

"This is very improper, Mr. Vale. Not done well at all."

"Don't talk, Watley." I looked around. This place was a palace. I stood in a room the size of my apartment and then some. Twenty-foot ceilings. Plush carpets covering a polished hardwood floor. Intricate moldings and massive bookshelves and ornate brass lamps . . . leather furniture . . . marble . . . There was even a finely appointed bar set into one corner, bristling with bottles and glassware. Down one of two halls connected to the living room, I could see what looked to be a dining room. The other hall was darkened. Faint big band music drifted through the bright, crisp air from somewhere.

"So how much does Eddie pay you again?" I asked, picking up a large clothbound book from the mahogany table by his chair.

"I think a better question might be how much is he paying you?"

I snorted out a little laugh. "Never enough."

"No, I doubt it will be."

I poked around through the room a bit more, trying to look like my efforts were concerted, but frankly, I was in awe of the opulence. I hadn't seen a place like this in years. Eventually, I began my little speech.

"Well, John, let's get into it, huh? Last time I saw you, you were wearing a blue button-down shirt and a pair of ill-fitting khakis. Now a fancy robe. Ed gets robbed, you live rich. And you don't seem all that surprised by my being here. See, what

I do is not what people tend to think of as detective work, per se. . . ."

I tapped my cigarette ash onto the wooden floor; Watley winced, looking pissed. "What I do is more like a research scientist. I make some observations—like, for example, I can see that someone has been robbing a warehouse. Then I make a hypothesis . . . like, say, I think maybe that someone is in this room and wearing slippers and a robe . . . then, I test my hypothesis. . . ."

I took a few steps and stood right before him. "I test it and make sure it tells me if it's true or not. It's pretty easy to do that. I have a lot of experience, see?"

Watley barely batted an eyelash. His skin was still a healthy tone, his breathing steady and calm. What the fuck? Most people are at least a bit on edge by now. Asking questions and talking fast. Not this guy.

"So I can start my line of questioning, or you—" Watley stood up and raised a palm to quiet me. Surprised, I actually fell silent. He strolled to the sideboard bar.

"Care for a drink, Vale?"

I sputtered for a second and then, trying to sound like a tough guy, growled: "Yeah, a strong one."

"Well, do come over and pick what you'd like."

On autopilot, I walked toward him and stared vacantly at the many foreign-looking bottles before me.

"No scotch worth much, I'm afraid. Here . . . try this cognac." He pulled a bottle from the front row and poured two fingers into a tumbler glass. He added three large ice cubes from a pewter bucket and handed the drink to me, shaking it from side to side so the ice clinked against the glass.

He held the bottle in his hand, looking down at the French label absentmindedly. I took a sip. It was delicious. Absolutely amazing stuff. He poured himself a glass, neat.

Watley looked up at me. Smiled warmly. He looked over at

a bookshelf next to us. I followed his eyes to a pistol lying on the shelf. A revolver. I looked back at him, and he nodded imperceptibly, and then raised the bottle a bit in his hand.

"There's plenty more where that came from," he said, his tone grave. "So drink up. Enjoy, Thomas, enjoy. Now come have a seat, and let's talk with a bit more civility. Let's keep it just two gentlemen chatting."

As if hypnotized, I complied and sat down on a soft, luxurious couch across from him. I sipped at the cognac.

"Now, you said you liked to conduct your affairs almost like a . . . What was your metaphor? Like a research scientist? Fascinating! I'll wager there are scientists who like to think of themselves as detectives too. Much more romantic. Detectives searching through layers of data for clues. Scientists in the lab searching for answers and the detective out in the foggy streets searching for—" He took a long sip from his glass. "—answers as well. So, tell me about yourself. Tell me about your case."

"Why don't you tell me about my case instead," I said evenly. It was not a question. I needed to regain the power, to not be cowed by his demeanor or liquor or even the pistol, though I'd not actually been threatened with a handgun in years. They're fabulously illegal. Extremely rare. The bullets alone cost a fortune, no less.

"What could I tell you? I obviously have no need of increased wealth. I want for nothing, really, other than perhaps a few more days of blue skies." He smiled a coy, reptilian little grin at me. His eyes flashed. I could have smashed my glass against his teeth if he'd held my gaze a second longer than he did. He looked away, his eyes drifting around his home. "So why would I take silly little things from a silly little place?"

"You wouldn't. That's part of the whole mystery here. See what I find the most . . . oh, not suspicious, of course . . . intriguing question, if you will, is why are you there in the first place?"

"Working for Edward, you mean?"

"You know that's what I mean. Cut the shit. I came here for answers. I've known you were dirty since I first laid eyes on you, Watley. Rich, fat, and happy—I didn't expect that, and it doesn't make sense. Yet. But what does make sense to me is that a wealthy man needlessly working a dead end job likely has just as much reason to steal as a poor, desperate man in the same place." I knocked back the last of my liquor and rose, stepping around the coffee table that separated us. I got between him and the gun, glancing over at it to let him see I knew my options.

"Mr. Vale, please . . ."

"Drop the polite shit! How did you know my first name? Talk fast or this fine cut crystal is in your forehead!" I wrapped my fingers tightly around the highball glass and raised it slightly, near his eyes. Calm as a lazy river. He almost looked melancholy, disappointed by my aggression.

"You really know much less even than you think you do. You really should practice more tact." He was looking past me into space. Watley idly raised one hand as if about to wave or gesture and then sighed, studying his fingernails before looking up at me.

Then it hit me—we weren't alone. He hadn't been looking into space at all. The dark hallway . . . he'd said something about "keeping it the two of us" when he'd first revealed the revolver earlier . . . calm when tacitly threatened with it. And then, as Watley sighed again and my thoughts began to race, I realized something else: The music had stopped. Shit.

I stepped away from him and calmly set my glass down on the coffee table. I sat back down on the couch. Forced a smile.

"I guess I can leave the streets outside when I step into this parlor, hmm?"

"One would hope so." His eyes were cold.

"Tell me, Watley, I was under the impression you had a wife, children. Where are they?"

"I don't spend all my time in the—" He paused, shifting slightly in his chair. "—in this residence. I have many."

"Must be nice."

He didn't answer, and I racked my brain to keep the conversation going long enough to make a smooth exit.

"What did you do pre-fog?"

"I gathered wealth about me. Many things. I did many things, and I gathered a life around me."

"Okay . . . I won't pry. In fact, I'll go. I don't get you. I don't get this—" I waved my hand around at the room. "—but I suppose it's true: Why would you rob a little guy like Eddie? No reason for it when you don't need wealth or items."

"Stay awhile. Let's hear your other theories on this mystery of ours."

I rose and walked straight for the door. Behind me, I heard Watley begin to rise quickly but then settle back down into his chair. I turned the knob, half-expecting to find myself locked in, and then pulled open the door.

In the hall, I paused and turned back. I waited to see if he'd say anything. He held my gaze. I watched his eyes for any movement . . . observed his breathing . . . his skin . . . any nonverbal response. . . . "John," I said quietly. He tilted his head to one side receptively. "I know it's you. I know it."

Nothing. The picture of tranquility. His lips curled up into that same smug bastard smile. "You know nothing," he whispered. I broke eye contact, grabbed hold of the massive door, and slammed it behind me.

MY APARTMENT WAS MORE DEPRESSING THAN EVER. A TINY CELL with a few cans of government-issue food and some cheap liquor. My stained and scratched-up pressboard coffee table. The bed with its never-changed sheets. Rust all over the bathroom. I looked around the place as if seeing it for the first time, as if I had stepped into someone else's home and thought, *How do you live like this? How is this your life?*

On top of my newfound loathing of the place, I also didn't feel safe there. There was no way everything today had been co-incidence. *You'll figure it out, Tommy. You'll figure it out. Always do. Always have, anyway.* I muttered some of this out loud; some I repeated in my head as I paced around my little home. I grabbed a bottle of scotch from under the sink and started taking small pulls from it.

My mind was racing but going nowhere. I knew it was a bad plan, that I wasn't secure in my own place and that I should have my wits about me, but getting a little drunk sounded divine. I had thrown my button-down shirt into a pile in the corner and now stripped off my T-shirt. The cloth stuck to my skin, damp from mist and perspiration, and it took some wriggling and twisting before I was finally free of it and bare chested. My breath came quickly and I stepped before the window and looked out into the gray black evening. My lips parted and eyes blazed, and for a while I felt as if something were about to happen—something outside of me or from within.

I looked over my shoulder at the small room. Nothing, of course. I pressed my forehead against the glass, but all I could see was the faintest outline of the street below in the pale yellow glow of the shitshop. My hands were trembling, and I realized I was still holding the T-shirt balled up in my left fist. I dragged it across my brow and then violently threw it to the floor. After a large gulp of scotch, I slammed the bottle down on the table and returned to the window.

I pushed both palms against the pane, arms raised above me. Slowly I leaned forward until my chest pressed against it too. The cold glass was soothing, comforting even, tangible. My life had been so stable, in its own way, for so long that these few days spent stumbling into the unknown were taking their toll. I didn't know what to do with myself. Did I just wait and see if Rebecca showed up tomorrow and politely ask what the hell she'd gotten me into? Rebecca whose last name I didn't know. Becca the lovely chameleon, the frightened lover, the little rich girl . . .

I pressed the side of my face to the glass. The skin by my right eye stretched and my vision blurred. The world was one half my living room, one half a swirl of yellow and gray. Then . . . I thought for just a fleeting second I had seen a man wearing a fedora on the street below me looking up. I took in a deep breath and let it out slowly, scanning the haze. A trick of the eye? *Must have been . . .*

Then I bolted for the door, grabbing the whiskey bottle—it being the only blunt object that came to hand—and leapt down the stairs, taking them four and five at a time. I burst out onto the street and stopped just off the sidewalk, my feet wide, arms up, looking from side to side. Silence. A faint breeze stirred the evening, swirling about me. I was still for a long time. Scarcely breathing. Nothing.

Then, from very far off, came the faint sound of receding footfalls. Not those of anyone trying to flee or be stealthy—just a man walking away. I craned my neck from side to side, trying to determine from which direction they came. I was sure it was right and then left. I stood upright, looked down at the whiskey bottle in my hand. The amber liquid was dark in the pale light of the shop's sign. I backed up against the bricks and felt them on my skin, cool and crumbling. I took a sip of scotch. It wasn't so foggy tonight. I could see three orbs in either direction. They shone like angry eyes, frowning at me half-naked and frightened and alone in the night.

I went back inside. I poured a tall glass of liquor and a small glass of water and placed three pills on the table. I gathered up the papers strewn about the place and stacked them in an uneven pile in a corner. As I rose, looking down at my notes and observations and scribbled theories, I thought that maybe I'd never touch them again. "Can't help you now, Eddie," I said in a slow whisper. Can't do anything but try to help myself.

I gulped scotch and took little sips of water and tried not to think about anything. Every time I made a connection, it only confused me further. The man in the blue suit with the piercing eyes . . . he had looked at me like one stares across the ring at his opponent, not like one examines something new. Watley hadn't seemed the least bit surprised by me showing up at his door. He seemed more like he had been waiting for it. Becca was lying about her lover. I was just trying to survive each day. Just trying to have a few dollars and a bed.

Before I joined the army, I had tried my hand at a few other things and failed like a champion. I worked in an office for a few months once. Or maybe it was weeks. Strapped to a desk and making phone calls and filling out forms, trying to get a few orders filled each day. Paper. The company sold raw paper to manufacturers. We'd sell the pulp that they would turn into cardboard boxes or posters or toilet tissue or whatever else. The management used to extol the virtues of our lowly enterprise, pouring aphorisms about greater good and necessary service and other such bullshit down on our heads. "Remember, everything you buy comes packaged in paper. Every idea is written down before it's carried out." I was twenty-one years old when I took that job and twenty-one when I quit.

I was a cog. I couldn't take it. If everyone in the company were essential to every part of the company as they would preach, fine, but anyone could be one of those everyone, and I could not. I stole pens and a coffee mug and left. Everyone wants to think of themselves as honest and good, but Number One comes first. Always. The person who tells you they are truly honest, truly pure—that person has just lied and torn their own ethos apart. Sure, I don't want to hurt anyone who doesn't hurt anyone else, but I'll take your bread if you won't realize it's gone. I too must eat bread.

For months I did nothing. My parents would call me and ask how life was and I would be as pleasant as I could force and then get off the phone. I lived not fifteen miles away from home yet hardly ever saw them. It was not for lack of love for them that I became a recluse; it was because of the confusion and disgust I felt with myself.

On my darkest days in those early years, nothing filled me with more revulsion and ennui than the knowledge that my self-loathing and listlessness were entirely not unique. My father had given me his old car. It was a reliable but wretched gray sedan with scratches all along the left side and a muffler that coughed and wheezed until I got into fourth or fifth gear. But it was my home on wheels. My room with a view. I would stuff a few beers and a pack of cigarettes into the glove box and drive out of the city into the fields and just roll along for hours. Sometimes I'd go fifty, sixty, a hundred miles in one direction before I realized I had to turn back.

I never really knew why I turned back. Turning back and driving home meant my same pungent mattress, my same mildew-covered walls, and my same smoky mirror, where I would stare into my same hollow, twenty-one-year-old eyes.

And then they were twenty-two-year-old eyes. I tried to find work as a driver—any sort of driver. I figured it would suit me well: time alone, time driving like I always did but being paid, no chicken shit. But the only offer I got was trucking sodas around town, and it was more time spent at delivery stops than on the road and would involve talking to scores of people all the time. I never had anything against people as a whole; I just didn't want to be around them that much.

Eventually my money ran thin and I was faced with the prospect of begging from my middle-class family. Then they died, and I immediately joined the army. I was older than most of the others. They were children who could scarcely grow beards. I was a child who could grow a beard. We ran and did push-ups and shot rifles and made our beds. They yelled at us and we yelled back. Then training was over and I was qualified to shoot a rifle and I knew how to iron my uniform and I could run wires to lumps of explosive clay and explode things and I marched around when I was told to and I was always surrounded by boys with the same haircut but I didn't have to think very much and it suited me fine, really.

The sickness came so fast, it was almost easy to deal with. Everything was normal one day, and then the next it was not. Its swiftness made it more tolerable than the fog, despite its horrors. The fog could be ignored at first—the disease could not. Whole towns' worth of people just started rotting. Some places were almost untouched; some were almost erased. Everyone I knew outside of the young recruits I slept beside and did not know died very quickly. They died in their homes or in hospitals or wherever the buses we were ordered to force them onto took them. They told us the buses went to quarantine and treatment centers, but I was sure they just took them off to die out of sight—I never once saw evidence of the "clinics" the officers and civilian advisors claimed had been established.

Those who wandered back into sight we shot, and it was just that simple.

And then shortly after that, we were corralled into the city and then it slowly grew misty.

I didn't ask for it. I didn't ask for any of it. If I could go back to the night of my conception, frankly, I think I would have told my father to roll over and go to sleep. It's amazingly awful not to desire to be alive, yet not to hate life quite enough to end it.

I always wondered what kept a guy like Heller going. Why Salk bothered waking up each morning to lament fate in his flowery prose and sell canned goods and illicit meds. I guess it must have been worse than this at times before. Plagues and pestilence and wars and floods and fires have laid waste to mankind for longer than we've bothered to record. I wondered if the whole world was like this. Pockets of humanity riding out the storm of disease and death in a thousand gray nests that were randomly spared. I wondered if there was any change to hope for. Hope is a dangerous commodity if it is in vain. Despair, at least, can lead to definitive action.

I was drunk. I had finished my glass, finished the bottle, and delved into the fifth of vodka. Rebecca's vodka, I ruefully muttered as I took another sip. I washed all three pills back with a pull of ice-cold liquor and gagged, choking the capsules down and coughing, hands on my knees.

I lay down on the carpet next to the door and pulled my pants off. Then my socks. I paused, feet on the floor and legs bent, looking up at my cracked and molding ceiling. There had to be more than this.

Even in times of hardship, the measure of success is always calculated against the level of others' misery. In a blue-sky world, would Watley have strolled among manicured hedges and well-groomed rosebushes while I drank cheap wine on a tenement roof? And would he have been as happy for that as he was for his high ceilings and polished wooden tables? I supposed a medieval peasant might have seen my little chambers and refrigerator with its meager but preserved rations and thought me something of a nobleman.

Noble. I laughed aloud as I stripped off my underwear. For all I knew, I would be killed in an alley, just like some scientist I'd never met, for asking questions. The only reason I had a few thousand dollars crammed into a hole in my bathroom wall was that most people were too scared to ask questions anymore. It was so easy to disappear in the fog. Fewer people would miss me than I could count on one finger. Maybe Adam the bartender would wonder for five minutes why his bottle of Cutty Sark was lasting so long. Maybe Rebecca was clean after all and would be upset, for a little while, that I'd never panned out. Maybe Heller would miss my occasional loans. And he'd want his Chopin back.

More likely, Watley would shoot me in the back and eventually, when my rent went unpaid for long enough, someone new would sleep in my wretched little home.

The pills were taking hold, and I rose and stood naked in the middle of the room. The blood drained from my head as I got up, and for a moment my vision swam. My temples pulsed and a dull ache constricted my brain. I stumbled into the kitchen and sucked sulfurous water from the sink. Only a few minutes left now before I was asleep or at least blacked out. I always feared the time right after those few minutes. What if my mind released before my body? What if I stumbled down into the night while out of my head? Coming to, somewhere out there in a misty alley, naked and confused and shivering. There would be no one to help me home.

I lurched toward my bedroom. Bounced off the doorframe and stumbled. Lay down. Couldn't find a pillow. The sheets were a messy pile, so I threw them onto the ground. Just the mattress on my skin. Rough and soiled. I was fading. Never told Watley my first name, never learned Rebecca's last. Never asked for any of it. Never tried to make a difference or get in the way. Just wanted to keep surviving until I was ready to give up.

I rolled over onto my back. Coughing. Then I was up on my knees on the bed. I clawed at my cheeks, my chest. Sweating and gasping. It was all so pathetic—so miserable. What the fuck were we doing running around in our little world until our hearts stopped pumping or our lungs filled with fluid or our brain cells were replaced with cancer? For what? Before, at the very least, you could change your scenery. Move someplace hot and dry to spend your dying years. Spend your life savings on things. The only point of living was to avoid death. Did everyone in this godforsaken city feel like this? What did the bureaucrat do to get his jollies? Did he have a lady to go home to and get inside? Maybe. Maybe that was enough. Maybe he read books or listened to music and escaped into a polychromatic land in his head.

The eight-hundred-pound gorilla lurking in the corner of my mind was knowing that had the fog never drifted in, had the sickness never spread across the land—the earth, for all any of us knew—I would most likely still be alone and drunk and sweating on a bare mattress. I would still have never once had sex with and loved the same person. Never shed a tear another could see. Never once experienced happiness that lasted longer than one drink or one orgasm or, long ago when I was younger and would drive around in my father's old car, one song. And that one moment of song, rolling along open roads with the windows down and the volume up on a crisp day . . . that one moment would never be replaced.

In the morning, the backs of my fingers were raw and sore. There were a few spots of dried blood on the concrete wall above my headboard. I didn't remember any of it.

6

"HI, REBECCA." SHE WAS SO FOCUSED ON A PIECE OF PAPER HELD close to her nose that she hadn't even glanced up as she passed within inches of me. I was leaning against the speckled granite wall by my office building's entrance. She gasped upon hearing her name.

"What are you reading?" I asked with an edge to my voice. She had crammed the paper into her pocket and closed her eyes, then took in a deep breath to regain her composure.

"Tom. Hi. Hello, I . . . you startled me."

"I was just standing here. Just leaning on the wall, perfectly still. Perfectly calm. What were you reading?"

"Nothing. Nothing important. To you, I mean. Just other things in my life.

I blew a short burst of air through my nose and looked away. "Well, that's kind of an answer. I'd like to talk to you about other things in your life, though, so I'm glad you brought it up."

I took her roughly by the arm and started walking down the

street. Her biceps was tense beneath the soft wool of her gray jacket.

"Aren't we—what . . . aren't we going to your office?" she asked, her voice growing higher as she spoke.

"No." I tightened my grip as she tried to pull her arm free.

"Tom, what are—?"

"Don't talk, okay." I spat laconically. I led her down the block. She kept looking over at me, but I kept my eyes forward, my face a blank mask. When we had walked maybe fifty yards, I abruptly turned around and pulled her along as I went back the way we had come. After covering half the distance back to the office, I stopped.

"Shhh," I ordered. She jerked her arm free and stood breathing quickly and staring at me. I looked into her frightened gray eyes for a moment and then stood still, staring off into the mist and listening for any sound. None came. A minute passed and then another and then, finally, I turned again and said, "Let's go."

She followed a few steps behind me as I walked quickly down the street. I knew this part of town well, so while it seemed no one was following, it would be easy for me to be sure. We passed an alley obscured by the haze, and I quickly turned left and entered it, looking over my shoulder to be sure she followed. Down another small street and then through a square we walked. I gradually led us in a circle, taking an illogical and winding path. We crossed the same square, and I was confident she didn't realize it.

Finally I led her out onto Saint Anne's Boulevard. The wide, clear-blown street was nearly deserted. I stopped in the very middle of the road and turned to look at her. I said nothing. Let her do the talking for a bit. Rebecca was nervous, confused. Good. It had been on her terms before. Now it was going to be on mine. Several times she took a breath as if to speak but was silent. She avoided my gaze, crossed her arms and hugged them tightly to her gray-clad chest. Finally, her voice steady but imploring, she asked "What's going on?"

"I really have no idea. But I want to know. I want to know very much. I want you, right here on this fine street in our fine city, to tell me."

Strands of her blond hair danced across her face in the blower winds, and she pushed them behind her ears. Looking up at me, her brow knit with concern, she seemed younger than she had before. Gone was the red-dressed vixen. Gone was the smartly dressed client offering fifty thousand dollars. Here was a girl wearing a white T-shirt beneath a cropped jacket and a pair of blue jeans. And me? I'd washed, shaved, and put on my nicest shirt and a brown suede blazer. Which was a bit pathetic, but lack of trust aside, she was disarmingly pretty.

"I don't know what to say, Tom. I thought you would be . . . doing the talking this time, I guess."

"I can start. What's your last name?" She hesitated a beat, her lips slightly parted. "What's your last name, Rebecca? Tell me your last name."

"Smith."

I snorted. "Right. And what's Fallon's last name?"

"It's Samson."

"Right—that's right, Fallon Samson. What kind of cigarettes do you smoke? When you do smoke, I mean."

She looked away, down to her left, and I immediately continued. "Don't worry about it. What color are Fallon's eyes?"

"They're blue."

I nodded. "Blue eyes . . . yeah. And here I am brown and boring. What have you—" I paused and took in a breath, leaned closer. "—what have you gotten me into, Ms. Smith?"

She looked around as if expecting to see something that could help her. "I don't know what to say to that."

"I spent all morning on the phone. There doesn't seem to be a Fallon Samson in jail. It's not easy to get information these days, sure, but it's something of a specialty of mine, and I came up dry. The police don't have a record of him. I know because it took me only three minutes to be told nothing—when there's information to be found, it's normally a slew of transferred calls and time on hold and questions asked of me before I'm told nothing. Every time I called today, I got no answer immediately. It was very unusual. But then I got to thinking, you see, and you know what I came up with? Do you know?"

She shook her head, her eyes downcast.

"Well, what I started thinking was, *Hey, Rebecca is lying.* Isn't that interesting? Twice yesterday, Becca Smith, twice I had to leave places in a big hurry. Very different places. It was unnerving. One of them was the offices of the Science and Development Research Department. I was there because of you, in fact. Strange that I'd feel compelled to rush out of such a dull, sober place as that, huh? The other place I felt I had to get out of was different. That simply *must* have been unrelated. But quite a coincidence, yes? Normally I go find people in places and I talk to them about things and then when I'm good and satisfied, I go home and sit on my couch. But when I was in that office yesterday, trying to find out about poor Mr. Samuel Ayers— well, Rebecca Smith, it was very unnerving."

"You can walk away if you want. I need help and I have the money, but maybe you want to walk away."

"You always confuse me. I've never met someone who brings three different faces to three different meetings. Who is Fallon? You're going to tell me all about him. Right now, here on St. Anne's. Tell me."

She bit down on her lower lip. Eyes shifting, as if she were looking for an escape. She spoke softly. "He's not a killer. And he's someone who I'd do anything to protect. He's a good man and somewhere out there—" Her hand traced a loose arc and then dropped to her side. "—is someone who is a killer and Fallon needs help and so I need help."

"Rebecca, you just told me nothing."

Her gray eyes flashed and her cheeks grew faintly red. She stared up at me but kept silent. I spun around, thinking I'd heard footsteps. No one. Nothing. Slowly I turned to face her again.

"What were you reading? What's on that sheet of paper in your left jacket pocket there?"

"Nothing you need to see."

"We're out of the traditional service provider–client relationship, Ms. Smith. I'm not asking you, I'm telling you. Give me the paper." Instinctually, she took a small step away from me. I put my hands on her shoulders, careful to be firm but not hurt her, and repeated myself. "Give me the paper." My voice was hung with icicles.

Her face twisting into a look of panic, she muttered something under her breath, then whispered aloud, "Fine . . . Tom, fine. I'll show you the paper. I'll tell you about Fallon. I'll tell you what I know about Sam Ayers."

I let go of her immediately and stepped back. She reached into her pocket, and I heard the crushed paper crinkle as she drew it out. She hesitated, and extended the balled-up sheet to me.

"Shit," she muttered as she dropped it.

It bounced and rolled a bit in the blower wind, and I quickly leaned over to grab it. As my fingers closed on the paper, I heard Becca whisper, "I'm sorry," and then her knee was rushing toward my face and then it was all stars and pain and a red black night before my eyes.

I heard her turn and run at full speed up the street. I was on my knees and shook my head, jamming the heels of my hands into my eyes and trying to get my sight back. Unsteadily, I rose and could just see her through my swimming vision as she turned and darted off into a foggy alley. I began to chase her but stumbled with each step. Slowly I jogged toward the street where she had disappeared, but by the time I got there, I knew it was useless to follow. She was gone.

My head throbbed as I staggered back to the place where we had stood moments before. I scoured the area. The paper was gone.

With no idea what to do next, I decided on some aspirin and maybe a few hours of sleep. I'd figure out what to do about Rebecca Smith once the headache she'd so thoughtfully given me faded. I coughed as I turned off the clear-blown St. Anne's Boulevard onto a gray side street and said aloud to myself, "Come on, Tom—there's no way in hell that's her name."

THE FOG WAS DENSE, AND IT WAS GETTING COLDER AS I GOT BACK into my neighborhood. The walk, usually not more than fifteen minutes from the part of town by my office, had taken me the better part of an hour. The more my blood pumped, the more my head throbbed, especially just behind my right eye, where her knee had connected with my temple. I had to stop a few times to let my heart rate fall.

I did my best to think of nothing. *Fucking bitch* slipped into my mind a few times, though. At one point, I passed two young men in a pocket of lighter mist, and both had recoiled upon seeing my face. I must have had a pretty good-looking shiner already.

I stopped a little way down from my door to light a cigarette. I figured my hobbled pace would leave me just about the right amount of time for a smoke. I struck several matches, but their flames kept going out. Finding a doorway, I stepped into it and struck another match, finally getting the cigarette burning. I started walking but thought better of it and stopped, leaning against the moldy bricks of the building. Probably apartments exactly like mine. Hundreds of rooms like boxes, where people like me stored themselves. Hundreds of people carrying on with their lives, lives that had very little to carry on toward.

I began to walk again, each step still sending a dull wave of pain through my head. It must have been five o'clock or maybe even six. The fog was changing into a deeper gray by the minute, though the orbs were still dark. Ahead, I saw the pale glow of the shitshop's sign through the swirling mist. I sighed. Home. It stirred no sense of relief in me. No promise of warmth and comfort. Just rooms in which to spend hours.

I drew nearer to the shop window. The sign was now fully visible, its pale yellow light casting a faint pall on the sidewalk. Sure enough, the old woman was there with her face to the glass. But then something happened that sent shivers down my spine. She spotted me, and for the first time I'd ever seen, emotion flickered across her round face. Her eyes went wide and her mouth agape. She leaned back from the bars and looked around frantically, and then her face gradually resumed its calm.

She leaned back between the bars, her eyes again narrowed and lips pressed together. She stared right into my eyes. Then she lifted her head very slightly and turned it left, her eyes looking in the same direction. As if at my apartment. She turned back to me and almost imperceptibly shook her head once from left to right, and then was still.

I was stunned. Frozen. I dropped my cigarette and looked up through the fog at the windows of my home. I could barely make them out. Unconsciously, I turned around and took one faltering step. I looked back at the old woman. Her face stayed placid, but her eyes widened ever so slightly and she nodded. I was still for a moment, numb, and then I nodded back and started walking away. I took a few slow steps, and when I looked back at the window, she was gone. Just me and the haze and the pale yellow light receding as I walked ever faster away.

I KICKED THE OUTER DOOR TO HELLER'S BUILDING OPEN, WALKED inside, and roughly shut it behind me. "Be here, man! Be here," I muttered over and over as I jogged up the steps to his apartment. I raised a fist to hammer at the door but instead knocked more lightly, three times, with my knuckles. I waited. Footsteps.

"What—who's there?"

"It's Tom. Tom Vale."

I heard him begin to fidget with the locks, and then the door swung open. I stepped in. He didn't look so bad. Blue jeans and a ratty brown sweater and no shoes or socks, but he looked better than last time. And I couldn't quite tell, but I thought the look on his face showed happiness to see me.

"Jesus, man. What the fuck happened to you?"

"What?"

He pointed to my face.

"Oh . . . yeah. It's kind of a long story. But it involves a girl's knee right at the end of it. I haven't even looked in a mirror yet, actually."

"You sure you want to?"

I nodded.

"Help yourself." He gestured vaguely over his shoulder. "I'll pour some booze, and you can shake me down for cash. Which I don't have, by the way."

I had stepped into the bathroom. "Debt's off, kid. Fuck it," I called over my shoulder as I flipped on the light switch. Harsh halogen light washed my skin a pale greenish white. The single bulb hummed above me. My eye looked like absolute shit. Black, gray, and blue around the socket and already inflated with blood and whatever other humors had seeped in. The right side of my face down to below my cheekbone was purple, blue, and red. I moved my jaw from side to side, and it ached. I did it more. Couldn't help it for a second.

Then I realized Heller was standing in the doorway. He held two glasses in his hands. Real glasses, not a mug or plastic cup or anything. He looked relieved, confused, and contrite all at once.

"The debt's off?" he asked, barely above a whisper.

"Yeah. I don't want to take your money, Heller. Keep it. Buy tapes and lots of liquor, and I'll stop by and drink it without feeling too guilty."

He smiled a bit and nodded, stepping back from the doorway and walking into his living room. I pulled a soiled rag from
off a nail in the wall and soaked it in cool water. Pain ripped
through my skull each time I dabbed at my eye or cheek, but I
had to clean any lesions. Partially satisfied, I resoaked the rag
and pressed it to my face, walking out of the bathroom. Heller
was on his knees by the tape player, sorting through some
tapes. He looked up, and then down at a glass on the table. He
pushed it toward me. Ice cubes clicked in the amber liquid.

"What's this?" I asked as I picked it up and held it to my nose.

"Bourbon," he said, returning to his stack of cassettes. I inhaled deeply. Been a while since I had bourbon—the first sip
was a warm, welcome change from the usual. I sat down on the
couch.

"So who's this girl that clocked you?"

"It's a fucking mess, kid. I honestly don't want to say anything about her. For your sake. I don't know, maybe I'm all
wrong about things, maybe I'm in way over my head. Could be
nothing. I don't know, but frankly—" I took a long sip and
trailed off. He looked up. "—I didn't feel safe going into my
own home this afternoon, Heller. I came here. Where the hell
else have I got to go in this fucking city? I won't stay long. I
just need to wait it out a bit."

"No problem. I'd just be sitting here listening to music and
drinking anyway. Maybe from a mug."

I gave a small laugh. He began to put a tape in the player.
"Are you in the mood to listen?" he asked, pausing with the
cassette raised in his hand.

"Sure. Why not."

He pressed the tape in and hit play. The warm crackle of an
overplayed album filled the room.

"What are we listening to?"

"Beethoven. The Ninth."

Then the music started. Christ, I recognized it. "I know this music," I whispered. He looked up at me, smiled, and raised his glass slightly. He took a sip and looked back down. The song drifted from the single speaker across the years, through the mist and sickness, and I closed my eyes. They were already filling with tears. Welling from my one good eye and trickling painfully from the damaged other, teardrops streaked down my face and I let them.

My father used to play this record. I remembered every rising swell, every melancholy fall, the sweeping strings and thundering bass. Pure wonder crackling through; Heller must have listened to this tape a thousand times.

It went on. Oh Jesus Christ was it ever beautiful.

The first movement ended and in the crackling pause, I opened my eyes and looked at Heller. He was staring right at me. He didn't look away when our eyes met. He didn't blink. Then the next song started and finally he looked off, toward his window. "I'll bet you know this one too. All of it, I bet."

He was right. And it was amazing to hear. How many years had I deprived myself of this simple pleasure? Simple? Maybe not. Memories—mostly visions—swam behind my eyes as each note played. Little glimpses of times gone by and suppressed. Green grass and smiling faces and auburn sunsets and naked pink flesh and snow falling on leafless trees and my hands gripping steering wheels and movie posters and city skylines at night and all of it. There, but hidden and now creeping back to the surface. It was amazing. It was too much.

"Turn it off, okay?" I kept my eyes closed tightly, but I heard him shuffling and then, abruptly, the room was silent.

I said nothing for a long time. Heller didn't stir. Once I knew they were dry, I opened my eyes and blinked.

"That was good to hear. I . . . thanks for playing that."

"Anytime."

"I think I could take even more of it next time too. I think maybe I've been a goddamn idiot for the past decade and a half, shunning music."

"It helps me hold on. Maybe it helps you let go. I don't know. I just like listening to it. It confuses me—fascinates me that people ever bothered to make such beautiful things."

I drained my liquor and he rose and walked to the kitchen. Wordlessly he refilled my glass and then his own.

"You read much?"

"Never. Not unless it's for work. Even then pretty much no. Never. You?"

"Yeah," he said quietly. "I read a lot. All the time. I guess maybe if I remembered more from before it got like this, I wouldn't. I think I wouldn't be able to take it knowing full well how fucked we'd all gotten. Knowing full well what was taken away. I guess for me when I go through books written before, it's like reading something about another world, huh? A book of fantasy."

"What—" I took in a breath. "—what's your first name, Heller?"

He raised his head sharply, then slowly turned it to look at me. His face went from mildly insulted to quietly amused.

"You really never asked me that, did you? You don't know. It's Tom, Tom. I'm Thomas Heller."

I shook my head in disbelief. "No shit." I said quietly, "Sorry I never asked before, Tom. Kind of fucked up, I guess."

"Yeah, well—just stick with Heller. It'll be strange for me if you change it up now."

I nodded. He swirled the whiskey in his glass and looked out the window. It was black gray now. Night had fallen. I lit a cigarette and took a long, deep drag. The smoke tickled the back of my throat, and I held it in for a second and then exhaled through my nose. Past the thin trail of blue smoke, I saw Heller's pale face framed by the slate sky beyond the glass. Thomas Heller. Just a kid and, I realized with gratitude and sadness, the only person left I could call a friend. Gratitude because he'd put up with my asshole self for what—nearly two years? Sadness for him, not for me. This was the best he'd ever know. An old drunken jerkoff like me and music made long before his birth.

"I'd better get going." I said, rising.

"Is it safe for you to go home? I won't pry—it's not my business . . . not my problem, but you can stay here for all I care."

"I appreciate that. But if I've got trouble to deal with, it might as well be now while it's fresh. Thanks for the rag and the booze," I said, placing the damp cloth and glass on the dark wood of his scratched, stained old coffee table. It must have been a beautiful piece once.

"I hate to ask, but . . . could you bring my Chopin back sometime? Soon? I've been missing it. And it's only been a day or two. Pathetic, huh?"

"No . . . that makes sense to me. I'll bring it tomorrow night, in fact."

He nodded, and we said nothing else as I let myself out and started down the stairs.

The fog was thick and cold. My skin grew damp and my hair wet after just a few minutes of walking down his street. One two three steps and an orb post . . . one two three steps and another. They led me along until I turned down an alley and made my way out onto windblown Eighth Ave.

I HAD TO SEE EDDIE. ASIDE FROM TOM HELLER, HE WAS THE ONLY one not mixed up in the parts of my life that were falling apart. I was sure he was clean. I was sure he was just as embroiled in it as me, and maybe talking to Eddie some would make a few things click together. For both of us.

My right eye was still badly swollen, but I could see well enough, and it hurt only if I touched it or when I bent over and blood rushed to my head. Not pretty, though.

I went to my office and lost several of my little points passing people in the halls. They gawked at my battered face and it pissed me off. It bothered me because one, hey, go fuck yourself, but two, because if anyone was asking questions, it would be a lot easier to remember some guy with a bruised-up face than it would some guy in his forties wearing a brown jacket.

I got into my office and shut the door behind me. After sitting quietly for a minute to make sure I'd be left alone, I pulled out my old phone. I plugged it in and dialed Eddie. He answered on the second ring.

"Eddie, it's Tom Vale."

"Thomas! Where are you? Can you—? I'm leaving here soon. Can you come by?" He was talking fast, his voice tempered by stress and fear.

"Sure, I suppose. Any people there with you, though?"

"What? None. No one; I'm alone."

Sounded true. I told him I'd be there in half an hour and left immediately, planning to show up in ten minutes. I went downstairs and hustled through the bright gray haze as fast as I could without breaking into a run. In the back of my mind, I knew I could have some serious trouble in the next few minutes. But without answers, I could get caught with my pants around my ankles. It was worth the risk.

When I got to his building, I paused long enough for one deep breath and went in. The doors were never locked during business hours, which was good—if Eddie was lying to me and wasn't alone, at least I could make my entrance unannounced. He had been telling the truth, though. It was just him. And really just him: the place was empty. File cabinets with their drawers removed, bare shelves, empty closets; it was just Eddie sitting on a wooden chair in a big, vacant room that had once held his life's work.

"Tom! Oh God, I'm glad to see you!" And he looked it. Relief washed across his face. It almost made me sick how happy he seemed. But then: "What happened to your face!"

"Nothing. Well, something, but tell me about you first."

He shook his head and studied my bruised cheek like some grandmother, clucking his tongue softly. Then, straightening up and turning to face the empty warehouse, he said with bright sarcasm, "Well, the police are back! They came by late last night. Poked around for a while, took pictures, and then left. Then the phone rang this morning—and it was so strange because for a few weeks now, you've been really the only one who calls—and they asked me if they could come by and take some evidence . . . evidence, they called it. Ha! I said they were a month late for that, but sure, come on by, and not thirty minutes later, six or seven of them showed up." He walked around the large room, pointing here and there as he spoke. "They had these big plastic . . . bins, I guess you'd say, with wheels on them, and they gathered everything that was left. All of it. Said they needed it all and would get it all back to me but that if the case were to be open, they had to have it. What could I say? I hope you don't feel like I went behind your back, Thomas," he said, turning to look at me and sounding so damn sincere.

"Of course not. What were you supposed to do, anyway? They don't like to hear no these days."

"When did they ever?" He shook his head. "You know what kills me, though? If it were the old days, I would just call up the insurance company and say, 'Hi! This is Edward Vessel and I've been robbed poor and then picked clean and what's my policy cover?' Now? I'm just . . . fucked, Tom." He locked his fingers behind his head and twisted from side to side at the waist. "I just wanted to help people out and get by. Now everyone who put their trust in me is lost. Now I don't have a pot to piss in."

I nodded even though he wasn't looking at me. He was talking mostly to himself, anyway. I walked around a bit, pretending to study the place, but there was nothing to see: it was surgically cleaned out.

Eddie wheeled suddenly to face me. "They asked a lot of questions about you too. They wanted to know all about you, Tom."

"Last night or today?"

"Last night, mostly. In fact, only last night, come to think of it."

"What did you tell them?"

"What? Well, I just . . . told them about you. About how I met you through that woman—what was her name? Susan something . . ." Susan Brewer. Her husband had been cheating on her, and she'd hired me to prove it and then scare the shit out of him. Which I did in an alley one night. She and her deadbeat man stored their family albums with Eddie. Or they had, at least. He took a few steps toward me, stroking his chin absentmindedly. "Susan Whatever, and how after the cops gave up on me the first time, I remembered you and called you and all. I told it just like it happened."

"Did you tell them you came to my house?"

"I . . . did. Yes, I told one of them that. One of them was asking all the questions."

"What did he look like?"

"Look like? I . . . He was pretty tall—taller than me, anyway . . . um . . . He had dark eyes. Penetrating eyes, you know? I could hardly look at him. His skin was pretty dark too. I don't know what to tell you—he was just some guy. No uniform, though. He was just wearing a suit."

"Okay." I nodded and walked over to a couple of chairs near the far wall. I sat in one and Eddie dutifully sat down in the other. I leaned forward and placed my elbows on my knees, intertwining my fingers. My head down, eyes on the floor, I said, "Ed, I'd like to see that note you have with my address written on it."

He opened his mouth to speak but said nothing, and then

rose and walked toward the adjoining office. He cast a sidelong glance at me as he passed through the doorway, his brow knit with concern. I lightly punched one palm and then the other as sounds of his rummaging came from the next room.

Then Eddie walked back in and toward me, his right hand held at chest level, a folded piece of paper in his fingers. He handed the note to me and I unfolded it and read it again. My street, my building number, signed *T. Vale*. Was that my handwriting? For the life of me, I couldn't tell. It looked right but felt wrong. Even in the depths of a binge—especially in the depths of a binge—why would I have given this to Eddie? Eyes still on the note, I asked, "When did I give this to you?"

"You didn't, exactly. It came in through the mail slot. You don't—"

I looked up at him, cut him off. "There are no numbers on my apartment door. How did you know which unit to find me in?"

"You . . . Thomas, really! You telephoned me. Last door on the left, you said."

"I don't remember calling you. I don't . . ." I trailed off, my mind starting to race. Then I glanced back up at him. "Did I sound drunk?"

"Not at all. I remember it well—so few people call me and it's you half the time, anyway, like I said. The occasional angry customer, but so few people even have telephones anymore, they usually just show up." He started in talking about them, but I persisted.

"You remember it well? What did I say?"

"You told me to come over in the morning, told me last door on the left. . . . That was all, really."

"Someone wanted you out of here. Needed to be sure you were gone for a while."

"You mean—?"

"I didn't call you, Eddie. I don't even have a phone in my

home, and I wouldn't have been drunk in my office. Plus you say I sounded fine."

"You did." He nodded firmly and sat back down beside me.

"And it was definitely me? Or sounded like me, at least?"

"I mean, my phone is old, sure, but yes—it sounded just like you."

I rose, pocketing the piece of paper. Pacing, I looked for any clues, anything left behind. The place was barren—they had been thorough, whoever they were. I was at a loss for the moment. But at least something had happened; there had been a big change in this Eddie situation, and with change comes either answers or trouble. Usually both. This time both for sure.

I closed my eyes tightly, pressing the tip of a forefinger and thumb against each eyelid. Walking in a small, aimless circle with my eyes still closed, I began mouthing my thoughts silently.

The phone rang.

It seemed deafening in the otherwise silent warehouse. Eddie's eyes opened wide, and he jumped up from his chair. He started toward the office as the ringer clattered noisily for a second time, but stopped short off my hard look.

"Hardly ever get calls?" I asked.

"Hardly ever." He shook his head solemnly.

I held his gaze for a beat, and then rushed for the door. "Lie for me, Ed—I wasn't here." I clapped him on the shoulder as I passed him. I stopped in the doorway to the office and turned back, saying over my shoulder: "It was Watley, by the way. I don't know exactly how and much less why, but he's the one. We talked." Eddie looked away, nodding slowly. I burst through the office door and leapt down the stairs, leaving Eddie standing there alone in a big empty room, hands limply by his sides and his eyes on the floor.

I HAD HALF EXPECTED THEM TO BE WAITING IN THE STAIRWAY. Whoever the hell they were. As I roamed aimlessly about the city at midday, on every face that appeared in the swirling mist, I saw the black-suited man from Research. Dark piercing eyes, dark skin. Close on my trail, and me not even certain what I was following that made my trail so hot.

I wanted to go home and pore over my old notes from the weeks I'd spent working for Ed. See if anything popped out at me. But I knew it wasn't safe. Couldn't go to the office either, I figured. The safest place to be was in the middle of the street, surrounded by gray, and where everyone keeps their eyes on their feet. I came to a corner and ran my hand along the cement of a building until I found the brass street plate of Cathedral Street.

Years ago, this was a wide, beautiful road lined with white birches spaced evenly along a broad brick sidewalk. The cathedral at the northern end of the street still stood, but was barred from public access. Its spires that had once challenged the sky had succumbed to the mist. It was effectively just a few large, moldy doors and old damp granite now. I've never been religious, but I used to go in from time to time. I still remember the smell of the stale, musty air. The smoke from candles mixing with incense and curling upward through colorful shafts of light . . . I wished I could have gone in again. Even without the brightly lit stained glass, I would have loved to sniff the air and just to be in a place so tall and wide that was free of fog. But the doors were barred and the windows boarded.

I was standing at the corner, absentmindedly tracing my finger through the letters of the sign over and over again. I stopped and stepped back, then once more ran my hand across the cool, wet metal. Turning on my heels, I headed up Cathedral Street at a clip. If I couldn't get inside, I could at least stand outside, feeling sorry for myself.

Parts of the sidewalk still bore the original brick. Cracked and crumbling now, there were still a few in good shape that led me along the way with their chevron pattern. Most of them had been ripped out and replaced with ash-colored cement. *You can't go home again,* I muttered to myself for the ten thousandth time. I passed a four-by-four square that was unpaved—just a loose mix of pebbles, dead soil, and refuse, and realized that a tree must once have grown there. Now not even a weed braved life.

I stopped walking altogether and lit a smoke. I needed to get out of the fog for a while. I made up my mind to go briefly home and grab a few things, and then head somewhere safe. Some dive of a restaurant or obscure shop or even just a blown-out street with my head kept low—anything to spend a few minutes out of the dampness.

I CHANGED MY ROUTE, AND IN ABOUT FIFTEEN MINUTES, I WAS AP-proaching my door from the south side of the street. Part of me wanted to overshoot and see if the old woman was in the shop window, but another part of me was gripped by fatalism: If someone was waiting for me, he would get me eventually. I went through the vented chamber and upstairs to my little home. It seemed fine. Just as I'd left it: a mess. I went immediately for the cupboard and a bottle of whiskey. The vodka sat next to it, and I smiled ruefully to myself. "Rebecca, may I offer you a drink?" I said aloud in a gentlemanly way. "Or would you prefer to just crack me upside the face?"

I took a sip of scotch from the bottle before grabbing a glass and pouring a few fingers' worth. I wandered around the place, into the bedroom, back out, and a moment later in again. If no external force ever made me change things, I would go on like this for another five years or ten or until I was dead. How else could I live, really? Nothing else made sense to me.

I went to the window and pressed my forehead against the cool glass, peering out into the midday haze. Not so bad out today. I could see the street below. I could almost see the inter-section off down to the south. I took a gulp of scotch and put the glass down still half-full. I needed to get to open space. Claustrophobia had been slowly wrapping its fingers about me for hours, and once it had me, it would be enough to trump my usual xenophobia. How people could ever have lived at sea—or even beneath it—or how every prisoner did not go mad . . . these things were beyond me. Four walls turn from sanctuary to cage with the slightest change in temperament.

I walked into my bathroom and pulled out the little white board by the toilet. I reached into the exposed hole and wrapped my fingers around a few wads of cash. As I stood, counting the bills, I realized that until I knelt to retrieve the money, I had not consciously decided to get it. Either intuition or paranoia led me to take almost two thousand dollars and stow the rest of the cash back in its nook.

I replaced the board and went into the kitchen. I grabbed a half-stale piece of bread and forced it down while rummaging about. A few pills—five or six, which I tossed into my jacket pocket loose. Some pens and a few sheets of yellow paper torn from one of my last two pads. I looked all over for knives with folding blades. I knew I had a few of them. So few things, yet still I could never find what I needed.

After digging for a good ten minutes, I relented and settled on a little paring knife. I wrapped the blade in paper and put it in one of the outer pockets of my coat. It would be next to useless, but at least it offered me a semblance of protection. Unless I was due for a bullet in the back. Either way or neither way, I wasn't going to stay caged in here. I started for the door, then stopped and turned around. I grabbed Heller's Chopin cassette and then left, slamming the door shut behind me.

I hit the street with purpose in my step, deciding arbitrarily that St. Anne's Boulevard was my first destination. I'd mill around by one of the blowers, smoking and watching for a tail, and enjoy a bit of dry air. I passed the shitshop window; it was empty. A ripple of unease went through me, and I moved as if to enter, but then shook my head and gathered my resolve. I was out to make something happen today, not to read into little things like the old woman's absence as baleful portents. I had a few stops to make, but my path was going to end in one place: Watley's. It was time to force a crisis.

7

THREE OR FOUR CIGARETTE BUTTS LAY NEXT TO THE ONE I HAD just dropped. St. Anne's was almost empty and was nice and clear. The fog had been growing thicker in the afternoon hours as the temperature dropped, but it still lingered fifteen or twenty feet above my head, dancing in the blower's wind. At first I had kept my chin tucked into my chest, my eyes down, warily watching for any signs I was being followed. None came and I was now leaning casually against a cement wall, feet planted wide apart and my head cocked to one side.

A bit more of the city was visible—almost a full second floor on many buildings. Some of those windows were boarded, but most still had their glass. I wondered what it must be like to live along a street with blowers. Looking down on pedestrians shopping and chatting and wandering along must've almost made it feel like old times. As long as you never looked up.

A family walked by, and as they drew near I straightened up to stand in a more "normal" position. All four pairs of their eyes stayed glued to the ground as they passed. I leaned back against the dry cement and spread my legs wide again. Strange that I cared what these strangers thought of me.

I absentmindedly fiddled with the loose pills in my pocket. Once it was dark, I'd be paying a visit to John Watley. I figured I could kill an hour or two at Albergue. My plan was to show up late and rouse Watley out of bed, drag him out of his little palace, wipe that smug grin off his face in a hazy alley.

I started walking at a clip toward the bar. Just a glass or two to get up my courage. Just a little while spent in a familiar place.

I PULLED SHUT THE HEAVY INTERIOR DOOR, AND AS THE HUM from the large vents was muffled I was met with the familiar soft music and musty leather-and-smoke smell of comfort. I walked up to the bar and took my old seat. There were two or three other guys sitting there, all of whom I recognized and none of whom I'd ever talked to. Adam wasn't there, but I had seen the bartender often enough, and he nodded in recognition to me and set down the glass he was wiping dry. Heavyset guy with small teeth he flashed around a lot.

"How you been?" he asked, stepping over.

"Just like always. Scotch, please."

He turned and scanned the selection of bottles, and then looked under the bar for a while. "Looks like we're out, my man. Sorry. What'll it be, then?"

I didn't like that. "Bourbon, I guess."

He poured a generous glass and I put a few bills down. He gave me a half smile and walked away, knowing it was enough for several rounds. I sipped at my whiskey and looked at myself in the smoky mirror behind the bar. Something caught my eye. I turned around on my stool.

There in the corner sat the old black fellow I'd passed on the street two days before. The same light gray suit and hat and dark sunglasses. I rose immediately and walked over to the booth where he sat. He didn't look up. He didn't even move a muscle as I stood glaring at him. Finally, I set my glass down roughly and slid onto the bench across from him.

"Howya doin?" he asked quietly, his voice barely above a mellow whisper.

"I don't know how I'm doing."

He nodded slowly and lowered his head, wrapping his gnarled fingers around a half-full bottle of beer. I waited for him to speak but he did not.

"I've seen you before. But not here."

"Hm." He grunted. "I've never seen you."

"You have, though. No one new comes here, and yet here you are. On the street one day and in my bar the next." I was resolved to drop any tact and get at the truth. He was here because of me, I was certain, and I had to know why. "What's your name?"

A smile slowly crept across his face. He sipped at his beer and then raised his chin. "People call me Lucid Jones."

"Lucid? That your given name?"

"Does it matter?"

"Well, what are you doing here, Lucid Jones? I'm too tired to deal with any bullshit. Just talk to me, man. I saw you on the street and now you're here. It's because of me. It must be."

"Well, maybe it is, Mr. Vale." My blood went cold. He smiled again and took a long pull off his bottle. "Maybe it is." Lucid slid the empty beer to the end of the table and raised his hand, one finger extended, for a long moment. As if reading my thoughts, he pulled off his dark glasses and looked up at me. Or rather raised his eyes to me. They were milky white. No pupils at all. Lucid Jones was blind.

"What are you having, Tom?" he asked as the bartender approached. I stuttered and he laughed a bit, putting his glasses back on and sniffing the air. "Whiskey? Let's have another round," he rasped to the bartender, who nodded and walked away to comply.

"A blind man called Lucid, huh?"

"It's the fog, Vale. The fog. Been blind since birth. Never seen a damn thing. So when the fog settled in on us, see, it didn't change much for old Jones. Now I can get around better than anyone, in fact. I practiced all my life."

"A blessing for some," I said sardonically.

"Oh, no. No, not at all. I miss the sun on my shoulders. I hate the way the air smells and tastes now. I'm always damp . . . cold. But it made a leg up out of a leg down, I suppose."

We were silent for a while. Our drinks arrived and he nodded his thanks.

"Why are you here, Jones?"

"Just a place to get a drink. Be out of the damp."

"Bullshit." I stared hard at his face before remembering that it was useless. Leaning back into the leather of the bench, I let my shoulders sag. "Bullshit. You're following me. Why?"

"Why does any man do anything?" he asked matter-of-factly.

I nodded to myself. "I have money," I said quietly.

He shook his head almost sadly. "Not enough, sir. Not enough, I'm afraid."

"Just tell me what you know. I promise you I have money. Thousands of—"

He held up a hand to silence me. "Just don't bother, Thomas. You ain't got enough tucked away down by your toilet to make it worth my while. I got nothing against you. I pledge that. But a blind man has to take care of himself, and so that's what I do."

We were silent for a while. But then it occurred to me: Why the honesty? Why tip his hand like this? The only thing I could figure was that old Tom Vale was near the end of his rope.

"How long have you been following me?"

"Long time."

"Weeks?"

"Mhmm."

"Who's paying you, Lucid?"

"Oh, Tom . . . I can't say that." He smiled brightly. "I mean . . . I got to get paid first, you know? I don't wish you any harm. I do not. I just don't ask too many questions, and I do what I need to get paid. To get by."

"So why are you here now? You must have known I'd find you . . . see you here."

"My work is done, Vale. I just got to bide my time."

"Can't I offer you something? Offer you cash on top of whatever . . . whoever else is out there?" My voice was tight, higher pitched than normal. I was expressing more of my growing fear than I wanted to but couldn't help it.

"I'm sorry. You really can't afford it. Or rather I can't, I suppose." He lowered his head and removed his gray hat, setting it on the table beside his beer. He had yet to take a sip. "It's all done now, anyhow. Wasn't an accident that you saw me on St. Anne's. I got no reason left to hide."

"Was it you watching me from the street outside my apartment? All those nights?"

He nodded slowly, solemnly. "Well . . . maybe not watching, exactly . . . but I always knew where you were."

"Jones, I . . . I never hurt anyone. Anyone innocent . . . I never tried to do wrong. . . ." I felt bile rising in my throat. "Can you just tell me—if not who or what—can you tell me why? Why me? What the hell did I do?"

He was silent. Still. Then, slowly, he put his hat back on. "I can't tell you a thing, Vale. I wouldn't go home if I was you, though. I just wanted to say that it ain't personal. That's why I came here. Knew you'd be by. I been following you long enough to, well, hell . . . I feel like I know you a bit. Wish no harm on you, but I always have to think first of Jones." He rose and nodded to me. "Good evening, Mr. Vale. Good luck."

He walked toward the door. I was stunned and didn't move at first. As soon as I was on my feet, he turned and said back over his shoulder, "Don't try to follow me, Vale. It won't help you a bit."

Lucid Jones stopped before the door. He reached up slowly and put a hand on his fedora. I couldn't tell if he was tilting it toward me or just readjusting it. He left and I sat back down, numb. His beer sat untouched on the table before me. None of the few other patrons seemed to have paid a bit of attention to our exchange.

Not knowing what else to do, I walked to the bar and ordered a double. I don't know if the bartender saw my trembling hands.

HOURS LATER, I WAS LOST AND DRUNK AND STUMBLING. WHEN I had left the bar, I turned away from home and walked aimlessly north, through streets and down alleys I had rarely if ever traveled. I was near the high chain-link fences and razor wire that marked the edge of my world. They hummed and occasionally crackled with electricity. Beyond them lay concrete walls and beyond that, the exclusion zone—the sickness. Who knew what it looked like anymore. Probably all gray, everywhere.

There were no residences at this far corner of the city. It was all warehouses and factories and greenhouses. Most of them had sat derelict for years. There was no longer either the material supply or the population to demand all they once produced. Not a soul was around. As I walked aimlessly, I was mumbling aloud, singing bits of songs I could remember, blubbering. Watley was nowhere in my mind. I had no plan. No idea what to do at all.

I vaguely remember reaching into my pocket and drawing out several pills. Caressing them in my hand. Holding them close to my face and then finally choking two or three down with the bit of saliva I could muster. Soon I was against a brick wall. Legs giving out. On the hard, cold ground. Fading and shivering and weeping. Entirely alone.

*　*　*

IN THE MORNING, I WANDERED THROUGH THE VACANT STREETS OF
the industrial northern quarter. My head ached from the pills
and booze, my body from sleeping on the concrete. My mouth
was dry, throat raw. I needed water. I needed to bathe and get
some real rest.

I walked beside the long, windowless brick wall of an old factory. It may have stood there for a century, for all I knew. The
doors I passed were all boarded shut—mismatched sheets of
plywood and scraps of planks thrown hastily together. Didn't
have to be pretty, just had to keep people out, I guess. The
fourth doorway I passed looked different, though. The wood
was much the same, but as I leaned in to study it, I could tell
that the door had been used more recently.

I gave the largest sheet of plywood a pull and stumbled a bit
as the whole mess of wood pulled away from the door. It had
been merely leaning there. I pushed it aside and tried to peer
into the charcoal gray interior. I could see nothing. Shrugging
to myself, I entered the factory.

It was much darker than even the pale light of the morning
inside, and at first I was nearly blind. As my eyes adjusted, I
could see that the air in this massive place swirled with mist,
but it was lighter than out in the streets. I could faintly make
out the steel bars and corrugated tin of the roof high above.
Old faded windows ringed the upper walls.

I made my way deeper into the building, in awe of the sheer
amount of open space before me. I had not seen so far above my
head in years. My eyes grew ever more accustomed to the gloom,
and I could see row after row of massive, decaying machinery
on the immense floor.

Hundreds of pieces. Each easily fifteen feet high and the size
of a city bus. Some sort of presses or molds, I guessed. Masses of
wires, pneumatic tubes, and cracked paint enshrouded by cobwebs and creeping mist. Old tools, caked in dust, lay scattered

about the floor along with scraps of rusting iron and other detritus.

I walked haltingly along a row of the hulking equipment, eyes passing from one great, crumbling machine to the next. Skeletons. That's all they were now. Skeletons no longer needed to support the works of man, left to rust just as bones bleach beneath the sun. I was walking through a silent tomb. A tomb and a monument to a time that had passed.

So still was the air that the fog seemed to hang suspended above and around me. Each step I took unfroze a few tendrils of mist, and like a following spirit they trailed me as I walked, dancing around my legs and arms. I wondered how long had it been since another man had walked among these hulking shells. The door had been forced open and deliberately left to look as if it were sealed, but that could have been months or even years ago.

If I had found this place sooner, I surely would have come more often. It had the reverent mournfulness of a graveyard, the breathless awe of an ancient church. A latter-day cathedral. It got my mind off Lucid Jones. I walked from one end of the enormous building to the other—it must have been a quarter mile long. I would gladly have paced the aisles all day, but was in desperate need of water.

I made my way back to the open doorway. Fog was slowly rolling in, and I made a note to myself to reseal it behind me if I ever returned. The day was much brighter now. How long had I spent inside? Not that it mattered. I kept close to the wall as I approached the first intersection. Before turning south, I sought out and found an old, tarnished nameplate on the factory wall. FOUNDRY ROAD. Made sense.

When I reached more familiar streets, I decided to go to a little diner I hadn't visited in many months. I pulled a few crumpled twenties from my pocket and transferred them to my jeans. Trying to catch my reflection in the glass of the restaurant's window was pointless—I could see only my shadow in a sea of gray. Maybe that was for the best, assuming I looked anything like I felt.

I must have. The homely young waitress who approached my corner table kept her eyes averted from my damaged, haggard face and even seemed to be avoiding my smell. I recognized her and hoped she didn't remember me.

"What do you want me to get you?" she asked quietly, an almost imperceptible pause between the words *want* and *me to get you*.

"Soup. Please. Any kind of hot soup and a glass of water. Two glasses, actually."

She turned and walked quickly away, and I looked around the place. It was as I'd left it. Ten, maybe twelve tables, though the room could have handled many more. Only one was occupied by two wizened old men who chattered to each other in hushed tones. One wore a faded suit and the other a heavy woolen jacket and a beige scarf, despite the fact that he was indoors and that it was still only early fall outside. As much as it was ever a season. Slightly colder or warmer was about all you got.

Most of the fluorescent bulbs were broken, and the diner was a patchwork of shadows and light. Everything was yellowed with age and disuse. But the air was warm and smelled of cooking. I suppose it was as comforting as it could be. The waitress returned with a piping hot bowl of vegetable soup and two tall glasses of water, pushing greasy ringlets of black hair behind her ears after setting everything down.

"It's three dollars," she mumbled, looking away and pushing her hands down into her apron. I handed her a twenty and she left.

The water was tepid but still wonderful. I never had any idea where water came from anymore. Always figured it was condensed fog but feared it was just treated and recirculated. It didn't matter; I was desperately thirsty. I drank one glass without setting it down and then sipped at the other. The soup broth was thin, but it was laden with noodles, potatoes, and carrots, and I ate it hungrily, sloppily. By the time the girl approached with my change, I was finished, and I pointed at the bowl to ask for another. She returned to the kitchen.

When the soup arrived, along with a third glass of water I had not asked for but very much wanted, I waved her away with the change. She gave me a fleeting smile and nodded wordlessly, retreating to the farthest table, where she sat and pulled loose fibers from her socks. I ate more slowly, with more dignity, and then rose and left, not looking at the old men or at her again.

My belly full and thirst slaked, I needed to bathe and rest, ideally in that order. Semi-consciously, I was on the way home. I had to go back there sometime . . . one more time, at least. At least it meant a shower and a change of clothes. Then I figured I could rest on a bench. In some doorway. Back in my graveyard factory. Any port in a storm. Part of me knew it was foolish—maybe even suicidal—but the rest of me was growing resigned to fate, and my legs kept carrying me south.

FEAR GRIPPED ME AS I WASHED AND SCRUBBED THE DIRT AND stench off my body. I dressed quickly, threw on my jacket, and left. The whole visit home lasted maybe twenty minutes. Everything had seemed in order but didn't feel that way. I thought I'd left my tape recorder and a pile of cassettes on the table, but they were stacked against one wall. And I couldn't find my bottle of pills. As I crept down the stairs and out through my building's doors, I clutched Heller's cassette through the fabric of my jacket like some talisman. I held it in my hand for a while as I made my way, for no real reason, north again.

It was nearing twilight, and I was determined to finally confront Watley. I followed a meandering course back in the general direction of Heller's apartment and the factory before turning sharply west and heading directly to the bar. Stupid, I knew. But I needed a bracer, anyway. Something to get my blood hot for what was sure to be unpleasant at best. I forced my mind to churn through all the mismatched facts I had. But all I kept repeating was: "This is it. This is it." Over and over again.

"No! No, that won't fucking help!" I chastised myself aloud, spitting the words out venomously. I scarcely realized I was actually speaking until I crossed a clear-blown street and caught the nervous eyes of the few people passing nearby. It didn't faze me in the least. I went on talking to myself to drown out my subconscious and sucked violently at cigarettes.

By the time I reached Albergue's street, I was near raving. How long ago had I left the bar, anyway? Was it even the same day? Stopping a block down from the bar, I realized that for perhaps the past ten minutes, I had been dragging at an unlit cigarette. Hand trembling, I tried to light it, but the filter was soaked with saliva and it wouldn't pull smoke through. I dropped it and crushed the paper and tobacco into dust. Then I set my jaw and walked up the street to my trusty old tavern. I reached out for the door handle and pulled on it for the thousandth time. For the first time ever, it was locked.

I LEANED AGAINST THE BRICKS OUTSIDE ALBERGUE AND LIT A NEW smoke. I had come up with a pathetic plan: Since I was a man without a country, I could at least be the architect of my own exile.

I sucked greedily at the cigarette and started walking. The orbs smiled at me as I walked. Orange-eyed spectators of my decline. I was heading southeast. A bit delirious with abandon. I kept moving, my fear replaced by fatalism.

"Fuck it, then!" I suddenly cried out into the night. "Fucking do it! Come get me, Jones! Come get me, fuckers!" I stopped walking and stood there, panting, my blood beginning to boil. "I'm right here! I'm Thomas Vale and I'm here!" I screamed as loudly as I could, my voice cracking. I drew the little knife from my pocket and lurched onward toward my destination.

I crossed clear-blown Eighth Avenue and found it empty. Pausing in the middle of the street, I leaned back and let out a long, ugly howl. My throat was raw, but I lit a cigarette and lumbered off down another street, slapping my palm onto each glowing orb.

Before me, I heard glass shatter. I stopped dead, my heart pounding. My bloodlust faded and I was terrified again. Silence reigned. The cigarette dropped from my hand and I looked down as its little orange glow fizzled out on the damp pavement. Then I was walking again, quickly, the tiny knife raised before me.

I passed an orb post and lurched toward the next. A shadow flitted past me in the haze, and then in a loud explosion of glass, the orb shattered before me. I let out a deep, animalistic growl. From behind came another crash. I wheeled round to find nothing but gray. I could see no orbs. Another crash came from down the way, and I set off running toward it.

I never heard a single footfall other than my own, but from out of the gray, now and then, came the shattering of the orbs, and I stumbled through black gray mist, chasing ghosts with my blade.

My breathing ragged and my energy spent, I collapsed against a wall. The entire street's orbs had been destroyed before me. I had neither seen nor heard a soul. As I sat there, coughing and moaning, I was confused and sickly overjoyed to find my mouth turned up into a smile. "Is that you, Jones? Is that you?" I called into the haze. "I'm right here! Vale is right here!"

Nothing.

Eventually, I got my breath back and rose. Fuck it all. This hadn't affected my plan. I just needed to make a detour, now that I was sure I could never go home again. Navigating against the walls, I found my way back down the street past the dead orb posts and on toward Salk's store. The three pills in my pocket weren't going to get me through more than a single night.

SURPRISE AND THEN A FLEETING LOOK OF DISMAY PLAYED ACROSS Salk's unsightly face as he looked up to see me standing before his glass window. I realized that it was barely a week since I had been here. I normally came monthly, if that. But here I was with my bruised eye and pale skin, out of drugs and asking for more. I thought to explain it to him, but his sad eyes made me feel very tired, very distant.

He looked down as he spoke to me through the grimy window. "Do you need more, Thomas?"

I nodded. He nodded back, very slowly. "It would be better if you came back later. Tomorrow or another day, even. It would be better if you weren't here right now."

"I can't, Salk. I need them now." *I can't go home,* I continued silently to myself. He sighed and looked around at the sparse shelves lining his office, shuffling slowly around in the cramped room. Then he put one hand to his head, rubbing his temples with a thumb and forefinger. Still in this position, he said, eyes closed, "Out back then, Tom."

I forced a smile and turned to walk out onto the street. The air was dark and thick. It would have been right about the time autumn began. It was cooler and the nights were growing longer. When raindrops fell through the fog all the way down to the streets, it would be winter. Spring came when it rained no more, and then very little changed—just the hours of darkness, really—until now: this invisible, barely tangible fall.

I stepped off the main street and into the gray alley that led back behind the pharmacy. My hand trailing along the brick wall, I came to the corner, turned and followed it until I found the back door. I waited. Salk was long in coming. I lit a cigarette, smoking slowly, my left hand in my pocket fiddling with my three pills.

Eventually the door opened and Salk stood there, his stooped shoulders and large, oval head framed by the soft yellow lights glowing within. I stepped closer to the doorway where he could see me. He smiled slightly and shook his head, as if dismissing a thought.

"I lost the rest, by the way. Not like I used them all."

"That's fine. Don't worry about explaining yourself to me. I'm the last to judge." He came out into the alley and shut the door behind him, careful to leave it an inch ajar. Salk dug into one pocket, looking up at me.

"What did you do before the fog, Tom?"

My cigarette hung limply in my lips. How to answer that question accurately? "I didn't do much worth writing down. I was in the army for a bit. Before, that I guess I just kind of stumbled through my youth. Why?"

"I never asked." He pulled a bottle of pills from his pocket. It rattled as he lifted it to study the label. "Here. Maybe this isn't what you wanted. I'm sorry."

I took the bottle and looked down at it, not comprehending. "I'm sure they're fine, man. No worries." I pulled out a few bills—forty dollars or sixty, I knew both would do and didn't care either way—and held them out to him. "Thanks like every time," I said, smiling.

"Not this time." He didn't reach out for the money, cleared his throat, and looked down. "This time is different. No thanks to me, Thomas. I'm so sorry." He rubbed his face with both hands, again muttering, "I have so many regrets, I don't know how to stomach another. I'm so sorry."

I lowered my hand slowly. "Salk . . ." He looked up and quickly reached out, placing a hand on my shoulder. He gripped me firmly for a moment, nodded, and then turned to go. As he pulled open the door, framed again by the softly glowing lights, he said over his shoulder, "Tom. You should do yourself a favor and don't take those."

He shut the door. I stood still as a statue. Then from the dancing mist came a series of sharp, mechanical clicks. From both sides of me. A low groan began: a deep bass hum growing ever louder and higher pitched. The air around me swirled more and more violently. The dollar bills dropped from my hand and drifted off in the breeze.

My heartbeat quickened. My knees buckled and my hands went cold. As the wind picked up and the hum turned into a howl, I realized I knew the sound: blowers. A loud, grating noise began, and suddenly the air around me was growing clear. I could almost make out a pair of blower fans up the way. They looked to be on the back of a truck bed. Shaking my head to snap out of my paralyzing trance, I turned to run.

Blinding lights burst on from down the alley. Silhouettes darted before them, and then the lights were so bright, I couldn't see. The blowers raged in the small alley, and the air rushed around me, clearing and howling. I fell to my knees. Could barely see the ground. Voices through the swirling air and then a pair of shoes were before me. I was panting, disoriented—terrified.

Slowly, I leaned back to sit on my ankles, rubbing my eyes. Then I looked up past the pair of still shoes, past a dark blue suit to see his face. The man from Research. He looked neither angry nor satisfied. There was even a slight smile in his eyes. I knelt there and he looked down for a few seconds, and then carefully hitched up his slacks and lowered himself to my level.

"Very predictable," he said quietly.

"What was?"

He shook his head a bit and then reached out, quickly but with a calm, steady hand, and stabbed a syringe into my left thigh. He pushed the plunger all the way down before I had time to react with so much as a grimace. I looked up at him. He drew out the needle and stood. Already I was growing faint. The gray crept back into my vision despite the blower fans, which were now fading to silence. I was vaguely aware that I was on my side, watching his legs recede. The lights grew dim and I felt, as my eyes closed, that maybe many hands were clutching at me. Maybe I was very alone.

8

MY HEAD POUNDED. I WAS SURE THAT MY EYES WERE OPEN, BUT I could see nothing. I thought to get up out of bed and stumble into the bathroom for a handful of aspirin. I needed water. Then the couch and sleep and no thinking. There was throbbing at my temples and behind both eyes. The bed felt so hard. I coughed and the pain in my skull turned to agony and finally my eyelids peeled open.

I was not at home.

White walls. The room was maybe ten by fifteen with very high ceilings. I was lying on a concrete floor next to a simple cot. The sheets and blanket on the cot were in disarray, used recently. I was on my back, and that was all I could see of the room. Slowly, my brain pulsing, I rolled away from the wall with the cot and looked across the room.

Two men sat on chairs molded of concrete on either side of an iron door. They wore gray fatigues and caps and were clean shaven, and each had a pistol holstered and a long rod that looked like a cattle prod hanging from their belts. One straightened up as my eyes met his; the other, on the left, didn't. He just stared at me.

My tongue, like a dry piece of leather, played across my chapped lips. I tried in vain to conjure up a bit of saliva. Finally, rasping and croaking, I slid up onto one elbow and said, "Hi, fellahs."

The one on the right leaned over to his compatriot and whispered something. The other nodded and then they were both silent again.

"So . . ." I winced as I pulled myself up to sit Indian style, leaning back against the cot. "What's um . . . what's going on?" Nothing. I raised a finger and, hand trembling, pointed to the guy on the right. "You . . . chatty Cathy . . . what's up with you?"

"Don't talk to me," he said.

"Okay, how about you?"

"Don't talk to him either," said the first one, leaning forward a bit on his stool. I hung my head and shook it from side to side. I guess I knew something like this was coming, but I had hoped it wouldn't be so clinical. So official. Matching uniformed guards with evil-looking tools. I turned and, using my arms as much as my legs, hefted my aching body up onto the cot. I sat with my feet on the floor and my hands clasped together, looking at the two stoic faces of my new friends. I decided to keep pressing my luck. Whatever was coming was coming, and I wanted to know about it or at least accelerate it as much as possible.

"Guys, if we can't talk, I don't know how we're going to get to know each other." I forced a shit-eating grin.

The guy on the left, the more stoic one with features shaped by a life of bitterness, rose and took a few steps toward me. He brandished the pole in his hand. It was thin, with a little fork at the business end and a thick handle at the other. He flicked a switch, and little tendrils of blue electricity danced across the tines held toward me.

"Keep talking, asshole," he said, his voice low and deadly serious.

"What should I talk about? I was hoping you jack offs would do the talking. . . ."

He took another step closer, raising the rod menacingly before me, and reached into one of the pockets of his trousers. He pulled out a syringe and removed its cap with his teeth.

"Would you rather a little wake-me-up"—he smiled, nodding toward the electrified rod—"or do you want to take another nap?"

"I'd really prefer a cigarette," I said quietly, looking down. It occurred to me then for the first time that I was still wearing my jacket. I patted my chest pockets and found that I still had my lighter and smokes. Incredulously, I realized I still had Heller's cassette and the pills too. My little knife was gone, though.

The guard stood there, feeling very tough, I'm sure. I slowly, deliberately drew out my pack of smokes and put a cigarette between my lips.

"Don't light that," the standing guard said. The other stood up behind him.

I thought about my options for a second, went with the one that made the most sense, given the less-than-ideal circumstances.

"Well, hey—" I smiled, flicking my lighter. "—fuck both of you."

I lit the cigarette. Got one deep drag. Then the closer of the two was on me, that goddamn pole against my chest. I heard the crackle of electric pain before it even registered. Then every muscle twisted in on itself, and I screamed like a wounded animal, writhing in anguish on the floor.

I'd never experienced more displeasure in so short a time. I convulsed on the cement as they stood, shoulder to shoulder, grinning down at me. My cigarette sat on the ground between their boots. Rolling onto my stomach and then rising unsteadily onto my knees, I reached out and picked up the smoke between two fingers.

"This asshole doesn't learn, does he?" The shock-happy guard flicked his pole to life again and very slowly began moving it toward me. Toward my face. I put the cigarette between my lips, rose up into a low crouch, and with everything I had, punched him square in the balls.

He crumpled like a wet tissue, howling and coughing as he fell. I grabbed the pole from where he'd dropped it and rose, waving it at the other guard, who stood looking nervously from his incapacitated comrade to me, hand on his holstered weapon. His other hand strayed toward the electric pole still clipped to his belt. I held the shock rod's tip near his chin for a moment, and he froze. Then I sat roughly down on the cot, threw the prod away, and smoked while staring up at him. The man on the floor got to his knees. He stared at me with hatred in his eyes, his face red and drenched with sweat from the pain in his crotch.

"You motherfucker . . . ," he growled between clenched teeth. He drew his pistol and leveled it at my chest.

"Easy guy . . . ," I said quietly.

"Rick, hand me your shocker," he said over his shoulder. The other guard stepped forward to oblige him. "Enjoy that drag." The kneeling guard smiled sadistically, his lips curling back to reveal mossy, piano key teeth. Then the prod was alive, and it was on my chest, my legs. I was blinded by the pain. The bastard went for my balls with it. My neck. I was racked by spasms, flopping around like a dying fish, smashing my head into the metal bedposts, screaming and nearly nauseated.

He finally relented and casually walked over to his seat to sit and watch me. The other followed suit. I was shaking and could smell burnt flesh in the air. I'd pissed myself. My coughing was so severe, I could hardly see. Tears stung my eyes, and then through the blur of pain, I realized the iron door had opened. It was him.

My vision was hazy, but I could make out his blue suit and

the line his jaw cut against the bright light spilling past him from the hall.

"What the hell did you do?" he said in a quiet but angry voice.

"He punched me in the nuts, sir."

"Just like that? He just woke up and hit you in the balls?"

"Pretty much. We—"

"Get out. Both of you. Get the hell out of here."

The guards exchanged puzzled, chastened looks and then rose to leave. Each had to turn his torso to slide past the man, who did not move an inch as they departed. When they were gone, he hitched up his pants and sat down on one of the concrete stools, sliding it a few feet closer to me.

"Sorry about that, Tom. Army guys—you know the type, I'm sure. No good without specific orders." He shook his head, glancing back at the open door. Then he leaned toward me. He reached into his outer jacket pocket and drew forth a bottle. "I brought you some water."

"That was . . ." My voice failed as I tried to speak. I took the bottle and sucked at the tepid water. I coughed and then tried again. "That was sweet of you. Why, you think of everything."

He laughed. "That's my job, Mr. Vale. I'm Anthony Kirk. One of the directors of the Science and Development Research Department."

I stared at him, finishing the water.

"I'm honestly sorry for how everything had to play out—if it could have been different, believe me, it would have. But . . . it's not." He studied me: my battered face, the urine stain on my pants, my damp, pale skin. His deep, intelligent eyes seemed saddened by what he saw, and for just a moment, emotion flickered across his dark complexion and it seemed he was about to say something. Then the fleeting look was replaced by clinical coldness. "I don't think your injuries are too bad, so we're going to get moving right away. Tonight, I hope—by morning, certainly. I'll get you some new clothes, of course. And you can shower if you want to and rest for a while. The cells upstairs are much nicer."

He rose and waited patiently as I clumsily did the same. Once on my feet, I eyed the slightly taller man intently and he held my gaze. "Tell me, Anthony. What . . . what did I do?"

"It's not so much about you, Mr. Vale. Or at least you personally. I know it's all very confusing and I empathize with your plight, but enough of it will make sense soon, I assure you. But we're very busy, and so please, for now be content to know that knowledge is coming. Let's get you cleaned up and rested."

He turned and stepped out of the cell and then waited for me to follow. The hallway seemed more like that of an office building than a prison, not counting the iron doors along one wall. The floor was covered by a thin, blue green carpet, and the walls were a soft beige. Fluorescent track lighting cast a cold brightness. The corridor was maybe a hundred feet long. At the far end, in the direction we began walking, the two guards from my cell leaned against the wall.

Anthony Kirk led me down the hall, walking briskly. As we neared the soldiers, he subtly waved his hand, gesturing for them to step to one side. They did, and he opened the door behind them. It was made of plain wood, painted white.

The guard I'd struck let out a low growl as I passed him, and I made a sudden feint toward him, my fist stopping just short of his stomach. He sucked in air and shrank from the phantom punch, closing his eyes tightly. He quickly reopened them and they filled with loathing as I smiled, looking back as the white door swung shut.

We were in a lobby. The three elevators before me looked fabulously familiar.

"We're in Science, aren't we?" He nodded. "You have jail cells in the Science and Research Department?"

"I know it seems odd, Thomas. Space is at a premium in the city." My mind went to the vacant factories and boarded-up buildings in the north end of town. As if reading my thoughts, he added: "Usable space, anyway. Very few buildings have steady power, water . . . Science was a natural fit, really. We use every square inch of this building for something."

I stretched my neck from side to side. Kirk stood before me, not looking back. I could have attacked him—could have thrown my arms around his neck or kicked his knee in sideways or just lunged upon him, fists flying. If this really was Science, if I immobilized him, I could very likely take an elevator down, run through the lobby, and be free. But I knew I wouldn't do it. What would I do then? Run out into the fog? That begged the question of what freedom really meant anymore. How long had they been watching me . . . Kirk and Lucid Jones and even Rebecca? Had she gone and convinced these guys that I'd killed their scientist, maybe? Then why the cordial treatment from Anthony Kirk?

The elevator arrived and Kirk ushered me in and then entered himself. He pressed the button for floor ten.

THE TENTH FLOOR OF THE SCIENCE AND DEVELOPMENT RESEARCH Department was an odd place. The elevators opened into a lavish room. Blue carpets adorned the floors, there were several leather couches and chairs set around finely carved tables, and most striking of all, large, live plants sat in clay urns along the walls. I stood looking around the room in something of a trance until Kirk cleared his throat behind me and I snapped back to the moment. I stepped out onto the soft carpet and he passed me with a knowing nod.

"We like to make a good impression on some of our first-time visitors."

"I doubt I fall into that category." He shrugged, distracted by a small device he held in his hand. It was a screen flashing with various images and text, none of which I could see clearly. Kirk cocked his head to one side in thought, and then abruptly lowered the device and began walking toward one pair of the large double doors that dominated each wall of the room. The doors were wood paneled and massive. Kirk pulled a keychain from his pocket and worked the two heavy brass locks. Then he tapped a code into a small keypad next to the doorframe and I heard a series of clicks. He pulled the door open. Its back was not wood. It was iron. The hallway it opened onto looked just like the lobby we had come from didn't: a prison.

It was a short hall. The floor and one wall were cement. The other wall held four sets of thick steel bars. Inclining his head as if in apology, Kirk bade me to enter with a sweep of his arm.

I said nothing as we walked down the hallway. The first cell was empty. The second was occupied. A young man—one or two years on either side of thirty, stood expectantly at the bars. He said nothing, but his eyes lit up with a knowing recognition that sent chills down my spine. I had no idea who he was, but he looked very familiar.

His sandy blond hair, his pale eyes . . . No way to dismiss the feeling as coincidence. He nodded imperceptibly as I passed. It all lasted maybe three seconds. Kirk looked over his shoulder as he walked ahead of me, and I snapped my head forward. I don't know if he could tell. The third cell was empty, as was the fourth, which he slid open. Obediently, I entered. I turned to face Kirk.

He stood by the open doorway, leaning against the bars and looking in at me. "The shower will warm up after a minute or so. There are towels, linens. I'll have clothing delivered to you. I strongly suggest you clean up and then rest. It's going to be a busy day tomorrow. And maybe a long night, even, if we get things moving fast enough."

"Anthony . . . you've got to tell me what the fuck is going on."

"No." His voice was harder than before. "I don't have to. I will, though, when I'm ready to." He slid home the metal grate and it clicked shut. I heard his rapid footfalls receding and something whispered to the other man. I couldn't make it out.

I turned and looked around the austere twelve-by-ten cell. There was indeed a nicer-looking cot. It had a thin mattress on it and neatly folded sheets and a pillow set on one end. There was a bar of soap too. The floor was cement except in the corner, where a showerhead stuck out above an iron grate. A steel toilet and sink were the only other accommodations. With nothing else to do, I turned on the shower and stripped. The air was cold on my tired, naked body, but the water grew hot as Kirk had promised.

I DON'T KNOW WHAT WOKE ME. I HAD NO IDEA WHAT TIME IT WAS, but I was instantly aware of my surroundings. A dim light from the hall cast striped shadows across the cell's floor. There was a pile of neatly folded clothing just inside the bars. I rose, naked, and went to the garments. As I sorted through them, a pit formed in my stomach—these were my clothes.

I raised a shirt to the light, seeing my own possessions as if they were some strange artifact. Slowly, almost sadly, I dressed. An undershirt, socks, shoes, one pair of pants, one button-up shirt . . . one outfit. Only one.

"Hey." I froze, unsure if I had imagined the soft whisper. It was perfectly silent; not even a vent hummed.

"Hey . . . you awake?"

I was scared stiff. My mouth moved, but no sound came out of it. Then, finally, I said quietly, "Yeah."

"How are you doing?" he said, his voice louder but still a whisper.

"Um . . . I'm not too good, man. Not doing very well." I thought to ask who he was and why he was here and all that. If he knew why I was here. But as I rose and gripped the bars, pressing my face between them, a thought hit me and was past my lips before I fully comprehended it.

"Fallon?" I said, my voice full.

"Yeah," he said, no longer whispering either. "You're Tom Vale, right?"

"Yeah."

There was a long pause. "I'm sorry, Tom. I'm sorry you're all mixed up in this shit."

"What am I mixed up in, Fallon?"

"I wish I could tell you. I don't know much, all things considered. I thought I got it, but turns out I don't really know a damn thing." He sighed. "I know none of it's your fault, though. You shouldn't have to be here. I know they're going to—" Just then, I heard the locks rattle in the door down the hallway. "Shit," Fallon muttered.

I pressed my face as far as I could between the narrow bars, struggling to look down the hallway. In the dim light, I could see shadows dance as the door swung open but nothing more. A man's voice called out, "No more talking! Don't. Talk."

Then the door slammed shut and it was silent again. The metal was cool against my face, and suddenly I thought of the old woman from the shitshop, spending her life just like this. Her face between the bars staring out into the haze.

I waited for a long time before venturing a whisper. "Fallon?"

"No talking!" a man's voice immediately boomed.

I stepped back from the bars. "Good night, Fallon," I said aloud.

"Good night, Tom," he called back. I lay down and was wide awake for hours. My thoughts at one point strayed to the new pills Salk had given me, and I rose quickly and flushed them. I wasn't sure what he had meant about not using them, but no reason to risk it in desperation—Salk had made a point of warning me against them. Back on the cot, I went from angry to scared to confused. Mostly I just wanted to know why. No one had ever taken the slightest interest in my life. Why did the first time I was in such high demand have to come with only one change of underwear?

IT FELT LIKE MORNING. THE LIGHTS WERE BACK ON IN THE HALLWAY and in my cell. I didn't remember falling asleep as I woke groggily from a dream. I had been floating on a river through a barren desert. The sun had shone but the sky was gray. The strange wasteland receded and was replaced by bars and concrete and men's voices as I came to.

I recognized Anthony Kirk's voice and Fallon's, and there were two more I hadn't heard before.

"Vale's in four," Kirk said.

"Okay, I'll go take a look," said a new voice. I heard heavy steps coming my way, and I stood up as a short, thick man wearing a white shirt tucked into khaki pants stepped into view. He was maybe sixty years old, with coarse white hair encircling an otherwise bald head. His brows were thick and dark and perched above eyes set deep into a large skull. His wrinkles pointed toward a life of frowning.

"Thomas Vale in the flesh, huh," he said gruffly. I gave no response. "All right, then," he said with a dismissive wave of his hand. He shook his head as he walked back out of view. He seemed almost disappointed.

The conversation continued down the hall, but I could not catch any of the words. Then the squat man's voice barked, "Hold up there, Fallon."

His gray eyes wide, Fallon rushed to my cell and gripped the bars. He stuck his hand through, reaching toward me. Numbly, I stepped forward and shook it.

"I'm sorry, Tom. Rebecca's sorry too." Hearing her name, something inside me stirred. I studied his face. "She's so sorry. She wanted to make sure you knew that. We didn't want any of it." Kirk walked up behind him and laid a hand on his shoulder.

"Let's go, kid," he said coldly.

Fallon held my gaze for long moment, then released my hand.

"Fallon!" I called as he began walking away. He shrugged off Kirk's grasp and turned. "What's your last name?"

Fallon looked at me incredulously. When he answered, it was in the matter-of-fact way one might tell you the time. "It's Ayers, Tom."

MAYBE AN HOUR HAD PASSED SINCE FALLON AYERS WAS ES-corted out of the cell block when I heard the heavy door swing open again. Several pairs of footsteps echoed off the concrete walls, and I rose from where I had been sitting on the bed. I hadn't known what else to do with myself, so I had folded my dirty garments and made the bed, and then just sat there waiting, smoking a single cigarette—I had only a few left.

Kirk and the squat man stopped before my cell with the less aggressive guard from the day before. The guard unlocked and slid aside the heavy bars. I picked up my jacket from where it lay next to my soiled but neatly folded clothing and stood in the center of the cell.

"Come on out, Tom," Kirk said softly. He was wearing a gray overcoat on top of a pressed black suit. I stepped out into the hall and we walked toward the doors, the guard leading the way and the other two men behind me.

"Where are we going, Kirk?"

"You'll find out soon enough, Vale," muttered the other man. I noted that he too had put on a jacket—a simple Windbreaker—over his white button-down shirt.

"And you are?" I asked over my shoulder.

"Callahan."

"Am I a dead man walking, Callahan?"

He snorted. "Nothing like that, Vale. Just stop asking questions, huh? It's too hard to explain to you, anyway."

I drew precious little comfort from his words. The guard

pulled open the large iron door, and we passed through into the opulent lobby. Several men sat around the room on the various couches and chairs. All of them wore rich suits and had perfectly manicured haircuts, close shaves, shined shoes. I recognized one of them immediately.

"Hey, John!" I called out with a bright smile and a wave. Several heads turned from their conversations. Watley's eyes widened when he saw me.

"Thomas Vale. So there you are," he said coolly, eyeing me and then glancing over at Kirk.

"Here I am. What brings you here, Watley?"

"Questions, questions, questions! Come on, Vale." Callahan clapped a hand on my shoulder and urged me toward the elevators.

"He's quite inquisitive, isn't he?" John Watley said quietly before turning back to his colleagues. They spoke in hushed tones, glancing at me now and then. They in their suits and ties, me with my jail cell five-o'clock shadow. All of them looked quite at home in the lavish room. Quite comfortable.

"Prick," I heard Callahan mutter as he jammed his stubby index finger into the elevator button repeatedly.

The elevator arrived and all four of us stepped on. The guard reached past me and pressed the button for number fourteen: the top floor. As the doors closed, Watley looked over at me once more, his face an emotionless mask.

"How do you know Watley?" Callahan asked, eyes forward.

"I . . . I was hired by a guy he worked for. I guess."

"He worked for?" Callahan asked with emphasis on the *for*, looking over at me.

"That's what I thought, at least. I don't know anymore, but if you asked me a couple days ago, I would have said he worked for a guy who hired me."

"That's . . . sort of accurate," Kirk said quietly. "I wouldn't worry too much about it."

"Well, that doesn't make sense. Asshole's an administrator!" Callahan obtusely pressed on, despite Kirk's clear attempt to end the conversation.

"One of the organizations that was deemed undesirable . . . Mr. Watley handled the assessment personally, Callahan."

"Why would he—?"

"Mr. Watley likes to do that kind of thing," Kirk interrupted.

I turned 180 degrees so my face was very close to Kirk's when I spoke. "What was it about Eddie's warehouse that you deemed undesirable, Anthony?"

He said nothing, looking past me. The elevator stopped moving and the doors opened. Kirk sidestepped me and exited the elevator with a curt "We're here."

Callahan followed him off, his face lighting up. "So, Tony, is that why . . ." He turned and pointed at me.

Kirk stood just beyond the doors in a simple white-walled room and glared at the short, thick man, his eyes ablaze. Callahan persisted, still pointing at me and shaking his head in disbelief and amusement. "That's why Vale's here, huh? Just happened to happen that way?"

"More or less. Enough," Kirk said icily.

Callahan laughed silently to himself as the guard led us to the only door in the room and opened it. My heart was beating quickly and my head was spinning.

"Hey, Callahan," I whispered, tugging at his shirtsleeve as Kirk passed through the door. "What does an administrator do?"

He looked askance at me, then turned and walked through the door while answering. "What do you think, Vale? City administrator? They run the city. Run everything. Make decisions, allocate shit around. That stuff. Like mayors, I guess you could say."

"How many of them are there?" I followed them through the doorway and could now see we were in a stairwell. A metal staircase led upward. We followed Kirk up as Callahan began to answer.

"Four, sometimes five if any special needs arise that—"

"Callahan! Just stop talking!" Kirk barked from above, leaning over the railing to look down at him.

Callahan raised his hands in sarcastic deference and trudged up the stairs, breathing heavily as we neared the last few steps. Kirk waited with his hand on the door.

"This can get disorienting. Just stay calm, and don't move too much." He pulled wide the door, and tendrils of fog rolled into the stairwell. Kirk stepped out into the gray, and Callahan bade me follow.

The wind whipped at my hair and face, and the mist swirled and danced more violently than I'd ever seen. "Are we on the roof?" I called above the howling wind.

Kirk nodded, and pointed toward the floor. There were two rows of orbs, not on posts, but rather set down on the concrete, leading off into the haze. It was daytime, but in the churning air, I could scarcely see more than three of the glowing orbs even though they were placed hardly four feet apart. "Stay between them!" Kirk shouted. He turned and set off walking along the glowing path, his shoulders hunched and head bent against the blowing fog. I followed him, looking back to see Callahan and the soldier behind me.

My steps were halting, uncertain, and soon I lost sight of Kirk. I inched forward half-blind, until suddenly his hazy figure was standing still before me. I took a few more steps and began to see the outline of something behind him. Something very big. I squinted as I drew up near Kirk, and then took a step past him. I could scarcely believe my eyes. A helicopter.

"Beauty, isn't she?" Callahan said, walking up beside me.

Quietly, my voice sounding like it came from somewhere far away, I replied, "I can't tell. I can't see much of it."

"Well, we'll take care of that. Trust me, she's a goddamn beauty. Great bird." He clapped me on the shoulder and pulled open both the rear and forward doors. Callahan gestured for me to climb in the back, and then he pulled himself into the front, sliding behind the stick. The soldier climbed into the other seat beside Callahan, and Kirk got in after me, pulling the door to the small cabin shut.

It was quieter inside, but much fog had swirled in and I could barely make out Callahan fiddling with the controls. Kirk took one of the two rear-facing seats, and I settled in diagonally across from him. The engine turned over several times and then roared to life. The craft shuddered and whined as the power came up. Callahan reached back past Kirk's shoulder and flipped a few switches on the ceiling. A new whirring noise filled that cabin. The fog dissipated, sucked out by a series of small fans I could now see placed around the aircraft.

"You all locked in back there?" Callahan called to us.

I said nothing. Kirk reached forward and clapped Callahan's burly shoulder and he nodded, adjusted a few controls, and then took the stick in his hand. The helicopter pulsed with life and trembled a bit, and then I felt it begin to rise, the engine roaring above my head.

Slowly at first, we ascended. My mouth grew dry. Fear tinged with anticipation. Maybe confusion more than anything else. As the craft lifted ever faster and higher, the fog seemed to be growing thinner and paler. Higher still, and it was just a fine mist and a very light gray.

Then we rose out of the fog, and above me was the bright blue sky.

"Oh my God." I whispered, "Oh my God . . . oh Christ . . . oh God . . . blue . . . blue . . . Jesus Christ . . ." Tears filled my eyes, and I began shaking. Callahan craned his neck around and looked at me. He started to laugh. I was barely aware of his laughter; hardly heard him turn to the soldier and mock me. Kirk silenced them with a sharp wave of his hand. I saw them all as if in a fading dream. For me, there was nothing but the sky. Oh beautiful deep azure sky. Soft clouds drifting here and there. Pure milk white—no trace of gray. The glorious sun. Blinding and beautiful brilliant sun. I stared right at it, squinting, overjoyed. Warming shining sun. Caressing my skin. And oh deep blue I knew only from flickering memories. And the lazy lovely clouds. I may have been speaking aloud, maybe babbling. I don't know. I didn't care.

I looked at Kirk with the joy of a child on Christmas. He awkwardly returned my smile. There was something in his eyes before he broke my gaze, and my thrill faded. In those moments of euphoria, I had not thought to look down. Slowly, suddenly terrified, I leaned over toward the curved glass of the window and pressed my face against it.

Fields! Rolling hills and trees! The winding river! Houses and roads and the familiar patchwork of perfect, everyday life. There was just so much color: white walls and green grass and black roofs and streets and bursts of orange and red from autumn trees. It was perfect, sylvan, suburban bliss. My joy returned. Briefly. At the same time, a small ember within me began to glow, began to burn hotter and grow larger.

"Where . . . have I been . . . all this time . . . ," I said very quietly, to myself. I was staring down at the land below me, but now turned to face Kirk. My voice wavering, I repeated myself more loudly. "Where have I been? Where have I been for all these years?"

Kirk sighed, his shoulders sagging. His face was grim as he looked toward the opposite window. I followed his gaze, looked back at him once more, and then hurriedly slid across the seat.

It was like one giant storm cloud nesting on the ground. The city. My city. My home of all these years. My prison all these years. One swirling mass of gray, pierced here and there by the tallest buildings. A massive bowl of gray turned upside down and placed over us all. Miles of swirling fog.

"Take me around it," I said, wheeling to face Kirk.

"What?"

"I want to circle the fucking city!" I screamed, lunging forward to lean past Kirk and getting right in Callahan's face. Kirk wrapped an arm around me and pushed me back into my seat. The soldier wheeled, his rifle up and trained on me.

"Calm down!" Kirk snapped at the man. He turned back to me, his eyes fiery. "I don't want to sedate you, Vale, but I will. Callahan, go ahead. Circle the city."

The pilot shrugged and nodded. He pushed the stick right, and we banked into a wide turn back toward home. As the helicopter straightened out, I could see the mist-enshrouded city more clearly through the cockpit. I leaned forward again, my knees resting on the seat by Kirk, head craned forward.

As we drew nearer, I began to recognize some of the buildings' profiles. Once these skyscrapers had towered above the entire city; now they barely crested the fog. Callahan drew us into a long, slow arc clockwise around the city. At regular intervals, tall, thin columns of steel stuck up through the hazy canopy. Hundred of little rods protruded from them.

I was about to ask Kirk what they were when something caught my eye. "The cathedral," I said aloud. I could just barely see the top two spires of the brilliant structure. They disappeared and reappeared several times in the swirling mist. Then we were past them. I was amazed to see that several of the bridges leading across the river into town were intact. I couldn't be sure if the one I had been assigned to destroy as a soldier was gone or rebuilt.

The more I looked down at the blanket of fog that for years had wrapped around my life, the more my confusion turned to numbness. Eventually I slid back into my seat and looked out the other window, up at the sky. Kirk said something to Callahan, and we made a sharp turn, heading away from the city.

I was silent for a long time, maybe ten full minutes. Then I turned to Kirk. He was gazing out the window.

"Kirk." My voice was even, strong. He looked at me. "What were those tall columns of metal?"

"It's what makes the fog." That's what I feared he would say, knew he would say.

"Why?"

"Wait a while longer." He turned back to the window. I was suddenly too overwhelmed to press the issue. A great weight had lowered itself onto my soul, crushing any fight I had in me. A long while passed during which my mind was all but blank. Every few minutes, I repeated silently to myself: *What the fuck? You goddamn bastards. How could you?*

I looked out the window again. There were no more houses below us—only green fields and swaths of woodland. Had we been flying that long—or that fast—to be already out in the country? Craning my neck to look in the direction we were traveling, I spotted a massive dam. Easily two hundred yards across, built into the side of a hill. The reservoir behind it was several miles wide. It was entirely new to me.

"Beautiful, isn't she? That's my baby." Kirk's voice was full of innocent excitement. "It was my first major design job with Research. Better part of two decades ago."

"Few years too late for nostalgia, Tony!" Callahan called from up front. Kirk ignored him. I was deeply unnerved. This place looked so familiar. The rise of the hills and the patches of forest—it was like something I'd seen in a dream.

"That's what generates all the power for the city. Every time you flicked on a light switch, it was power from that dam."

"It powers the vents too, I'll bet," I said quietly.

"Yes. Them too. Should have tried it when we had the chance. I should have pushed harder for it. It might have changed everything," he muttered, easing back into his seat and looking down at his hands. "But nothing would have changed." Kirk snapped out of his reverie, glancing at me and then out the window beside him. "It probably wouldn't have generated enough wattage for all the suburbs. So there it sat, a dam on paper."

"Why did you make the fog?"

He looked over at me. "I didn't."

"We'll be setting down in less than five, boys." Callahan called over his shoulder, "May want to buckle up before we do."

9

THE HELICOPTER TOUCHED DOWN IN A LARGE FIELD, ROCKING BACK
and forth a bit as the heavy skids dug into the soft grass. Callahan
powered down the engine, and with a dying whine all was silent.
I sat staring out the window at the lush green grass. It was over a
foot high and bent that length again back down to the ground
under its own weight. Wild flowers dotted the verdant carpet in
millions of places along the miles of sun-drenched, gentle hills.

The clicking of harnesses and an opening door snapped me
back to the moment. Kirk was waiting expectantly by the open
door. I crouched and slid past him and out of the helicopter.
The land beneath my feet . . . the air crisp but the sun in my
eyes and on my shoulders . . . it was surreal. The smell of the
moist grass washed over me, and I was assailed by countless
memories. Rolling in it at one age, using a lawn mower at another, crawling along with a rifle on my back still later . . . I took
a few halting steps toward nowhere, overwhelmed.

"Should we cuff him?" I heard the soldier ask. I turned and
faced the three men.

"No need for that, I'm sure. Right, Vale?" Kirk asked me.

"Where am I going to go?" I shrugged.

"Now that we're here, I suppose I can answer that, in fact." He took me by the arm and led me around to the front of the helicopter, pointing up a small hill. Among a stand of trees painted bright by autumn sat a charming home. White bricks and a wraparound porch and dark green shutters. About halfway up the hill, the grass was cut short and there were manicured hedges and bright flower beds. It was beautiful. Norman Rockwell perfect. A postcard from the past.

"I'm going to explain this very directly because I feel you deserve that much, but I don't want you to ask questions or protest or anything. Just listen and then comply, okay? It's a bad lot, Tom. I'm sorry. We're going into that house. You are going to touch what we tell you, and then we're going to leave. That's it."

"You're framing me." I said it matter-of-factly at first. "You're fucking framing me, Kirk? Is that Ayers's house? Tell me, goddammit!" I shouted, taking hold of his lapels.

"Yes," he said, knocking my hands away from his jacket.

"I won't do it. I refuse."

Callahan walked up behind me. "Hey. Tom. If you put up a fight, we can always just cut your hands off and use them anyway." He sounded more serious than before. So I kept silent.

"Come on." Kirk turned and walked up the hill. I glanced back as I began to slowly follow him. Callahan trailed a few paces behind me while the soldier stood attentively by the chopper, a rifle slung across his back.

At the crest of the hill, I could see a gravel driveway leading down to a narrow road. The pavement did not pass the driveway; it started right at its bottom and then continued across the fields and out of sight.

"Pretty private out here, huh?" I muttered.

"Wasn't always. They cleared the land years ago," said Callahan, wheezing behind me after the short walk uphill. "This was a suburb at one point. Been a while, though."

I stopped walking and turned to face Callahan. His face, flushed red, rose and fell with each heaving breath. "What did you do pre-fog, Callahan?"

"Me? Ha! I was a soldier. A sergeant for years."

"I was a soldier too. Why have you been out here and me in there?"

"I don't know, Vale." He looked off across the meadow. "I guess I was a good soldier. I never asked too many questions, I can tell you that. I kept my head down—still do." He nodded to himself as if in confirmation.

"What's going to happen to me after you smear my prints all over this dead man's house?"

"Not my business. I have no idea. I just flew you here."

"Thomas!" Kirk called out from behind us. I turned to find him standing on the porch, the front door wide open behind him. Aside from his dark overcoat and suit, one might have thought he was welcoming in neighbors for a Sunday supper. "Come on in," he said, turning and walking inside and out of view.

The interior of the house was dimly lit, but it smelled clean, fresh. From the foyer, I could see furnished rooms and pictures hung on walls and shoes on a little rack by the door; it felt like no one had lived in the house for some time, though. Rather, it seemed as if someone had been maintaining it for something. For my arrival, I guess.

I had not been in a house for years. The off-white couch with a knit blanket draped across its back fascinated me. The rough-hewn wooden end tables were beautiful. A rustic throw rug here, a dining nook there. Despite the sterile feel of the place, it was a lovely home.

I could sense Kirk wanted to start talking, but he let me explore for a while uninterrupted. Callahan stayed in the front room, fidgeting nervously about. He muttered something about "here in a couple hours," to which Kirk gave no response.

I scanned all the framed pictures in the hallway. People smiled out at me from the past. Then it dawned on me—some of these pictures were not from the past. I pulled a framed photo of Fallon off the wall and studied it. He looked to be the same age as when I had seen him in the cell, here standing in a sun-dappled forest. Another picture showed Fallon with an older man by a waterfall. It was Samuel Ayers. I recognized him from the file photo from Research, and I could see in his face the features of his son, standing there beside him.

Reverently, I returned the frame to the wall. There were several bare spots where a photograph had clearly been removed. I turned to ask Kirk about them, but as soon as our eyes met, he waved for me to follow and left the hallway. We went into the kitchen, and with a touch of remorse in his eyes, he drew a piece of paper from his pocket and unfolded it. After reading for a moment, he pointed to the sink.

"Please turn both the hot and cold handle on and then off. Then open this cabinet—" He pointed to each object he listed, careful to keep his own hands to himself. "—this drawer, that drawer, and then lay a hand on the doorjamb."

"No," I said flatly. He shook his head, sighing, then looked past me and nodded. I spun round just as Callahan touched a shock rod to my neck. I howled in pain and my knees gave out. My head bounced off the tile countertop as I went down.

Callahan leaned over me. "Don't fight, Tom. Don't make this shit worse than it has to be. For any of us." He grabbed me under both arms and hoisted me back onto my feet. I stood unsteadily.

"Turn on the faucet, touch the cabinet, open the drawer—"

I cut Kirk off. "Fuck. You. I'm not—" The prod crackled against my spine, right above my pelvis, and I stumbled forward. Kirk sidestepped, letting me crumple to my knees. Callahan walked over to me and jammed the shocker into my left thigh. Shrieking, I went down, my vision blurred by the pain.

"Vale. Comply. This is all going to happen, so just deal with that knowledge and comply." Kirk and Callahan together stood me up as Kirk stared into my eyes.

"Okay . . . Okay, asshole, I'll do it. I'll touch wherever and whatever you say. But afterwards, you've got to tell me everything you know."

"All right." He nodded.

They led me around the house, laying my hands all over the place. I rifled through drawers, opened and closed cabinets and closets. I took a piss and flushed. It was all a goddamn farce. In the living room, I thought I made out a rusty bloodstain on the oriental carpet but thought better of asking.

Their attitudes had changed. Kirk was cold and businesslike, Callahan all too happy to use the shocker. After half an hour, they seemed content with my print-planting, and Kirk led me back into the living room.

"Sit down," he said, pointing to one of the two couches in the rustic, cozy room. "Go ahead, Tom. Ask me whatever you want."

I leaned back against the cushions of the couch, moving a hand-embroidered pillow from under my arm. The unfinished wood of the frame rubbed against my flesh. I had taken off my jacket and draped it over a chair in the corner. Across the room, Kirk watched me from where he sat in a corduroy upholstered recliner. It seemed so odd—almost funny, really—that we would leave behind the foggy city and the jail cells and all of it and sit here, in this warm country den and discuss the why of everything.

I sat up again, resting my elbows on my knees and clasping my hands together. Callahan was clattering around in the kitchen. "I don't know where to start."

"Well, we're not going to hang around here all day, so find a place," he said without venom.

"I . . . I haven't seen the goddamn sun or a blade of grass or any of it in fifteen years, and here we sit." I pressed the heels of my hands to each eye for a while. "Jesus fucking Christ, can a guy get a drink or something?"

"Callahan! Bring some liquor and two glasses!" Kirk called out. "Now, ask away, Tom."

"I guess I'll start with the fog. You say you didn't make it. Someone did. All those metal spires or towers or whatever you call them."

"We call them stacks."

"Like a smokestack?" He nodded. "Okay. Why did you—why did they make them? Make the stacks. The fog. Why did you do it?"

"I was in energy. Nothing at all to do with that. Initially, anyway. But to answer your question, at first it was for protection. Everyone's. Yours and mine."

"What? Protection from what?"

"Radiation." He held my gaze for a second and then shouted, "Callahan! What's the holdup?"

"I got it, I got it," grumbled the squat man, entering the room with a bottle of liquor and two mismatched glasses. He handed one to me and the other, with the bottle, to Kirk. Kirk nodded thanks and then waited until Callahan left the room.

"Cutty Sark." He said quietly, "Your brand, yes?"

"Yes," I answered quietly as he rose and filled my glass. He sat back down and poured a few fingers for himself. Kirk looked out a window as I sat, staring at the side of his head. "Radiation?"

"Sixteen years ago. Well, it started before that—it started over twenty years ago. The Department of Energy commissioned a new nuclear plant to replace all the coal-fired operations. All of them, you see? This was a test. A pilot program. It failed."

"Sixteen . . . years ago?"

"Yeah," he said, barely above a whisper.

"It was radiation. It . . . sixteen years . . ."

Kirk was silent for a while. My lips trembled and my chest grew tight. I took a large sip of scotch, choking on the amber liquid.

"I fought for the dam, okay? We could have phased out coal and used hydro and tested the new gear on a smaller scale. I fought it. My team lost."

"It was radiation," I said again.

"Yes, Tom."

"My family . . . everyone . . ."

"Almost everyone for over three hundred miles. Not you. Not me. Not some of us. Everyone else. My wife and newborn daughter."

I was numb, dizzy. My head spinning, I set my glass down on the little table beside the couch. Kirk sat resolute as the room swirled before my eyes. Finally, barely audibly, I whispered, "Why the fog?"

"Fallout. The isotopes didn't penetrate it. They would swirl back into the lighter air. Those of us who survived the first week and got everyone into town started off using smaller machines near the meltdown site to tamp down the fallout. Someone made the connection between the death rate dropping and heavy air from a weather system a few miles north, so we stuck the foggers on the backs of trucks and drove around the city, blasting mist twenty-four hours a day. People stopped getting sick, so we made more fog. We didn't know what else to do—it was all so big. So horrible."

"Sixteen years, Kirk. We're sitting here in a house surrounded by fields and grass and sunlight . . . sixteen years gone by. Why?"

"To keep people safe. We had to at first. No one understood cold fusion. No one knew how long the synthetic iridium would radiate. The brightest minds thought they had the future all wrapped up, and now, almost two decades later, we're still scratching our heads."

"What the fuck is cold fusion?"

"It's supposed to be the antithesis of what happened. Supposed to be safe. Nearly endless power at room temperature. This was just the beginning, Tom. Plants big enough to fuel the country and battery cells small enough to run a car for years without new iridium. That was the problem. Iridium is more rare than platinum, so—why am I explaining this? Does any of this make sense?"

"No." I practically gasped.

"I suppose not. Anyway, when the research team began to experiment with a synthesized metal to replace the raw element, they fucked up. It wasn't inert. And it blew up and hell rained down. That's the short story."

He took a small sip of liquor. I picked up my own glass and downed it. He continued. "Then we—fucking Christ—then two years had passed and we'd built all the stacks and everything was stable. I thought it would be a generation before the area was safe. Maybe fifty years, maybe more. But the half-life wasn't nearly as bad as we thought, and eventually . . . eventually people had dealt with it anyway. The fog. Their lives. So they—we decided to keep the program running while we cleaned up and then . . . then it was a decade and a half later."

"Why didn't you just tell us?"

He sat forward quickly, his face flashing with anger. "Tell you what? Tell you all we fucked up? Tell the twenty thousand poor bastards living in gray that it was all because of a mistake? Tell you millions died because of a design flaw? Tell the world that? Tell our enemies we fucked up and oh, by the way, here's how to make a superweapon! Sorry! We blew it and now, hey, fog for these poor assholes! You don't grasp the magnitude of what happened at all, my friend." His jaw was clenched, his eyes flashing. "Cold fusion has been the dream of geniuses and dictators alike—we were so close. Maybe on a different day, it would have worked. Maybe one decimal was off in some equation. But now . . . now it has fallen to me and a very small group of others to make damn well sure no one ever finds out. Finds out about the science or the catastrophe. Tell you about it? Don't be so naïve. Or go ahead and shake your fist in righteous indignation—frankly, I don't give a rat's ass anymore. What happened, happened; what's done is long since done and almost forgotten."

I leaned back on the couch, slowly sliding down until I was lying sideways. His chest rose and fell rapidly as he stared at me. "I bought it. Bought it all, Kirk. The sickness and weather . . . the talk about—what did you all call it? Hemorrhagic fever? Yeah, I remember it now. Somehow related to new pressure systems, right? It doesn't make much sense, really, does it? But none of us ever questioned too deeply. We just bought it." I laughed sadly.

He shook his head slightly and took in a breath to answer but exhaled wordlessly. "Why would any of us poor fucks have guessed anything else? We were traumatized—too scared to guess anything else. We thought we could trust you types. Thought you were looking out for us."

"I was!" he exclaimed sharply. "I tried to! Junk science! I fucking knew it, and I said it." Veins stood out on his neck, and he took in a long slow breath to calm himself. "I never wanted the plant, but they built it and it melted down. When we figured out that mist could protect people, I supported it. It saved lives. And it's a sustainable system, at least. You were all safe. Turn on the stacks at two fifty-seven every morning, ease them off at midnight, everyone lives, no more sickness, no—"

"The fog turns on at two fifty-seven every morning?" I interrupted, my voice distant.

"That's when we found that statistically the fewest people were awake. There's a hiss for a minute when the stacks come on, and the haze gets noticeably thicker. We didn't want to scare anyone."

"Two fifty-seven . . . ," I said to myself. "And here I thought three was my special time."

"What?" I said nothing, and after a moment Kirk looked away. "Anyway, now you know, Vale."

"I need to know more."

"Well, time is precious. You're going to have to content your-self with this much."

"No. I need to know more. I need to know why me?" He had been sitting forward in his chair as if to rise but now leaned back, his shoulders sagging. "Why me, in the midst of all this shit? You just framed me as a goddamn murderer. Why?"

Kirk looked down and sighed, closing his eyes. He shook his head slowly, as if this were the part he'd most hoped to avoid. He poured more liquor into his glass, then shoved the cork into the bottle. Motioning for me to catch it, he tossed the scotch to me, saying, "One more drink." Kirk rose and walked over to the large bay window overlooking the front porch and the land beyond. "You, Thomas, because of bad luck. Because of Watley. You stuck your nose around things you shouldn't have sniffed. Anyone would have done fine, really; you just ended up being perfect."

I took a swig from the bottle while he was looking away and then refilled my glass. Kirk turned to face me. "We're not go-ing to do this forever, Vale. We're not evil. We just got in deep, that's all."

"Who's we?"

"We. Them. Us. The ones who were in control before and didn't die. I'm just an engineer at heart. A scientist by trade. There are other scientists and there are soldiers and administra-tors. There's a structure—a hierarchy that runs the city. Your world. And we are the liaisons to the few out there who know the truth."

"What's out there?"

"Out there?" He pointed out the window and then swept his arm in a circle. "Life. Normal life. The world over. Progress and history and families and babies and cars and music . . . divorces and love and pain and wars and joy—nothing changed out there."

"No one asked what happened? Where we went?"

"Why would they? The world knows exactly what happened: You all died of an airborne plague. The whole area is still infected and likely will be for, say, another thirty, forty-five years. That's what they know. For a few years, people tried to sneak in, tried to find loved ones. That was the hardest part, I think. Healthy people—people who should never have been involved— trying to come in from outside. We . . . we couldn't let them get back out, and we couldn't let them spread word within. So . . . more losses. But it convinced others that the virus was very much real, when no one ever came back."

Hot tears stung my eyes, and I blinked them back. A deep black rage began to seep into my soul, and I knew soon it would cloud my thinking, turn me into an animal. I held it at bay for now. I needed to know. "Why me?"

"Like I said, we're not evil. This whole . . . experiment . . . this project will be finished in fifteen, twenty years. A generation will be dead. People sterilized. Memories will be hazy for those now young. That's why we're starting to clean out all the operations like what's-his-name's . . . Vessel?"

"Eddie?"

"Yeah, Eddie—that's right."

"What do you mean cleaning up?"

"No one wanted all this to happen. Me less than anyone. But it did, and we're going to make damn sure no one ever finds out about it."

"So you're destroying the past? Erasing people's lives?"

"The way I see it, we're setting people free. People have lived through plagues and wars and all of it, Vale. They'll deal with this. Every day, people adjust a bit more. Let go of a bit more. Eventually, they'll feel liberated to live in the present."

"Instead of robbed of their past," I added coldly.

"Yes, if you need to frame it like that. Anyway, Ayers was killed, and we needed someone to blame. We'd been following you for weeks, and bad luck, Tom. It was two birds with one stone."

"Weeks? Who was it, Lucid Jones? Rebecca?"

"What? How—?" He looked up at me sharply, his guard dropped for just a second. Then, more calmly, he asked, "How do you know about Jones?"

"He introduced himself to me. The night before you jabbed that needle into my leg, in fact. Was that just three days ago? Time flies, huh?"

"He introduced himself. . . . That's unusual. . . ."

"Why's that?"

"He'd been on you for weeks, but we never told him when we planned to apprehend you. He'd been on you since you first started sniffing around Eddie Vessel's. Back before we knew a damn thing about you."

"The blind leading the blind," I said with a bitter smile. "Well, I guess he just sensed a change in the air."

He looked ready to retort but instead continued calmly. "Anyway, when it's all over, years from now, there will need to be records of certain people who lived both on the inside and outside. Certain of those records wouldn't reflect too kindly on me, on Watley. Remember, in the eyes of the powers that be, we're the good guys. If you weren't so obtuse, maybe you'd understand. No matter. We forced a pretty girl to plant an idea in your head. Figured maybe you'd let some facts slide about your other case to her. It turned out that you basically didn't know anything, but that's beside the point." He chuckled softly. "You were close, that's the point. Some of the pictures and documents you took from that warehouse; if you'd had any idea what you were looking at . . ." He set down his glass.

"Samuel Ayers is one of the few people who lived in both worlds and will have a historical record, you see. It will be about his work studying the atmosphere in the exclusion zone. Samuel Ayers's record will end stating that he was killed in his own home by a disgruntled soldier named Thomas Vale."

I sucked in air, and Kirk looked up at me; then his gaze shifted and I realized Callahan was standing in the doorway. "We should get moving," he said gruffly.

"True enough," Kirk said, checking his gold and silver wristwatch. "I hope this has been informative if less than pleasant, Tom." He began to rise.

"Wait a second, Kirk. Allow me three more questions." He lowered himself back down and looked at me attentively, raising one palm and gesturing for me to proceed.

"The exclusion zone—how big is it? How far away is . . . everyone? Everyone else?"

"It's about a two-hundred-mile radius. Outside that, life starts up again rather abruptly. It gives me a slight shock every time, to be honest. Next. And hurry, please."

"Why was Ayers killed, and what's next for me?"

"The first question doesn't concern you. The second, you'll know very soon. We need you for one more thing, Vale." He stood up quickly and walked over to where I sat, picking up my jacket and tossing it onto my lap. I didn't move.

"It doesn't concern me? Doesn't concern me, Kirk? I'd say it does. I think it concerns me very, very much. Profoundly, even."

He stood looking down at me, his face cold. In his dark eyes, there was no flicker of compassion. There was only the hard gaze of a scientist working out an equation. "Perhaps my word choice was poor, Vale. But we're out of time. So go ahead and be concerned, but stand up. I didn't have to tell you a thing, but instead I told you everything. You want to find out what's next? Let's go."

I stood up and faced him. My heart began to beat more rapidly as I stared at Kirk, the slight hint of a sneer on his calm, composed face. His suntanned face. All that I had just learned churned in my head, and my anger grew. Turned to fury. It was academic for Anthony Kirk: just facts and problems to be solved with hydroelectric power and fog stacks and glowing orbs and all the rest of it. Not so for me. Not so for all of us. He held my gaze. My parents. My time. Any chance for happiness. My life.

I slowly pulled on my jacket. As I did, Heller's cassette slipped from the pocket. Chopin. The tape bounced off the carpet and came to rest between my rough brown leather boots and his polished black wingtips. He looked down at the tape, bemused. I knelt to pick it up, my eyes on his face.

Something deep inside me cracked as my left hand closed around the tape. Kirk smiled down. My chest tightened, and before I knew it, my right hand had curled into a fist. The backs of my fingers trailed across the carpet. My torso began to twist as I rose. Fifteen years of stumbling through the gray compressed into one action as my fist began its arc up from the floor. Kirk's eyes widened the instant before I hit him. I struck with every fiber of my shaken soul.

My hand connected just below his cheekbone. The punch was so hard, his feet left the floor and he hung parallel with the ground, falling, eyes rolling back, until he landed in a pile, head first, then feet, then the rest of his dead weight. I stood over him and then heard the crackle of Callahan's prod. He jammed it into my back. I went down to my knees and then it was on my neck. Then my cheek, my knees, my balls. I was curled into fetal position, screaming, howling, mucus flowing from my nose and blinded by tears. He just kept coming. Nailed my crotch again, the bastard. Then he kicked me savagely in the back and I rolled over, my face inches from Kirk's.

He was conscious, but just barely. His eyes focused briefly on mine, and even as Callahan jammed the shocker against me one last time, I smiled at Kirk. His eyes closed.

* * *

THEY HAD CUFFED ME BEFORE LEADING ME FROM THE HOUSE. Kirk was unsteady on his feet as we walked past the lengthening shadows on the soft green grass. Callahan shoved me roughly into the back of the helicopter, handing Kirk his prod once he was seated across from me. Already his face was swollen and bruised. I hoped I had damaged his teeth. Better yet a concussion. He kept his jaw shut tight, his eyes on mine.

Callahan got the helicopter powered up, and in a few minutes we lifted off. I leaned against the window and looked down at the verdant fields as we rose ever higher. Kirk leaned forward and whispered, "Take your last look, Vale."

"Oh, let's not let a little thing like your jaw get in the way of our friendship, Tony."

He leaned back again, looking away. Through clenched teeth, he rasped, "I said we needed you for one more thing. That thing is your corpse." He faced me again. "Take your last look."

Maybe he was right. I pressed my face to the window and took in the beauty below me for a good long time. The sun shone through the glass and warmed my face. From above, the trees formed a palette of orange, red, and yellow. The sky was still deep blue. The fields were vast and green, and far off in the distance I saw the familiar sprawl of houses and shops and offices—of life. If it was going to be my last look, I was determined to make it theirs too. *No going softly into that dark night, Tom.* I smiled to myself, squinting in the sunshine. The anger and bitterness I felt just minutes before were replaced by profound resignation. At least there had always been a world out there. At least others had felt the sun on their shoulders or the grass beneath their feet. I took what was possibly to be my last look and then turned, calmly, deliberately, and faced forward.

Kirk was looking out the other window, paying no attention to me. The soldier was nodding off. It was time. I took two deep breaths. Then I leapt forward, slamming one knee into Kirk's chest as I threw my arms around Callahan's neck.

It all happened fast. Kirk coughed for air, and again I hit him with my knee, this time in the face. Callahan's fingers clawed at the short length of chain between my wrists, and I leaned left to slide my right leg between the seats, firmly planting my foot on the stick and jamming it forward. The aircraft shuddered and then began dropping violently, rolling forward and to one side.

The soldier came to in a panic and fumbled with his rifle.

"Too late, asshole!" I shouted with joyful madness. Too late. A grating whine filled the cabin as the motor strained and then failed. Then only the sound was men shouting dampened by howling wind. The ground rushed up to meet us. I looked back and saw Kirk's eyes wide with terror, and then there was a dull crunch and then silence.

10

GASOLINE—ITS ODOR CURLING AROUND ME. ALL WAS SILENT SAVE
for an occasional drip. I was in no pain. I could see nothing.
The fetid smell grew ever stronger. Liquid dripped onto my
forehead. Slowly the world went from black to dull red. Rust
colored. Then a bit of pain. Just in two places, really: both
wrists. Then I snapped awake.

I was hanging by my wrists, the cuffs still wrapped around
Callahan's lifeless neck. My feet hung past the back bench. I
stepped onto the backrest to ease the pressure on my wrists and
then gingerly raised the handcuffs off Callahan's corpse and
over his seat. Slumping down onto the back of the bench seat,
I was very near Kirk. His body was bent double at the waist,
neck twisted, and one leg stuck out at a horrible angle. Not
that it mattered. He looked good and dead.

The skin of my forearms was ragged and bloody. Everything
worked, though; I made fists and wriggled my fingers. The helicopter must have rolled at least twice—the tail section was
gone entirely and the cabin was resting with its windshield

pointed directly up at the sky. The glass on the right half of the cockpit was all missing, as was the soldier who had presumably been thrown clear.

I was still in a daze, my thinking cloudy, but the gasoline worried me. I had to get out. Again my eyes fell upon the man in the dark suit. "Are you dead, Kirk? Huh?" I kicked at his torso, my toe connecting roughly with his ribs. It felt divine. I kicked him again. And again. Ribs cracked. "Are you dead, asshole?" He was. Very much so. I dropped back down onto the seatback, coughing and sucking in ragged breaths.

I tried the cabin door but the latch was bent and it wouldn't budge. After a few solid kicks, I got the door open and crawled outside, lowering myself gingerly onto the grass. New pain seeped in. Both legs, the left side of my chest and my neck. I had a dozen little cuts where shattering glass must have caught me. But I was alive. I walked in a circle around the destroyed chopper and was amazed to be so.

The rotors were gone. The tail lay a good fifty feet away. The skids were bent, the engine nearly ripped off the top. It was bent, cracked, and dented all over. I found the soldier lying facedown about thirty feet away. The massive patches of crimson on his gray fatigues left little doubt that he was dead, but I turned him over anyway. He still bore the shocked expression of his last living moment; his eyes were wide open, mouth agape. Poor son of a bitch. It could just as well have been me if things had been different. He was just doing what he was told.

I could see Callahan's round, dead face through the glass on the side of the craft. His eyes bulged out and his yellow teeth were bared beneath curled lips. His neck was ripped to shreds where I had hung from it. There was blood on my jacket—must have been his. I wiped at my face and my hands came away streaked with crimson. The handle on the pilot's side door was just within reach if I stood on my tiptoes. I tugged at the latch, and the door popped open. Carefully placing one foot on the open frame of the rear door, I pulled myself up to stand eye to eye with the dead man.

His body was stiff beneath his clothing as I dug through his pockets. I found the keys to the handcuffs in his pants and jumped back down onto the soft grass. I freed myself and tenderly massaged my wrists, looking up at the purple blue sky. The last rays of sunlight were just leaving the distant hills. The air was cool, fresh—amazing.

I took the rifle and, rejoicing at my luck, three packs of cigarettes from the soldier. *Thanks, brother.* I nodded as I straightened out his limbs so that he could lie in some manner of repose. He had a small kit that I looked through briefly—some water, ammunition, a pocket knife, a walkie-talkie that had cracked nearly in half, and a few protein bars. Not much, really, but better than nothing. I peered into the ever-darkening cabin to see if there was anything that looked useful, but the acrid stench of fuel was much stronger now. I could see a small pool of gas collecting on the back windows.

I retreated to a safe distance to light a cigarette. I smoked about half of it, staring at the shattered tomb of a helicopter. Then I ratcheted back the bolt on the rifle and clicked off the safety. It was the same model they'd handed me a decade and a half ago. Aiming into the air, I let fly a single round: a salute for all of us these bastards had left behind. Then I trained the rifle on the ruined helicopter and began firing. The engine exploded on the eighth shot, and flames engulfed the craft. I took one last drag from the cigarette, threw it down, and set out walking toward the hills.

The sky was now a brilliant canvas of colors, stretching out from the western orange purple end of day to the eastern blue gray of night's approach. I started humming Beethoven's Ninth.

One by one, stars crept through the shimmering canopy above.

* * *

TRUE DARKNESS. THE SKY BETWEEN THE THOUSANDS OF STARS was black. I could scarcely see my hand in front of my face, much less the lay of the land. As night had taken over, I picked a cluster of stars as my beacon and followed them diligently for hours as they crept away across the night sky.

As it had gotten darker and more stars winked to life above me, I nearly lost my little constellation many times before the firmament once again grew familiar. The sky that I had not seen in fifteen years was helping me along my way. Before it all, I had never once navigated by the heavens, never even thought to. Now after all these years, I was back to the elemental ways of things. For all that time, the stars had hung above me, waiting for the chance to help.

It must have been horrifying, I thought while stopping to rest, to have journeyed through the night in the past. The sailor adrift in the middle of the ocean at the mercy of the wind and guided only by the brilliant map above must have lived in constant fear. He too could be ruined by fog. If mist obscured the stars above, he was lost. If he strayed too far from his course, he may never have found his way again.

But I had emerged from the fog. I had my stars before me and I followed them on my course. It was a cold night, but it was an honest cold. The chill wind was biting but crisp. There was no moisture in the air, and even while shivering I relished the night. But my fingers were growing numb and my joints tight, and I knew I could neither stop for long without a fire nor continue on all night without rest.

I decided to walk awhile longer before settling in for the night. I had no idea if others would come looking for me. The thought of being missed was darkly amusing—no one had much thought of me in . . . ever. Now here I was, as alone as I could possibly be and surely more sought-after than ever before in my life. Watley was probably sitting at a large oak conference table right now, discussing Kirk's failure to return. I expected to hear helicopter blades slicing through the air any minute.

I passed through a small copse of trees and paused to pick up a few of the branches that cracked beneath my feet. The treetops—some barren and leafless—reached up to the sky like skeletal hands. I ran my palm along the rough bark. When I had gathered a large enough load of wood to last me for a few hours, I selected a grassless patch of soil under a towering oak and began to make a fire.

It was a calculated risk to have this beacon burning in the middle of such a dark night, but I was too cold to rest without fire. I broke twigs into roughly even lengths and made a small bier on which I set larger sticks. I had no paper for kindling, so I crouched low and shielded the lighter from the wind with my body. Finally a few small embers turned into a feeble, dancing flame. I gently blew on the little fire, urging it to spread. Stick by stick, the licking flames crept upward and grew into a warming fire. It came to life like an orb in the haze, starting as a pale yellow and soon changing into a warm orange.

I wondered how many thousands were, at that very moment, walking along in the gray guided by glowing orb posts. Maybe it was better if they never found out. Just let them live out their lives and die thinking they had made the best of it. "No. No!" I said aloud. No. They had been robbed. I had been. If the whole of the last decade and a half could not be returned, at least there was a brighter future if all those in the city could be freed.

It was academic thinking, and I gave myself very slim odds. But even if this night were my last, I was glad for it. I had never cherished the stars and the cold air and the dancing tongues of flame so much as I did now. The air was sweet and the ground felt good under my back. Soil and grass. I had felt nothing but concrete for so long.

I watched embers wheel and swirl in the night air, spiraling up from my fire to join the stars hanging above. For thousands of years, thousands of peoples had looked up to the sky and prayed to the many gods for rain. They burned offerings or let blood or danced, begging rain to fall so that they might live. Now we could throw a switch and fog in an entire city. For millennia, we gathered close around the fire so that we would be warm, that the night would not be so dark. Now our mighty power plants electrified the world, and when one failed, we could always build another.

How horrifying but pure it must have been to live for rain and crouch by flames. There was no design flaw in rain or fire. No meltdown possible. If it rained, crops would grow and you would eat and thrive. If it was dry, you would not eat and you would perish. If the fire went out, you would freeze. As long as it glowed, you would be warm. It was perfect for the sole fact that people had no part in it. You can make fire, but you cannot make fire exist. Fire has always and will always exist whether or not we start it. Rain will fall when it chooses to and cares not if it is upon our fields or far away. We had come much, much too far. Decisions such as these were never meant to be made by man.

The fire burned low, and I added several larger branches. I lit a cigarette off the glowing embers of one of the dying logs. Just before putting the pack back in my pocket, I looked down at it. The white box with the simple block letters reading CIGA-RETTES across the front . . . Other people all this time had been walking into stores and selecting myriad brands of smokes, and all I had were CIGARETTES.

I put the pack away. My fingers brushed against Salk's pills. I had forgotten all about them. I pulled one out and rolled it around between my fingers. Then I threw it into the fire and dug out the other two. I burned the second, eventually slipping the third and final pill back into my pocket.

Sleep took me gently. No pills. No drinking. Just clean air and the fire burning low. It was the first time I had slept beneath the stars in sixteen years. It was deep and pure. I didn't even dream.

I AWOKE WITH A START BUT IMMEDIATELY REMEMBERED WHERE I was and all that had happened. It was just before dawn. There were still a few stars in the gray blue sky above me, and a pale golden glow crept ever closer from the east. The fire smoldered and I was cold and stiff, but my head was clear and I felt healthy, vigorous. Alive.

I rose and stretched, my body popping and cracking all over in the chill morning air. With my foot, I dispersed the remnants of the fire as well as I could. Then I set out walking in the soft morning light. I could see the group of hills where I was headed. They looked to be only a few miles farther. I kept my pace brisk, not knowing if I would be quickly apprehended or if I would never be thought of again.

The sun crested the horizon and began its brilliant ascent, warming me as it rose. Gradually the blue fields turned deep green as the light crept across them. Soon I took off my jacket and threw it over one shoulder. I'd covered a lot of ground the night before. It was less than an hour of walking before I stood at the long winding driveway that ran up to Ayers's house.

I started up the hill, cavalierly walking in the center of the gravel driveway. If anyone had been looking out across the land, I would have been visible all morning. When I drew near the top of the hill where the house sat, I stopped short and leapt behind a large bush. There was a red pickup truck parked next to the house. Someone was home.

After lingering behind the bush and looking for anyone in the windows, the rifle cocked and ready in my hands, I approached the house. There was no cover in the yard, so I moved swiftly until I was pressed against the porch, down on one knee. Crouched low to the ground, I made a slow circuit all the way around the house. The backyard was largely taken up by a garden of fresh vegetables, and I momentarily forgot where I was and went for a planter boasting several ripe tomatoes. My mouth watered, and a memory of Salk flickered through my mind, his pocked face cast downward, moaning in his sorrowing baritone about tomatoes. Hopefully I'd get a chance to have a few later; I had to keep focused now. I eased around a large cylindrical tank—likely for sewage or gas—and slowly raised just my eyes above the porch floor.

There was a long bank of windows across the back of the house and I could see a figure moving within, but the rooms were dark and my eyes were used to the bright sun. Not that it much mattered—I was going in anyway. I continued around the house and then, without pausing a bit, rose to stand fully erect and quietly but casually walked up the front steps and tried the door.

It clicked open. I pushed the door slowly inward and entered the house, gun barrel tracking from side to side with my eyes. It was quiet. I could smell something cooking. I leaned into the living room, where the day before, Kirk had unraveled my world. It was empty. The chairs and pillows sat as we had left them. Moving down the hall toward the kitchen, I realized that the picture frames that had been removed were now all back on the walls. I leaned in toward the photographs, trying to discern which were new in the gloomy light, but then there was a clattering in the kitchen. A woman cursed.

I lowered the rifle and stepped into the warmly lit kitchen. "Hi, Rebecca." She screamed and leapt up from where she was gathering pots off the floor. Her face turned white, and her gray eyes were wide above flaring nostrils. She was dressed in a T-shirt and shorts. Despite the terror on her face, I couldn't help but think that she looked amazing. I'd never seen her legs before. Her skin was taut and smooth. Her breasts rose and fell with each rapid breath she drew. She backed away from me, stopping against a cupboard, her palms pressed against its wooden door.

"Tom! You . . . you're not . . ."

"Dead?" I said quietly, slinging the rifle across my shoulder. She was silent, then looked away and nodded.

"Does that upset you?"

She immediately looked up and right into my eyes. "Of course not! No. I just . . . I can't believe it. . . . I . . . what happened?"

"I think that's a better question for you. I need to know from the start. What did happen?"

She slowly slid down the cupboard until she was sitting Indian style on the ground. She ran her hands through her long blond hair and looked up at me, her face heavy with emotion. "I'm so sorry, Tom. About everything. I hated every second of it. I . . . I don't know if I can ask you to forgive me."

I sat down at the kitchen table, laying my weapon across my knees. "Worry about that kind of thing later. I'm hungry. Thirsty. And I need to bathe. Is it safe here?"

"Yes. I mean, it always was. Why, are—? How are you here?"

"They made me come here. Made me put my fingerprints all over the place." She nodded sadly, knowingly. "On the helicopter ride back to the city, I figured that was it. I was dead. So I brought the chopper down. I lived. No one else did."

"What? Who?"

"Government assholes. A soldier."

"Who?" she asked again, imploringly.

"The soldier, I don't know. Just some poor bastard. There was a scientist named Anthony Kirk calling the shots and a monkey named Callahan."

"Callahan's dead?"

"Very."

For a moment her face was a mask, and I didn't know what to make of her. She looked away and then gradually her lips twisted up into a bitter smile. "Good. I hope he's already burning in hell. Goddamn him."

"So I guess you knew him, huh?"

She looked up at me sharply. "Yes. If I'd ever met him again, I would have killed him myself."

"What did he do?"

"Callahan is the one who shot my father."

"Your . . ." My head reeled and I rose suddenly, setting the rifle down on the table. Her eyes did not follow it, so I turned and walked hurriedly into the hall. I searched around for a light switch and, finding it, bathed the wall of photographs in light. There she was. With him. And Fallon. The happy, smiling Ayers family. It all finally made sense. In some of the pictures of a much younger Becca, there was a beaming, blond-haired woman with the family too. She stepped into the doorway behind me, resting her hands on the frame above her, head tilted to one side.

"Your father . . . your brother . . . you." Rebecca nodded slightly. I pulled one of the pictures off the wall and studied it closely. The two siblings and father smiled brightly out at me from a thickly wooded, sun-dappled forest. "You all look so happy."

"We were happy."

"What did your father do, Becca? Why is he dead?"

She let her hands drop from the doorframe and reached out, taking the picture from my hands. Looking down at it, her eyes welling up with tears, she said quietly, "My father made the fog."

I BATHED, WASHING EVERY INCH OF MY BODY OVER AND OVER again. The cuts and scratches from the crash stung and my ribs throbbed, but it felt divine to clean myself so thoroughly. The bathroom was spacious and finely appointed: cream-colored tiles along the bottom half of the wall and light brown wood paneling covering the rest. A large window above the sink let sunlight pour in, and the whole room was bright and airy. Rebecca had started to tell me about everything in a rush, her voice cracking, her sentences stumbling and jumping. I had stopped her. It was too much to take while tired, caked in another man's blood, and smelling of sweat and gasoline.

I dried off, looking at myself in a full-length mirror. The sunlight washed over me, softening wrinkles here and scars there. My skin was pale, almost luminous in the natural brightness. The fading bruise on my face was washed out by the sun. I stood there, staring at my naked self. It was as if I was looking at a stranger. Or rather an acquaintance I had not seen in a long, long time.

I left the bathroom and crossed the hall wearing a soft, luxurious towel. In the bedroom Becca had offered me, I found a fresh set of clothing lying on a wide, four-post bed. Blue jeans and a T-shirt, socks and a light gray sweater. I hoped they were Fallon's and not Ayers's, but assumed the latter. I knew it would bother her to see me in her father's clothing.

I dressed slowly, just as I had bathed. The scent of food cooking filled the house.

I padded downstairs as quietly as I could and stopped in the doorway of the kitchen. Rebecca still wore only a plain white T-shirt and gray shorts. Her hair was up in a ponytail. She was frying bacon and scrambling eggs, and there was bread peeking out of a toaster. A good, honest breakfast. She seemed to sense my presence and stiffened slightly, so I entered the kitchen, saying, "It smells amazing."

"Just bacon and eggs. I wish I had more here but . . . I don't."

"No, this looks perfect. Thank you." She nodded without turning around.

"There's coffee. I don't have cream, but there should be sugar."

"Black is fine. Can I pour you some too?" I asked, lifting the small coffeepot off its hot plate and pulling two mugs from the shelf behind it. Both the mugs were white and had black rims and bases. Becca looked over her shoulder and whispered yes, her eyes travelling up and down my body. I assumed it was seeing her dad's clothes on a living man that made her face twist into an unhappy grimace. "Sorry about your eye. I'm sorry I hit you."

"Oh, that's— No, it's fine. I mean, I wish it hadn't happened and all, but it doesn't even hurt anymore. If I had a nickel for every . . . you know . . ."

She forced a smile and turned back to the stove. I stood in the middle of the kitchen, awkwardly holding both mugs of coffee. Eventually I set hers down on the counter beside her and stepped back again as she nodded her thanks. This felt so pleasantly domestic . . . like something from an old TV show, almost. The coffee was warm and rich. I took in a breath to speak, but it came out as a sigh.

"I'm gonna go smoke a cigarette, okay? Then maybe after we eat we can talk?"

"Of course," she said quietly, her shoulders tense. I walked down the main hall and let myself out onto the porch. At first I could hardly see without squinting. It was a brilliant autumn day. The air was crisp, the sky a perfect cerulean blue, and the clouds frozen in dramatic clusters. Slipping off my socks, I walked down the steps onto the soft grass of the yard and lit a smoke. The blades of grass were damp and chill beneath my bare feet. Taking long drags, I wandered around the house slowly, my eyes shifting from treetops to rolling hills to the bright green carpet of grass below me. This was how she had lived for these last fifteen years. How Ayers had. And Kirk and Watley when he wasn't in his palatial city dwelling. It felt like, on some small scale, feudal Europe. *Keep them in their places.*

I didn't blame Rebecca for it. For anything. I somehow felt that she was outside the system. But that was likely inaccurate: her father was one of the architects of my life, after all. The need to know—the need to know every detail and motivation and all of it . . . about the whole city and why me —was less pressing in my mind now. Everything made sense in a macabre, general way, and I worried that more facts would just cloud my thinking and blunt any pride I had left. I had been a pawn. No man likes to be a pawn. While I had never loved my life, at least I thought up until a handful of days ago that I was in charge of my own destiny.

"Do you want to eat on the porch?" Rebecca called out to me.

I was startled back to the present by her voice. I blinked in the sunlight, realizing that I had been standing still with my eyes closed for several minutes. My cigarette had burned out. I turned and replied with a weak "Sure."

She went inside and I dropped the butt and walked up the porch's back steps. There was a little wrought iron table with two chairs sitting around it. I set my mug of tepid coffee down and sat in one of the chairs.

Becca came back outside balancing two plates of food, silverware, and her coffee in her arms, and I rose to help set down the meal. I followed suit as she draped her napkin across her lap and then in silence we began eating. I ate slowly, deliberately enjoying each forkful. She kept her eyes down, taking small, rapid bites. As soon as we were finished, she rose and cleared the table, waving for me to remain seated with one hand.

After a minute, Rebecca came back outside with the coffeepot. She freshened both our mugs and then sat. "All right. Anything you ask, I'll try to answer."

I leaned back, raising the front feet of the chair off the cherry wood deck and looking out over the countryside. "It's ironic, isn't it. . . . In twenty-four hours time, I'll learn everything I've wanted to know for fifteen, sixteen years, and all of it here at this little house in the country."

"It used to be the suburbs." I looked over at her, and she nodded. "The house sat on maybe an acre when I was a little girl. There were houses on either side and a park out back there past where the grass is cut. My school was a half mile away. They spared this house only because Dad made them. Threatened to leave the department. So they scrubbed and cleaned and tested the house for almost a year, and then we got to move back in. I was eleven then. Maybe twelve. Everything around was just bare dirt and a few trees. They bulldozed the buildings, burned most of the brush . . . even ripped up all the grass. It was like the moon. For miles and miles. We couldn't play outside without Geiger counters until I was almost fifteen." She took a sip of coffee and looked out at her yard, her eyes glazing as she slipped back into memories.

"This was all suburbs?" I whispered incredulously.

"Yeah. Mostly. Some trees and fields, but yeah, there were homes all around us."

"Where did . . ." I trailed off.

"There's a band around the city—about fifteen miles wide most places—where there's just nothing there. Some of it used to be towns; some was woods. Now it's all just grassland. They tried to tell us it was for decontamination. But that was bullshit. It was to help them catch the escapees. The forests and abandoned—"

"People escape?" I cut her off.

"All the time. They don't get far, mostly. But a few times a year, we'd see someone running across the fields. Or faces watching as we drove through the ruined towns. Sometimes then you'd hear helicopters or little prop planes circling, searching."

I shook my head in disbelief. Not at what she was saying, but at the moral fortitude of those who had broken free. The brash will. I'd never once even thought to venture beyond the barricades and fences—I swallowed it all down. I thought of what it must have been like to emerge from the haze on your own two feet. Amazing that someone might have found the answers I'd been so close to but missed.

"I guess no one ever got all the way out, huh?"

"I doubt it." She sighed. "Everything would have changed then, I guess."

We sat in silence for a while; then, quietly, I asked, "Rebecca . . . what did your father do?"

"He was a scientist. Wanted to be since he was a kid. Right out of college, he got a grant to study pressure systems and wind cycles. It fascinated him. He'd talk us to sleep night after night, trying to explain this or that. He was on the state board of research when it happened."

"The meltdown?"

"Yeah. On the second day, a natural fog bank rolled in over a smaller town about fifty miles from the city and the death rate dropped. Dad was the one who made the connection. So he and his team were tasked with getting as many places . . . as many people fogged in as fast as they could. So many people had died that it wasn't even worth trying to save the little towns or the farmhouses or any of it. So they herded everyone into the city. Me too, for a few months. It was horrifying. I was just a kid, you know? Then when we got to go home . . . it was never the same. I cried all the time. I would clutch my mom's nightgown to my face and cry for hours and hours."

"Did . . ." I trailed off again, wishing I had never started the question. Becca nodded sadly, understanding, her eyes welling up. I furrowed my brow and looked away. "Mine too. Both of them. It's tough."

"I'm sorry."

"So am I. For you and me." She put her elbows on the table and rested her face in her hands, breathing heavily, obviously fighting back tears.

I nodded, drifting back to those days in my mind. "I enlisted to be a soldier then," I said very quietly. "When they were moving everyone into the city I was . . . out on the roads . . . guarding . . ." She looked up at me and I lost my train of thought. I sat there staring deeply into her eyes, fascination etched into my face. She blushed and turned away, smiling slightly.

"What?"

"Your eyes. They're blue."

Becca looked at me quizzically. She blinked several times,

long lashes flitting before her soft, sky blue eyes. "They've always been blue."

"In the city they were gray. I guess everything was. But you have . . . They're beautiful." She looked away again, bashfully. We shared a moment of warm silence, but eventually her expression changed. I took a sip of coffee, avoiding the question I most needed to ask for a second longer.

"Why did they kill him?"

"Because he was a good man. Because he was honest. And foolish enough to trust that others were too. He never wanted any of this, Tom. As soon as it was obvious that we weren't dealing with some temporary quarantine . . . that it was being lied about and covered up . . . he hated it. He protested. They told him to keep quiet. That was years ago. Dad never drank more than a glass or two of wine a week—even after Mom died—until then. He tried to keep his head down. Tried to take comfort in at least knowing that people would be safe and that his children were safe . . . He always felt like it was his fault. All of it." Her lip quivered and a tear ran down her left cheek, sparkling in the sunlight. "He was such a good man. He thought it was all his fault, and he couldn't take it."

Another tear followed the damp trail of the first, and I grabbed the green cloth napkin off my lap and reached out, half-expecting her to lean away. She closed her eyes and I gently, tenderly wiped away the tears. Her head dropped forward as I withdrew. Her right hand was resting on the table, and I slid the napkin under it, lingering for a moment with our skin pressed together. My chest fluttered at the feel of her soft, warm flesh. She opened her eyes and smiled at me, whispering a barely audible thank you and dabbing at her eyes with the napkin.

Her voice stronger, she continued. "A few months ago, Dad decided he couldn't bear it anymore. He decided that they had to know. That . . . you all did. Everyone. He thought I didn't know how he felt . . . what he was planning . . . but I knew. I was working at the Science Department, so I heard things." I looked up at her quickly when she said this, and she shrugged, guilt and remorse in her eyes. "I was a research assistant. It was just so I could be near my father. He was determined to stop the fog, stop the lies—all of it. He told Kirk about it. They were friends, he thought. They'd worked together for years. His wife and kids used to come to our house. . . . They all died, though. He told Kirk about the letters he was drafting to all the newspapers . . . to foreign governments. He was going to drag it all out into the light in one play. Asked Kirk to help him . . . and then, two weeks ago, Kirk had him shot in the head in his own backyard." Her face was a mask when she said this—she displayed no emotion, but her knuckles were white, gripping and stretching the napkin.

"I got home to find an army truck outside and Callahan in the kitchen smiling as he held a gun to my brother's head. He told me Dad was dead just like you'd tell someone the score of a game. Said Fallon was next. Jesus Christ . . . I'd barely even seen him in two years. Fallon's been so busy with his work in the city for so long, and I hated him for so long because he was becoming like them, and then . . . there he was on his knees in the kitchen, bruised and crying and I started crying and Callahan laughed. He fucking laughed at us."

She finally broke down, crossing her arms and lowering her head between them onto the table. Sobs racked her body. I sat there like a deer in headlights. It all made so much sense in that instant. She made sense. The seductress in the red dress, the snappily attired business woman . . . Everything was just a mask covering a frightened girl who missed her father, who would do anything to protect her brother.

I rose and stepped around the table, kneeling beside her. Gently, unsteadily at first, I began to massage her shoulders and neck with one hand. "It's okay. I don't want you to keep talking about it anymore. I just . . . if there's anything . . ." I trailed off pathetically and after a moment took my hand off her back. Without so much as looking up, she reached out, found my arm, and guided my hand back onto her shoulders.

I rose and stood behind her, firmly but tenderly massaging her neck, upper arms, shoulders, and back. It was amazing. Sensual. Satisfying. I could have rubbed her pale neck and run my fingers through her soft, golden hair for hours, forever. From time to time, she let out little sighs and whimpers. I leaned down and took a long, deep breath of her essence. Honey sweet and fresh, young. *She's just a kid,* I thought to myself. Maybe a young woman, but still, a twenty-something orphan with the weight of the world on her shoulders. And my forty-something hands. I had to help her as much as I could. I owed her that. She had done exactly what anyone would have for as long as she had to, and then, at the first opportunity, she had been honest. Her honesty had set me free. If more than a third of my life was robbed from me by their lies and their fog, if everyone I knew died by their failures, so be it. At least I knew. At least I would never again wander through the foggy streets with my mind in a haze.

It saddened me to know that the most helpful thing I could do for her was to disappear quickly and forever. Maybe five minutes had passed as I ran my hands along her back and through her hair. Reluctantly, I patted her softly on the left shoulder and drew my chair around the table nearer to hers. I sat, my hands clasped between my knees, looking at her. After a moment, she slowly raised her head a bit, resting her chin on her folded arms. Her soft blue eyes were red with tears, and her hair fell around her face. I could scarcely believe this perfect, innocent young woman was the same person who had reeled me in not two weeks ago.

She stared off into the distance for a while and then turned to look at me, dabbing at moist eyes with my napkin. "Thank you. That felt great."

I leaned toward her, not wanting to change the mood of the moment, but I felt it was incumbent on me to tell her what I was thinking. "Rebecca . . . as long as I'm here, you're not safe. I was just some asshole to be framed and dealt with before." She winced slightly as I said this, and I held up my hands and inclined my head slightly to say, *It's okay,* and then continued. "But now it's a lot bigger than that. I know about everything now. I . . . I've killed people now."

"People who had it coming," she said sharply.

"Yes, but their people. City people. If they find me here, you and Fallon are in more danger than ever. I need to leave. Immediately. Now."

"No! Tom, no!" She sat up and grabbed both my knees. I sat back rigidly in surprise. "I don't want you to leave! I have no one! Nothing! I . . . I'm just here in this house alone and now, I'm out of eggs and I . . . I don't know where to get them. . . ."

Her lip began to quiver, and instinctively I reached out to grasp her shoulder. She sprang forward from her chair and wrapped her arms around my neck. Her hair fell across my face, her lips grazed my ear.

"Don't leave me. Please."

"I don't want to . . . but I want you to be safe. You're so young. You need to be safe. I can't be caught here and let you throw your whole life away."

"What will you do?" she whispered, her soft lips brushing the skin of my cheek.

"I don't know. I mean . . . there's still a world out there, right? I'll get to a city. Blend in and disappear."

"How much harder is it for two people to disappear than one?"

"Becca," I said, drawing her up off her knees and into my lap. She kept her arms around my neck and nestled her head against my chest. I looked out over the rolling, sunny hills. Her scent mingled with that of the pure, open land. "You don't want to follow me. I'm just . . . just a tired, homeless man almost twice your age. And a wanted one, at that. There's a mark on my head. If I can get away . . . slip out of their system and into another world . . . well, then maybe I'll have something of a second chance. Thanks to you. But you don't have to take the risk. You can do whatever you want. You don't want to follow me. I'm a mess."

"You're a good man," she said quietly, stroking the hair on the back of my neck. "You tried to help me even when you knew I was lying to you."

"You have nothing to atone for. You did what you had to."

"They would have killed you. I . . . I'm so sorry. They would have killed you because of me—"

"No," I interrupted. "Not because of you. Because of them. It's all them. You're perfectly innocent, Becca. Perfect . . ." I trailed off again. We sat like that for a long time. I rocked her gently in my arms, already beginning to formulate my plans. I would leave at dusk. It would be awful, leaving the first thing I had cared about in years, but it was necessary. To care about her was to leave at once.

I wasn't sure if she was even still awake. Then, after maybe ten minutes, she leaned away from me and looked up, her eyes clear and bright. "I'm still hungry."

11

SHE WAS UPSTAIRS IN THE SHOWER. SHE HAD LEFT THE BATH-
room door ajar and I stood at the top of the stairs spellbound
by her silhouette bending and twisting behind the pale curtain. It felt wrong—perverse, even—but I could not pull myself
away. I was caught somewhere between voyeurism and admira-
tion as the strength and powerful loneliness of this girl became
ever more clear to me.

I had thought to scrawl a quick note and leave while she
bathed. It was the only way to be sure she would not follow
me. But lovely little Becca deserved better. Suddenly the water
stopped running, and in a panic I turned and hurried downstairs as quickly as I could without making noise.

I paced aimlessly about the house, looking at a picture here, a
painting there. The woodwork of the furniture was first rate, the
carpets rich and intricate; everything was exactly as it should
have been. I felt like something of a stranger visiting a museum
in a foreign land. The chairs made sense to me. They were chairs.
You could sit in them. But coming from a life of concrete and

folding metal furniture and rusting zinc-lined shower stalls, a finely wrought piece made as much sense to me as a throne to a beggar.

The thin, checkered curtains of the living room rustled as a midday gust came through the open windows. I was captivated by them. Here too was something so innately familiar yet now amazing—a novelty. They actually hung to block sunlight. There was a soft cool breeze blowing across the land. I reached out and took the fabric between two fingers and rubbed it gently. I could feel the seams and change in grain where the pattern turned from stripe to box and back again. I pushed one of the curtains aside to squint out across the vast, rolling fields. My chest grew cold.

I turned and barreled upstairs, not even remembering that Rebecca would be changing. I tossed wide the door to her room and caught a fleeting glimpse of her nude body as she threw her towel around herself with a gasp.

"Does anyone know you're here?"

"I . . . mean I suppose . . . yes . . . ," she stammered.

"Do you expect visitors? Ever?"

"No," she answered, concern laced through her voice and across her face.

"Well, you've got one." I led her to the bedroom window that faced out across the front yard and the hills beyond and pointed. Far off down the road—the road that ended at this house—a truck was heading our way.

"Oh my God . . . ," she said, choking up. Her arms fell to her side, and the towel drooped, revealing one of her perfect breasts. I reached out and straightened the cloth around her, covering her up again. She scarcely noticed. "That's the same kind of truck Callahan and the soldiers drove. At least it looks like it—I can't tell. Oh my God, what do we do?" She turned from the window and looked up into my face, fearful, searching for help.

I turned back to the window. It was still a few miles out. And very much alone. "Is there anyone . . . anyone good who would be visiting? A friend of your father's or anything like that?" She shook her head. "Get dressed. We'll deal with this and then make a plan. I walked from the room, pausing at the door. Over my shoulder I said, "And you should pull together some warm clothes and pack them."

It had happened faster than I expected. When both the helicopter and this truck failed to return, they wouldn't send another single-vehicle mission out. They'd send an army. I wouldn't make it far enough to get away in time; the house was too small to hide in for long. I grabbed the rifle and my jacket, making sure the pockets were still stuffed with extra rounds. Peering out the living room window again, I estimated I had three minutes before they were in range. Four if I waited until they were close enough for kill shots.

"Becca! We have four minutes until the world is on its way here, okay? Pack us some clothes and get some blankets! Your truck works, right?" I shouted up to her.

She came to the top of the stairs, nodding, frightened. "What are you going to do?" she asked, her voice cracking a bit as she saw the gun in my hand.

"I'm going to buy us some time. Get food too." I pulled on my boots and slipped out the front door. It was crisp and sunny outside. Silent save for birdsongs and an occasional breeze; eerily idyllic. I jogged across the bright green grass, keeping hedges and trees between myself and the road. I'd make sure she was safe and then get out of her life. I'd only fuck things up for her. Crouching behind a bush, I eased myself around it slowly, parting the brambles and peering between them so as not to let my profile stick out from the shrub.

The truck was close now. I recognized the model—I'd ridden in that same vehicle many times. We were taken out onto the highways in them, in fact. We lay across their roofs to gain a better vantage point for reconnaissance, to get a better shot. So now I had come full circle. There could be as many as eight troops in the back and three up front, so I'd need to disable the vehicle. No way would I be able to take all the men, even if it were only half-loaded.

I slid behind the bush, the coarse leaves scratching at my unshaven face. After rolling onto my back, I did a quick check of the rifle to make sure the action was sliding smoothly and the sights were lined up. It had been sixteen years since I'd done that. I pulled one of the loose shells from my pocket: 5.56 millimeters of high-grain lead with a little red titanium tip. That's what would do it, let me punch through the quarter inch of glass and take out the driver. If I waited until they were on a turn, maybe I could get the truck to roll. Maybe we'd have enough time to actually make a break for it.

I turned over onto my stomach and crawled forward past the edge of the manicured lawn and into the high grass. They'd be in range in less than a minute. I yanked back on the bolt and released it. It clicked home, chambering a round. Shooting at people again . . . not something I ever wanted to do. I hated it. I hated it so much. These poor fucks, just following orders. But it was for her. And it was against them. Not the soldiers, but all of them. There are times when blood must spill. Even if some of it was to be innocent blood, I was determined to have not a drop of it be Rebecca's. Not today. No one asked for my permission when they fogged me in; no one asked for my approval when they plucked me back out . . . framed me . . . would have killed me.

"Well, you should have done it when you had the chance, Kirk. Watley. All of you." I rose up on both elbows, the fingers of my right hand wrapping slowly around the grip and trigger, my left hand sliding forward into a shooting platform. The black metal stock of the rifle was cool and mildly damp against my skin. The old familiar sent of oil filled my nostrils, strangely comforting amidst the confusion. Blood pounded in my temples. I squinted against the bright light and lined up my sights on the truck, tracking it slowly.

Every few seconds, the windshield flashed in the sun as the vehicle made slight turns one way or the other. "Sorry," I whispered aloud as the truck entered a turn toward me. It was maybe half a mile off and coming down a long, gentle slope. The sun flashed again off the glass of the windshield. I took in a deep breath and began slowly exhaling it, steadying my muscles.

The curve tightened. The sun danced across the truck, and I fired two shots in close succession. The reports crackled through the hills as the rifle bucked in my arms. Nothing. Still driving smoothly. I took in a sharp breath and again exhaled, this time making sure both eyes were open wide. Slowly, steadily, I led the truck along with the front sight of my weapon and let my conscious thinking subside. It was silent after those first two shots. Not a bird singing or leaf rustling in the breeze. The scent of the fresh grass mixed with the lingering odor of cordite. The sun was hot on my back, and my hands were steady.

Before I knew I had committed, I squeezed off three shots in a tight group. The sun glinting off the windshield disappeared. For a moment, the truck kept following the curve it was on, but then it wavered and began to drift onto the grass. The vehicle lurched back onto and then across the road, far overcorrecting, and began to tip. With a great thunderous crash and grinding of metal, it went over, rolling off the road and into the lush field, where it came to rest on one side.

Then all was silent. I glanced back at the house to find Rebecca peering through the partly open front door. I smiled at her and pointed to the ruined truck, proud of myself. Her brow knit with concern, she withdrew back into the house. Chastened, I turned my attention back to the wreck. This would be the hard part, both emotionally and tactically: dealing with potential survivors. At first, there was no sign of life. A thin trail of smoke rose from the vehicle.

Then from behind the crash stumbled a single man. He wore the gray fatigues of a soldier and looked badly hurt. He took a few uneven steps and then fell to his knees, one hand going to his head. For a long time he stayed there like that, on both knees and with a hand over his face. Then finally he slumped down to sit Indian style. I drew a bead on him and wrapped my finger around the trigger, but I could not bring myself to fire.

I lowered the weapon and looked away. When I turned back, I found the man now lying down on his back. I couldn't tell if he had reclined or sagged. I moved the barrel slightly to the right and fired a single round at the exposed belly of the truck. It caromed off with a loud metallic clang. The man did not move. I was torn. If he was alive enough to crawl, he was alive enough to use a radio. Shoot again?

I rose to a crouch and backed up toward the house, keeping my eyes on the crash scene the whole time. Nothing stirred. Inside, Rebecca was sitting on the stairs, looking down at the floor. "Are they all dead?"

"I don't know. I hope so." She looked up at me reproachfully. "Can I have your keys?"

She rose and walked into the kitchen, and I heard her fumbling in a drawer and then the familiar jangle of a keychain as she returned. She extended her hand to me but kept her fist closed. "Do you remember how to drive?" she asked.

"I think so." She opened her hand and dropped the keys into my palm.

"Do you want me to do it?"

"No. Thanks. I don't want you down there." She nodded and I turned to go.

Then her hand was on my shoulder. "Be careful." Her eyes were soft, forgiving. "I know you had to. I just hate it."

"I hate it too." I placed my hand over hers and squeezed it gently, then removed it from my shoulder and left the house.

I SWERVED BACK AND FORTH ACROSS THE ROAD. I WAS SIXTEEN all over again, narrowly avoiding skids and rollovers as I tried to steady the big red truck. Going fifty miles an hour felt like the speed of light. It was exhilarating, liberating. Just as my muscles were remembering how to control a vehicle, I was at the crash site. At the sight of the body sprawled out on the grass, my mood darkened as quickly as it had lifted.

I pulled the pickup alongside the ruined truck and jumped out, rifle cocked, raised, and ready to fire. I went first to the man I had seen alive. He was very much dead now—the right half of his face and skull were covered in deep lacerations. Blood stained his uniform from lapels to bootlaces. Next I peered through the shattered windshield. The driver hung limply from his seat belt, a gunshot wound in the center of his chest. The passenger was slumped against the side window that rested on the ground, his knees near the roof and head down below the seat.

Walking around the back of the truck, I strained to listen for any noise from within, but there was none. A crow's ragged call and my own tense breathing were the only sounds. One of the back doors was ajar. I slowly slid the rifle barrel into the open doorway and grabbed the latch with my left hand, swinging the door wide open. My fingers came away bloody.

The interior of the truck was dark, and I could see nothing with the bright sun in my eyes. I shielded my face and leaned into the truck. As my eyes adjusted, I could see two soldiers lying dead, their bodies bent and broken into horrible poses. A third man was hanging from his harness on the opposite wall. He wore a gray blazer and khaki pants with a bloodstained shirt tucked into them. He was thin, nearly bald, and had a bookish air about him. He was moving.

His fingers were trembling as they dangled in space. His

head jerked from side to side erratically. He was in shock. Badly hurt.

"Can you hear me?" I asked. He turned his head and looked at me, his eyes unfocused. There was a horrid gash across his neck. "Can you understand me?"

He tried to reply, but it came out only as a sickening gurgle. He was racked by coughs. Blood and phlegm dripped from his face as his head sagged back. He was finished. In agony. I set my jaw and raised the rifle to my shoulder. The man tried to reach inside his jacket but was too weak. His hands flopped uselessly at the ends of broken arms. He gurgled once more, and I put two bullets through the side of his head. Flecks of blood spattered onto my hands and forehead, and I recoiled from the deafening reports and the gore. Behind me, the crow took flight and cried out balefully as it soared away.

I took a knee and dropped the gun beside me. My hands were shaking.

"There was no other way," I repeated to myself several times aloud. I lowered myself roughly to sit in the grass, realizing as I did so that I was inadvertently mimicking the motions of the soldier I'd watched from afar. His legs were sticking out past the back of the truck. The drying blood was crimson as it soaked into his slate gray trousers. I crawled over toward him. His eyes were open, staring up at the sky. In one of his hands he held a crumpled pack of cigarettes. That just about broke my heart.

I leaned closer to the dead man and gently closed his eyes. He couldn't have been a day over twenty-one. Just another little soldier boy they handed a gun. Well, it was done now. I steeled my nerves and tried to stop thinking as I took the smokes from his hand and placed one in my mouth. I sucked on it unlit and rose, returning to the back of the vehicle. I reached in and dragged out the first soldier by his boots, being careful not to look at his face. No more remorse, no more sentiment. The second soldier's head was closer to the door, so I hooked my arms under his shoulders and pulled him out to lie facedown beside his comrade.

Then I placed one hand on the chest of the civilian I'd euthanized and lifted him a bit to take the pressure off his harness. I clicked it open and let his body drop down across my shoulders. He weighed no more than 120-some pounds. Had bones like a bird. Him I laid faceup. There were five rifles strapped against the far wall of the truck and numerous clips of ammunition below them. All of this I took and threw into the back of Rebecca's truck.

There was blood and bits of human body all over the front cabin, and I decided not to bother searching through it. I could see through the shattered windshield that there were no weapons up front with the driver and passenger. Five unloaded rifles for five soldiers. These guys hadn't been looking for a fight. Which led me to believe that they had no idea I would be there with Rebecca Ayers.

My mind racing, I jogged back around the truck and began rifling through the pockets of the little blazer-wearing man. In one of the two larger pockets of his jacket, I found an old, yellowed envelope. Folding it open, I pulled out several photographs. One was of the little man with Samuel Ayers. Two of them were photos of Ayers with Becca and Fallon when they were kids. The last one was a picture of a little girl who had to be Becca with both her parents smiling from atop a tall brown horse. One of her front teeth was missing. A sinking feeling grew in the pit of my stomach. I stuffed the pictures back into the envelope and pocketed them and continued to search the man. Pens. A notepad. A handkerchief . . . and then I found it.

Macabre relief washed over me. In his inside jacket pocket, the little man had a spring-loaded syringe filled with a pale, cloudy liquid. I held the needle close to my nose and sniffed at it. It smelled faintly of sweet almonds. Cyanide. He was on his way to eliminate Rebecca.

There was no making her safer by putting distance between us. Selfishly, my first reaction was brief elation. As I quickly searched the other bodies and the wrecked truck—finding little of use except cigarettes—my happiness turned steadily into a profound dread. If they were going to kill her with or without me, they were going to kill Fallon. They'd probably go after poor old Eddie and the phlegmatic, resigned Salk. Heller. I hoped those guys wouldn't be sucked into all of this, but there didn't seem much I could do for them now.

SHE WAS SITTING ON THE FRONT STEPS WHEN I PULLED UP. I SAT in the truck's cab for a minute, watching her. Her eyes were cast downward. She had put on blue jeans and an olive green sweater, and her hair was pulled back into a ponytail. Eventually she looked up, and I killed the engine and got out of the truck.

"Were they all dead?" she asked quietly.

"Yes."

"I heard shooting."

"I . . ." Looking away, I whispered, "I was just being sure."

"Who was it?"

"Soldiers."

"Just soldiers?" Her eyes searched mine, saw the blood on my face.

"There was someone else too. Listen, we need to get moving. I'll tell you about it on the road."

"Where are we going?" she asked, standing up.

"I have no idea. That's going to be your department. Somewhere safe." I walked past her and entered the house.

She followed me and put a hand on my arm, turning me to face her. "So it's not safe here anymore?"

"No. It's not safe here. I'm sorry."

She dropped her hand and looked around the foyer sadly, her eyes sliding past photographs, a painting, an old wooden chest. "Okay, well . . . I packed clothes for wherever we go."

"How far is it to the next city? To anywhere where there are lots of people?"

"Almost two hundred miles. Maybe a bit less, I guess. There are only two intact roads, though."

"Dammit." I sat down on the stairs and massaged my eyes with the heels of each hand. "That's no good, then."

"Who else was in the truck?"

"Another man. A civilian. We need to figure out where we're going. There are still a few hours of daylight, and if they send helicopters—which they will—we're fucked. We don't have much time."

"Why wouldn't they have just done that in the first place?"

"They don't know I'm here, I guess. That I'm alive. Let's load up. Do you have extra gas tanks?"

She nodded. "We have lots of them. They ration how often you can get fuel, so Dad always took lots of containers to fill."

We were going to need to drive hard and fast. Away from the city, but beyond that I had no idea. We had to chance it off road. One checkpoint and we'd be done, and they'd be watching the roads even if there weren't any official checkpoints. The red pickup could be spotted for miles from the air. I entered the kitchen, drank water from the tap, and wiped at my face, trying to get the flecks of blood off.

"Dad always used to take us camping. The place is only about an hour away. Maybe we could go there?" She stood just outside the kitchen in the hallway, looking at the wall of pictures.

"That's a good idea." I smiled at her.

She showed me where the jerry cans full of gasoline were tucked away under the porch among random tools scattered about—shovels, a hammer and pick. The ground beneath the stairs had been recently turned. It looked as though someone had been digging for something. I tried to shrug it off and loaded several cans of gas into the truck. She had set our packed duffels on the porch, and I stuck them on the bench behind the two front seats.

Rebecca came outside with a canvas bag stuffed with all the food she could find. A bit of pasta and rice, tomatoes, some dried fruit, random cans. It would do for a while. It would have to, at any rate. She loaded the food into the truck and then took a few steps back toward the house. Her face was placid, but her eyes were pained as she stood in the middle of the bright green yard looking up at her home.

"I'll never see it again, will I?"

"You might. I hope you do." I came up to stand next to her and studied the side of her face. The sun, just beginning its afternoon descent, highlighted the line of her nose, the pout of her lips. She wore a gentle golden halo around her face. Memories must have been swirling through her mind. Her shoulders rose and fell, and her eyes gently closed.

"Were you digging for something under the porch recently?" I asked as quietly as I could. She made no reply, her eyes looking a thousand miles away.

Finally, meekly, she asked, "What?"

"Nothing. Take your time," I whispered, walking toward the pickup. Moles or whatever. I was growing more restless by the second, but I couldn't bring myself to rush her. I leaned on the side of the truck bed and took stock of our supplies. Five rifles back here and one in the cab. Enough fuel for a few days of driving. Food for maybe a week if we could augment it with something. A mix of checkered and plaid woolen blankets. Clothing.

I thought to run inside and grab a few bottles of liquor, but there was no way I was going to push past this heartsick girl for booze. *Sorry about your life being ripped to shreds, sweetheart. Take your last look at childhood as I come down the porch steps with a few bottles of Daddy's cough medicine.*

I reached into my pocket to grab a smoke. Just then, Rebecca turned and walked to me with quick, confident steps. I let go of the cigarette pack as she stopped before me.

"Okay if I drive?"

"Sure." I handed her the keys. "I'm a bit out of practice."

"I noticed. I was watching you head down there." She smiled, walking around to the driver's side.

"Hey, a decade and a half without getting behind the wheel . . . I thought I was pretty good."

I climbed into the passenger seat, pulling off my coat and settling it on the seat between us. One of the rifles sat there too, close at hand. She turned the key, and the engine rumbled to life. The big, heavy tires tossed gravel about the yard as Rebecca stomped down on the gas. We flew down the driveway at over forty miles an hour. I guess she wanted to get the leaving over with fast. I couldn't blame her. It was easier just to head out into the world one day and realize later that you would never go home, that things were to be eternally different.

Every few minutes, she dabbed at her eyes with the sleeve of her dark green sweater. I almost started talking a few times, but she seemed to bristle whenever I took in breath to do so. I gave up and leaned my head against the window glass, watching the trees and fields roll by. The shadows were growing longer. The sky had turned from the deep azure of day to a lighter, powder blue. I could see a sliver of the moon hanging ashen gray in the afternoon sky, waiting silently for the sun to recede.

We crested a small hill, and miles off to the west was the dam. The highway was heading roughly toward it. I grew nervous, thinking pictures of our faces had been spread out across the land. I was about to tell Rebecca but held my tongue as we drew ever closer to the massive dam. There were no buildings surrounding it. There was no infrastructure to speak of at all, really, save for the mighty gray edifice itself. The same strange unease

I'd felt from the air washed over me again. The steep hills on either side of the dam looked so strange, the rest of the land so familiar. I suppressed a thought as it began to form.

The highway drew near and then ran parallel with the river formed at the dam's base. I craned my neck back between the seats to look at the thing. There was one small tower near the center and a service road running up to it from the highway. Four mighty waterfalls poured forth from its walls in utter isolation. It was as if some unseen hand had ordained this gigantic creation and then withdrawn to leave it forever churning out power for a dead and forgotten people.

"Kirk's dam," I muttered.

"He told you about that, huh?"

"All about it. Sounded like a father describing his valedictorian son."

She nodded, a rueful smile on her lips. I turned back to look at his scion once more and then faced the highway again. I had no idea how far we were going, but I hoped we got off this road soon. It was the only trace of human life for as far as the eye could see: a vast expanse of pristine, rolling hills bisected by this perfectly maintained two-lane strip of concrete. The rhythm of the truck's wheels rolling across the seams in the road gradually began to sedate me. My eyelids grew heavy, and soon the gentle beat of the highway was all I was aware of.

SAND BENEATH MY TOES. SO ODD—IT DIDN'T FEEL LIKE SAND . . . more like a carpet or even a bolt of silk. But there it was, milk white before the blue green sea. No sun or sky to speak of: all was pale beige and cream above the placid water. I was standing and then I was walking toward the water but I never got to the water. I knew she was behind me. In her red dress. I wanted to turn and see her, but when I did she was behind a wooden fence between the sea and the forest.

Her pale blue eyes peered over the fence at me and I could

see her delicate feet gliding from side to side below the fence. Then the red dress slipped around her feet and I was walking toward her and her eyes were closed. I walked around and around the fence but it never ceased and she was there with her eyes closed and then she was not there and there was no beach and no fence and only a forest. I was not in the forest though I was not on the beach and I could see nothing but the trees and then from the trees came Kirk, walking slowly toward me. His face was tan and healthy and smiling, but his suit was torn and there was blood on his shirt.

He stopped just outside the trees and, still smiling, asked if I would join him. I walked to him and he turned and went back into the forest and then I was in the forest and he was gone and I was frightened then and growing more so by the second, panicked, running tree to tree and ever darker and "Kirk!" and running, seeking, "Dad! Father!" finding no one, screaming little child with hot tears blinding everything and then the trees parted and there was Heller sitting on the ground with knees drawn up to his naked chest and face cast downward and flesh gray and I, little child, ran up to him and he looked at me through watery eyes and tried to smile through golden teeth and from his smile came notes and chords and it was wondrous and I was not frightened and I was not a child but he was growing faint and harder to see as mist seeped down from the treetops and crept along the forest floor and Heller turned and crawled away and I ran to follow but I could not follow and the notes and music in the forest surged and clawed their way into my mind and then . . .

. . . I AWOKE WITH A START, GASPING AND CLINCHING MY FISTS. Rushing air and colors. I coughed and shook my head to clear it. Okay. I was in the truck. With Rebecca. It was nearly dusk now. We were on a smaller road.

"Are you okay?" she asked with concern.

"Yeah . . ." I muttered, still half asleep and disoriented. Was I still—? "What is . . . music? What music is this?" As I came to, I realized that it was Chopin bridging the gap between my dream and the waking world.

"I don't know. I found it in your jacket."

"It's okay." I leaned back, catching my breath and trying to slow my heart rate. "It's Chopin."

"I didn't figure you for a classical kind of guy." She smiled.

"Just him. Just this one tape, really, to be honest." I took in a breath to add, *and Beethoven*, but exhaled without speaking. I'd keep that for me.

"It's beautiful."

"Yeah," I said, turning away and taking in a quavering breath. Tears welled up in my eyes, and I fought to keep them in. One ran down my cheek, and I nonchalantly wiped it away. She saw, though. For a moment I thought she would let it pass, but then she reached out and began to rub the back of my neck.

"What's wrong?" I shook my head. "Talk to me. Please."

"It was a friend's tape. I'll never see him again. No way. The last thing we did was listen to this music." She reached out quickly and pressed the stop key on the dash. "No, it's okay. I want to hear it." I studied the glowing controls but could not figure out how to restart the music. A sad smile on her face, she took my hand and guided my finger on one of the buttons.

"Fancy new stuff," I muttered, half-smiling.

"Actually, this truck is ten years old. They don't even make cars with tape players anymore."

"Yeah, well, thanks. That makes me feel a lot better."

Her hand returned to the nape of my neck. "I guess ten years old is six years in the future for you." I nodded. We were silent for a while, listening to the gentle strains of a slow, mournful movement. Then she looked over. "Will you tell me about him? Your friend? I know it's hard, but it helps to talk."

"Yeah . . . it does. That's just it. For almost fifteen years, I had no one to talk to. And then this poor kid I'd been chasing for money and roughing up and all—one day I got to talking to him and . . . turned out he was a friend just waiting to be recognized. . . . I didn't have anyone to talk to for all those years and then I had him for just a couple of weeks . . . Heller. Tom Heller was his name." I pulled a pack of cigarettes from my pocket and jammed one in my mouth. "You mind?" She shook her head, and I lit the smoke and rolled down my window an inch. The cool evening air felt good on my face.

"I just get the feeling he's going to get hurt. Maybe killed because of me. Because of all of this."

Her face twisted into a scowl and she looked away, arms tense on the wheel. "Then you mean because of me," she said quietly.

"No! No." I said firmly, laying my hand on her thigh, "Not you. Them. Me. Not you, Rebecca. What you did, you were forced to do. No one forced me to rope Tom into my mess of a life. No one forced me to drink his liquor and listen to his music and go whine and moan to him. You had no choice. He had no choice. Same as you . . . you there in a red dress . . ."

"I felt so disgusting. You must have been revolted by me. Stupid slut in a dirty little dress. I kept crying and redoing my makeup . . . I hate myself for it."

"No . . . don't. You're so young—your dad—what else could you have done? I'm sorry it happened too, but it's not your fault—"

"It is my fault!" she shouted, pounding her fist on the steering wheel. "I didn't have to jump through their hoops! How many people are going to die because I was just a scared little kid!? How many have already died? It is my fault."

The truck was slowing down and drifting. Sobs racked her body. I put a hand on the wheel to steady the vehicle. "It's okay, sweetheart. . . . Just pull over, okay?"

She gradually eased us to a stop and sat there, eyes closed with her hands gripping the wheel. "They were going to kill you too. They're still trying. Won't stop." Her cheeks were bright red. I unbuckled my seat belt and got out of the truck, running around to her side. I pulled open the door and reached toward her to wipe off her face with the sleeve of my shirt. Suddenly she threw off her seat belt and came stumbling out of the car. She fell against me and wrapped her arms around my neck.

Her lips were at my chin, a cheek, on my neck, and finally they found mine and I did not fight it. Her tongue forced its way violently between my teeth. She pressed her face to mine, hands clutching at my neck, my shoulders. Slowly she relaxed. Our lips gently swirled around each other's, and my hands were on the back of her head in her hair, holding her close.

We drew apart, and she buried her face in my shirt.

"It's okay, Becca. It will all be okay."

"How?" Her voice was muffled by my chest.

I thought about it for a minute. "I've got no clue. But it will be. We'll stay together." I wrapped my arms more tightly around her. "How much further do we have?"

She shrugged and pulled back from me a bit. Her eyes were drying. "Maybe half an hour. A bit less probably."

"Let's get moving. I'll drive." She fixed me with a cautious smile. "Don't worry, it'll be fine. You need to rest anyway." Nodding, she walked back around the truck, and I climbed up into the driver's seat. "Which one is the gas?"

She smiled and I turned the key. The engine rumbled back to life.

12

I HELD FIVE OR SIX THICK LOGS UNDER ONE ARM AND A MASS OF twigs and brambles under the other. It was nearly true night, and I could see very little around me in the dark forest. The small stream that ran near our campsite gurgled in the blue gray haze, but I wasn't sure if it was to my left or right. I had lost my bearings entirely. It was almost silent, save for the flowing water and the occasional chirp of a bird. Every once in a while, there was a rustling or crackle of dried leaves disturbed by some unseen creature.

Each noise sent shivers down my spine. I used to love forests, but on this night, the woods felt as foreign to me as the ocean's floor. I felt trapped in some endless catacomb beneath the thick canopy and among the encroaching undergrowth. *Just little squirrels and possums and things,* I told myself. *Crickets and owls. Just get back to camp.*

Becca had directed me off the paved road and onto a little strip of dirt at dusk. We followed the neglected path a few miles into the hills and finally into the outskirts of the woods.

The dirt road had ended abruptly in a clearing, but she knew the way well and had taken the wheel, inching us another half mile through the trees and thornbushes and undergrowth until finally we could go no farther. We set up camp about a hundred yards from the truck beside the stream as the last light left the sky.

I strained to hear her, but no promising sound came. I'm not sure why I was so frightened to call out, knowing the only things that would hear me would be timid little animals, but still, any words were stuck in my throat. I began to walk toward where I thought we'd made camp. My heartbeat quickened. I crossed a little clearing and stumbled as my foot caught on a root. There were a few stars visible through the gap in the foliage above.

I took in a deep breath and knelt, trying to calm my nerves. Three stones, all about equal size and alabaster white, rested by my boots. I rose to my feet, tasting bile. All around me, the same pale hue shone through the dried leaves and brambles, reflecting the moonlight. To the left was another pile of the strange stones; one, less buried, was cracked in half and I could see that it was hollow, concave. The remains of rotted teeth. A skull. I took a faltering step backwards. Something under my heel broke with a sickening snap. Gasping and coughing, I lurched out of the clearing and back into the forest.

I stood very still for a few minutes to regain my composure. I was determined not to let her know anything of what I'd seen. Finally I worked up the nerve, and throat still dry with horror, I croaked out her name.

For a minute, no response came. Then, about fifty feet away from me, a little flame came to life in the forest. Drawn like a moth, I practically sprinted toward the light. She was kneeling, looking up toward me as I entered the campsite. She lifted her thumb off my lighter, and again we were in darkness.

"I'm freezing," she said softly, rising to take some of the

wood. Her hands found my arms and slid down to the twigs and brambles, and she took several of them from me. "Can you hold the lighter while I make the fire?"

"Sure." I set down the rest of the wood and reached out to find her. My hand grazed past her breast. "Sorry!" I whispered quickly. I could sense her smiling as she put the lighter in my hand. I flicked it and knelt, illuminating a little space she had cleared in the dirt. She worked quickly, breaking the smallest twigs into kindling and stacking sticks around them into the shape of a little cabin. Or bier. We did not talk for several minutes.

When the fire was set, she took the lighter from me and touched it briefly to the bottom brambles. They crackled and twisted, and soon the larger branches were smoking until one by one, they burst into flames.

"You build a hell of a fire," I whispered.

"Dad taught us. He used the same kind of scientific approach to the simplest things." She leaned in close to the flames, blowing gently on the embers. Her face flickered in the dancing light, orange and red playing across her eyes and tinting her golden hair amber. "I swear he would have eaten his breakfast with a compass and protractor if there had been a way to."

I smiled and leaned back from the fire, my legs crossed before me, palms on the cool forest floor. The flames licked higher into the night. Three rifles glinted where they leaned against the closest tree. I'd left the rest under the back bench of the truck. No sense in hauling them all out here. We had brought the blankets and some food, leaving the rest locked in the vehicle. The water from the stream was cold and sweet, and Rebecca assured me it was safe. Her father had done the same for her years ago.

With the fire crackling and Rebecca at ease, I felt relaxed out here in the forest. It was profoundly dark, and through the treetops, I could barely make out the stars in the sky. She seemed more comfortable than I had ever seen her, and it rubbed off on me. It was a temporary peace, though. Whether we stayed camped out here for a night or a week, we could not sustain this indefinitely. What tomorrow would bring concerned me, but at least for tonight I felt safe and secure. I did my best to banish thoughts of an uncertain future and lit a cigarette as I watched the light dance across her angelic face.

She looked up at me and I did not look away. She smiled.

"You're beautiful."

"Thank you," she said with sincerity, holding my gaze. "So what now?"

My heart skipped a beat, not sure what she meant by that. Her face was earnest and concerned. Not a come-hither look if I'd ever seen one. But her eyes fixed me with an intensity I would not have recognized before. She was a complicated girl. Probably more confused and conflicted than suited her intelligence. I was resolved to be nothing but a protective, positive force. In my mind I put ice on my loins—injected them with novocaine and ordered them to bed. But the curve of her neck . . . the hint of cleavage peeking out from her low-cut sweater . . . the firelight dancing across her and turning her flaxen hair into a waterfall of amber and gold.

"We'll need to travel by dark. At least it's getting on toward winter and dark for so long . . . If we drive hard, we'll make it only fifty miles a night at best, considering all the off-road we'll have to do, avoiding checkpoints and searchers." Her eyes settled on the fire. A vacant veneer crept over her face. Maybe she had meant the *What now?* I would have liked. But the moment was gone.

"The next town—the first place where they're not in control . . . You know how to get there?"

"I guess," she said quietly. Then, her voice more firm, "Yes, we can get there. There are lots of checkpoints and only one road for the first hundred miles, but the truck should be able to handle the fields."

I nodded. We exchanged no words for a long time. It was a painful silence. I wanted to level with her, to tell her she was amazing and beautiful and that I yearned for her . . . lusted for her. . . . I wanted to tell her I had bought a bottle of vodka for her. I'd masturbated to a specter of her red-dressed alter ego, and here she was before me, alone in the forest . . . and I would not act.

I wondered how much all cities had changed since I had been stuck in my own, since I had been stuck in time. I assumed everything would look just about the same. That bothered me more than a brave new world of flying cars and pneumatic tubes would have—it was like I had been in a drug-induced coma, and now, for reasons no more cogent than it had begun, it was over. She was still watching the fire.

"What are you thinking about?"

She looked up at me and smiled. "You."

"That won't take long," I said, looking away. I hoped she couldn't see the blood rush to my cheeks in the flickering light.

"I was just thinking about how I feel I know you, but I know so little about you. Don't know what were you like as a kid. What sports you played. What you were afraid of."

I sighed and rubbed my eyes with a thumb and forefinger. "I was always scared of being alone. Of being lonely. So I worked my whole life to be all alone and not need anyone or have anyone need me, so that I could never be abandoned. That's what I was like as a kid. That's . . . it's—"

"How you are now?" She finished for me.

"Yeah. That's how I am," I whispered.

Rebecca rose and walked around the fire. She knelt behind me and began massaging my shoulders. "Will you tell me about yourself? What you've done . . . seen . . ."

"I don't know. . . . What do I say?"

"Say one time I went to the beach and I found a shell. Say

once I saw an elephant. Tell me about skinning your knee in a soccer game."

"Once I went to the beach and skinned my knee. There was an elephant there too. He found a shell."

She laughed, her voice rising into the cold dark air. It felt divine to have inspired that wondrous noise.

"Okay, I'll tell you about me."

I told her everything. I told her about Salk's giant nose and about his pills. I told her about the two girls who had broken my heart. I told her about bruising ribs and smashing in faces for handfuls of wrinkled dollars. I told her about guarding the roads as part of a squad of boys unwittingly tasked with delivering death. I told her how I dreamt of her so many nights and of how I had watched her through the shower curtain. Her hands wrapped more tightly and sensuously around me at that, sliding forward down my chest. I was losing myself in her. Soon there was nothing but the warmth of the fire on my face and the ministration of her hands on my body. I was talking to her, to myself, to everyone. I dictated my autobiography—I babbled out a diary entry for every event I had so long sought to suppress. It was euphoric—it was awful. I was scarred and healed all at once. Maybe for twenty minutes, maybe an hour did I carry on until finally I realized she was talking to me and that I had been silent for some time.

"Tom . . . Tom, what is it? Tell me. Please. What are you thinking about?" She was by my side, holding my right hand in hers and wiping the tears from my face. With great strain, I lifted my eyes to hers.

"The people on the roads . . ." She nodded, her face receptive, saddened. "It was radiation. The meltdown. When I learned from Kirk that it was all radiation, I knew in the back of my mind . . . Radiation isn't contagious. They made us shoot them so the truth would die, not a virus. . . . We killed the truth."

She wrapped her arms around me, and I buried my head in

her chest. Slowly we rocked back and forth. She whispered in my ear, trying to comfort me, saying it wasn't my fault. Her skin was warm and smelled faintly sweet beneath her sweater. My cheek lay against one of her soft breasts. Gradually my breathing slowed and my head stopped spinning with flashes of long-ago death. I lifted my head and looked into her eyes, inches from my own.

"Thank you," I mumbled. She kissed me on the forehead. It was as if she had absolved me of my sins. I gently disengaged myself from her arms and leaned away, stretching my neck. The fire crackled loudly as a thick log split. I rose and grabbed a few more large pieces of wood and tossed one on top of the flames. A great cloud of embers broke free and rushed skyward in the night, swirling like a flock of angry fowl. I watched the last of this cloud of sparks rise upward until each had burned out and disappeared, followed every few seconds by a glowing ember or two that rose when the fire snapped and popped.

"Just like life," I said quietly.

"What is?"

"I was just thinking about the fire . . . the embers. They glow brilliantly for a little while. They're alive and in motion and they're warm, then they burn out. Then they don't glow ever again. Sometimes there's this big surge of them. Once that's risen, shined and cooled, there are a few more following all the time . . . drifting up more slowly . . . less sure of where to go because they have no group to follow. . . ."

"That's us," Rebecca said quietly.

"Yeah, that's us. We didn't get caught up in the fire's hottest flare-up, so now we have to drift free and alone, until we burn out." Another branch cracked in half and a few more embers rose. One of them, slightly larger than the others, began spiraling upward clockwise with the group but then seemed to catch its own breeze, drifting laterally and then down and coming to rest on the forest floor. It sat there, still glowing a faint, dying orange for several seconds before fading into ash. I glanced over at Rebecca and saw that she too had watched this cinder.

"I guess sometimes some of them do make it back down still burning. Still alive."

"Sometimes," I said, trying to return her hopeful smile. "Every once in a while, they can even start fires of their own."

THE FIRE HAD BURNED LOW. IT WAS JUST A FEW SMOLDERING embers now, faintly glowing orange beneath ashen shells. Rebecca's body was curled almost into fetal position, her back pressed against my chest. I had one arm around her. Still half-asleep, I blinked my eyes in the darkness and tried to figure out if anything had awakened me. It was perfectly silent, and I could see nothing amiss by the fire's dying light. I eased away from Rebecca. She sighed softly and pulled the blanket more tightly about her neck.

I rose stiffly in the cold air and stretched my legs and back. There were still a few logs left, and after stepping over Becca's slumbering body, I placed one down into the coals. Kneeling, I blew gently onto the embers, coaxing a little life out of them. Eventually a few tongues of flame licked upward and caught one end of the new piece of wood. I sat down beside the fire and held my hands out to it, warming them.

The thick branch crackled and snapped as it became ever more consumed by flame. Each time a pocket of air exploded into sparks, I jumped a bit at the sharp, violent sound. It seemed too loud, piercing the silence of the night. Slowly I felt hairs rise on my neck and on the back of my arms. It hadn't been quiet when I fell asleep; there had been insects humming and animals flitting about in the darkness. Now there was barely a breeze.

I stood slowly, bile rising in my throat, and padded softly over to where the rifles leaned against a tree. I grabbed one and racked back on the bolt, the metallic click impossibly loud. I strained to hear anything, moving away from the fire a few more feet. Animals are silent like this only for a reason—that much I knew.

My breath came out in plumes of mist, quickly dissipating in the flickering light. I could hear my heartbeat and feel my hands trembling. I squeezed more tightly on the gun's grips and took in a deep breath, holding it and closing my eyes. Silence . . . and then . . . very faint. Very far away . . . I exhaled and breathed in again, listening.

It almost sounded like distant thunder at first. Maybe a series of rumbling explosions very far off. Slowly the noise grew more steady, ever louder and finally pronounced. Helicopters. Once I placed the sound of rotors chopping through the freezing air, engines started whining beneath the blades, their sound was drawing closer, growing quickly.

Hastily I lay down the rifle and dashed back to the fire. "Becca," I said firmly but trying to sound calm. "Wake up, sweetie." I rolled the fresh log, now burning brightly, out of the fire with my foot and began trying to claw dirt from the frigid ground to throw onto it.

She came to slowly, muttering. "Tom . . . what—the fire. What are you doing?"

"We need to get it out. Now."

"Why?" she asked, sitting up and rubbing her eyes. I kept frantically kicking and scratching at the ground.

"Listen," I said, pausing. She sat still and cocked her head to one side. The rhythmic bass of the thumping rotors gradually filled the clearing.

"Is it thunder?" she whispered.

"Thunder would suit me just fine. It's helicopters."

Her eyes went wide and her hands instinctively flew to her neck. "Oh, Christ! What do we do?"

"Just help me get the fire out. Then, nothing. It's a big forest, we're just two people. We'll sit tight." It was the truck I was worried about. Lights would reflect off the glass in the clear, dark night. Oh well, not a damn thing to do about it now. Together we managed to get the flames tamped down, and then I covered the glowing coals in more loose dirt and gravel so nothing would flare up. Becca sat with her knees drawn to her chest, her face stretched tight with terror. I was frightened too, and a lot less new to this kind of thing than she.

I lay my rifle across my lap and sat beside Rebecca, barely able to see her in the little bit of celestial light filtering through the trees. Her eyes stared vacantly into the night. If there were four-hundred-some miles to the diameter of the exclusion zone, then they weren't likely to be looking in this area randomly. Tire tracks or some sort of surveillance or something, I guessed. Who knows, maybe they were just traveling along the roads and wouldn't think to follow a little dirt path through some fields and into the woods. That was entirely possible, even.

"They're probably just following the highways," I whispered.

"Do you think that, or are you just saying it?" she replied, her voice cracking. I could see tears beginning to run down her cheeks.

"I hope it, okay? It's very possible and . . . I hope so." They drew ever nearer. Had to be six, seven choppers at least. Big birds. The forest thundered with their roaring blades. Then, a few hundred yards off, powerful shafts of light pierced the canopy above and began to streak the forest floor. Rebecca screamed and threw her arms around my neck. Her voice was carried away as the rotor wash began to stir the air around us. Three and then four different beams strafed the forest, and I caught glimpses of still others far off to the sides. The howl became deafening. The lights were scarcely a hundred yards away, bouncing around among the trees, illuminating the night.

I looked down into her eyes and saw not fear but a great sadness and resignation. She pulled my ear down to her mouth and called out above the din, "I'm so sorry, Tom. I'm so sorry."

I looked at her, holding her cheeks between my hands and

shook my head. Then I pressed my lips to hers and her mouth opened eagerly. Her hands were on my back, my thighs, my ass, and then up my shirt. She peeled off my jacket and then pulled her own sweater over her head.

"You don't want this, Becca!" I shouted, stopping her hands as she began to strip off her T-shirt. She shook loose and pressed one hand over my mouth, peeling off her shirt with the other. She grabbed the bottom of my shirt, trying to get it off me. I pulled it off for her, and by the time it was on the ground, her pants had followed. I stripped naked, and then she fell on top of me, her breasts near my face. Like some starving infant, I pressed them to my mouth. She moaned and I felt her lips on my forehead, one of her hands snaking down between my legs and taking hold of me.

Our lips met. She was on fire, biting, licking, her tongue flitting about, serpentine. I grabbed her about the waist and flipped her onto her back on the pile of blankets and shoved my face down into her crotch, the bristled skin of my cheeks dragging roughly across her soft, tender flesh. No matter—she screamed with pleasure amidst the howling winds and thunderous roar and slashing lights, and then I slid upward and was inside her.

The world could have collapsed in that instant and not taken us with it. Galaxies twirling and smashing into one another would have had to take a seat and wait until we were through with each other. Thrusting and moaning and in ecstasy from head to toe. Her eyes opened briefly and met mine, and it was pure joy. Bliss. Her nails raked across my shoulders and she arched her back and her screams drowned out the helicopter blades. I rose up on my forearms and threw back my head, driving ever deeper until I too cried out into the night, cried out so that I could hear nothing but my own victory yell and feel nothing but a perfect warmth and joy spreading from my loins to my very fingertips.

I fell down on top of her, and her tongue found mine. Our

lips stayed together for a long time until finally, breathing more steadily, I realized something. "They're getting farther away," I whispered in her ear.

As we made love, it had seemed the lights and thunder were all around us, circling and zeroing in. But now the roar was slowly fading away into a distant rumble, and the searchlights were a dull glow, ever receding. She wrapped her arms tightly around me, eyes staring upward attentively. Slowly she relaxed and her grip loosened, her hands running gently across my sweat-covered back. She looked up at me.

"Thank you," she murmured.

"Thank you . . . thank you . . ." I stammered back.

"Will you stay in me for a while?"

I nodded and slumped downward, partially supporting myself with my elbows. Her hands gradually slowed their ministrations across my back.

"Are we safe?" she asked, her voice sounding very small and far away.

"We're safe for now." A faint smile grew on her face and stayed there as she drifted off to sleep. Slowly I withdrew from her, sighing with pleasure. I wiped myself off on the sleeve of my shirt and then wrapped several of the blankets tightly around her lovely sleeping body.

Dressing, I stood up to stretch and lit a cigarette. We had been lucky, but it was our first day on the run. The remaining nights were limited. No doubt about that. I had the makings of a plan in my head, and I paced to think it through, careful not to rustle too many leaves or snap twigs that could awaken her. My mind kept wandering, though; I had just had sex with her. From the red dress to the blazer to the girl cooking me eggs . . . I had just had her. And it felt pure, righteous. I wanted to spend the rest of my life with her. To wake up beside her and listen to her slumbering breaths. To feel her fingers running through my gray hair. I wanted to protect her forever, however long that was and whatever protecting her ended up meaning. Her chest rose and fell as she took long, slow breaths, and her face was perfectly at peace. It wasn't going to be easy.

I HAD BEEN AWAKE FOR ABOUT A HALF HOUR. THE SKY WAS PALE blue, and in the forest all was cast in a muted, dreamlike purple gray. I could see my hands but not the veins and scars criss-crossed along their backs. I could see the shapes of the trees but not their colors or textures. The air was bitter cold but crisp. It felt wonderful to be alive. I was lacing up my boots, careful not to wake Rebecca. We were going to have a long day ahead of us.

I slinked away from our campsite and made my way through the awakening forest to where the truck was parked just inside the last stand of trees. The fields beyond the woods were still gray and dormant, but a touch of gold had crept into the east-ern sky. I walked past the truck a few yards and stood leaning against a young sapling, looking out across the land. It was silent save for the occasional songbird.

There was no sign of human life. Not even a hint it had ever existed. I knew it was a false, bittersweet landscape, but I liked it this way. Better than the purgatory from which I had escaped, certainly, but in the darker corners of my mind, I had always felt that I was born at the wrong time. I should have lived a thousand years ago—maybe more. I would like to have had no concerns beyond the only three that counted for a damn any-way: sustenance, shelter, and sex. Everything else is padding, clutter. Even the pleasures derived from reading or a glass of scotch or a sunset or all of it are superfluous if you're fed, safe, and have two sets of genitalia willing to collaborate.

Perhaps a greater connectivity to others is virtually essential. Sustenance, shelter, sex, and a bit of conversation, then. I had that now for the first time in my life, in an odd way. We could hide in the forest, live off the land, make love, and then lie back and whisper together. My ship had come in, but the port was on fire. Soon enough, we would sink back into the gray depths again. Unless we acted rather than waited, rather than stood by, hoping.

I turned away from the brightening countryside and walked back to the truck. After opening the door, I leaned in and rifled through our rations. I grabbed a little bag of dried fruit, a can of black beans, and about a cup of rice. The concussion of the slamming door echoed through the trees and I winced, berating myself for the carelessness. There was no one to hear—I told myself that several times. It was just us and a million acres. My hope was that for them having patrolled this area last night, we would have at least a day of relative safety. I needed just one day.

Rebecca was sitting up, swaddled in blankets when I got back to the campsite. I noticed that one of the rifles was resting conspicuously close by. She seemed relieved to see me but nervous nonetheless. I set down the food and knelt beside her. She leaned in and kissed me gently on the lips. It felt so strangely domestic, even out here in the cold forest at dawn.

"Do you know how to use that?" I asked, rocking back onto my heels and pointing at the rifle.

"Not really. In theory . . . but I've never actually— No. I really don't." She looked from the gun to me, a sheepish grin on her face. I smiled and told her we'd get to it after eating.

I gathered twigs and brambles and in a few minutes had a little fire burning. I set the can of beans down close beside it. Rebecca dressed, which I watched with pleasure, and then we sat nibbling on fruit, waiting for the beans to warm. Once they were ready, we took turns eating out of the can. When it was empty, I filled it with rice and water and nestled the can down into the glowing coals.

We tidied up the campsite as the water came to a boil, gathering blankets and the remains of our humble meal and sharing the bland rice. "Well, this is . . . caloric," I said under my breath.

"That's what counts." She smiled back, her mouth full of rice. I nodded. It was indeed what counted, after all. Sustenance. We finished the meal in silence, and then I picked up the folded blankets and two of the rifles.

"You take this one," I instructed, handing her the third weapon. "So you can start getting used to the weight."

She lifted the rifle and hefted it a few times in her hands to get its feel. Her fingers explored the bolt, trigger, and safety. I was nervous—a gun in untrained hands is a dangerous thing. But she was a smart girl, and I was sure she'd be a quick study. I was also banking on her never having to fire the thing at anyone.

We made our way through the thorns and brambles back to the edge of the woods. It was fully morning now—the fields rolling away and down across the hills were verdant beneath a striking cobalt sky punctuated here and there by wispy clouds. I tossed our blankets into the cab and then walked to the very edge of the tree line. My eyes slowly scanned the countryside, then the horizon and finally the skies. We were utterly alone.

"Okay . . . before long, you're going to shoot this," I said over my shoulder, holding aloft the empty bean can and walking about fifty feet out into the field. I rested the can on a small moldering stump and returned to where she stood by a large pine. I grabbed a rifle from where it was slung across my back and held it at the ready, indicating for her to do the same.

"Pretty simple overall, okay? Clip goes in here, this button releases it when spent." She followed along as I showed her each part and its action. "Ratchet back on the bolt like so, and you chamber a round . . . you've got thirty of them per clip . . . safety off . . . squeeze and fire." I whirled rapidly and fired three shots at the can. The third knocked it off the stump. Rebecca let out a little gasp at the loud reports.

"Sorry . . . showboating," I said.

"You're allowed."

I handed her the rifle and walked toward the stump, saying over my shoulder, "For the record, no shooting right now."

It took a while for her to work up the courage to take a shot. The noise bothered her. Finally I convinced her just to squeeze a few rounds off into the air, said she could even turn her head away and close her eyes. Soon she was a professional at shooting with her eyes closed tight and her face averted. It took a lot longer to get her eyes down to the stock and sighting along the weapon. But she got there. I coaxed her along, reminding her now and then that our situation was neither ideal nor elective.

"Just look between the rear sights, put the forward iron on the can. Let your finger close slowly on the trigger. . . . Wait, stop!" Her eyes were closed again. "You need to keep your eyes open. It's the anticipation that bothers people—not so much the actual shot."

"The actual shot isn't a whole lot of fun, Tom," she said snippily.

"Better to be on this end of it."

"Yeah, okay." Becca lowered her face to the rifle again. She fired three shots. The third knocked the can from the stump. She let out a little yelp of surprise.

After she had fired fifteen or twenty rounds competently if not accurately, I decided it had been enough. She was visibly shaken, unaccustomed to the loud crack of the weapon and of the violence inherent in its use. We walked out of the open field and back toward the truck. I put two of the rifles in the bed and two in the cab and then turned to face her.

"Now you know how to use a gun in case you need to. For any reason." Her pale blue eyes stared deeply into mine. She understood completely. I absentmindedly slid a hand into my jacket pocket, seeking cigarettes but finding the syringe I'd taken from the man in truck. That would work too, if it would keep her from pain. I withdrew my hand empty.

"They'll kill us if they find us, won't they?"

"Yeah. They can't afford not to."

"Do you think—" Her voice cracked, and she took a wavering breath. "—do you think my brother is dead?"

"I don't know, Becca. I hope not." Tears welled in her eyes and I drew her to me, stroking her soft tangle of hair. She did not weep, merely sighed over and over again for a few minutes. Finally she leaned back and looked out across the sunlit hills.

I followed her gaze along the peaceful, empty land. Its vastness gave a false sense of security. I was certain they could find us easily and was scrambling for a way to make it out alive. It had kept me up for most of the night. Watley and his kind would not stop searching. Even if we made it to a new city—a different country, even—and tried to start a new life, they would follow. We would have to blend in and disappear and live forever in fear, forever looking over our shoulders and afraid of things that go bump in the night.

Any romantic notions I had held of slipping away from it all and never looking back were fading. Besides, I'd long known that even if the fog had never come, even if none of it had happened, my life would not have been exceptional. I was born to get by and not much else. Maybe that had changed now. Maybe I could rise to the occasion once. At least I had to try—for her if not for me.

She had walked a few steps toward the meadows. I grabbed my pack of smokes and drew out a cigarette. There were about fifteen left in the pack. Then I was done. Shaking my head, I lit one and took a long, deep drag. A gentle breeze had stirred up, and I watched the smoke dance skyward in frenetic little spirals until caught by a more powerful wind and blown away.

"So what do we do now?" she said without looking back.

"Well, first we clean up the campsite. Got to make it look like no one was ever there. I'll take that," I said, reaching for the rifle. She handed it to me, and I put the weapon in the cab. She turned and headed toward camp as I grabbed one of the jerry cans from the truck bed, then stamped out my smoke and poured fuel into the gas tank. Impulsively, I reached into my pocket for the cigarette pack. My fingers closed instead around Heller's cassette tape. I pulled my hand from my pocket as if shocked, looking down at my fingers. For no discernible reason, I found myself fighting back tears. The things I knew now and the conversations I'd had with the kid—fuck, it seemed they were separated by years. Slowly I eased my fingers back between the rough folds of cloth in the jacket and caressed the tape. For several minutes, I was motionless. Chopin. I'd said I'd bring it back to him. If I died out here, Tom's music would die with me. I shuddered involuntarily and thrust the tape back into my pocket, taking the empty jerry can in both hands and turning to the pickup.

I tossed the gas jug back into the truck bed. It made a jarring, unpleasant clatter, made my spine shiver. I positioned it more carefully among the others and looked up. Something was off. I could feel it. Sense it. After a long moment, I knew it. Hadn't taken them long at all. I sighed, shaking my head slowly. A low rumble crept across the hills. The rhythmic chop of helicopter blades was unmistakable. I turned to walk back into the forest and stopped short.

Two soldiers stood smiling at me, rifles trained at my chest. I instantly recognized one of them as the broad-shouldered guard from the jail cell in Science. The other man was middle aged and stone faced.

"Go call the birds and tell them where to put down," said my friend from the prison. The older soldier hurried off along the tree line, jogging south, away from Becca.

"Thanks for all the shooting. Saved me a lot of time." I cursed myself. "Where's the girl?" the big man went on, his smile fading.

"What?"

"First take a step back from the cab and those guns. That's better. Now . . . where is she?"

"Dunno. Keys were in the truck when I stole it. I owe the bitch a black eye—it's the least I could do." I tried to act confident, defiant. "Say, how're your balls doing?"

He spit on the soil, advancing. "Never better, Vale." He stopped within arm's reach of me, the rifle barrel still aimed at my chest. "I hope you enjoyed your time out here. We sure did miss you back home."

I started to reply, but that's when I saw Rebecca. She stood, petrified, not twenty feet away. Her blond hair and wide eyes shone brightly in the morning sun against a backdrop of dark forest. She was directly behind the soldier. I looked at her for less than a second, then kept my eyes on him, my gaze being the only thing that would give her away.

"Never heard *home* sound like a dirty word before you said it," I muttered. "Just tell me what the fuck to do, asshole."

He took another step toward me. The gun's muzzle grazed my chin. I thought of knocking it aside and leaping for him, but it would have been in vain—his partner couldn't have been far off, and the din of the choppers was growing louder. Besides, if I could keep the focus on me, maybe I could help her escape.

"If it were up to me, you'd be on the ground right now with a bullet in you."

"You know what? If I had my say, I'd probably ask for the same," I shot back, retreating a step and brazenly reaching into my pocket for the pack of smokes. As I drew it out, I let the keys fall to the ground. I made as if to retrieve them but then straightened up, kicking them away. "Doesn't much matter now, huh?" I snorted, placing the unlit smoke in my mouth. Over the soldier's shoulder, I saw Rebecca set her jaw and begin walking toward us. She wasn't going to let me go down alone. I couldn't allow that. I grabbed the cigarette back out of my mouth, raising my voice to mask the crunch of brush beneath her feet.

"Stop! Stop with the bullshit. Just tell me what to do, man!

Do I just walk out into the field and jump in one of those chop-pers?"

"That's about the whole of it." He nodded.

"Fine. Fuck it. Here I am, all by my lonesome. You boys win." I leaned toward him and raised a hand, palm out. "I guess this is good-bye. Too bad." I paused, drawing in a long breath. "But I promise"—my eyes locked on to his—"my little friend . . . I promise if I can, I'll see you again. You and I are not done here." He cocked his head to one side, confused, but he didn't seem to realize my voice had caught on the word *promise,* that those words not meant for him. Both of Becca's hands were pressed to her face as she stood still, watching me. Finally she crouched behind a thicket of brambles out of view. The last glimpse I caught of her was of those two brilliant blue eyes closing as she knelt. I wheeled and walked out across the soft green grass. Toward the rapidly approaching fleet of chop-pers. Away from her.

After I'd covered about a hundred yards, not once looking back to see if the soldier was following me, I paused and turned around. He stood a short ways down from the forest's edge, watching. At least that meant he hadn't found Rebecca. Yet. As I watched, he wheeled and went to the truck and began to rum-mage about in the cab. I stopped in fear, knowing she was a scant fifteen feet away. When I saw him reemerge from the truck and head into the forest, my heart skipped a beat. He looked back once, and I took the only chance I had to protect her. I broke into an all-out run. Away, across the fields. Had logic been an attribute of his, he'd surely have known my flight was point-less, his shots hopeless. Nonetheless, I heard several reports ring out behind me. That's what I'd wanted: focus on me. Out here.

I ran as hard and as far as I could across the meadow directly toward the helicopters. There were three troop carriers and a gunship. They were done fucking around. Only once did a lit-tle patch of turf erupt within twenty feet of me as the barrel-chested bastard plinked away with his rifle. I ran until my lungs seared and my legs begged me to stop. Then I kept on some more. Eventually I was more staggering than running. Soon just walking, doubled over.

"I'll miss you," I wheezed aloud. "I love you." Then even my own thundering heartbeat and hacking were drowned out by the four mighty engines now hovering above. Wind whipped around me, tossing the tall grass this way and that. Three of the choppers set down in near perfect unison, forming a large triangle with me at its center. The gunship circled, a savage thirty-millimeter cannon in its nose trained on yours truly. It'd be a painless way to go, I thought for a fleeting second. But I'd just made a promise I hoped to keep.

Four soldiers leapt from each of the helicopters and formed a loose circle around me, slowly closing in. Twelve gun barrels pointed at my chest. I raised my arms above my head very slowly. They inched closer. Twenty feet. Fifteen. Hard faces and tense fingers.

"Relax, guys!" I called above the din of the engines. "Where the fuck do you think I'm gonna go?"

13

THEY HAD STRAPPED ME INTO THE BACKSEAT OF ONE OF THE helicopters by both ankles and wrists. Smart on their part. Two soldiers sat across from me, stone faced and weapons ready. I hardly noticed them. I focused only on the cloudless sky above me and the expanse of green fields below. Tried to take in the colors. The open space. My eyes kept turning involuntarily to the ever-nearer city.

I shifted as much as possible against my restraints to look out the other window, and realized we were flying over a reservoir, and then I could see Kirk's dam. The four waterfalls spilling past the dark retaining wall gave the whole structure the look of a mouth smiling up at me. Or baring its teeth, rather. Sneering as if to say, *I told you so*. I craned my neck to stare at the dam for as long as I could. I was relatively certain by now that my hometown—the house where my parents had raised me, the parking lot where I'd first had sex, the shitty elementary school that always smelled like ammonia, all of it—was under those still black waters.

I pictured a younger Anthony Kirk standing before the dam, his chest swelling with paternal pride. I could neither blame him nor feel remorse anymore—I could see now how inevitable it all was. This thing they had created. We were all just parts of the machine.

As we drew within a few miles of the city, I thought that just maybe, if I couldn't break free from the machine, I might yet be able to break down my little piece. If I could be the right faulty cog, maybe the wheels could still be ground to a halt. An idea took root somewhere deep in my mind. Outlandishly optimistic though it was, I nursed this new fantasy as the helicopter began to descend past the highest buildings. Then wisps of fog licked at the windows. In a matter of seconds, the world was gray. I closed my eyes, hoping she was okay.

THE SKIDS HIT CEMENT ROUGHLY. BOTH SOLDIERS ACROSS FROM me snapped upright in their seats. The guy on the right, clean shaven and maybe all of twenty-five, leaned over to his older compatriot and whispered something. Then they both got out through their respective doors. Mist poured into the chopper as the rotors slowed with a dying whine. That goddamn familiar scent wafted in. Moldering life. My skin grew damp. Then the pilot and trooper up front hopped out of the chopper, and for a minute I was left alone.

I could hear voices colluding in the fog. Then the older of the two soldiers leaned into the helicopter and trained a pistol on me while he unlocked the four cuffs holding me to the seat. He waved for me to follow and I stepped down, surprised to find the black pavement of a street beneath my feet. Through the heavy air, I could hear footfalls and the occasional whisper or cough. It sounded like I was surrounded, but the only person I could see was the soldier beside me with his gun barrel trained on my chest.

"Mind if I smoke?" I asked quietly.

"Those things'll kill you," he answered without irony. I snorted out a short laugh and dug in my pocket for cigarettes. The smoke tasted different here in the fog. Very familiar, but in no way comforting.

"How's Watley?"

"Who?" the soldier asked, looking over at me.

"Nothing. Forget it," I muttered back. I had taken seven or eight slow drags when a new gray-clad man materialized from the fog. He had the insignia of a major on his lapels. And the lines of a life free of pleasure cut into his face.

The major had a shock rod in his hand but held it down against his thigh. His tone was all business, but not menacing. "We're in a lot off St. Anne's, Vale," he said, staring through me. "Follow me."

I looked over at the soldier beside me. His eyes betrayed a lack of knowledge. With resignation, I dropped my smoke and walked behind the officer as he turned and set out through the gloom. After twenty or thirty yards, I saw the telltale dance of mist swirling before a blown-out street. Then we were through the undulating haze and I recognized the storefronts and benches of St. Anne's Boulevard, once my refuge from perpetual twilight.

The major wheeled to face me. He dug in a pocket of his jacket and produced a sealed letter. I kept my hands to my sides as he held it out to me.

"Take it."

"What is it, a sentence?"

"I don't know."

"What's next?"

"Don't know," he repeated laconically. "Don't read this until I'm out of sight."

"Why not?" I asked defiantly.

"I'm not sure, Vale. Orders." He raised the letter before my eyes, and finally I grabbed it from him. "For what it's worth, I remember you from basic training."

I studied his face carefully, and he stood there, letting me do it. I didn't recognize him at all. "I don't remember you." After a pause, I added, "No offense."

"No, none taken." He looked me in the eyes, then walked past, quickly receding into the haze. I looked down at the envelope in my hands. It was beige and without markings. I held it up to the diffuse light of the sky, somewhere above, and then tore off one side.

The letter within was handwritten on plain white paper.

Welcome home, Thomas. You're free to do as you please. For now. But I think I'll be seeing you soon nonetheless; you'll have a choice to make.

J.W.

I turned 360 degrees, scanning every window and doorway in view. There were a few passersby, and in the shops and homes, all appeared to be the same as ever. No one paying attention to me. No one watching. I took a few tentative steps down the street, then stopped in the middle of the broad boulevard. There had to be a catch. No way was I on my own. I reread the letter twice. Free to do as I please? Choice? What the fuck was I going to do?

They were playing with me. He was. I had expected inquisition or execution or at the very least imprisonment—this was far worse. Trapped but free, just as I had been for fifteen years, but this time with the knowledge that there was more out there and that I was anything but in control. Kirk and Watley and all the rest of them had planned every fucking step of the way for me. The brief forays I'd taken off their established track had been for naught: I was back in the goddamn fog. And with Rebecca out there alone, I couldn't think only of myself—I couldn't be reckless. Bastards. "Just kill me now," I muttered.

Clearly that was in the future. The sword would fall. This stay only made it that much worse. Maybe that was their only plan. Watley had to know I would go down fighting. Would go down trying. I guess he just wanted to watch me do it. That, or they hoped I would lead them to something. I'd have thought it clear by now that I hadn't known a goddamn thing, but still, it was possible. If that were the case, the joke was on them. Though I tried to keep the thought at bay, I knew well that the only other thing they needed was her. Rebecca was the last loose end. At least I could assume she was safe—if they had her, I imagined I'd already be dead.

I was walking aimlessly down St Anne's, my eyes on the street. I'd never noticed the perpetual din of the blower fans before. And even on this clear street, the air was heavy and stale. I understood now more clearly why Ayers couldn't take it, why he pushed back against them despite surely being aware of the danger.

Fifteen minutes later, and I was on my street. Where else could I go? Sure, it was an obvious destination, but they had just set me "free," so I figured being there would be as good as any-where. No need to hide. I didn't have keys, but a few solid kicks would do just as well. I neared the shitshop and slowed down. Something was wrong. I stopped under the sign and peered up at it. Even in the pale gray of afternoon, I could see that it was not illuminated. And the grate behind the window, for the first time ever, had been slid aside. Inside, the shop was dark.

I could have gone home anyway, but I didn't. I turned and walked away. I could have gone to Albergue. I could have tried to hide out—maybe in the abandoned warehouse, maybe just wandering the foggy streets with my head kept down. But no . . . delaying it would be futile. I knew the second the major walked away from me where I was going, really. I had just wanted to shit, shower, and shave first. I was headed for the fences up in the northern quarter. They were the oldest. The weakest. I didn't know if the voltage was lethal. It didn't matter. Watley obviously knew I would try to make a run for it now that I knew there was somewhere to run to, but maybe he wouldn't anticipate me doing it so fast. No going home. Not a drink at the good old bar. It wasn't like I'd be taken seriously if I told anyone what I knew. And if I was, I would only imperil more people. Sentence them to death by knowledge. Maybe that's what they wanted. They'd expect me to look for Watley. To try to strike from within like the caged animal I was. But no . . . I'd just start climbing or digging—keep trying to get out of the cage—and then at some point, they could shoot me in the back. Be it in some gray alley or out in the sunlight again.

I began walking quickly north by northwest. When I got to Forty-eighth Street, I turned left, sighing as I passed a blower, and plunged into the mist. Part of me felt like I was leading the wolf home behind me. I would make it a painfully short visit, but I had something I needed to return to its owner. I trailed my hand along the bricks and after a few paces found the slick, damp brass plate engraved RIVER STREET. My friend's street. Once more I set into the familiar rhythm. One two three steps and an orb post . . . one two three. . . .

THE OUTER DOOR TO HELLER'S BUILDING WAS AJAR. THAT WAS unusual but not unprecedented. I wrote it off—what else could I do? Inside, I shut the door gently and stood still, listening. The humming vents and nothing more. I started slowly up the stairs, each creak and groan cutting through the air like thunder in my ears. *It's just paranoia,* I told myself as my pace slowed and heart rate quickened. *Nothing up there but Heller.*

I was taking one step every few seconds by the time I crested the last flight. Still silence. No signs of anything amiss. But my mouth was dry and the hairs on my arms had risen. I inched toward his door and knocked three times quietly. After a moment, I heard movement inside. Then nothing.

"Heller?" I called out.

More movement, and then came his voice. "Tom? Is that you?"

"Yeah, it's Vale."

"It's open." Open? All three locks open? I tried the handle, and sure enough the door swung inward.

"Why is it unlocked, kid? Are—?" Then I saw him. "Jesus Christ, Heller . . . what happened?"

He was lying on the couch, wearing nothing but his soiled old linen pants. One eye was bruised nearly shut. His lips were cracked, chest and arms black and blue all over. His left hand was wrapped in a wet rag, the beige cloth stained rust red with blood. He smiled weakly at me as I stood in the threshold, jaw hanging open.

"I fell."

I slammed the door behind me and went toward him. Sitting down on the coffee table, I leaned in. "Tom, what happened?"

"I, uh . . . I was drinking, and I don't really know. . . . I must have rolled down the stairs, I guess. . . ."

"Bullshit. Tell me."

"Better not to, buddy."

"Heller! You—"

He held up his good hand to silence me. His battered face took on an aspect I'd never seen before: pain and grim resolve mixed on his brow and taut lips, twisting his bloodied visage. He looked older, weary. Very slowly, very firmly he repeated: "Better not to tell you, Tom. I know that's the last thing you want to hear. But the more I say, the more you're going to run off and get yourself into trouble."

"This is my fault."

He sat up, wincing. "Don't blame yourself. I don't. I promise you I won't blame you for any of it. Get—" His voice failed him for a moment as he swung his legs down to sit fully upright, agony dancing behind his sad young eyes. "—get me a drink, would you?"

I rose, nodding, and walked to the kitchen. I grabbed two glasses and a bottle of bourbon from the cabinet. It was clear the place had been ransacked, now that I glanced around. Not that it looked that different than usual, but someone other than Heller had been here. I looked over my shoulder as I filled the cups. He was looking down at his left hand, shaking his head mournfully. The fingers were mangled, ruined. I turned away and took a sip from the bottle, pretending not to have seen. The liquor burned my throat.

"Did you bring back my Chopin?" He hid his hand and looked up at me, eyes pleading as I sat back down on the table and handed him one of the two glasses.

"Of course."

He leaned back and let out a sigh of relief. "Could you—?" He gestured to the tape player with his glass. I nodded and pulled the tape from my pocket, popped it into the machine, and pressed play.

The warm crackling began. Heller took a sip of liquor, coughing a bit as it went down, and leaned back. When the first notes began, he closed his eyes. I studied his battered face. Poor fucking kid. I had to help him.

I leaned back, then rose and moved over to the wall, lowering myself onto the ground to sit on the bare concrete. I'd give him his time with the music, then get to Salk's for whatever first aid supplies he had. Then I was going to make Heller talk. And once he told me what he knew, I would tell him what I did. But the thought of it pained me: telling this man-child his sunset dreams and blue sky memories were more than just that. Would he be elated or shattered? I sat staring at his tightly shut eyelids and could scarcely fathom what just a few words could do to him.

He took small furtive sips from his whiskey, eyes never opening. His breathing seemed to be in tune with the sonata, chest rising as the music swelled, sinking each time it fell. I wanted to get moving, but there was no way I could interrupt him.

My thoughts drifted and soon were carried far away by dulcet strains formed in the long-dead composer's mind. Green grass and floating clouds. My eyes left Heller and spent a while on the glass of bourbon and cigarette in my hands. I barely remembered lighting it. I took a drag and exhaled through my nose, closing my eyes. How many millions of people had been touched by the same music? How many had sat, transfixed and moved at the same time, by the notes Chopin scratched out onto the page? I felt very small. My life was a fleeting one. I had been destined for little and touched few. Here I had brought pain. The thought that had reoccurred to me a thousand times—in moments of desperation and as the destruction of rare moments of happiness—was that most people were insignificant, and I was one of them.

I read avidly in my youth to allay my loneliness. I traveled as far as I could afford to escape from my lack of purpose. As I aged beyond the years where listlessness was romantic, I became a professional dilettante, drifting from job to job, briefly seeking out communion in whatever social circle fell to hand. Then I joined the army like so many who crave nothing more than direction—any direction. Had that been a few years earlier, maybe I would have been the major with Watley's letter. I slipped a hand into my jacket and touched the folded paper. No matter— sickness followed by fog snuffed any lingering chance I had of a worthwhile life. And one night, years after the mist had settled down over my quarantined world, while I was crouched next to a staircase outside a decrepit apartment complex, waiting for a man who was cheating on his wife, it all became clear to me through the haze: My only escape was to be escapism.

The woman had promised me five hundred dollars for one night's work. I was to beat her husband—not badly—and frighten him into never straying again. I was thirty-four, maybe thirty-five years old, and there, leaning against the peeling paint of the cheap vinyl wall of the building, I had given up on ever achieving anything but survival. That was the first night I took pills.

I have never thought of suicide. Indeed, even in my darkest hours, I derided those who chose it. With no potential joy to aspire to, at least I could yearn for its aspiration. At least I could enjoy poisoning my body and stumbling through the night like a half-wit. And I had long ago admitted to myself that despite the base nature of my sordid professional life, or perhaps because of it, for fifteen years I took some measure of satisfaction in what I had done. Inflicting pain and causing fear in those who deserved it may not be righteous, but it had felt just. And I had never, at least as far as I knew, brought harm upon an innocent. I would hate myself if I ever did; I would be *them*.

I sucked in a sharp breath. My last thought froze, turned, and lashed out at me. Heller. Tom Heller. Wayward young drunk . . . I had brought harm down upon him. I opened my eyes. Through one lid nearly swollen shut and the other wide, Heller was staring at me. He did not blink when I looked up at him. We held each other's gaze. His battered face, his bruised chest, and broken hand . . . they sat before me like a testament to my failure. I opened my mouth to speak, but no words came. The music had stopped—I knew not how long ago.

He forced a smile, and I lamely tried to return it. "Do you want me to flip the tape?" I asked.

He shook his head slowly. "That's okay."

"Listen," I said, rising to my knees and resting my elbows on the table, "I'm going to go and get some stuff for you. Some antiseptic and bandages and something for the pain, okay? I'll be back in an hour." I stood up, and to my great surprise, he rose as well.

"No . . . no, that's okay, Tom. I have liquor for all that. Let's just have a drink out on the balcony."

"Heller, you're a mess. You need to let me help you. And I need to tell—"

"I don't need your help. I appreciate your company, that's all." He walked, unsteadily and breathing in short, strained gasps, into the kitchen. Grabbing the bottle of bourbon off the counter, he tucked it under the elbow of his left arm, turned, and pointed at the bedroom door. "Please, after you."

I stood still for a second, and then nodded. He followed me into the bedroom, where I switched on the fan above the balcony door and then slid it open, stepping outside. Heller followed and sank roughly into his chair, groaning.

"Fuck me," he muttered under his breath. Heller rested his glass on one leg and unsteadily filled it with whiskey, spilling liquor onto his pants. He shivered in the chill, damp air and then handed the bottle to me. I took it and poured myself a few fingers of bourbon. He sipped slowly at his glass a few times and stared out into the gray evening. A hundred questions danced through my mind, but I knew I should bide my time and let him speak.

I lit a cigarette. Heller looked over and wordlessly reached across himself toward the pack. I pulled out a smoke for him. He put the cigarette between his swollen lips, and I held a flame to its tip. "Thank you, Tom," he said, his tone strangely formal. We smoked in silence for a while, his eyes staring vacantly, mine looking askance at him.

When half his cigarette was gone, he looked over at me. "I never resented you. Even when you were slapping me around or whatever, I never disliked you." He took a slow drag. "I wish everything was different, but it's not. Even when you were first coming around for money or to shake me down or whatever, I always had a sense that in another life, we would have been friends."

"I like to think we are," I said, my voice tarnished with remorse.

A smile played briefly across his face. "Agreed." He held out his glass, and I quickly tapped mine against it, spilling a bit of whiskey on the concrete. He raised his glass and held it in front of his face, staring at it as though it were consecrated. Then Heller took a sip and, leaning over slowly with his cloth-wrapped hand held tight to his ribs, set it down.

"Some men came by and did this to me. They asked about you. I told them nothing, okay? I told them I owed you money and then I paid it and that was it. One of them said you'd have some things to tell me, but I don't want you to, okay? I don't want to know a fuckin' thing they want me to."

"Who?"

He shook his head, dismissing me. "I think the less I say, the better for you. They told me to tell you something and I don't think I should, but I'm going to. I think it's going to put you in more danger, but I'd want you to tell me."

"Heller . . . Tom, don't try to carry this yourself. I'll listen, but I do have things to tell you. I can help you. I need to— I need to help myself, for Christ's sake."

"I don't want to know a thing. Not a damn thing. Just lie low. Hide."

"I can't do that!" I raised my glass but paused before taking a drink, and then lowered it again. "Look, I hardly know what all I'm involved with anymore, okay? But I know things now that you need to know." He looked over at me, his one good eye wide but not perceptive. There was a glaze to his visage: the look one gets when too drunk or . . . or very near . . . I trailed off for a moment, again unsure if telling him what I knew would set him free or crush him beneath the weight of the whole goddamn world.

"Look," I continued lamely, "there are pieces that must fit in some logical way, and I need help to . . . to see the forest for the trees. What happened to you?"

He was silent, motionless. Then, with deep sorrow weighing

down his voice, said, "You know, I never really saw a forest. At least that I can remember at all. Just some pictures in a book I read in this goddamn city. I'd give anything to get out. Listen, I'm going to ask you to do me a favor. One favor, and you just have to say yes, okay?"

"Heller, I don't—"

"You're just going to have to say yes. It's just one little favor, Tom. Give me your word. Say yes!" He coughed, and I saw flecks of blood on his lips.

"Yes."

He nodded and thanked me, looking over. Then he looked back out into the gray. "You can have the apartment. Take all the tapes—take whatever you want. Don't fight them, Tom. Just lie low and try to be forgotten. That's the only chance you've got."

"Kid, you have to tell me what happened."

"No. Just what they said. Just that and the one favor, okay? I always liked you. I blame you for nothing. I always respected you. What they said is, 'She's next.' What you have to do for me—" He rose suddenly to his feet. "—is go downstairs and finish me off if I need it." He clambered over the railing and without a moment's hesitation leapt out into the void.

"Heller, no!" I screamed, my voice cracking as he fell out of view. A dull thud sounded from the street below. My knees buckled and I dropped my glass. It shattered beside his, still sitting half-full where he had set it down. I gripped the railing for what felt like an eternity; maybe it was ten seconds.

Then I wheeled and threw wide the glass door. I charged through his apartment, out the door, and leapt down each flight of stairs. Barreling through the vent chamber, I stumbled headlong out into the street, panic mixing with dread. I ran in frenzied circles, trying to find him in the misty night.

"Heller! Heller, please!" I cried out, knowing it was in vain. Finally in desperation, I fell to my knees and began crawling back and forth across the street, covering every square inch. Then before me out of the swirling air was his leg. I froze, petrified to have his death confirmed.

"Heller . . . ," I whispered. "I'm so sorry. I'm so sorry, Tom."

I crawled forward until I was beside him and could see all of his body. He didn't need me to finish him off. He had landed with his damaged left eye down, and the side of his face I could see looked peaceful. His exposed eye was half-open, and I gently pushed the lid closed. From beneath his chest seeped blood, black in the night haze, slowly fanning out around him in all directions.

He had died because of me. Trying to protect me, even. Finally he had escaped. At least he had achieved that.

"Thank you, Tom." I rested my hand on his pale, narrow back. His skin was warm. "I'm sorry." I stood up slowly and looked down at Heller, knowing that image would be indelibly burned into my mind. His one leg bent, his hands, palms down, near his head. His face.

I turned and went back upstairs into his place. For some reason, after standing still in the spartan apartment for a long while, I had carefully made Heller's bed. I cleaned up the shards of my shattered whiskey glass and poured out the rest of the liquor from his, cleaned the cup, and put it away on a shelf. I took the Chopin cassette from the tape player and Beethoven's Ninth from a pile on his table and left forever.

Before seeing Heller's broken body, there had been two options open: Run away, or face them full-on. Now the choice had been made for me. It was Watley's choice, but I didn't give much of a fuck anymore. I just needed to get close enough to wrap my hands around his neck. It was straight back to the Science and Development Research Department for me.

14

THERE WERE SIX ARMED GUARDS IN THE LOBBY OF RESEARCH. None of them seemed particularly surprised by my arrival. None even drew a weapon. The biggest of them, a boulder of a man with a pockmarked white face, took a few steps toward me and fingered a shock rod, but he kept it on his belt.

"No problems, right?" he growled.

"If you take me to John Watley, no. No problems."

The man nodded slowly, then looked over his shoulder at the group. "Call ahead." He turned back to face me and pulled a pair of handcuffs from his jacket. "Standard practice."

I nodded, feigning resignation, and held my hands out before me. Hell, they worked pretty well on Callahan's neck. Seven pairs of boots echoed in the bare lobby as the guards walked me to the elevator. The doors opened without anyone pushing a button. Like it was sent from on high. I sighed and stepped in. The elevator shuddered as each man entered; then the doors slid silently shut, and the big guy punched the button for floor ten. Figured it was back to the good old jail cells.

I was wrong. When the doors opened, revealing the same richly appointed lobby, empty for the moment, I was led not right to the holding cells, but left toward the opposite set of imposing wooden doors. Four of the guards held back in the lobby while the big man and an older guy approached the doors. The older guard knocked on the door, paused, and then turned the handle. Both doors swung inward.

Watley I was not surprised to see. He stood in the middle of the large carpeted room—empty but for a big screen on one wall and a stack of folding chairs—dressed impeccably as always. Fallon Ayers's presence was a bit less expected. He stood beside Watley, eyes on the ground, wearing a gray suit and pressed white shirt with no tie. I missed a step in confusion, and then walked into the room and stopped a few paces from the men, staring at Watley. He held my gaze for a while, then turned abruptly and pulled a chair from the pile.

He unfolded it and set it down, gesturing for me to sit. I did, and Watley repeated the action for Fallon, who also sat. He caught my eye for a fleeting second. His gaze was hard, and I couldn't tell if he meant me to read hatred or solidarity. Watley got a chair of his own, then waved the big guard over. He knelt beside me and took off my cuffs. No one had said a word yet.

Finally Watley cleared his throat. The patrician air was gone from his voice when he spoke. "We're going to watch something." He gestured vaguely at the screen mounted on the wall. "But first, I wanted to ask you if you went to visit your Mr. Heller?"

"Yeah. I did."

"Tell us how your friend looked." Blood flashed behind my eyes. I took in a long, slow breath and said nothing. "Did you tell him . . . anything?"

I shook my head.

"Did he give you my message?"

I nodded. Watley leaned forward, elbows on his knees and fingers intertwined. He glanced at Fallon, who lowered his eyes.

"Why don't you go ahead and repeat it."

"You're next."

Watley leaned back in his chair. "That's not quite what I instructed him to say."

"I know," I whispered. "That's my message to you."

Watley's face was implacable. Then slowly the corners of his mouth rose into a sneer. His eyes were unsmiling. "You'd be a psychiatrist's dream patient, Vale. Really—I mean that. So cavalier in the face of desperation. It's like you've managed to totally block out reality."

"I'd say you're the one who did that."

Watley laughed. He gave a toothy, genuine smile. The goddamn bastard was smiling at me. The muscles in my neck grew tense. My legs were coiled springs.

"The message, Fallon, was, '*She's* n—'" I was upon him. I dived full into his chest, trying to find an eye socket with a thumb, my other hand on his neck, teeth seeking flesh. His head bounced off the thin carpet. Watley shrieked and tried to push me off as I drove my forearm against his throat.

"Get him the fuck off me!" he rasped.

"Do I shoot him?" the guard shouted.

"Just hit him in the head, you stupid goddamn—"

THE ROOM WAS AS SIMPLE AS A ROOM CAN BE. ONE DOOR. A WINdow in one wall. Two chairs and a table. The door was unpainted wood and the walls were white. Four recessed lights filled the room with bright, soft light. Beyond the window was nothing but gray. I had woken up slumped in a corner with a pounding headache. There was matted blood in my hair and on my shoulders; some of it was still damp.

Nearly an hour later, still I sat on the floor, the pain subsiding when I didn't move. I had gotten up once to look around. The door was sturdy and double bolted. The table, made of cheap pressboard, had a single drawer containing two sheets of paper, one envelope, and a pen. Doubtful that they'd been left there inadvertently. Eventually I had sat back down in the corner and slipped into reverie.

If only Fallon had been shackled and dressed in rags. I couldn't make sense of this anymore. Couldn't fathom son against father. Against sister. My first thought upon waking was of the smiling family in the picture in front of a waterfall. Then I had thought of nothing but Rebecca for a long time.

"She's next." And Fallon sat calmly beside that bastard. I fought back tears, thinking of them hurting her. Just a few more seconds, and maybe I could have snapped Watley's trachea. Broken his skull against the floor.

Suddenly the room went pitch black. I heard the locks click and the door swing open. Someone entered, and then the door slammed shut. As quickly as they had been turned off, the lights came back on. It was Fallon. Still in his suit and dress shirt. He looked around the room, studying it as if for the first time. I doubted that it was, though. I stood, wincing and pressing the heel of my right hand to my temple.

"Nice suit," I muttered.

Fallon took a step toward me and took in a breath to speak but let it out again.

I snorted and looked away, shaking my head. "Just tell me what to do next, kid. I don't fucking care anymore."

"I know the feeling," he said quietly, his voice sad and distant. Slowly he unbuttoned his shirt halfway. Then he pulled it open. His chest was a covered in burns, bruises, and lacerations. I sucked in a breath. Most of them were older, nearly healed. A few looked fresh.

"What did they—?"

He quickly held up a hand to silence me. Fallon lowered himself into one of the two chairs, and after a standing still for a moment, I slid into the other across from him.

"Are we still in Science?" I asked.

"Not sure." He shrugged, then leaned forward and turned his head ninety degrees. "I tried to help." His crown was cracked and bloodied, just like mine.

"Thanks." I put my elbows on the table and held my face in both palms. "Shouldn't have doubted you. Sorry."

"You were right to. They wanted to use me." And I would have let them. He didn't say it, but I knew he meant me to understand it. I didn't begrudge him for it—she was his sister.

"The last time I saw her—" Again Fallon silenced me, this time emphatically, with both hands. He pointed to one ear and then gestured around the room, mouthing the words *every-thing . . . everywhere*. I nodded, understanding.

"So with plan A out—" Fallon pointed to the gash on his head. "—here's their plan B: We're each supposed to write out a declaration. Yours is everything that happened after the helicopter crash. And what you know about where Rebecca is." He leaned back and reached under his jacket, pulling out a pistol and setting it on the table between us. "Have a look," he said barely above a whisper.

I picked up the gun and dropped the clip free. One bullet. I reloaded the pistol and set it down. "Got it," I said.

"Only one of us can leave alive."

"What's your deal, Fallon? Why are we even still alive now?"

He sighed, long and heavy, as if it were squeezed from his lungs by the weight of the world. Resting both elbows on the table and his chin between his palms, he looked up at me. "Until a few weeks ago, they still thought I was on their side. I think maybe I was. I grew to hate my dad, Tom. I thought he was a fool. An optimistic, rosy-cheeked fool. I became part of all of this. I . . . Jesus Christ . . ." His voice cracked and his face twisted into an awful grimace. He held his head in his hands.

"I was working on sterilizing people. That was my fucking assignment, and I took it. The water . . . medicines . . . I was sterilizing human beings." He looked up at me again. His eyes were red and his lips trembled, but he held my gaze. "I thought I was right. I felt righteous, even. It took Dad's fucking murder to show me I wasn't. It all became very, very clear."

I jumped as Fallon slammed a fist down on the table. "I was wrong! It's all wrong. Now look at us." He laughed sadly. "Just fucking look at us now."

"Well, here we are. What do you think should we do?"

Fallon shrugged dismissively, his face saying he had no idea. He stood up and walked around the table, kneeling next to me and opening the drawer. He pulled out one of the sheets of paper and the pen and began writing:

Is she OK?

I took the pen and paused. I had been about to write that I didn't know, but looking into his broken young eyes, I couldn't do it. I nodded and set down the pen. He smiled, then tapped the pistol and began writing again:

That bullet is for me. There's no reason for them to let me live so I'm sure they won't.

His handwriting was small, even, and clear. Confident.

They still need you for something. Not sure what but something, so you can help her.

I looked over at him. Shook my head no. *How?* I mouthed silently. Then I wrote:

What could they need me for? I know nothing. I'm worth nothing. You're her only shot.

He waved to cut me off, taking the pen.

You saw her last. You know more than them. Only reason you're alive still.

Then, pointing to his chest: *Dead man.* Then to his head: *Know too much.*

"Me too," I muttered. "Just enough to be too much."

"Maybe," Fallon replied in a normal voice. "But Watley told me the door won't open until that bullet is in one of our heads."

I went for the gun. He must have anticipated my move because he sprang forward and swept it off the table. "Wait!" he shouted, a hand on my shoulder. I dropped back down into my chair. Fighting to kill myself—never expected that. He was right, though. They'd be fools to let him live. That was abundantly clear now. I still had the syringe in my pocket. Maybe we could go together. Or take someone with us.

He leaned over me again:

Under the porch stairs at Dad's house are documents, photos, all of it. Laid out in detail. You need to live, Tom. No matter what it takes. How long it takes.

I sighed, my heart heavy.

When did you bury this stuff?

He spelled out:

Dad did. Last spring.

That's what I had feared. "It's gone, Fallon. They already got them."

His eyes went wide; then his shoulders sank. "Jesus Christ," he muttered.

"I've got a plan, though. Stupid long shot, but hey, why dream if you ain't gonna dream big, right?"

Just then the locks clicked. I grabbed the sheet of paper and jammed it into a pocket as the door swung open. Watley entered, backed by two soldiers.

"Already got what, Vale?" I stared daggers at him. "What's this plan? Already got what! What plan! Already got what, dammit!" he shouted, his shoulders quivering with fury. His cheek was gashed where my fingernails had caught him, and his throat was black and blue.

"All right. Fine." He regained his composure and turned to one of the men beside him. "Kill Ayers."

"Wait!" I yelled, leaping to my feet. Without hesitation, the guards raised their rifles. I got between Fallon and the guns.

"You're just wasting time," Watley said coldly.

"It's okay, Tom. Let them get a clean shot, though." Fallon laid a hand on my arm. I shook off his grip and dropped to my knees, grabbing the pistol from where it lay on the floor. I trained it on Watley.

"Go ahead. It won't save either of you. Or her. Only I can do that. Now step aside so Fallon can say hi to his dad."

I smiled. Then I put the barrel of the pistol under my own chin. "Still need me for anything, John?" I asked, my voice low.

He faltered.

"Figured."

"You think this will help her, Vale?"

"Not sure. I know it won't help you, though." I held Watley's gaze for a moment, then looked back at Fallon and gestured for him to lean in close. I put my lips near his ear and whispered.

He smiled. "Wouldn't that be great."

"Nice to think about," I said. Then I wheeled to face him and pressed the pistol into his hands. "Send him along after me if you can, buddy." With that, I ran one two three steps across the room and dived through the window, the glass shattering into gray.

TALL, LUSH GRASS SOFTENED MY LANDING. IT HAD BEEN ALL OF A four-foot drop. Utterly confused, I lay still, blinking in the bright sunlight. I was surrounded by shards of glass. A large sliver sat inches from my nose, and I could see that one side was painted gray. I rolled onto my back, returning to the moment as shouting came from the within the window. Watley and Fallon's voices. The window was set into a simple one-story building. It looked like a long shed, with corrugated tin walls and a plastic roof. The building sat in the middle of a large field, bordered on all sides by dilapidated shops and houses.

I rose to my feet and made for the window when a shot rang out. The shouts turned to screams, and then seven or eight louder reports followed in two tight bursts. Rifle fire. I wheeled and ran along the side of the shed away from the gaping window. Around the corner, I found a third soldier scrambling to get out of a hole he had been digging. A slightly larger one sat finished beside it. Graves.

He froze when I came into view; I kept moving. There were two trucks idling behind the man, and against one rested a rifle. He tracked my trajectory a second too late and made for the weapon but slipped coming out of the grave, and then I had the gun in my hand. I ratcheted back on the bolt and trained the rifle at the man's chest. Young guy. Drenched in sweat and with his mouth hanging open in fear. He was still holding a shovel, which he wrapped his hands around tightly and brandished at me.

"I've got a rifle; you've got a shovel. Fuck's sake, man—start running." Without missing a beat, he did just that. Tossed the shovel aside and hauled ass away from me back around the little building. I pumped a few rounds into the front and rear tires on one side of the first truck then ran for the second, throwing wide the door and jumping in.

Blinking monitors, a switchboard of toggles and buttons and complex, arcane gear cluttered up the dashboard, but fortunately there was still a good old steering wheel and gas pedal. I jammed the clutch in gear and shot off across the field, the door slamming shut with acceleration. No idea where to head, just away from the hail of bullets that was surely coming. Only as I shifted into third gear did I finally look up and realize that before me, not more than a mile away, sat the great gray city. Wrong way. I made a sharp turn to the right. The heavy truck rumbled across the uneven land, losing traction. I eased up on the wheel as the squat vehicle began to roll. I swung widely about and then pressed home on the gas pedal.

Heading west, I made for a wide gap between a white-walled church with a collapsed steeple and a cinder block warehouse. The engine roared as I mashed the gas pedal against the steel floorboards. I passed the church and pulled onto pavement. The street was pocked with cracks and holes and covered by debris, and the vehicle bucked and skidded but stayed true upon thick tires.

I needed to keep heading west. I tried to drive toward the setting sun, but at every turn I was blocked: a broken-down eighteen-wheeler here, a building collapsed across the street there. Many times I had to jam the unwieldy troop carrier into reverse and back up blind.

From the air, the sprawling suburbs had looked intact, whole. But up close, I could see that it was one big ghost town. Weeds had overtaken the pumps at a gas station. Most every streetlight and power line had toppled. Barely any windows still had panes. The few remaining doors hung from their hinges like beaten-down souls, too tired to carry themselves upright.

A flurry of memories assailed me as I realized a shattered edifice I'd flown by at fifty miles an hour was the movie theater where I'd had my first kiss. Erin Shuler. Some stupid horror flick.

Finally I found a broad, smooth street and I threw the stick into fourth gear—the top gear of this lumbering piece of shit. In the side-view mirror, it was a straight line back to a bridge across the river and into the city. Before me, I could see the highway. It looked intact. I sped up to seventy-three. The engine screamed and the whole truck rumbled and wouldn't give me even a mile per hour more. I couldn't be sure, but I thought as I sped past a run-down house with a sagging roof I'd seen two faces peering out from behind a curtain.

THE BETTER PART OF AN HOUR HAD PASSED. I WAS SEVERAL miles into the cleared zone. The skies were empty and the road behind me clear, but I was sure that at any second I'd see helicopters above or vehicles on the horizon. I'd kept the truck near top speed the whole time, rolling through the late-afternoon sun. The gas tank was more than half empty; I had to ease up. As I crested yet another hillock and slowed, from the recesses of my memory came a quote I'd read back when I still bothered to read. It was Aristotle, Socrates, or Plato—one of those three men who lived thousands of years before my birth and will be remembered thousands of years after my death. I kept trying to get the words right in my head but remembered only the notion: something to the effect of "We are what we repeatedly do; excellence is not an action, but a habit." A habit of excellence. It sounded like a condemnation of my life: a forgettable childhood, an unwitting murderer as a young man, and then years stumbling around, making money by whatever means came easily to hand.

I remembered the family I had seen that day a couple weeks back on their way to church. I had judged them—derided them, even. God aside, at least they were trying to do something bigger with themselves. Even with all the misfortune that had been thrust upon us poor bastards, Eddie had opened a business; Salk worked a legitimate job and helped people out on the side. There were restaurants and stores in the fog. There were people in relationships. There was goodness.

I'd never considered myself corrupt, but I had become pathetically neutral, my moral compass twirling wildly according to each situation. I used to threaten and beat the only man I had called friend. I'd held knives to throats because someone offered me fistfuls of crumpled bills. I would have jumped Becca and shaken her up, scared her shitless, done whatever had been asked. She could have been just another bit of cash.

The thought that most frightened me was imagining who I would have been and what I would have done had I been one of the few chosen to be a part of the new order. If I'd been called into some briefing room fifteen years ago and told all the facts and been ordered into complicity, I can't be sure I wouldn't have said, *Yes, sir,* and laced up my boots. I'm sure Kirk and Callahan and all the rest felt justified and righteous in their pursuits. Maybe every bit as much as I did in fighting back. But I was right and they were wrong. I had to keep telling myself that. Samuel Ayers stood up. Fallon was surely now dead for trying. Rebecca saw the truth. No matter what might have been, this was where I had landed, and for once, I was determined to go all the way. To practice excellence—or try, anyway.

I rolled to a complete stop on top of the next hill. I was on the right road. I left my hands on the steering wheel and sat there, looking at Kirk's dam.

I COULDN'T BELIEVE THAT THE WHOLE COMPLEX WAS NEITHER staffed nor monitored, but it seemed that was the case. I had driven to within a few miles of the dam and then pulled off the highway into a stand of trees. The truck would have been visible from the dam for a good fifteen, twenty minutes, yet here I was nearly at the foot of it unmolested. Fifteen years of inaction had bred extreme complacency. Or so I hoped. I leaned against a tree, smoking cigarettes and surveying the massive structure for almost an hour.

When the sunlight was no longer on the fields, I grabbed a gray soldier's jacket that had been folded on the shotgun seat and set out on foot. The trees on the highest hills were painted with the afternoon's gold and the sky was still a pale blue, but soon it would begin to grow dark. The temperature was dropping. The dam was easily two miles away, and it was a tough trek to make before night fell. I needed to get there before that happened.

I stopped and looked back several times, marking the spot where I'd left the truck in the trees. I could still see the outline of the vehicle and specific trees the first few times I looked back, but soon it was just a distant copse of gray shadows. I wondered at the lack of bullet holes in the back of the truck—it was like they hadn't even tried to stop me. I hoped I could find my way back.

I adjusted the rifle strapped across my back so the bolt would stop digging into my spine. I had a few additional clips of ammunition, a half pack of smokes, and my wits. I would need at least two of those. This was my one chance to carry out what I'd whispered to Fallon. I needed to get inside the structure to find its weakest point. Every work of man has its Achilles' heel.

My lungs burned as I pressed on toward the dam. Now and then, I had to slow to a walk and was racked by a hacking cough. I stumbled along slowly for a few feet and then willed myself to speed up again. There was a finish line at the end of this race—no more aimless drifting for me.

The sky was the color of slate in the east and a swirl of violet and orange to the west when I reached the narrow river that started at the dam's base. The land was formless and gray behind me, and even though I was now quite close to the structure, I was confident no one would be able to see me if they bothered to look. I jogged along the riverbank slowly enough to regain some energy. Ahead of me was a narrow, one-lane bridge that ran across the water, connecting the dam with a road that extended off into the hazy twilight. The sound of crashing water had gradually grown from a distant hum to a deep bass, a constant rumble.

I slowed to a cautious walk as I neared the bridge and swung the gun down off my shoulder. I chambered a round as I reached the head of the bridge. It was a remarkably simple design: three concrete pylons sank down into the river, supporting a simple post-and-lintel-style stretch of concrete. There were no walls, and the bridge itself was perhaps ten feet wide. It was clearly built for an extremely low volume of traffic. The concrete was pale, shining like alabaster in the fading light. I hurried across it so my dark form would not long be framed against the white bridge.

I was scarcely a hundred yards from one end of the massive, concave structure. It stood easily two hundred feet high, sweeping dramatically between two steep ridges. Water spewed forth from four large slots, each placed about halfway up the dam's face. There were several tiers, each wider but shorter than the one below it. I moved off the service road itself but followed its path toward the structure. Above me, countless power lines, each as thick as my leg, stretched off into the distance. They crackled and hummed above, carrying power to my former world.

It looked as though the road disappeared into the lowest level of the dam. That was where I needed to go. I needed to find its heart, to rip it out. Somehow.

Moving quickly, I closed the distance between me and the large, cavernous door where the road ended. It gaped open like the mouth of a corpse, not caring who stopped to peer inside. I paused just outside the thick concrete walls and looked back over the twilight fields. Orion's Belt shimmered in the heavens just above where I figured I had left the truck. I knew that the stars would would be moving all the time and before long I would have no way to know what direction to go. Taking a few quick breaths and clicking off my rifle's safety, I walked into the gloom.

AT FIRST I COULD SEE NOTHING. THE ROOM WAS DAMP AND MUSTY, and the muted thunder of crashing water rumbled all around me. Far ahead was a pale, formless light issuing from somewhere, but I could not even see my hand in front of my face. I took slow, halting steps toward the distant light. My left hand swung back and forth before me, and I kept the gun barrel up and ready. My breathing was shallow; my skin cold and growing wet as sweat mingled with condensation.

The ground beneath my boots was covered with loose bits of gravel and dirt, and it seemed that no one had traveled down this hall in a long time. The very air was stagnant and fetid. My vision slowly adjusted, and though I could see nothing in detail, some forms and shapes began to coalesce around me. The ceiling, some twenty feet above, was curved and covered in moldering tiles. There were light fixtures lining the tunnel, but they all looked to be broken and rusted. The soft light drifting down to me was coming from an open door seventy or eighty feet ahead. There were other doors here and there set into the walls, but all were iron, bolted and rusted shut.

My feet crunched and slipped on the dirty floor, and I made my way forward slowly to keep quiet. The deep bass roar of water from above grew softer the deeper I went, and I figured I must have been heading into the center of the structure. I was only a few feet from the door—from the ethereal light. There was a large retractable grate set into the back wall next to the doorway. I leaned against the cold metal of the grate, secured the rifle against my shoulder, and pressed my right cheek down on the stock. One breath, and I stepped into the next room. There was no one there. But there had been. I had entered a small, simple room, perhaps fifteen by fifteen. One wall was lined by old lockers, the kind that might be found in a gym. There was a door in one of the two walls, an identical retractable grate in the other. A small table sat in one corner. On the table lay the light source, a naked bulb connected to a simple handle and extension cord. Next to the light, there was an open book and a half-eaten sandwich.

I walked over to the table and lowered my rifle, flipping the book over to look at its cover. *The Adventures of Huckleberry Finn,* by Mark Twain. I hadn't seen or even thought of that book in twenty years. I set it down, open to page 110, where the reader had left it. I gently pressed my thumb down into the bread of the sandwich. It was still soft.

"What the hell are you doin'?"

I wheeled and dropped down to one knee, drawing a bead on the source of the gruff, scratchy voice. The old man's hands flew up and he stumbled backwards, eyes wide above a hoary beard.

"Hey! Hey, calm down, man! Jesus Christ!"

"Who are you?" I kept the gun trained on him and rose to my feet.

"I'm Hank Verlassen. I'm the operator! Why's your goddamn gun out?"

I lowered the weapon, realizing that he was not the least bit startled to see someone but rather confused to see someone armed and ready. I let out a sigh as if releasing tension and studied the man. He must have been in his late sixties. His skin was wrinkled and weathered, hands gnarled by a lifetime of work. His eyes were dark but vacant, set far back into his skull beneath salt-and-pepper brows. The blue uniform he wore was soiled and stained with oil.

Verlassen took a step toward me once I had the gun off him. "What's going on here, fella? Where's your team?"

"My what? Sorry . . . just a bit shook up here." I had to buy time and fish for information from him without tipping my hand.

"I heard choppers earlier but then no one came and then you show up alone and all trigger-happy—what's the story?"

"We had an accident. Everyone's fine, but we had to put down a few miles away." His eyes traveled up and down me, taking on a quizzical aspect as he noted my boots and blue jeans and jacket.

"My pants got some gasoline on 'em. Didn't seem safe."

He nodded, his face again placid. He seemed perfectly satisfied after this cursory explanation. I had to learn all I could about this man—he had to know almost everything about this place.

"Sorry if I interrupted your dinner," I said, gesturing toward the sandwich. "Feel free to finish." He sat back down, folding over the corner of a page in *Huck Finn* and putting the book aside, still open.

"So are you here for a resupply?" he asked through a mouthful of food. "Seems I'm about due for it."

"Yeah. That was the plan, anyway. Probably tomorrow."

"Good. I'm all out of milk powder and eggs."

I crossed to the wall of lockers and leaned up against them, watching him in profile. "How long have you been here, Verlassen?"

"Here? At the dam? About four years. Just shy, actually, I think. Who's counting? When I hit five, they'll ship me out and that'll be that. Watching the calendar just gets depressing, y'know."

"Who's they?"

He snorted and then dragged a sleeve across his nose. "That's a good one! You're they, bud!" I smiled and shrugged as if to say, *Just kidding*. "Say, what was your name again?"

"I didn't give it. Sorry—it's Thomas. Tom Heller."

"Nice to meet you, Tom. This your first time at the dam? I

mean it probably is—I ain't never seen you, but this thing's been here years."

"Yeah . . . yeah, it's my first time."

He nodded and took another giant bite of his sandwich, leaving just a crust behind, which he balled up in a napkin and pushed aside. The napkin fell open, and the remnants fell out onto the table. He made no move to clean up.

"Well, I'm gonna go for a smoke. Care to join?" I nodded and straightened up. "Then you can check all the dials and gauges and whatnot you boys always do and leave old Hank all by his lonesome again."

I followed him through a heavy iron door. It led into a small square room with a spiral staircase in its center. The thunder of the falling water echoed more loudly in here, and the air was quite damp. Dim track lighting running up one corner of the narrow room cast shadows across the walls and stairs. I followed Verlassen up dozens of corkscrew turns.

Eventually he looked back at me and spoke over the dull roar. "Imagine trying to sleep hearing this shit every night! Ha! Takes a while."

"You said at five years, we'll ship you out. . . . What'd you mean?"

"You are new! That's my contract length." We reached the top of the stairs, and he threw wide a door connected to a metal grate landing. Darkness penetrated at points by stars framed the doorway as deafening thunder washed over me. Verlassen waited for me to step past him and then pulled the door closed. He shouted to give me bearing as I blinked and rubbed my eyes to adjust them to the dark.

"I would have taken a longer contract, but it ain't safe, I guess. I never felt sick or nothing, but what are you gonna do, right?"

I nodded, not really understanding. He pulled out two cigarettes and handed one to me. On the front of the pack in his hand, I could clearly see the word MARLBORO. I accepted his lighter and cupped my hands around his in the dancing winds. The smoke was rich and fine.

We were standing on a thin ledge, maybe four feet wide, which curved outward along the dam's wall before disappearing into the haze. A thin, rusting iron railing stood between us and a long drop.

"What brought you here, Hank?" I called out, leaning near to his ear.

"Money. Good money. Gets lonely without even a phone, but man, you deal. I worked most every day of my life, and I'll make more in these five years'n all of it put together, bud!" He took a drag off his cigarette and nodded to himself. "I'll head home and retire and never lift a finger again."

"Where's home?"

"California. Way up north by Oregon. Lots of rivers up there. I worked on every dam north of Frisco, I'll bet."

"Oh yeah? I bet you know all about these things, huh?"

"You think I could run this sumbitch alone if not? Oh yeah, I know rivers and dams, Heller. Shasta, Monticello, Lake Oroville . . . tension or cantilever or cement, no prob." He leaned in conspiratorially, lowering his voice only slightly over the crashing water. "I'll tell you, though, this baby just about runs itself. It's got more fancy computers and machines and all—I just make sure they keep clicking and whizzing. Which they always do. Piece of pie here. Ain't like the old days."

He leaned away again and continued more to himself than to me. "But I've read all my books. I don't mind being alone, but it makes me sore not having nothing new to read."

I was silent for a moment, feigning attention and trying to figure out how to prolong the conversation and turn it my way. Verlassen was clearly not the smartest man, but I sensed a worldly awareness about him that would smell foul play if I didn't tread softly.

"Where are we right now, Hank? What part of this thing?"

"Just above the powerhouse below the main retention wall." He pointed down and to the left. I followed his gesture but could see nothing in the gloom. "The reservoir's up behind us. Almost six miles long and half that wide most parts. Whole fuckin' thing is man-made." My stomach turned over. "You should see it, Heller—biggest earthworks I've ever seen or even heard of. I go up there and look out over it sometimes. Only for just a couple minutes at a time, of course," he said, glancing over at me with a knowing nod. I returned the gesture, uncomprehending, and he went on.

"The excess water sluices out of channels over there—" He hooked a thumb to the left, then pointed the other way, and as I leaned over the railing, I could make out falling water in the pale moonlight. "—and there. That's why it's so loud right here. We're kind of near the middle of the bowl, and all the echoes come right here. I love it. Normally ain't up here for a conversation, though."

He flicked his cigarette butt out into the darkness. I wondered how many of them littered the ground below us, how many times he stood there, smoking in the dark and utterly alone.

Verlassen motioned for me to follow him back into the stairwell and shut the heavy iron door behind us. In the relative quiet, he coughed and then asked, "Well, I guess you want to take your readings now, huh?"

"Sure. I should try, at least. The other guys know a bit more about it than me, though. They should be along tomorrow."

"Tomorrow? They're gonna spend the night out there?"

"I suppose so. Got to get the helicopter working."

"Ain't safe," he said, shaking his head and turning to lead the way back down the spiral staircase.

"Why not, Hank?"

"What?"

"Why isn't it safe?"

Verlsassen stopped and turned to face me. "I get that you're new to this stuff, but come on, Heller. The sickness all over. I'm sure you boys got your pills and all, but . . ." He trailed off. "Well, you couldn't pay me to spend a night outside." He continued down. I was struck by his words and forgot myself, standing perfectly still, one foot raised slightly to continue my descent. They fed the same line to everyone, inside and out. Dead to the world as the world had been dead to us.

Verlassen looked back over his shoulder at the sound of my heavy footfalls echoing off the metal steps. He waited at the bottom of the stairs and held the door to the antechamber open for me. Stepping past him, I made a point of taking the rifle off my back and leaning it in a corner of the room. To show him trust.

"Okay to leave that here?"

"Ain't gonna be any visitors unless they came with you."

I nodded and Hank walked over to a control panel set in the wall next to the large sliding door. He turned a key that was already sitting in its slot and then pressed the uppermost of three large black buttons. With a groan, the door began to rise, its metal slats clicking together. A dull hum grew louder as the grate rose into the ceiling. Beyond it, I could see massive machinery.

I followed Hank into the cavernous chamber as the door locked open with a loud clank. He started off across the floor, and I followed at a very slow pace, marveling at the enormous machines before me. They looked remarkably similar to those I had seen in the warehouse. Twenty of them painted bright blue and red and churning and grinding away rather than rotting beneath a veil of cobwebs. Each had a large base penetrated all over by cords and pipes; the upper half of the contraptions was shaped much like a giant top hat, slowly revolving beneath a thick cable that led up to the ceiling.

I didn't realize Verlassen was standing beside me until he spoke. "Lots of watts, as we always say." He chuckled to himself. "Lots 'n' lots of watts. Come on—I'll show you to control."

We walked down the row of humming, groaning behemoths toward a thin wooden staircase that led to a small landing. Verlassen led the way up, and past him I could see a wall of windows overlooking the machine room floor. He nudged a door open and stepped into the room beyond it.

I followed him and for a moment could see nothing but flickering lights and pulsing screens here and there. Then Hank flipped a switch and the room was bathed in a cool blue light. There were dozens of monitors, gauges, dials, and control panels. I walked the length of the small room while Verlassen stood back, arms crossed, looking almost paternally out over the instruments.

"Everything's ship shape, Heller. Always is on my watch. Poke around."

"I don't doubt it." I said, "You know more about this kind of fancy shit than I ever could anyway."

He nodded and grinned, walking to a small shelf in the corner. There he sorted through some bags and produced a nondescript bottle of pills. I watched askance as he cracked it open and poured one into his palm, pausing before he recapped the bottle.

"You had yours today?"

"What'd you say?" I asked over my shoulder, pretending I hadn't seen.

"Your dose. Antidote pills. Good for you and good for me to have you nice and healthy while we're sharing the same air. I got plenty stockpiled."

"Not a bad idea . . . It has been about twenty-four hours, I guess." He walked over and handed me a pill. It was a large clear capsule filled with white powder. Hank walked back to the shelf and replaced the pills in a little satchel, producing a bottle of water. He raised it to offer me some.

"No, dry is fine, thanks." I mimed taking the pill and slipped it into my jacket pocket. Walking slowly from gauge to gauge and glancing at all the monitors in the room, I made little grunts in the affirmative and pretended to study the intricate system that kept the city alive. I had no clue what I was looking at, but at least every dial's needle was squarely in the center of its circumference and each screen was full of words like STABLE, READY, or NOMINAL. *Well done, Kirk,* I thought to myself. *Well done.*

"Everything looks good to me, Hank."

He smiled and held up both hands to indicate, *Well, what can I say.* I followed him back down the narrow wooden steps and onto the floor of the machine room. "What are these doors along here?" I asked.

Verlassen kept walking, answering over his shoulder. "That leads down to the penstock, this—"

"The what?" I interrupted.

"The penstock. It's a big kinda underground tube of water. Gets forced through the main turbine." He pointed to the next set of steel double doors as he continued on. "Which is down through there."

"Can I see it?"

He stopped walking and laughed, turning to face me. "Ain't nothing to see unless you want to swim through twenty thousand cubic feet of water and get chewed up by fan blades the size of a truck." He continued laughing and pushed hard against the silver blue metal doors. They swung open, revealing darkness within. "There, take a look," he said as he turned and started off again. "Big empty tunnel next to a big tunnel full of cold water."

I stepped in front of him, putting a hand on his shoulder. "Wait, I want to understand. The water flows through the pen. . . ."

"Penstock. It goes in a big ol' intake and down into the penstock to the turbines."

"So what's all the water spilling over up top?"

"Out them four chutes? That's just runoff. Some days there

ain't a drop; some days it comes out like lightning. Depends on the rain, the snow."

"But the power is always steady?"

He looked at me as though I'd asked which hand was left. "Well, yeah—that's why the intakes are deep down in the reservoir. Not always, actually, I should say. Hell, you should see the Shasta Dam way up near Oregon. Got its intake spillway in the center of a lake. It looks like God reached down and put a drain right in the middle of the water. Biggest spillway in the world—it's forty feet across."

"That sounds like something, all right."

Verlassen nodded and began to turn again.

"Let me ask you, Hank, just because I'm new to this stuff, I heard some of the other guys talking . . . Could this thing ever break down? I mean, just one guy monitoring it all . . . What if there was a fire or something up in that control room?"

"Nah, there's sprinklers and all. Don't you worry, Heller— we're safe."

"Is there any way you could shut it down? Turn the power off?"

He looked hard at me, his dull eyes flashing for a fleeting moment. "No. Christ, hell no. I couldn't shut it down if I wanted to—the controls are all redundant, see? Here and far off who the hell knows where else—they don't tell me for security, I guess. And I don't ask. This thing provides my power too, y'know? I want my air and water filters plugging away just as much as they want theirs."

"Theirs . . . You mean the city?"

"City? There's nothing but a couple research posts out there, man!" He seemed offended by my question. "Maybe I wouldn't have come here if not for the money, but I sure as hell hope they find out what the fuck happened out there too. Stop it from happening again."

He was the lone sentinel of a forsaken world, and he didn't

even know it. I figured I could get nothing further out of him. I just had to come up with a way to get him out of here for a while. We walked back to the small room where he had first surprised me, and I slung my weapon as he shut the heavy grate, sealing off the generator room.

"I'll walk you out, Heller," Hank said, flipping a switch next to the line of lockers. The long corridor through which I'd earlier stumbled lit up in a patchwork of shadows and flickering pools of light.

We walked down the tunnel together in silence, the gritty floor crunching beneath our feet and the dull thunder of falling water all around. As we reached the end of the tunnel, I stepped out onto the road and into the cool night air. I figured the one chance I had to keep Hank safe and out of the way was to play upon his fears.

"Listen, Hank, I have to level with you. I wasn't here for a resupply, and as you may have noticed, I don't know a goddamn thing about dams or the gauges or any of it." He eyed me quizzically, and I went on. "Tomorrow we're going to do some tests in the area. We think it may be safe again around here—safe to be out and about. To live. But to be sure, we have to take some air samples from a lot of places, and one of them is in there." I pointed back down the tunnel. "So I need you to clear out for a while tomorrow. From sunup to sundown. They weren't going to say anything, but you seem like good people, Hank, and I don't want you in any danger. It's safe out here for a few hours. Just take a double dose and clear out for the day, huh? Take a long walk. Maybe around the reservoir—I don't know. Might be a nice change of scenery."

Verlassen's eyes studied my face. His lips tightened behind his beard. He didn't believe me—he was going to radio this in. . . .

"Take a walk?" He slowly stroked the long whiskers on his chin. "Well, that sounds just fine, Tom. I ain't spent more than fifteen minutes further than just right here in four goddamn years!" He smiled and clapped me on the shoulder. "Four years," he repeated softly.

I let out a breath I didn't know I had been holding and reached out to shake his hand.

"Hey, where are you from, by the way?" he asked.

"I was from around here, actually. I had to go away for a while, of course, but I was from here." He frowned knowingly and then bade me a safe trek back. I thanked him and set off down the road, searching the sky for my beacon of stars, wondering how far they'd slid across the firmament. Hank Verlassen stood in the mouth of the tunnel—the door to his world—for a long time, framed by pale gray light from within. As I crossed the bridge, I looked back once more and he was gone.

I set out across the fields, coughing and wheezing in the cold air. I rubbed my hands together to warm them. Then I remembered something I had noted to myself earlier. I stopped walking and pulled out the pill Verlassen had given me. Rolling the capsule in my fingers, I gently separated the two halves and poured a bit of the white powder into one palm. The little mound shone starkly against my flesh in the moonlight. I took a pinch and put it on my tongue. Sugar.

15

I SWITCHED OFF THE ENGINE AND STEPPED OUT INTO THE COLD night air, stretching my legs and back. I slung the rifle over my shoulder and leaned against the warm hood of the truck, looking across the low valley between me and the Ayers home. With the same sense of fatality that had led me to Science and Research before, I started off down the hill. There was no other choice to choose. Following a route directly across the grassy fields that would give wide berth to the wreck and the soldiers' bodies below, I made my way toward the house. The windows were dark. All was silent; not the slightest breeze stirred the cold night air. I had no idea what to expect—the best I could hope for was nothing. Well . . . maybe not the best I could hope for, but hope had never helped me out that much.

The house seemed quiet. I circled all the way around it once and was crouching in the tall grass below the manicured yard. There were no lights, no sounds, no vehicles, and no fresh tracks. Finally, slowly, I began to ascend the hill. I kept my rifle at the ready, cocked and with the safety off, my finger resting on the trigger guard, but I felt no fear. The night had gotten colder as it wore on. Icy air sneaked in between my clothing and skin. I shivered and picked up the pace; I had spent too long sitting still, observing the house, and was chilled to the bone.

As I crossed the threshold from rough, wild grass to the trimmed yard—just now beginning to grow out of control—I slowed again, peering carefully into every window I could see. The glass panes reflected starlight. I hurried across the open stretch of land between the last hedges and pressed my back up against the wicker siding of the deck. Maybe it was all paranoia, but if there was actually a visitor, I wasn't going to be caught relaxing now.

Bent low, I approached the front of the house and eased up the wooden steps onto the porch, ending up with one leg firmly on a step, the opposite knee on the deck. Once more I waited for a good, long time, gun at the ready. Then I rose and moved to the door. Gingerly, I tested the knob and it twisted in my hand. The door clicked open and swung inward with a quiet sigh.

It was still within. Silent. I entered the house, sucking in a breath as the floorboards creaked beneath my feet, and began to sweep through the main floor. The living room was clear—exactly as we had left it. The dining room and halls showed no signs of disruption. I could hardly see a thing in the gloomy, windowless study, but sensed no intrusion. I padded up the stairs and stuck my head and gun barrel into every room and then every closet. Finally I was content. I turned on a few lamps—one at the top of the stairs and one in a downstairs hallway—that would cast little or no light through the windows, and then walked back to the front door, easing it closed.

I stopped dead. I heard a noise. Something between a distant breeze and a muffled whimper. I took a few painfully slow steps toward the stairs. For a minute all was silent, and then I heard it again, more distinct. Gentle weeping. Rebecca. Foolishly, overjoyed and not thinking of the shock it would give her, I cried out her name.

Then I was barreling up the stairs, calling out, "It's me! Becca! It's Tom!" I looked into her room and found it empty. No one in the guest bedroom or bathroom either. Then I heard her wavering voice.

"Tom . . ."

I leaned back into her doorway, and in the dark room I could just see her tearstained eyes peering above the bed. Then she raised her head and I could see her face. She looked exhausted, confused, and frightened but unharmed. I had fought back thoughts of them finding and hurting her all day. Emotion washed over me and I dropped my rifle roughly to the floor and went to her, and she rose and fell into my arms. For a long time, we held each other in silence.

"What happened?"

"They took me back. Back into the fog. Then they—" What could I say? Tell her about Heller? About her brother? "—then I got back out. So I came to you."

"Just like you said."

"Yeah." I leaned away and looked down at her, studying her face and chest and arms. "Are you okay? What—how did you get away?"

"They never even searched for me," she answered, looking up into my eyes. "The big guy shot at you some and then just stood there watching until you flew away, then he walked off. A few minutes later, a truck drove out of the woods. That was it." She shook her head, looking away, her face expressing her own disbelief. "I sat behind that bush for hours, then I just . . . I drove away. I didn't know where else to go. What to do. When I got a couple miles from here, I pulled over and hiked back in. There were a few trucks out front, but they left, and eventually I got the pickup and just . . . drove home." She looked up again.

I smiled wearily down at her, fatigue replacing the tension I'd borne with me all day. "Well, here we are again."

"You look so tired. Are you hungry? Or thirsty?"

"Yeah, I do need water. And sleep. But we don't have much time."

"Just relax for now. Come on, I'll get you a drink and see what food we have left."

I followed her downstairs. I was shocked that they hadn't looked harder for her. There was nothing left to chance—I knew that. Surely they were watching or had followed and would soon return. Most likely they already knew where I was. There was no time left. At the foot of the stairs, she went into the kitchen, I into the living room. I sat down on the couch, the same place where Kirk had revealed the world to me. I was overcome with exhaustion. It seized me the second I leaned my head back on the cushions. I couldn't remember the last time I had slept. Just a day? I hated to lose even a minute, especially while it was dark, but I had to rest. I slid one arm awkwardly behind my back to stave off sleep, but my thoughts began swimming.

Then came footfalls in the hall. As I sat half-asleep, an apparition swam before my eyes. Callahan. His ragged neck, his jacket dark with blood . . . he reached out, loomed just in front of me, and then suddenly with a spasm I was wide awake.

Rebecca stood in the middle of the room, looking down at me. "You okay?"

"Yeah . . . Jesus Christ . . ." I rubbed my eyes with both fists. "I started dreaming the second I sat down, I guess. . . ."

"Here." She handed me a glass of water and a few stale crackers. "That's about all we've got."

I thanked her and drank thirstily. I had no hunger but forced the food down anyway. She sat beside me. "You shouldn't have come back here, honey."

"I know. It was so stupid. I just wanted to take a few things with me. Then I was going to leave again. I didn't know where

I was going and I know it was stupid but I just wanted some pictures and my book."

I nodded, understanding. I longed to tell her everything.

I told her only some. About going back into the fog. About Tom. About the room with the white walls and the window painted gray. But I said nothing about Fallon. On this, what could be our last night together, I just couldn't see more sadness in those pale blue eyes.

Then came the question I had most dreaded. After a long silence, her fingers tracing through the hair on the back of my head, Rebecca whispered: "What next?"

I sighed and answered softly. "I'm going to destroy Kirk's dam."

"What?" She turned sharply to face me, her hands pressed together in her lap.

All I could think to do was nod. "Tomorrow morning. Tonight if I can. I just need to rest. Then I need to do this. For us. For everyone."

"It's suicide. Insane."

"It's the only way."

"Tom, we'll tell people! We can tell the world!"

"You think anyone would listen? And do you really think we could reach anyone, anyway? The few hundred miles between us and the outside may as well be a million."

She sighed in resignation and turned away. "How are you planning to do it?"

"I still need to figure out the details, but it can be done. They trained me for this—something like it, at least. Everything has a weak spot. Anything that can be built can be destroyed."

"You're not doing this for us, are you? Is it for the people back there, or is it revenge?"

"For us, for them. All of it. And it's the only way to keep you safe. Us safe. Permanently. They won't be able to hide it anymore. It will all have to end."

"Okay," she said, still not looking away from me. I leaned closer and rested my hands on her shoulders. She settled back into me, and I wrapped my arms around her chest. Her hands slid back around my head, lacing into my hair and drawing me forward until our lips met.

"How are we going to do it?" She subtly emphasized the word *we*.

"Where's the pickup?"

She pulled the keys from her pocket and dropped them on the table before us. "I parked it down the back hill a ways. Out of sight from the road, I figured."

"Good move. Your house is so remote—there's no way you're on a sewer or gas grid. . . . That tank in the backyard— is it propane? Gas for heating and the stove?"

She nodded slowly.

"Okay. Then we've got our bomb."

"What? How are you going to use that?"

"I'll figure that out. I'll make it work. Necessity breeds a method."

"Or leads people to die trying," she whispered, slipping from my arms and leaning away to study my face. She had me there. I nodded almost imperceptibly, my thoughts drifting to the dam. The penstock, specifically. I had taken Kirk's life, and now I would take his greatest accomplishment—I would tear down his memorial. I wouldn't be some disgruntled, murderous sol- dier in some historical footnotes. I was going to write a whole new chapter.

As much as I demurred in telling Rebecca the details—it did sound like madness out loud—she persisted in asking. So I told her. About Verlassen. About the penstock and the turbines and how I could stop it. Alone . . . What I didn't tell her was that she was staying at home. I didn't tell her I was fairly certain I would be caught up in the concussion blast that would rip through the structure.

Once it was done, they would have no reason left to hunt her. Becca was a flickering candle of truth to be snuffed; if I could do this thing, live or die, Watley's world, his lies, would be burned down by an all-consuming fire. She could sense I wasn't being completely honest.

I looked at the clock sitting across the room. Two fifty-five A.M. A few dozen miles and a world away, the city was just about to be blanketed in a fresh layer of fog. Little spurts of mist would keep it thick all day. For at least one more day.

"What is it?" she asked quietly.

"What?"

"You were smiling."

"I didn't realize. I was just thinking about . . . It's two fifty-five right now. I always woke up right before three. Most every night. I always thought something was wrong with me—I took pills for years just so I could sleep. It's just . . . It's not funny—but I was just thinking about how isolated I felt. I bet there were thousands and thousands of people waking up each night, thinking the exact same thing as me. I want all those people to know what I know. It makes me happy thinking about it, I guess. But it shouldn't. I wonder if maybe a lifetime of ignorance would be better."

"You would have chosen to stay?"

"No. Christ—no way."

"Neither would I." Rebecca rose and then bent double, kissing me on the forehead. "Let's go upstairs."

In her bedroom, I collapsed onto the soft mattress. She began undressing beside me.

"You're beautiful," I whispered, reaching out to touch the smooth skin of her thigh. Then I yawned.

"You need to sleep."

"I know. I don't want to, but I won't make it long without passing out."

"Come on. Sit up," Becca said, helping me out of my jacket.

I unbuttoned my shirt, leaving it hanging open, as she undid my belt and zipper and slid my pants down.

"I should probably take my shoes off first."

She laughed and I leaned off the side of the bed pulling off my boots and socks and then allowing her to ease off my pants. I rose and pulled her shirt up over her head and then took off my own. She finished stripping and stood before me naked.

"Goddamn." I whispered, "I want you, Rebecca. Like nothing I've ever felt." I sat back down on the bed and stifled another yawn.

"Get some sleep, and maybe then we can do something about it." She smiled.

I made no protest as she pulled back the covers and waited for me to climb under them. She slid in beside me and we kissed. I ran my hand down the length of her back. Her skin was smooth and warm. Her fingers ran through my hair, and already I was drifting off again. As my consciousness receded, it seemed she was softly humming.

IT WAS A BRILLIANT DAY. THE SKY WAS A RICH AZURE SHADE OF blue, the clouds perfectly defined in the cold air and the sun bright. I figured it to be somewhere around eight. I stood in the yard, looking out over the hills and fields. I was filled with bitter sadness thinking of what had been in the face of what would come. Wondering whether or not I would have another day to look out across the sunbathed world.

Either way, I had much to do and was already on borrowed time. I walked to the side of the house to inspect the propane tank. It was about seven feet long and maybe five in diameter. It would fit into the pickup's bed with the gate down, if I could get it there. There was a large shutoff valve and a hose on the end nearest to the house. The hose, a thick, wire-mesh encased tube that barely moved an inch when I tugged at it, looked to be screwed to the tank. That was good—it allowed for a clean, safe separation. A small wheel, like that used to seal a ship's hatch, sat just above the hose. I needed to leave a tiny crack open and insert some sort of detonator. I had no clue yet what I would use. A gun barrel was my last resort.

There was a gauge on the long axis of the tank indicating that it was over 70 percent full. The massive cylinder sat on four concrete posts that held it some three feet off the ground. I stepped back to think about how I could make this work, digging in the back pocket of my jeans for the open pack of smokes I took from the soldier who had crawled from the troop carrier. I shook my head while tamping the pack against one palm. *More dead man's cigarettes.* It didn't feel right, smoking what he had reached for as his final act. Then I got the idea about how to load the propane tank onto the truck, and the guilt cleared from my thinking, replaced by motivation. If it worked, maybe no more bodies would be added to the pile. Or maybe just one. I drew out a cigarette as I walked down the long hill behind the house and around a copse of trees to where the truck was parked. I jumped in and lit my smoke, taking a long drag before bringing the truck to life. I drove it slowly up the slope and around to the side of the house. In a four- or five-point maneuver, I got the tail of the pickup lined up a few feet from the tank.

Getting out, I nodded to myself. There were only eight or nine inches' difference in the levels of the truck bed and the propane cylinder. I had seen various shovels and picks strewn about under the porch by the jerry cans. Next to where Sam Ayers had hidden his proof. Whatever it was. Wherever it ended up. I wondered if he added anything personal—a letter or something, perhaps addressed to the rest of the world. To posterity.

I crawled under the porch and selected a few tools, wiping cobwebs from my face. I backed out from under the deck, inch by inch so as not to hit my head or make too much clatter with the shovels, sledgehammer, and pick I was dragging. Back in the yard, I straightened up on my knees and leaned over to stretch my back. My eyes came parallel with Rebecca's shins.

She was standing on the steps to the porch wearing a bathrobe.

"Good morning." I smiled up at her.

"Morning, Tom." She sat down, her face now level with mine. I could see the smooth inside of her left thigh almost all the way up where her robe draped open. "When did you get up?"

"Maybe an hour ago."

"I heard the truck."

"Sorry. I should have thought of that—I didn't mean to wake you."

She looked away, her eyes panning across the fields. "No, it's okay. When I heard it I thought . . . you know."

I shook my head. "I'm right here."

She smiled sadly at me and started to speak, but closed her mouth again, instead reaching out with one hand and squeezing my shoulder.

"It's beautiful out today," I said, rising to sit beside her on the steps.

"It's perfect. If it had to be one temperature, to have the sun in one place and just so many clouds and the breeze—if it had to be one way forever, I'd pick this."

Her words rang in my ears. She was right—it was perfect. The day, the silent peace, her beside me: I would have stopped time forever.

She glanced over at me and let out a soft sigh. "What were you moving the truck for?"

"The propane tank."

"I figured. When are we leaving?"

"I don't know how long it will take for me to get it loaded . . . but soon, I hope."

"Do you need help?"

"No." After a pause I added, "I may—not now, though. Just relax. Enjoy the morning."

"I'll make coffee and see if there's anything worth eating." Rebecca rose and turned to walk back into the house. I stayed seated. After a pause, she walked down the steps and turned to face me, leaning down until her eyes were inches from mine. She said nothing, just looked at me. I held her gaze, but her look made me uncomfortable. My heartbeat quickened. Finally she leaned in and we kissed; then she walked up into the house, her fingers trailing through my hair as she went.

I stood and gathered my tools and walked back to where the truck was parked. My plan was simple enough: Dig two narrow ditches for the pickup's wheels to roll down and ease the bed under the cylinder. Once I had a portion of it on the truck, I'd use brute force to knock out the first set of concrete pillars and then repeat the process.

I selected the heavier of the two shovels and set to work. The ground was cold and my progress was slow at first, but I kept at it and soon had one track running down to the first pillar. I pulled off my sweater and tossed it into the truck cab, sweat trickling down my brow. I felt like taking a break but immediately put the thought out of mind and set in digging the second ditch, the unmistakable sound of blade striking earth echoing off the house.

I DON'T KNOW HOW LONG SHE STOOD THERE WATCHING ME. I HAD stripped to the waist and was swinging the sledgehammer wildly, bashing away at the propane tank's last remaining support column. I was exhausted, delirious—shouting and swearing as my aching arms hefted the nine-pound hammer again and again. Finally, with one more chunk of cement knocked free, the post began to crumble. The massive cylinder dropped down into the pickup's bed, the truck groaning from its full weight.

"That's right . . . motherfucker . . . ," I wheezed out, hands on my knees. Eventually I straightened up and turned and there she was, holding a sandwich and glass of water. Her face was knit with concern—fear, almost. She looked at me like I had done something wrong. My shoulders rose and fell as I got my breath back, and I wiped at my sweat-soaked face and neck.

"What's wrong?" I asked quietly.

"Nothing." She took a step toward me. "I could hear you shouting in the kitchen."

"Sorry," I said, taking the glass of water from her. "I didn't realize."

"Want something to eat?"

"I still need to unhook the gas line and get the tank secured. What time is it?"

"I'm not sure. Ten, maybe." She looked away, out across the field.

I finished the water and closed my eyes, stretching my neck from one side to the other. "Sure." I picked up my T-shirt and pulled it on. "Let's eat." She gave me a small smile and turned to walk inside. I followed her, glancing back at the truck and the cylinder.

Inside, we sat at the kitchen table and she brought me more water and got her own sandwich. It was made from the loaf's end pieces. She kept one hand resting in front of the sandwich as if she thought I wouldn't notice them. I wiped the sweat off my lips with a napkin and leaned forward to kiss her forehead. Then I grabbed the bread from the top of my sandwich and hers and switched them. She flushed red but grinned.

"What are we having?"

"Um . . . a whatever-shit-Becca-could-find club, I guess. Some cheese, a bit of onion and lettuce. Probably better not to ask— it's the last in the house. Fresh tomatoes, anyway."

I laughed a bit and took a big bite to reassure her. It was okay. Calories, at least. We ate in silence. Whenever Rebecca's eyes were down, mine were on her. Within the hour, I'd be gone. She would be here. I still didn't have the heart to tell her. It was safer not to, I rationalized. If she didn't know when I was leaving, she couldn't try to fight it. She would not be anywhere near that dam when I set to work. I had to lie to protect her. I knew she would forgive me someday, no matter what happened. I had told myself that over and over again as I drove the sledgehammer into cement. *She'll be fine.* Over and over with each swing. *She'll be fine.*

I finished eating and rose to wash my hands. As I stood at the sink, she came up behind me and slid her hands around my stomach.

"Do you want to go upstairs?" she whispered. I did. Desperately. I wanted nothing more, really. But wants and needs have a way of getting mixed up, and I needed to get on with things. I still couldn't believe no one had come for us yet. Every second counted.

"More than you could fathom," I answered, sighing. I lay my hands over hers and she rested her head against my shoulder. "But just let me finish up outside. Just a few minutes. Then I'm all yours."

She let go of me and I wheeled to face her, afraid I had hurt her feelings. But there was understanding in her eyes. She told me it was all right and began to clear the table.

"I'll be right in. I'm sorry. . . . I just . . . I have to know I'm ready—that we're ready."

I walked back outside and around to the pickup. The few random straps and lengths of rope I'd found in the truck bed were all I had to secure the massive cylinder. I set about lashing them together and to the truck and tossing the makeshift cords over the tank. I secured it as best I could, which was not well. A serious bump, and I would be fucked.

I climbed into the cab and reached for the ignition, intending to test the vehicle's capabilities under the load. My fingers lingered over the keys for a moment, and then I shook my head and got back out. I couldn't stand the thought of her heart skipping a beat, again wondering if I was leaving her behind. I returned to the back porch and looked through the kitchen windows for her. She was out of sight. I let myself in quietly.

"HAVE A TOAST?" I WHISPERED FROM THE DOORWAY. REBECCA was lying on her bed, wearing only a bathrobe. She looked up in surprise from a book she was reading. I was leaning against the doorframe, holding two highball glasses of whiskey, water, and juice: the only palatable concoction I had been able to make.

"We haven't shared a drink in a while," I went on, "and I figured this was probably as good a time as any."

"Probably better," she answered with a fleeting smile. I went to her and sat down on the bedside, handing her one of the glasses. She sat up, drawing her legs in beneath her, and took it from me. We tapped them together and each took a sip.

"What are you reading?"

"It's stupid," she said, sliding the book away from me.

"No, what is it?"

Reluctantly, she handed me the book. It was a worn copy of *The Little Prince* by Antoine de Saint-Exupéry. The cover was blue with a drawing of a small blond boy and an airplane flying toward him in the background. Large, cartoonish stars filled the sky. "My dad used to read it to me. To us."

"I've never read it."

She turned away, trying to mask a tear that had formed in the corner of her left eye. I slid my hand under her chin and gently turned her head back toward me, wiping the tear away with my other hand just as it began to slide down her cheek. She took in a faltering breath and then a big sip of her drink, as if to chase down the emotions that were threatening to rise.

I drained my glass and set it down, slipping off my shoes and easing fully up onto the bed.

"You can have mine," she offered. "No offense. It's fine," she quickly continued "I just . . . if you want."

"I want you to have it. I know it's nothing special, but I made it for you."

She smiled and took a few more sips, finishing the glass with a slight grimace. I took it from her and set it beside my own.

"This is different from our first drink, huh?" she said softly.

"Everything is different." I lay back on the soft pillows, sliding one arm behind my head. With the other, I reached out and gently stroked her hair. "You know how they say live every day like it's your last? I'd take this, Becca. I never need to see another city, another face . . . anything. Just a soft place to lie beside you."

She turned and lowered herself down until her head was on my chest. With one hand, I continued stroking her hair and with the other I wrapped her up in an embrace. We were silent for several minutes.

"I'm sleepy, Tom," she said eventually.

"You can sleep. Just take a nap."

"But don't you want to . . ." She trailed off.

"Sure I do—but rest now. There's all the time in the world."

"I just . . . I don't feel like myself. . . . I can't . . . I need to sleep. . . ."

I eased her off me and onto her pillow and picked up *The Little Prince* from where it sat open facedown on the bedspread. Kissing her on the cheek, I sat up and began to read aloud to her. She sighed softly. I read for five, maybe ten minutes before her breathing was deep and steady. Then slowly, carefully, I got up off the bed and walked downstairs. Now I had none of Salk's pills left, and I hated myself but it was the only way. I searched around for a pen and paper.

16

IT MUST HAVE BEEN NEAR TWO. THE SUN WAS PAST ITS ZENITH, bathing the land in a golden glow. The sky was blue, cloudless. I hurtled along the empty highway. The bright red truck and massive white gas tank would be visible for miles if anyone was looking. And they had to be looking. More than another half hour would pass before I would crest a hill and see the dam. I kept the pickup just above seventy-five—it shook when I got to eighty, and shaking was not good for the propane cylinder.

I fought to keep my mind blank. Which worked poorly. Again and again, I pictured Rebecca waking up. Groggy at first, she would roll over and find herself alone. I imagined her checking the bathroom. Then she'd hurry downstairs, hoping to find me in the kitchen or living room. I imagined her heart rate quickening as she ran outside barefoot in her robe, slowing as she circled the house to confront the inevitable: I had left her. Abandoned her, or so it would feel.

I lit a cigarette and cracked the window. Cold air blasted into the cab. I had come to terms with dying two nights ago in the forest. I had no fear of it and was ready to put more effort into accomplishing my goal than preserving my life. What I had given hardly any thought to was potential success. If I could do this thing—could destroy or at least disable Kirk's dam—what then? Was it over? Certainly not. It would be just beginning. How long would it take for the world to realize what had happened, what all these years meant?

I didn't want to be any part of it if I survived. I just wanted it over. I would gladly have passed the torch to anyone willing to take my place. I would have wished them well with a smile and a pat on the ass and sat back to watch with a beer or two. But there was no one else. There were two people in four hundred miles with the knowledge and wherewithal to fight back against them. One of them was drugged and sleeping so she could live on and tell her story later. The other badly needed a shave.

My face itched under its week-old beard. I glanced at myself in the rearview mirror. I looked weathered. My hair seemed to have grayed more in the past few days than it had in years. The lines beside my eyes cut more deeply than before. My skin was damp and sallow. Maybe it was a touch of fear—or at least foreboding—that weighed heavily on me the closer I drew to the dam. I felt a great sorrow when I thought of her thinking of me. I wasn't worth her tears. How long would those thoughts sting? How long before she could think back on all of this and then, moments later, wonder about tomorrow's forecast. We're nothing if not resilient, dead if not adaptable. By the time I got out of the mist, I barely remembered life before it. Barely cared. I guess some of it was suppression, but mostly it was acceptance. When you're out of options, taking life as it comes is quite tolerable if far from ideal.

At least Eddie Vessel would be happily out of work. It was time for people to make new memories. Perhaps tomorrow, the sun would rise on a day of euphoria. Certainly many would feel bitter, seething anger for the years lost to them, but those feel-ings would fade. It had taken me only a few days, after all, and I think my pent-up rage was a fine litmus test for other city dwellers.

How long had the Roman Empire stood? Six, seven hun-dred years? And Egypt for thousands before it. And for tens of thousands of years before that, what had men done? So many billions had died and been forgotten, but they had at least lived to give us a chance, to pass on one more generation of fertil-ity . . . one more round of potential. Were any of them great? If you die leaving no trace of your history other than rotting bones, can you be considered significant? To be sure, human history did not begin with the record of human history, but for all the semantic arguments in the world, it might as well have.

Dying anonymously didn't much bother me. Living a point-less life did. Maybe in some twisted way, I owed thanks to Wat-ley and Kirk and even the reluctant Ayers. Had it not been for their work, I would surely have led a quiet, desperate, pointless life. Then again, at least it would have been my fault—my choices and my failures.

The seams of the highway drummed methodically under the tires. I glanced down at the speedometer and realized I was going only sixty miles an hour. I had lost time in my reverie. I sped the truck back up to just below eighty, easing as the pile trembled. I slid Heller's Beethoven cassette into the tape player and rolled up my window.

The cab filled with the warm crackling promise of music to come. Then it came. I turned the volume as high as it would go and covered the last few miles of perhaps my last drive singing as loudly as I could and totally off-key but with reckless, joyful abandon. I was ready.

THE TRUCK AND PROPANE TANK EASILY FIT INTO THE DAM'S LONG, dark tunnel. I flicked on the parking lights. They cast a soft orange glow about the corridor. I drove slowly, careful to avoid pieces of fallen ceiling and letting my eyes adjust to the dim space. The door at the far end of the tunnel was closed. In daylight, the dam had loomed above the land like some medieval castle. Its massive gray walls and crenellations and the four waterfalls crashing through the concrete had unnerved me when they came into view. I had almost lost my will.

I inched up to the heavy sliding door at the tunnel's end and turned off the engine. The bits of broken tile and dirt crunched beneath my feet, and the dull thunder of rushing water echoed through the cavernous corridor. I slung a rifle across my shoulder for good measure and then walked to the smaller iron door. The handle turned smoothly and the door clicked open.

I stepped into the little room. It was exactly as I had left it. The light, the book—even the crust of Verlassen's sandwich, now rotting, sat on the little table in the corner. I grabbed *Huckleberry Finn* and found the book still turned to page 110. The hairs on the back of my neck went up. Something felt very wrong. There was nothing to do but press on. I scratched an itch on my cheek that seemed to travel down to one shoulder and soon was everywhere. My palms grew damp. I went over to the control panel in the far wall and turned the little key clockwise as I had watched Verlassen do, then pressed the highest of the three black buttons. The door beside me retracted upward, clicking and groaning as it rose. From beyond it came the sounds of the massive machines clanking and churning and pumping out the electricity that kept the city from waking up.

I bent double to step under the metal door as it continued to slowly rise and straightened up on the other side. I took a few steps before glancing to one side. I stopped walking.

"What the hell are you doing here, Hank?" Verlassen was leaning against a blue plastic drum, hands tucked into his pockets. He wore the same soiled workman's clothing as the day before. Same rip above the right knee. Same oil stains all over his shirt. But there was something new. His head was turned slightly to the right and lowered, his chin pressed against his chest and eyes looking askance at me. I took a slow step toward him. He averted his eyes and turned his head farther away. As my eyes adjusted to the harsh fluorescent light of the room, I could see the blood in his beard.

"I, uh . . . He told me to stay right here," Verlassen muttered, his voice a quiet rasp.

"Who did?" I drew nearer to him, and he finally raised his head and looked right at me. The right side of his face was bruised and gashed. Dried blood matted the coarse white hairs of his beard and stained the side of his neck and his collar. He shifted his weight and groaned, pulling one hand from a pocket to clutch his ribs. The skin of his knuckles was flayed.

"Who did this?" Again he lowered his eyes and let out a long sigh, his shoulders sagging. With a trembling hand, Verlassen pointed past me. He suddenly flinched, and I wheeled to follow his gesture just as a torrent of pain crashed through my head. I felt the ground rushing up at me and then I was a crumpled heap on the floor. Throbbing agony and the taste of blood. I could see nothing but flashes of black and red. I heard heels click on the concrete floor and felt the strap of my rifle rub against my neck as the weapon was pulled away from me. I wrapped my arms around my head and struggled to get my knees under my body. Slowly my vision came back, but I could hardly think through the pain.

"Take your time." His voice was low, calm—almost friendly. Familiar. I finally managed to roll over onto my side and rise up on one elbow. A pair of polished black loafers stood inches from my nose. I slid away until I could get a clear look up. The gash on Watley's cheek had turned a sickly crimson. That much brought me pleasure through the pain. He looked down at me with a faint smile on his lips. His eyes were hard, though. He wore a light gray, neatly pressed suit over an open white shirt. There was even a handkerchief peeking out of his breast pocket. He had a pistol in his left hand—likely the source of my headache.

"So, how's Ms. Ayers?"

"I should . . . ask you the same thing."

"But you know the answer, and I don't. You think I don't recognize that truck? I've driven that goddamn truck before, Vale."

I pulled my legs under me to sit nearly upright. "Ah, fuck you, John."

"Aren't you brave? Aren't you one tough bastard?" He leaned in toward me. "The road ends here. It can be abrupt or protracted. Where is she? Still at home like she was last night? You think we weren't watching? I know you know where she went, so we can move on from that game to this one." He pressed the barrel of the pistol against my right foot. I reflexively drew it back. His lips curled into a cold, ruthless sneer as he straightened up and aimed vaguely at my heart.

"Don't like that game? It's one of my favorites."

"I'm more of a solitaire player myself."

"Oh, believe me, I know. I know you are. I know all about you, Vale. So much more, even, than you think." He straightened up. "Since the first day you stuck your fucking nose into my business at Vessel's warehouse, I've known all about you. All I wanted was just to soften a few memories, take the sting out of the past. To look forward, Tom! But you had to fuck things up. See, I know it all."

He looked over at the old man. "Don't I, Hank? Don't I know all sorts of things about him? About his mother and dead friend and all?"

Verlassen looked away and shivered involuntarily. Watley walked over to him and stood looking down at the quavering oldtimer. "You two don't know a goddamn thing, though. Between the two of you miserable pissants, you haven't got half a clue."

He turned to look at me again, shaking his head in disapproval. "What did you think, Vale? Did you really think you'd come here and put a stop to it? You think you can change any of it? You're a pawn. He's a pawn." He pointed to Hank. "I'm the one playing chess, not you. We move the pieces." Hitching up his slacks, he crouched, his face near mine. "She's back at the house, isn't she? I thought you'd bring her along for the ride, but I guess she's all alone again. Probably clutching daddy's shirt to her cheek and weeping. Is that where she is? Just tell me and save us both time, Thomas. We're going to check there again, of course. I have men fanning out all over. The house. Your campsite. Just save me time. Save yourself pain. It's almost over now, you see. Your little race is run. Nice try, but we win. With Sam's truck out there, it means she's near home or near here—doesn't take a scientist to guess that. I figured you for the type to return to the scene of the crime, anyway."

"It wasn't my crime."

"Semantics to be lost on the ages. Besides, one of the last few people who knows that will be dead soon enough."

"Then get on with it, you bastard."

"Careful what you ask for. See, I don't need you anymore. At all." Watley straightened up and trained the pistol on my stomach and held it there for a moment, seeming to weigh his options.

"So Fallon missed, huh? Shame."

"The shame is that he didn't just drop the gun. I was hoping that bullet would end up in you. Not so long ago, I felt almost like a second father to that young man, you know."

He walked away a few feet and began pacing in a loose figure-eight pattern, thinking. Hank had slid down to the floor and sat Indian-style, his face in his battered hands. Watley added: "Not anymore, though."

"He's dead?"

"Coma. Four shots in the chest. No one's holding their

breath." He stopped pacing and glanced over at Verlassen, shivering on the floor. "As much as it may shock you, Mr. Vale, I actually don't like it when people get hurt. I don't like death." He looked over his shoulder at me, holding my gaze for just a second. "Anthony Kirk was a friend of mine. Sam Ayers too, once. You're not."

"Well," I muttered, "with friends like you, huh?"

"People change. Facts don't."

"Now, you of all people know that's not true. Not the second part, at least."

I rose unsteadily to my feet. He stopped pacing and faced me. Our eyes were locked together for the better part of a minute. Saliva welled up in my mouth, and when I was good and ready, I spit directly at Watley's face. He stumbled backwards reflexively, clawing at the spit on his nose and cheeks. Then his hand was rising and the pistol was on me and I spun away as he fired.

The report echoed throughout the mighty hall despite the clatter of machines and the din of rushing water. I felt only a dull pain at first, as if I had stumbled into the edge of a table. Then heat spread through the right side of my lower body. I stumbled backwards, frightened to look down, and crashed roughly against the cement wall, barely keeping my feet. I pressed one hand to my right thigh as the heat turned to searing agony. My fingers came away dripping with crimson. Finally I looked down to see a dark stain spreading over my right leg from just below my waistline.

I slid sideways to the floor, hands already beginning to tremble slightly. He hadn't hit my artery. I was sure of that. Bones seemed intact. But I also figured this was it. No way to fight. Nowhere to run. He smiled coldly at me.

"The next one can be fatal or not. Your choice. I say again, I take no pleasure in violence. Not for its own sake, anyway. I just relish order and control. You tried to damage those things I love."

"You . . ." I coughed and stuttered at the pain. "You could have stopped me a long time ago. . . ."

"And I would have, had things not grown so complicated. It's not my fault you roped your friend into your miserable little life. Not my fault you went back for Rebecca. No matter. Now we've moved on to the mopping-up stage."

He turned suddenly to face Verlassen. "That reminds me." Watley walked over to the seated old man. Hank raised frightened eyes set into a gnarled, beaten face. "Shame you got mixed up in Vale's mess. I sincerely hate to do this."

"No!" I shouted as Watley fired three bullets into Verlassen's chest. The old man's hands flew to his neck as he fell sideways. He struggled to suck in a breath but could only gurgle and wheeze through his ruined lungs. Blood bubbled from his mouth and flowed from his chest, and his arms slumped to the floor. Hank's eyes locked on to mine as the life faded from them. One more ragged sigh drifted past his white beard, and he was gone.

"Fuck you, John. He was an innocent old man."

"You brought this all about, Vale. Not us."

"Me! Me? You motherfucker! I didn't kill thousands of people! I didn't keep those people trapped in the goddamn fog, wondering if everything and everyone out there was dead and gone. Wondering why the fuck we get up every morning! I just tried to have enough to eat and a place to sleep, you miserable piece of shit! I didn't bring on a fucking thing!" My shoulders heaved with each breath I drew. Rage blocked the pain from my leg. I struggled to rise, almost getting to my feet before Watley took two quick steps toward me and jammed the gun barrel into my ribs. He pressed hard against me, and I slumped back down.

I coughed, then lamely swatted the weapon away. "What were you going to show me? The video back there in Research."

"Ah, yes!" he said with what seemed like genuine pleasure. The patrician crispness returned to his voice as he spoke. "We were going to sit and watch a newsreel. A little something from the archives. The clip I thought you'd most enjoy was from fifteen years go, in fact. I thought it may interest you to see what the whole rest of the world thought had happened here. And how thoroughly they'd forgotten about you all."

"And I'm sure they're putting you on a stamp, you miserable prick."

"This will be where the next shot goes." He dug the tip of his shoe into my stomach. "Then you'll beg for death. I'm no stranger to pain, Thomas. Cancer. Twice. Lots of people have gotten it. Not surprising at all, of course, but still—it's a miserable experience. I disconnected my IV to blow air bubbles into it and end myself once, the pain got so bad. I passed out before I could do it. Which I suppose was for the better. That was the first bout. When it came back, I thought I would be ready to handle it—to fight it heroically. But before long, all my thoughts were of death. Release. For you—" He leaned closer to me and I shrank away, lying flat on my back on the hard cement floor. "—it can end remarkably fast. And why not? Maybe you deserve that much, after everything. So just tell me if she came with you, and if she knew your stupid little plan."

His eyes blazed as he spoke, standing over me. I flopped onto my side and turned my head away, feeling the cool concrete on one cheek. Hank's lifeless face lay not six feet from my own. The old man was already pale. The crimson pool of blood around his neck had stopped spreading. All he ever wanted was a new book to read. Institutionalized sociopaths.

My body ached. I wasn't sure if I could muster the strength even to sit up and die properly. Watley stood up to his full height and looked down at me. His gaze traveled with mine to Verlassen's corpse. He snorted and shook his head, pinching the bridge of his nose between two fingers. That was all I got; it was all I needed. With strength born of abject desperation, I sprang to my feet and swung at him. I put all I had left into it. My hand connected squarely with the side of his head. He stumbled backwards, hand clutching his cheek but never even lost his feet. Recovering quickly, Watley planted a solid kick in my gut. I was thrown backwards against the wall and then crumpled to the ground, my right elbow cracking roughly down on the cement. He was on me in a second, fingers tightening around my neck. I tried in vain to push him away, but my injured right arm was near useless, my left pinned beneath his perfectly shined shoe.

"You're not long for this world, Vale. You should have stayed back in the other one and not asked questions."

"You should have blown those bubbles into your IV." My fingers slid into my jacket pocket.

"No. Wrong. They need me. They all need me. Ayers hated it. Kirk tolerated it. I love it. It's a perfect world, Vale. It's contained and sustainable. We should all be so lucky."

"You created a monster, and now you don't know how to stop it." I winced as he pressed the pistol barrel against my temple. My right hand was sliding out of the pocket.

"We created utopia. We just need a few more memories to fade. And even if you were right, you can't just stop a monster. . . . You have to kill it. Maybe that's the answer."

"Truer words I've never heard, Watley," I coughed out as I jammed the syringe of cyanide into his thigh. His eyes went wide as he looked down and saw the needle, its plunger all the way depressed, sticking out of his suit pants. First fear flashed across his face, replaced immediately by rage. Already his eyes were growing glassy. The pistol trembled near my face. He was swearing, muttering. Spittle collected at one corner of his mouth as his legs began to fail him.

"Just let go," I coughed out. "Let it go."

He bared his teeth at me. I used what little strength I had left to push him aside just as he collapsed, firing a single shot past my head. The blast deafened me, and I was momentarily blind. In a haze, I rolled his dying body off me and struggled to my knees, crawling away from him. Through blurred vision, I saw his legs spasm twice, and then he was still. I sat there gasping for breath, aching and bleeding. My hands had begun to tremble. I managed to light a cigarette and take a few drags.

IT TOOK ME SEVEN OR EIGHT TIGHT TURNS, REVERSES, AND RE-tries to get the truck maneuvered before the penstock's access tunnel. I clambered out of the cab and limped over to the heavy steel doors, pulling one open, pausing and then throwing the second wide as well. I peered into the gloom, barely able to make out the bottom of the passageway some fifty feet below. I wasn't sure if the propane tank would clear the doorframe. Only one way to find out. And probably not a surplus of time. I had lost a lot of blood. My vision swam, the brightly colored machines swirling together, voices seeming to whisper beneath their mechanical droning.

I got back into Samuel Ayers's bright red pickup and threw it into reverse. Leaning out of the open door, I could just barely see down the steep tunnel by the truck's reverse lights. I drew in and then slowly let out a deep breath. My foot came off the brake and pressed home on the gas. The vehicle lurched backwards. The cylinder just cleared the tunnel doors, and a split second later I was driving down through damp darkness. I estimated as best I could what thirty feet felt like while driving backwards and then violently smashed my foot onto the brake pedal. The tires squealed as I watched the massive propane tank fly off the truck bed and crash violently into the back wall. I sat perfectly still for a moment, waiting for either an explosion or a rush of icy water or both. When neither came after a full minute, I figured I'd cleared the first hurdle.

I drove back up the steep corridor and steered around several of the clanking turbines, finally stopping the truck just before the raised metal door connecting to the main tunnel's antechamber. I hobbled down from the truck and over to Verlassen's body.

"Sorry, Hank," I muttered, crouching painfully next to him. I hooked my hands under his shoulders, rolling him flat onto his back, and tried to straighten up to drag him toward the truck. Shooting pains racked my right elbow and thigh. My ribs ached under the strain. I let go of him and stumbled backwards, coming to rest against one of the turbines. After getting my breath back, I tried to lift him once more. It was no use. Too many parts of me were too badly damaged for my body to work as a whole. I'd wanted to drive him out of the dam a ways to where someone would find his body. He deserved to be properly buried. I justified leaving him here to myself as best I could—he had spent the better part of his life in and around dams; he may as well be buried in one. It bothered me to entomb Hank next to Watley, but I had little choice.

Again I slumped against the turbine, sliding down to the concrete while digging in my pocket for a cigarette. It was my next to last. I put it in my mouth but then took it out again as something occurred to me. I crawled over to Watley's rigid corpse and pried the pistol from his hand. I ratcheted back on the action, expelling a shell onto the floor. Picking it up, I sucked in a sharp breath. I bit down as hard as I could on the bullet with my back teeth, twisting the brass casing in my fingers. After a moment, I felt the metal begin to give and then suddenly the bullet popped free of the shell. I spit it out and rubbed my aching jaw.

Not much of the black powder had spilled from the casing. It would probably be enough. It had to be. I ripped the filter off my cigarette and tossed it aside, sliding the unfiltered smoke into the brass case. I rose and limped as quickly as I could back toward the penstock. Excitement helped to dull my pain. Excitement that my plan to detonate the gas tank by jamming a gun barrel into it had been replaced. If it didn't work, I always had martyrdom.

The cement was damp and slippery beneath my unsteady feet

as I made my way down to the propane cylinder. I flicked my lighter now and then to see, keeping each burn brief, as I was nervous that gas might have been leaking. Reaching the bottom of the tunnel, I leaned for a moment against the heavy steel panel the tank was resting by. I could hear water rushing past on the other side of the cold sheet of metal. The walls vibrated and groaned with it—the lifeblood of the city. Now it would spill.

I took a long look at the tank's main valve by the flickering flame of my lighter, then worked by feel in the dark. The aperture widened in a spiral pattern as a disk around it twisted so that the gas flow could be regulated. I took hold of the adjustable disk and turned it about 180 degrees. Immediately, I could smell propane wafting out at me. I checked the size of the hole I'd made with my index finger, and then slid the back of the shell casing into it. Gingerly, I twisted the valve closed until it held fast around the brass casing.

I leaned back against the damp steel wall to relax and to let the escaped gas dissipate until I could smell nothing but the musty air. I pulled the lighter from my pants pocket and wrapped my fingers around it, holding my fist to my lips. It felt as though I should think of my mother and father or something else from before, or Heller or even just Rebecca, but as I tried to let my mind wander, I thought only of lighting the cigarette and getting to the truck. No matter what happened, the die had already been cast, the machine was running . . . all was in motion, and I was for the moment nothing but a cog in my own design.

I flicked the lighter. Its pale, dancing light cast strange shadows on the walls. I cupped my left hand around the flame and slowly raised it to the cigarette protruding from the shell. The patterns of my left palm stood out in the shimmering orange flame's light—grooves cut deeply into dry, weathered flesh. I paused for perhaps two seconds, looking at my hand. In those seconds, I did see many things from my past. Then I held the flame to the cigarette tip. With no breath to draw life into it, the ember took a moment to catch. Then it glowed gently in the dark. I moved the lighter away and paused for a moment to make sure the cigarette was burning. The stale sweet smell of tobacco filled my nostrils, and I nodded to myself and then stumbled up away from the penstock and time bomb and millions of gallons of rushing water.

I got up to the turbine room and threw shut the heavy steel doors that led down to the propane tank, hoping to maximize the blast. Lurching toward the truck, I took one last wistful and hateful look at Hank and Watley, respectively. Then I was at the truck. I had left the door open, the keys in the ignition. The engine came to life, and then I was flying through the little room, past *Huckleberry Finn* and Verlassen's last supper. Down the long, dim corridor, my eyes darting back and forth from the rearview mirror to the tunnel's end.

Then I was outside, the setting sun in my eyes. I stopped the truck a few yards from the entryway and rolled down the window to listen. Nothing. I could hear birds calling and gentle breeze and falling water. From within the dam came silence. I sighed in resignation. I climbed from the truck and began limping back inside. I figured I may as well have one more stroll.

The few working lights in the long corridor shone down above me, pale and mocking. Tile crunched beneath my feet. I walked back through the little service chamber, glancing over at the open book on the table. I grabbed the book and carried it into the turbine room to rest it, still open to page 110, on Hank's chest.

It occurred to me there was no reason to save it at this point, so I drew out my last cigarette and lit it. Looking past Verlassen, I noticed my rifle in a corner where Watley had thrown it. It was better than the pistol. I limped to the rifle and hefted it, feeling the old familiar grips for the last time.

The cigarette was sweet and rich. Blue gray smoke curled up from my nostrils into the still air. My leg throbbed and my elbow ached, but it was easy to take. I would have killed for a taste of scotch. But there was nothing to do but get on with it.

I checked the bolt and the action on the rifle, and everything seemed to be working smoothly. One last deep drag of the cigarette and I threw it aside. I walked slowly, minimizing my limp, to the penstock doors. Pulling them open, I could hear the murmur of water below. I could just see the large white cylinder in the gloom.

I planted my feet and switched the rifle to fully automatic.

Secured the stock against my shoulder.

The metal was cool against my cheek.

A faint smell of oil.

My left arm trembled for a second and then was steady.

I exhaled.

My right index finger wrapped around the trigger lightly.

Then I stopped breathing and drew the trigger all the way home.

Reports sang out and from below came a bright surge of roaring fire and I was drifting away from it and then all was black.

BY NOW, REBECCA WOULD HAVE SEEN THE NOTE I LEFT ON THE kitchen table. It was shorter than I'd wanted, but words had failed me. Surely tears streamed down from her soft blue eyes, leaving damp trails along her lovely face. Those eyes that had once been gray . . . reading my final scrawling:

I'm sorry, Rebecca. I'm gone. I care about you too much to worry about your feelings; I care only that you stay alive. If I cannot do the same, please forgive me. Please know that I love you. Know that you're the probably only thing I ever loved.

It was not enough, but perhaps she would understand. I was so far away. All my life, I had been so far away from everything.

From everyone. Principally myself. I saw it now. I had known it always, but only now would I have been ready to look someone else in the eyes, and see into rather than seeing past. See into another rather than seeing my own reflection.

Water gently lapped at my face. It was frigid but welcome. I smiled weakly at the water. I could not see. Then my arms knew the water and my legs and my fingers. It was all around me, gently flowing and gurgling. I was on my back in the water. Not floating, but I could feel nothing but its cold embrace. I tried to bring my hands to my face. After what seemed like an eternity, they got there and I explored my face, hardly comprehending what it meant to have one. All the parts seemed like they were there. All the parts of my hands were there.

Slowly I began to feel the pain. It crept in out of the icy water and wrapped around me. All around me. I was not dead. The idea seemed absurd to me. Foolish. But as I lay there slowly reintroducing myself to life, I quickly became convinced of it. I was alive. My thoughts coalesced. The water . . . the absolute darkness . . . There was no power. I smiled faintly to myself. It hurt to smile, but I could not stop.

I lay there in the darkened turbine room, aching and groaning, for perhaps ten minutes, maybe more. Finally I pulled myself up to my knees. The water was slowly rising. I could barely move my legs, so I half swam, half crawled around the room until I found a wall. I picked a direction and drift-crawled along it until finally I found the large space that led to the outer tunnel.

It took me more than twenty minutes to work my way toward the pale silver aura at the corridor's end. Water was flowing out of the tunnel and down across the land. There was no sound of the four crashing waterfalls from the far side of the dam. The red truck sat patiently in what looked like hazy twilight or morning. I crawled to the pickup and slumped against one tire, finally looking down at myself. My hands were blistered and burned. My pants were shredded, as was the skin beneath. My chest was riddled with lacerations caused by bits of metal and concrete. My palms came away from my face stained with blood. I was growing weaker. Tired. I wanted to just rest there, beside the dead giant.

But there was something I needed to see. I set my jaw and heaved myself up and into the truck. The engine rumbled to life and I set off. Sure enough, the sun was rising, not setting.

17

THE CITY'S SKYLINE WAS PERFECT. IT WAS EXACTLY AS I REMEM-
bered it. Backlit by dawn, the tall buildings cut sharp, crisp patterns into the sky. The thin, towering fog stacks glinted in the
sunlight like a crown atop the city. All the buildings were dark;
not a single light shone in any window. I was passing through
the shattered suburbs.

It was a strain to keep my eyes focused, and my head dipped
forward frequently. The steering wheel was slick with blood.

I could hardly feel my fingers or toes.

I thought I saw people peering out from the shadows along
the road.

I was fading.

I kept my foot pressed firmly down on the accelerator even as
I crossed the river into town. There was a massive concrete bun-
ker at either end of the bridge and a series of gates, but they were
all raised and unmanned. A thick metal door, easily fifteen feet
in height and double that across, was swung wide open at the far
side. It was the last barrier before the city. Or first for those

within. I slowed as I entered town and rolled down a wide open boulevard. Getting my bearings, I turned onto a side street. I desperately wanted to get to the cathedral . . . to see its wondrous facade one more time.

I turned down what I figured was River Street and had to abandon the truck. Orb columns ran down the center of the road. They looked absurd now in the light of a clear day. I laughed breathlessly to myself as I climbed out of the cab, wincing immediately afterwards.

I was home. As much as I had ever felt at home anywhere.

My legs gave out after less than a block. I crawled for maybe a hundred yards and then pulled myself along with just my elbows for a few feet more. The pavement behind me was streaked with blood. I figured I was in the last few moments of my life, so what the hell—stop crawling.

Rolling onto my back, I looked up at the sky . . . the blue sky. There were a few clouds and the sun was bright, warming. I lay there staring upward for a long time. The buildings around me were all dilapidated above their first few floors—cracked paint, boarded-up windows, old signs, and bare flagpoles that no one had seen in years.

It was warm and bright in the sun, and there wasn't a soul around. Everyone was terrified and hiding. So I had the street and the sky to myself and I lay there, bleeding and broken and probably moribund, and I was happy as hell. I had never felt such joy, in fact. Ever. I was . . . satisfied.

28 Day Loan

Hewl&   _ibrary
Hewlett, New York 11557-0903

Business Phone 516-374-1967
Recorded Announcements 516-374-1667